The Landman

Ray Parks

For my wife, Dianne

and family

I am the basis of wealth and the heritage of the wise
I provide joy, comfort and security to those who possess me
I provide the foundation for living
I am cherished as having great worth
I provide the choicest fruits of the forest
I am the source of all elements
I survive flood, fire and famine
I am always here with you; time is not my enemy
Yet, I am common and often exploited; many tread on me, wipe their feet and
unknowingly pass me by
Who am I?
I AM LAND!

Anonymous

*****

"The Great Spirit, in placing men on Earth, desired them to take good care
of the land."
Chief of the Cayuse First Nations People, USA

"Mother Earth is a living being."
Leonide Vargas
Andean Culture, Bolivia

"The land is the mother and we are of the land; we do not own the land,
rather the land owns us."
Dennis Foley
Gai-mariagal and Wiradjuri man and Indigenous Elder, Australia

Glossary

Australia is an island continent, relatively flat, with its highest point at 2228 metres on the eastern seaboard.

Spring – September to November
Summer – December to February
Autumn – March to May
Winter – June to August

The Dry: In Winter, cold fronts from the Southern Ocean bring rain to the southern coastline. These fronts do not penetrate the continent's northern regions, which remain dry and hot. Locals in the north refer to this period as The Dry.

The Wet: In Summer, the cold fronts retreat to the south, leaving the southern regions in dry, warm weather resembling a Californian climate. At the same time, monsoonal storms sweep in from the Timor Sea, drenching the northern region. Locals in the north refer to this period as The Wet.

PART 1
Lucille

Legalities
2016

The January summer promised a hot day in Perth.

Cord took the early ferry from South Perth to the city, even though it was the Monday rush hour and crowded with office workers and students. It was history repeating itself, but this time, he was going alone to meet his solicitor, Harold Foy, unlike that ferry journey in 2013 when he and Rodney Cao travelled to meet Miriam Manx at Manx Mooney Attorneys.

He sat watching the bow wave agitating the still water. The serenity of the river under the bright blue sky did little to alleviate his concerns. The Swan River is a peaceful river, always calm as it meanders along in no hurry to get to the sea. The crisp city skyline came closer, shimmering in the approaching heat. The ferry trundled into the berth and Cord checked his cell phone. The weatherman predicted thirty degrees and it felt like it was that already.

Cord McCullum was in good shape for his forty-one years. The years of surveying in the field, with a jigger over his shoulder and constant walking up hill and down dale ensured he didn't need an artificial gym; he didn't even own a pair of lycras. Strong of build but fair of skin, he avoided unnecessary exposure to the sun, a funny thing for a surveyor. He never really took to the water either, but this short trip across to the city reminded him of Penang and his time on the tugboat *Spree* with Gert Koch, the skipper. That was how he got the nickname 'Landman'. He remembered being grey and squeamish one black night, early in the piece, perched over the plotting table as the vessel rolled and pitched.

Gert was at the helm, laughing and slapping him on the back, "Cord, *mein Junge*, you're a Land Lubber. My advice, stick to the land, man." He laughed louder as Cord rushed from the bridge to relieve his heaving stomach. From that day forward, the crew called him 'Landman'.

He eventually found his sea legs, but those days and nights in Malaysia still lived in his memory; the tugboat bouncing around in sloppy, uneasy seas in the Penang Straits with the smell of diesel in the air and the cook coming up from the galley with a can of slops to throw overboard.

He studied the ferry passengers around him, deep in their own thoughts, most concentrating on mobile phones, the dull throb of the diesel engine the only other sound to break the monotony of the journey they did every day. He waited for them to disembark. He wasn't in a hurry and although he had a busy day ahead, he was early. The sun beat down as he crossed the foreshore esplanade to the Terrace, already busy with traffic and bustling people. In one of the small arcades off the Terrace, he sneaked into a pint-sized coffee shop and settled back in a padded corner booth. He ordered a flat white from a pretty Asian waitress. Her dark almond eyes reminded him of Mia.

He was here for Mia. Cord had been her guardian for five years since she was twelve. Today, he would meet his solicitor regarding the sudden turn of events that was about to affect their lives. He ordered another coffee and sat back pensively, contemplating the past and pondering what the future might bring. He felt a twinge of sadness at Rodney Cao's passing, that's all. How long had he known Rodney, Mia's father? It was a long time, not quite twenty years, he mused. For the second time that morning, it took him back to those days in Penang.

He looked at his watch; time for his appointment. He nodded and smiled at the waitress, who smiled back.

Outside, the day was heating up. He deviated through several arcades to stay in the shade before emerging outside the high-rise that housed the solicitor's office. The directory in the foyer displayed Foy and Foy, Barristers and Solicitors, Fourth Floor. The lift doors opened onto a tastefully furnished waiting room where a well-groomed receptionist welcomed him.

She gestured to a leather chair, made a short phone call and advised, "Mr McCullum, Mr Foy will be with you shortly. May I offer you a tea or coffee?"

Cord declined and was glancing at the morning newspaper when Harold Foy emerged from his office. He was a tall, grey-haired man, impeccably dressed, with an equally impeccable reputation in the legal fraternity. Offering his hand, he ushered Cord into his office. Foy knew the details of

Cord's guardianship, as he had drafted the contract documents all those years ago.

"How are you, Cord? I was sorry to hear of Rodney's death. He wasn't an old man. Forty-six, you said when you rang."

Cord took Foy's hand in a strong shake, "Yes, it's quite a shock."

The office was spacious and opulent. Foy gestured towards several leather lounge chairs in one corner of the room. Through the large plate glass window, Cord could see the river, blue, unruffled, unperturbed.

"Sure you won't have a coffee or tea, water?"

They sat facing each other, Cord nervous and anxious, wanting to get quickly to the issue that was worrying him. Calm, collected and sensing Cord's concern, Foy said, "How is Mia taking her father's death? It must be distressing for her. That was a nasty business Rodney was implicated in a few years ago, but it all cleared up satisfactorily."

"Yes, it turned out okay."

Cord thought of the circumstances of Rodney's death and the email he'd received the previous week from Bobbi Hahn, Rodney's lawyer in Kuala Lumpur. It appeared that Rodney had died of a drug overdose, but results were inconclusive, circumstances he wanted to keep from Mia. If Rodney had committed suicide, Cord knew of one dark secret in his past that may have driven him to this act. The tragedy of death and dying was an experience he wanted to shield Mia from, but how and when to break the news to her troubled him. She'd drifted away from her father over the years; after all, Rodney seldom visited, claiming his business in Malaysia kept him busy, but he kept her well provided for.

"I haven't told her yet."

Foy raised his eyebrows and was about to speak when Cord added, "I wanted to see you first. The email from the lawyer said he and Mia's aunty would be here in a few weeks to formalise matters and deliver sealed letters to Mia and myself. I guess the letters are to release my guardianship and appoint her aunty as guardian. Mr Foy…" He corrected himself, "Harold, I want to oppose that release. Mia is very much part of my family. My mother, father and sister Corrine are her family now. I have known her since she was nine. What can I do? I can't let her go, just like that."

Foy didn't comment. It seemed a long time before he rose, went to his desk and picked up the phone.

"Changed your mind? Would you like a drink now?"

"Thanks, no, I'm okay."

Foy spoke on the phone, "Claire, would you please bring me a coffee, the usual?"

He retreated to his chair, nodding deep in thought, "Mia, how old is she? Seventeen, I think?"

"That's right."

Claire entered the room with the coffee.

Foy sat with cup and saucer in hand and sipped the hot liquid. There was a long pause before he said, "And she'll be eighteen this year?"

"That's right, in November."

"Hmm," mused Foy. There was another long, thoughtful pause.

"Cord, there are a few issues we must consider before we go down the track you're suggesting. In my opinion, pursuing legal action to retain guardianship is not practicable. As you know, this guardianship is a loose arrangement, really only a contract between two parties for services. Even if we could start today, it'd be difficult to get the application for custody before the Family Court until later in the year and if there were an appeal of the verdict by either party, by the time that was determined, Mia would be eighteen. Then, if she is of sound mind and body, as I am sure she is, she'll no longer need a guardian and would also be independent of her father's will."

Cord contemplated the soundness of his solicitor's advice. He didn't know what to say.

Foy placed his cup on the side table. "Where does her aunty live? In Australia?"

"No, in America."

"Well then, it's possible she may not want to have custody, especially for only a year. She can renege on the request. It's a position that's not obligatory. Are she and Mia close?"

"No, they're virtually strangers. Casual contact, birthday texts, that's all."

"It's a good thing you haven't spoken to Mia yet. Find out how she feels about the matter. She may decide to be with her aunty, especially if that's her father's dying wish. There's the blood connection to consider, of course, and that would count in any dispute we might raise over custodial rights. I think you should let Mia decide where her duty to her father lies. It'll be a clear indicator as to how you stand in her affections. My advice is not to pre-empt things pending the lawyer's visit. Let's let the matter lie for the moment and wait to see what the letters contain."

Foy rose to shake Cord's hand, "Keep me informed."

The consultation was over.

Cord rode the afternoon ferry back to the apartment. A fresh sea breeze made the journey more comfortable. His business occupied the entire ground floor of the building, but rather than make his presence felt with his staff there, he quickly took the lift to his apartment upstairs. He opened a bottle of local Shiraz, filled a good-sized goblet and relaxed on the balcony overlooking the river esplanade, realising his next job was to tell Mia.

"I saw you sneak into the lift, Pa," Mia said.

She had come onto the balcony and surprised Cord. How beautiful she looked, standing there in the company outfit; even in her work jeans and crisp blue linen shirt, she looked spectacular. She sat beside him.

"What's up, Pa?"

He felt powerless, so close to her and yet so far away. The years that saw her grow from a child to the verge of womanhood merged in his memory. It was hard to believe it may all end in just a few weeks. From a child reliant on him, she had blossomed into a self-sufficient, strong-willed, gentle person, popular and driven to succeed no matter the venture. Those dark eyes, clear and intelligent, creamy flawless skin with full curved lips that always seemed half smiling exemplified her beauty and Eurasian pedigree.

She flipped back her ponytail of long black hair, gazed at him and said again, more concerned, "What is it, Pa?"

Cord drew her to him, hugging her softly. He hesitated, "I'm so sorry, sweetheart, your father's passed away."

There, he'd said it. He couldn't say 'died'; it sounded abrupt, not peaceful like it should be.

She pulled away from the embrace, staring at him incredulously for what seemed a long time. Tears welled up in her eyes, and sobbing, head shaking, with hands to her face, she turned away, with a breaking voice, "When, how, where?"

"In KL, a few days ago. He had complications, that's all I know. I don't know anything else except his lawyer's coming here in a few weeks to attend to his estate."

"His estate?"

"That includes you, honey." Honey, sweetheart, words he'd hardly used before.

"Your aunt's coming here too; you might now come under her care."

"What! Why? Aunty Lucille lives in America."

"I don't know if you've met her. Have you?"

"Yes, Father took me there to visit her before I came here."

Cord's thought of Mia seeing her aunt so suddenly in this new situation alarmed him. He wished he didn't have to say it, but it was important and he did have to raise it.

"You're her only blood relative, apart from your grandparents."

"I want to stay here with you, Pa," she cried, her eyes still tearful.

'Pa'; he was reminded of her wish to call him 'Pa' soon after she came under his care. Rodney had initially introduced him as 'Uncle Cord'. Mia didn't take to the 'Uncle' label and Cord was flattered when she suggested 'Pa'. It made her more comfortable with her school friends and Rodney didn't seem to mind.

"What about my degree and helping you in the business? I have friends here."

It was a sad and awkward occasion and he tried to make the best of it. "They have degrees in America and the business will look after itself."

They lapsed into silence, holding hands, watching the sun slowly sinking below the horizon. The last crimson rays vanished, dusk became evening and eventually, the city lights glowed softly, mirrored in the tranquil river.

Cord reflected on the first time he met Mia all those years ago. He hadn't heard from Rodney since he left Penang and was surprised when Rodney rang him saying he was in Perth, staying at the Crown and could they meet; he had some business to discuss, something to do with buying property. Cord went more out of curiosity than necessity. That's when he met her. It was 2007 and she was a little girl of mixed blood, just nine years old. Tell-tale deep dark almond eyes, a fine pointed nose, creamy porcelain skin, slender face and chin, her beauty set her apart even then.

"Your daughter?" Cord was surprised and tried not to sound incredulous.

It appeared completely out of character for Rodney to have a child. It didn't seem possible for the austere, business-focused Rodney to have a daughter or that Rodney would ever have had a romantic interest. Rodney's motto was 'Business before pleasure', and he meant it.

"I don't think you met Ruby, her mother."

"No, no, I didn't."

"Pity. We shifted our business to Kuala Lumpur twelve years ago when tobacco declined. I met her there. She was in marketing, English and, well, family circumstances, you know, we never married, but we had Mia. Ruby didn't want a child and returned to England following the birth. She never had contact with Mia and sadly died in a car accident several years ago." He paused, then added, "Anyway, I'm exploring the possibility of buying a property here. I thought of you and I'd appreciate your advice."

"Sure," Cord said, not knowing what else to say.

*****

Eventually, Mia woke Cord from his reverie. The lights of the city sparkled in the river. She brought the bottle of Shiraz from the cabinet, poured him a top-up and sat beside him.

"I don't want to leave home. I have friends. I don't even know Aunty Lucille."

"Come on, Mia, you do know her."

"I only met her once, perhaps twice. She sends a card on my birthday each year, that's all. Father said she gave me Daisy, my cuddly cow, when I was a baby. I suppose she did, but I don't remember much."

Cord hesitated; he didn't really want to hear what she might say as it would, no doubt, stir up old, happy, but sometimes bitter memories.

"Well, what do you remember?"

"Oh, I remember she was beautiful. Nice. She had a high-powered job in the Federal Government in Washington, D.C. and lived alone in the best apartment. I liked her, but she seemed a little sad and no fun. She was big into Land Rights for the Native American Indians. I remember all her study walls were covered in clippings and photos of some Human Rights Commission, really heavy stuff. I could tell she and Father weren't close, although she loved seeing my grandfather and grandmother. Funnily, amongst all the clippings, she had a photo of herself laughing. It was when she was young and there was this huge butterfly clinging to her hair. It's preserved in a box on her mantelpiece. It had an unusual name. The Chocolate Man ... no. Something ... I forget. I asked her about it and she just shrugged and said it was better times then."

The image struck home. Cord knew it was the butterfly, the Chocolate Sailor.

"So, she lives alone?"

"I'm not sure. She could be married now, she's pretty enough. Can't you do anything about this, Pa?"

"I've seen our solicitor. He advised to wait till your father's lawyer comes here. It's all in the melting pot. Your aunty may not want to be your guardian. She can opt out, you know."

"Well, I hope she does." Mia rose from the chair. "Chinese tonight?"

He nodded.

She paused and responded, "Okay, I'll order in. You've met Aunt Lucille, haven't you, Pa?"

"Once."

She pursed her lips, frowned, nodded and left the room.

He rose and went to the hi-fi, flicked a switch and selected a track on the CD. The moody sound of *Cavalleria Rusticana* floated into the air. The music soothed his troubled mind. Cord reclined on the couch; it'd been a long trying day.

He raised his arms, folded them behind his head and reflected. He knew Lucille once, a long time ago. How had it all started?

Memories flooded back. It seemed only yesterday when he flew into Penang, a raw twenty-three-year-old surveyor on his first big job.

The Spree
1998

The 747 came out of the high cloud and Cord could see the blue waters of the Penang Straits from his window seat. At age twenty-three, this was his first time in another country. The plane turned on a last broad sweep, descended and was soon skimming close to the water on its approach to the airport. The sea was alive with craft of all descriptions, plying in what seemed a haphazard fashion, their wakes criss-crossing each other, whipping the water into complete confusion. Suddenly, they were over land and the lush green vegetation bordering the runway came into view. With a final bump, they were down and he was in a strange new country.

The six-hour flight from Perth became longer as it took another hour and a half to pass through customs. As he went through the doors into the airport, he was relieved to see a man casually but smartly dressed in a short-sleeved shirt and shorts, holding a placard with several names on it; one of them was McCullum. There were seven others, none of whom Cord knew. When they were assembled, the man brusquely ushered them outside into a humid and sultry tropical February afternoon. There was an avenue of palm trees and in a parking bay, a small bus waited with its engine idling; emblazoned on its side was a motif that read *Penang Port Commission*.

On board, the man introduced himself as Rodney Cao, Contract Project Manager. Cord only briefly listened as he absorbed the sights and sounds of this new foreign place. He was surprised to see a myriad of motorbikes passing by with pillion passengers holding bags of produce. There were doorways full of people, sometimes spilling out into the street, keeping their driver on edge, constantly tooting. The odour of fried cooking floated through the air and into the bus. Even a short, sharp, torrential shower with lightning and muffled thunder didn't seem to disturb the ceaseless activity or override the noisy traffic. Cord felt alone and, for a moment, wondered what the hell he was doing there.

The bus turned off the narrow street and passed through a forbidding wrought iron gate into a spacious garden surrounding a large two-storey house. Cord later found out it was a colonial manor house built in 1810 for a British tobacco tycoon. It had recently been renovated and retained by the Malay Government because of its historic significance. Somehow, it was on loan to the Port Commission to house the project team over the course of the project. It was in a convenient location near the port, in a side alley just off Lebuh Downing and close to the main thoroughfare, Lebuh Light.

Several assistants helped unload their baggage and they were escorted into a spacious entry hall that reeked of past opulence. The arrivals stood around uneasily, not talking; no one broke the ice to introduce themselves. A middle-aged woman entered the hall. She wore a house frock, her hair in a bun and horn-rimmed spectacles. She was clearly not Asian.

Rodney spoke, "Gentlemen, let me introduce Mrs Brown, our housekeeper manageress."

She smiled, nodded and the new guests nodded in reply.

He continued, "You have two days to settle in. On Monday, in our George Town Office, there'll be a briefing with Gert Koch, the skipper of the boat you will be working on. I'll send the bus for you, pick up at 8 am sharp. Be outside. Welcome to Penang."

With that, he was gone, leaving them with Mrs Brown.

She spoke in a broad Scottish accent and quickly explained the house rules, mealtimes and policy for visitors, which, by the look in her eye, meant these should only be official visitors of the same gender. There were fifteen rooms and seven shared bathrooms. There were twelve personnel in lodgings, four of them women who were billeted in a separate wing, whose bathrooms were off limits to the male guests. It was clear Mrs Brown did not encourage fraternising amongst the sexes. She reminded Cord of his mother.

"In your comings and goings, make sure the main front gate is closed behind you. The Rawson's house down the road was robbed last week as a couple of beggars sneaked in through the gate when the guard wasn't watching. So, be careful. Any questions?"

Again, no one spoke, just nodded heads in acknowledgement. It was early days and the questions would no doubt come later.

"All right then, I'll show you your rooms."

She led them up a blue marble staircase to the first floor, saying as they went, "You're well catered for by the project managers. We have six house staff attending to cleaning, etcetera and two full-time cooks. You can have coffee, tea, Milo, whatever, anytime in the dining room, located to the right of the foyer. There's always food in the fridges if you're hungry. You can make it yourself, provided you clean up afterwards. Remember, breakfast is from 6 to 8:30 am. As you'll be in and out with shift work, there is a smorgasbord of meals throughout the day from noon till 9 pm. Your linen is changed each week on a Monday. I have an office on the ground floor below the stairs if you need help to settle in. By the way, no drugs, alcohol or visitors."

She emphasised 'visitors', leaving no doubt as to whom she was referring.

It was over quickly and she said, "Goodnight," and left.

Cord was thankful to be alone at last. Bewildered and tired, he sank fully clothed onto the bed, closed his eyes and slept, oblivious to the clamour and commotion rising from the street below.

He awoke with a start. It was 5:30 am. "Damn," he said to himself, seeing that he was still in his clothes. He crossed the room to a set of French doors that opened onto a small balcony. The sounds of the city were subdued at this hour but still there. A soft breeze wafted through the curtains, cooling the room as he carefully unpacked his suitcase, placing the contents neatly into a large wardrobe and chest of drawers. He tried to remember the direction of the bathroom and, fortunately, when he found it, it was empty. It was 6:30 am when he finished showering; he decided to go down for breakfast at 7:30 am, so he sat on the balcony to welcome his first day in this strange place.

The room overlooked the front gate and was fully exposed to the sights and sounds of the city that were beginning to gather momentum. Already, there were parades of people passing by. Women in wide straw hats, barefoot men running, pulling, and pushing fully laden rickety carts, children in ragged clothes with wheelbarrows, some with trinkets, others with bananas and pineapples. Motorbikes buzzed past tooting, avoiding those on bicycles. On the opposite side of the road, seemingly out of place, was a car dealership. The gleaming new vehicles in the showroom contrasted starkly with the tarnished world outside. Cord shook his head and wondered again what he was doing there.

Cord had been with JKSurveys since obtaining his license to practice surveying. He'd mainly been involved in residential development and was surprised when John Keep called him into his office just six weeks before, to offer him this new job.

"Cord, I'd like you to go to Malaysia for around twelve weeks on marine navigation work in the Penang Straits. We won a subcontract to the international resource group, ConsatUK, to provide personnel. You're my best field man, so I'm offering you the job first. What do you say?"

Cord was taken aback. It wasn't what he expected; questions flooded his mind. He'd never been overseas or to another country. He couldn't speak the language and knew nothing about boats and the marine environment.

Yet, he said, "Okay, yes."

"Good, here's the heads-up. You're to go to Sydney for a two-week course on the new encrypted Trimble GNNS equipment currently being installed on the workboat you'll be working on. You'll not only be responsible for operating the system but also for maintenance."

"Just me?"

"No, there will be three others in the navigation team; who they are, I don't know. It's a government contract, so there won't be any problems getting you a passport and a work permit. It's double your salary with all accommodation and meals thrown in and the Malaysian government pays a bonus for finishing the job early. I know I can count on you. See Marie at reception to start the ball rolling; she has all the details."

Cord left the office bewildered but elated, excited about this new venture.

The two weeks in Sydney with technicians from the Trimble system designers went smoothly, and now, four weeks later, here he was, sitting on the balcony of this manor in downtown Penang, surrounded by the continuous cacophony of sounds, wondering what he had let himself in for. Working on a boat in a marine environment was, to say the least, unfamiliar to him. Was this something he could handle? He felt fearful but vibrant and very much alive.

*****

It was 7:30 am, time for breakfast. Several others were in the dining room, including one of his fellow travellers. Cord took a tray, poured himself an orange juice and was preparing a bowl of cereal when a voice behind him said, "Glad to see a familiar face. I flew in with you yesterday. I'm Brian. Are you a fellow surveyor?"

Cord nodded. "Yes, Cord, Cord McCullum."

They shook hands. Cord gauged he was a man in his thirties, tall and athletic.

"Brian Thomas. Good. For a while, I thought I was alone. Are you new to Penang?

"Yes, this is my first time."

"I've been here before, but only as a tourist. Missus and I came over on a cruise a couple of years ago. Watch out for the pickpockets and the hawkers; they're bloody pests."

They found a table near the others.

"I'm from Sydney. Where are you from?"

"Perth."

"Yeah, I've been to Perth. Nice place. Have you been to sea before?"

"No, never, just to Rottnest."

"Oh," Brian laughed, "I've been there too. Never been on a tugboat in the open water, though. I've only got a dinghy for fishing, that's all."

They sat in silence while they ate.

"Would you like to take a stroll downtown later, take in the sights, say after lunch?"

"Sure," Cord replied.

Gert
1998

They had two days to settle in and Cord and Brian wandered the streets and alleyways of George Town, savouring the sights and sounds of this new exotic place. They consumed the sizzling spicy chicken dish, Curry Mee, cooked by the obliging and jovial hawker in Lebuh Chulia and bargained in the alley markets for trinkets to send home. After dark, the streets lit up with strings of coloured lanterns strung from building to building and amongst the hustle and bustle, ladies of the night approached the pair, offering favours for a fee.

Their wanderings took them to the waterfront, to the quaint Church Street Pier, a memento of the historical colonial past, and to the ferry terminal alive with noise and activity. Tooting ferries painted in a variety of vibrant yellows, reds, blues and greens nosed into narrow gaps in the quay. For decades, these craft transported passengers and vehicles on a quick turnaround trip of three kilometres across the straits between George Town and Butterworth but were soon to be retired.

The navigation team members became acquainted at mealtimes and Cord realised that over the next few weeks, he'd be working closely with each of them within the confined space of the tugboat. Apart from Brian, there was Simon from England. He was five years older than Cord and had hydrographic surveying experience. He was brash, overbearing and Cord soon realised the man was not just there for the money but, from the way he spoke, also for otherworldly experiences. Sachin, from India, was a quiet, well-mannered man in his thirties. He was a marine engineer with naval experience and well acquainted with the early Global Positioning Systems, clearly the most experienced member of the team.

Then, there was Dixie; she came to their table at dinner the first night at the manor.

"Are you the nav boys?" she asked. "I'll be on the boat with you. I'm the geologist doing the proline drilling."

She did the rounds shaking hands and Simon was particularly courteous, holding her hand a little too long. Cord reckoned she was in her thirties, slim, not tall, an attractive brown-eyed brunette.

"I'm Dixie," she said brightly and grinned, "Not from Dixie down south but a Connecticut Yankee from Milford."

In time, Cord found she had an extensive background in exploration drilling, particularly regarding analysing drill core samples and had worked in Australia in Outback Queensland. It seemed she'd worked all over the world, from the Arctic to Antarctica. Cord liked her; she brought glamour and humour to the table and the boat.

The bus arrived on Monday at exactly 8 am to take the navigation team on the short journey to meet with Rodney at his office in a small prefab building near the Lim Jetty. The building was temporary accommodation for the duration of the project, the main Penang Port Commission office being at Butterworth on the mainland. There were several rooms, including a plan room with charts pinned to the walls, a kitchen/lounge area and an office. A woman, Rodney's assistant, ushered them into the plan room. They waited, lolling on several stools, except for Cord, who stood browsing the maps.

They could hear Rodney in his office in earnest conversation with another man. Eventually, Rodney and the stranger joined them, the stranger smartly dressed in brown shorts, a matching short-sleeved shirt with shoulder epaulettes and a captain's hat. Rodney seemed overly concerned and agitated when he introduced the man as the Master of the workboat. Clearly, words had passed between them, but the skipper appeared relaxed and self-assured. He was fortyish, tanned with blue eyes and a shock of fair hair showed under his peaked hat.

"Gert Koch," he said smiling, his direct gaze appraising each individual as they shook hands. He paused with an even broader smile when he took Dixie's hand and she smiled back.

Rodney spoke with great urgency. It was an intense briefing and Cord felt his confidence ebbing in this new and unfamiliar maritime environment. Rodney emphasised that timelines had to be met, that time was money and there was a fixed budget. With bewildering speed, he pointed to the various wall plans that detailed the extent of the project. The big picture was the modernisation of the port. The old wooden ferries were to be replaced by faster, larger diesel passenger catamarans, leaving goods and vehicles to be transported by a new system of an undersea tunnel and several bridges. It was a long-term project, but the initial contract was to provide a comprehensive map of the geology of the seabed and precise locations of port facilities and existing navigation structures.

He concluded, "We have estimated ten to twelve weeks' field time for this first stage, and we are confident you'll bring it in on time. You're the best in your respective fields and there's a bonus for early completion. I'll leave you with Gert to run through job specifics."

Cord realised Rodney was a man of few words; short, to the point and above all, a moneyman. He was not old, around thirty, Cord guessed and already a dynamic businessman running the family tea plantations on the island and mainland. His political persuasion and drive led him to be appointed to oversee the port redevelopment. He was influential, a man who got his way and very, very rich.

While Gert waited for Rodney to leave, he eye-balled each man to reinforce his rank and authority.

"Welcome, crew. Let's get this straight. Rodney used the term workboat, but this boat, my boat, is more than a workboat. It's a custom-built tugboat designed to work in both open and closed waters. She has a multitude of capabilities beyond that of other conventional tugboats. Her name is *Spree*. Gentlemen, I never want to hear the word 'tug'; I only ever want to hear you use her name with respect. Do that, be good to her, and we'll get along fine."

With a wink at Dixie, he went on, "Who's worked on boats before?"

Everyone, except Cord, nodded they had.

"Who hasn't been to sea before?"

Cord raised his hand.

Gert laughed, patting him on the shoulder, "We'll have to get you some sea legs then."

Cord liked the man.

It was a day for organising work rosters and going over general procedures for safety at sea. The naming protocol on board was on a first-name basis except for Gert, who was always to be addressed as 'Skipper'. The ship operated on a twenty-four-hour basis, with the nav team rotating on eight-hour shifts when at sea with an independent four-day break ashore for each man. Dixie was not included in the rotation and would come and go by tender independently.

Rodney didn't join them for lunch, choosing to remain in his office, either head down, on the phone, or both. Gert and Rodney spoke briefly before the team was on the bus to the Lim Jetty, where the *Spree* was moored. On board, Gert introduced his officer crew as Hardy, the Mate and First Officer; Max, the Engineer; and Jon, the Cook. There was no formal introduction to the several other crew members bustling around the deck.

The *Spree* was built in Norway and launched two years ago. Gert was well known in the region and had done good business around the ports and seaways of Malaysia and the Philippines over the years. It was said he skippered a tugboat through a cyclone when many others were lost. He named the boat after the Spree River that ran through Bautzen, his home town in Germany. As a boy, he had traversed the river many times in his dinghy yacht, the river that had launched him on a maritime career.

Gert left Hardy to show them over the vessel, expounding details of six hundred fifty tonnes dead weight, thirty-five-metre length, draft at six metres, beam at fifteen, engine size, capacity and so on. The bow wasn't pointed like a conventional ship; it was broad, rounded and protected by massive rubber fenders. Wide decks surrounded a tall central bridge structure. Four winches were located, one on each side of the bow and one on each side of the stern. The spacious bridge, the outside painted bright yellow, had a panoramic view of the decks.

The Trimble Electronics system, which most interested the nav team, was installed in an alcove close to the ship's steering and beside a plotting table, well away from interference by the ship's radio. All agreed that Sachin, who didn't have a say, was the right man to fire up the system for its first run when they set sail.

The vessel had bunk accommodation for ten crew and separate cabins for the skipper, mate and engineer. There was one spare two-bunk compartment, which was Dixie's berth when she came aboard. The nav team shared a four-bunk cabin. It was Cord's home away from home for the next few weeks.

They finished the initial tour in the spacious galley, where Jon provided hot muffins and coffee.

Gert met them on the bridge to explain the ship's rules, "Now listen up. It's Monday; we put to sea on Thursday 5 am. I expect everything to be shipshape and running when we leave. You can come and go as you please; Hardy has dock gate passes for each of you to come aboard. Don't lose them. You know your rosters. No alcohol on board. Any breach of that and you're out. Also, no females allowed, except project team members."

Simon muttered, "Bugger" under his breath.

The coffee was hot and relaxing and the comforting smell of yeast as the bread baked filled the galley. Cord thought it wasn't bad so far. He liked the *Spree*.

Rodney had company cell phones ready for each of the team and on arrival back at the office, Cord noticed a sleek, black Cadillac Eldorado parked outside, complete with driver in peaked hat. They waited in the plan room until Rodney appeared with the most exquisitely beautiful woman Cord had ever seen. She hugged Rodney, kissed his cheek, nodded and smiled at the gob-smacked nav team as she left. Cord caught her eye and at that moment, his very being lit up with fireworks.

Later, he lay in his room, remembering her. An oval face, cream skin, dark almond eyes, a pert nose, full lips and black hair pulled back and tied with a red band. She wore a traditional Malay yellow sarong and an embroidered full-length blue silk shirt that showed her figure to advantage. He remembered her perfectly. Cord was smitten and ruefully thought how lucky Rodney was.

Sea Legs
1998

Gert pushed the men hard. He was strict, uncompromising and tough. The proline drilling for seabed core samples tested the crew, demanding the highest degree of teamwork. The Global Positioning System (GPS) equipment worked well, but winching the *Spree* into position on a heaving ocean to the prescribed half-metre tolerance required skill and coordination. Gert couldn't tolerate sloppy performance and repeated the activity until it was perfect. For several days, Cord battled with bouts of nausea and ate little. Sometimes, his concentration lagged, but he willed himself not to let Gert or the team down.

A couple of weeks into the job, on a black, stormy night, he was at the map table plotting the next fix and still feeling uneasy when Gert entered the bridge.

"We're in for some weather," he said, shucking off his oilskins. "You've finally got your sea legs, Landman. We're on the Butterworth side, so we'll refuel there in the morning and lay off for a few days for the weather to blow out."

Cord thought it was not like Gert to let a little weather interfere with the task at hand, but one didn't question the skipper's decision.

Dixie came onto the bridge and Gert repeated the message to her. She nodded and seemed pleased. It was evident that Gert's decision had something to do with her and Cord suddenly realised they were a couple. It was then, and for the first time, that Gert spoke outside the work environment.

"You've got a girl, Landman?"

Cord shook his head.

Gert winked and laughed, "I've got one in every port; I take her with me every time."

Cord stopped plotting and puzzled. "My girl! The *Spree*," Gert laughed again and slapped Cord on the back.

"Got a message from our friend Rodney. We're ahead of schedule, so we're invited to a banquet with his family at their home in the hills when we return. A real privilege."

Cord broached the subject, "His family? I saw his wife at the office but don't know her name."

"Wife?" queried Gert. "Wife? Rodney doesn't have a wife. He hasn't got time for a wife. Must have been his sister, Lucille. Pretty little thing about twentyish?"

Cord's heart rose, skipped a beat, the sea calmed and the underlying nausea left him. He couldn't get her out of his mind. It was all right to fantasise about this woman, but to approach her, get to know her, was something new and daunting. There had been girls before. Brief entanglements in the backseat of his dad's car and in the previous two years, serious relationships with Celia and Rachel; but nothing had stirred him like this. Why had the brief sight of her affected him so much? It must be the real thing, he thought.

It was as if culture, religion and nationality had nothing to do with it. Would his parents accept an Asian girl? Dad would and his twin sister Corrine would, but he knew his mother would object. Other questions filled his mind. She'd have a suitor and probably wouldn't like him, ignore him, humiliate him, so he had to be on his guard in her presence. But it always came back to the very thought of her. It was love at first sight for Cord and he had to do something about it.

He didn't see Gert or Dixie during the stopover; they were both ashore and when the storm blew out, Hardy was in command and supervised the refuelling. After another long week at sea, they were back in George Town.

*****

The route to the Cao family home followed the coastline along the Jalan Tanjong Tokong road to the small village of Pantai Aceh on the northern coast of the island. The property was inland in the rainforest, adjacent to the Penang National Park. The large and impressive house sat on high stilts to encourage airflow. Cord noted three adjoining buildings, wooden with high-pitched rattan roofs and windows opening onto a surrounding veranda. Everything was natural, no paint, just raw materials that blended with the bordering jungle.

The bus with the nav team, excluding Simon, who chose to go to Butterworth, stopped at the staircase to the middle building. Rodney was waiting there, dressed differently to his usual business attire. He wore an embroidered crimson-coloured sarong over a lounge suit of light fabric in a more subdued colour. He was smiling and relaxed.

"*Selamat datang*," he said, bowing.

On the way, Gert briefed them on paying respect to Malay customs.

"They don't drink alcohol and remove your boots when you enter the house. Above all, bow to Rodney's parents; do not shake hands. Do that and you'll get along fine."

"Welcome," Rodney said, this time in English, as he led them into a spacious lounge area covered with colourful casual couches, large glossy ceramic flowerpots with bamboo and palm arrangements and stands of sculptured wooden figures. In the centre of the tiled room was a small pool, the water covered with floating lotus flowers. It was the most opulent lounge Cord had ever seen.

Rodney was at his gentlemanly best.

"I'm sure you'd like some tea to refresh. Father and Mother will be with us shortly. Please sit. Make yourself comfortable."

Cord was disappointed that Rodney's sister hadn't appeared. Perhaps she wouldn't be there after all.

A maid in a bright green sarong brought them tea and coconut biscuits.

"Ahead of time, four days ahead of schedule," Rodney clapped his hands in delight. The terseness Cord had experienced between the two men in the office had disappeared for the time being.

Gert responded, "I've a good crew; it's coming along well. We'll concentrate on dropping marker buoys next time out as the weather's looking good."

Rodney nodded and was about to speak when his parents and sister entered the room. He stood and the nav team did the same.

"Please meet my father and mother and my sister Lucille," he said.

Everyone bowed and for the first time, Cord looked directly into Lucille's eyes. They were dark and captivating and caught him in the moment. She smiled. He wanted to say something, anything, but couldn't speak. She'd taken his breath away. Lucille was in Malay dress, a bright red full-sleeved blouse over a long pinkish skirt embroidered with roses. A scarf of hand-woven fabric with gold thread covered her head and neck. She was stunning and Cord had difficulty not to keep staring at her.

The parents didn't speak English and nodded as Rodney introduced each person in turn before ushering everyone into a large room that opened out onto the veranda with spectacular views over the jungle valley. There was a long table already laden with food. Lucille spoke with a melodic English accent, explaining each dish with their Malay name. Cord wanted to sit close to her, but Dixie sat between them, so all he could do was eat and listen.

"We have our *Nasi Lemak,* a rice dish with coconut milk and sambal sauce. *Hokkien Hae Mee,* shrimp noodles, *Nasi Campur,* a traditional vegetable dish and *Ikan Bakar,* steamed fish from our coast served with a sour sauce. This is *Satay,* grilled curry chicken on skewers. Sweets are a banana, mango concoction I made." She laughed, pulled a face, "I hope they're okay. Anyway, Father and Mother say, *'Selamat menjamu selera'* or Bon Appetit."

The dishes were shared and Cord tried every one, including the delicious sweets. He mumbled a thank you to Lucille as they left the table and was pleased when she offered to show the guests around the property. Gert and Dixie stayed in the house talking to Rodney; the parents retired to another part of the house. Cord, Brian and Sachin strolled with Lucille around the extensive gardens. Later, Brian and Sachin decided to relax on recliner loungers on the veranda while Lucille offered to continue the tour and show Cord the pond where her father bred tortoises.

At last, Cord was alone with her, but he fumbled as to what to say; it was awkward. What on earth could he say except that he wanted desperately to see her again?

They were at the pool watching a large tortoise lying on the bank when Lucille said, "This one is *Malik,* which means *king* in English. He is sixty years old, the same as my father. Do they have tortoises in Australia?"

"I'm not sure," Cord replied, "I know we have turtles."

"I'd like to go to Australia one day," she added wistfully.

She pulled the scarf away from her face and Cord noticed the delicate shape of her neck. Her dark hair flowed loosely and elegantly around her shoulders.

"Did you guess I was Australian? Is it my accent?"

"No, I have my spies. My brother tells me everything. You're here for only a short time. What do you do in Australia?"

She was an avid listener as Cord volunteered information about his career, his family, a little about Perth and his interest in music and leisure activities.

"So, you like hiking," she said.

"Yes, we have some good walk trails where I live and I've walked most of them. We have one called the *Bibbulmun,* named after the aboriginal people who travelled it in their seasons. It's iconic. If you come to Australia, I'll take you on it."

She laughed, "Well, then you might like to hike the Moongate Trail here, through the Botanic Gardens. I'll give you my cell phone number and take you on it when you're free. That's if you wish."

If you wish, Cord thought. He couldn't believe his luck. It's just what he wanted; another opportunity to be with Lucille.

"Sure," he said, "Great! Perhaps next time I'm back in port."

"Perhaps," she said, smiling.

The others were waiting to leave when they returned. Everyone bowed again. As they stepped onto the bus, Dixie gave Cord a pert smile.

Gert winked and said quietly, "Watch out, Landman, this is no ordinary *Fräulein* you're playing with."

Cord wasn't sure what he meant, but he felt good.

The bus drove down the driveway. Rodney and Lucille waved from the veranda, and when it was out of sight, he turned to her, "You're not to have anything to do with these men; they're drifters, especially that Australian hayseed. I could see his eyes on you."

"I'll do what I want," she replied.

Rodney exploded, "You'll do what the family wants. Honour your obligations to Father and Mother; remember your marriage to Kim Li's eldest is arranged. You know our merger with their family business is important, so don't jeopardise it."

He turned and strode angrily into the house, leaving her standing alone.

Moongate
1998

It was another two weeks at sea before Cord was back in port. He called Lucille's cell phone with a lover's trepidation, hoping she'd answer and was elated when she did.

"I'm hoping that offer is still on for the hike."

"Sure. We need to start early. The jungle's no place for hiking in the dark."

Cord thought, with you, it'd be okay.

The nav team had access to two Volvo sedans for personal use around George Town. Cord commandeered one for the drive to the national park entrance where they had arranged to meet. Mrs Brown went out of her way to help him prepare a light snack for lunch. She supplied a water bottle for his day pack and a can of bug spray. She really did remind him of his mother.

"So, you're meeting Lucille?" she asked.

Cord nodded.

"I wouldn't tell Rodney," she added, looking him directly in the eye.

It was a harrowing drive through George Town to the highlands. In the previous few weeks, Cord had driven from the manor to the port office, just a short trip, but this trip was a nightmare with roundabouts, cyclists, all the way to the foot of the national park. Arriving at the Botanic Gardens parking area, he could see Lucille dressed in hiking gear, talking to a group. She smiled warmly as he approached, held out her hand and introduced him to the others as members of her hiking club. They spoke in Malay and it was evident they were taking a different route to Lucille and Cord as they donned their packs, waved goodbye and set off down the road and onto a track leading into the jungle.

It was his first time seeing Lucille in Western clothes, albeit an outdoor outfit. She wore an orange fabric hooded jacket over a taupe green shirt with matching waterproof pants. A light day pack, Salomon hiking shoes and a pair of carbon fibre trekking poles completed her attire. She looked sensational and Cord wanted so much to hold her. He felt a little underdressed for the occasion in his khaki work shorts and short-sleeved shirt, but what could he do? He was in unfamiliar territory, but at least he had brought his hiking boots.

"Do you have a jacket?" she asked. "It can get wet in the rainforest and there will be mosquitoes. I'll give you some spray."

Cord nodded and patted his day pack. "I've got some."

"Good, we start over there at the Moongate," she said, pointing to a spot on the other side of the parking area.

"It's roughly a three-hour walk, can take longer if you're not fit. It's steep in parts with steps, ladders and hand holds. We cut through some dense forest with waterfalls and across rock faces that can be slippery. When we reach the top of Penang Hill, if you don't feel up to descending, there's the funicular railway to take you down. It's popular with tourists."

This is a bloody setup, Cord thought. She's testing me out to see what I'm made of. I won't be taking any bloody funicular railway out of here, that's for sure!

They climbed steadily on a narrow trail through dense forest with Lucille leading and Cord following, delighting at the female form before him. They stopped at a small waterfall for a drink. Other hikers were there and Lucille joined them in animated conversation. Several of the guys looked slyly at Cord as if he had done something wrong, but he proudly realised they were looks of jealousy.

Lucille had given Cord one of the walking poles from her pair, which he was grateful for as the trail became steeper and narrower, following a ledge in the rock face. Once again, they stopped to drink and admire the sweeping views out towards the coast.

"I enjoyed lunch with your parents," Cord said, feeling stupid, not knowing what else to say.

"You're welcome. Rodney is pleased with developments and it does a lot to please him."

He felt it was the right time and blurted out, "I was hoping we could have lunch or dinner together sometime."

She looked away, thought about it, turned to him and said, "Yes, lunch would be best."

"Tomorrow, while I'm still in port?" he said hopefully.

"Yes, let me know where and I'll meet you there."

"I saw resorts and cafés along the coast when I drove up. Have you a preference?"

"I'll let you know," she replied.

They walked on in relative silence, Cord ecstatic at the prospect of seeing her again.

They reached the top of the hill at lunchtime. The place was busy with tourists who took the railway to the top and others who were just leaving. They found a table in a lawned area. Lucille poured an orange juice and they shared the cup.

"Can I have that as a souvenir?" he joked.

She fluttered her eyelids.

"Oh!" Lucille exclaimed when she saw Cord unpack his lunch from his pack. "I brought a snack for you."

"Well, Mrs Brown insisted I bring my own. If you don't mind, I had better eat hers for the sake of peace."

"No problem. Do you want to take the railway down? It's got spectacular views."

"No. I'd rather walk with you."

She smiled.

The way back didn't take as long and they were back at the car park by early afternoon.

She held his hand at the big waterfall.

"Going up on the slippery rock is okay but coming down is tricky."

He loved her delicate fingers and the softness of her skin. He felt her hand fit his like a glove and belonged there.

"You okay?" she said.

"I'm good. Great walk and thanks for the guided tour." He didn't want to overwhelm her; he wanted to hug her but just shook her hand.

"You're welcome."

She opened her car door and paused. "Cord? Rodney calls you Landman. Why is that?"

"It took me a while to get used to the ocean. You know, it's up and down in the swell. The name's a bit of a joke, but I'm used to it now. I don't mind."

"I like it, it suits you. I've never known a Landman before. Until tomorrow then. I'll call you later."

He watched her drive away.

Mrs Brown quizzed him about the walk. She rolled her eyes when he confided they were meeting for lunch the following day as if to say, watch your step.

Cord thought, Gert, Dixie, now Mrs Brown; what is their problem? Tomorrow will be a great day, he mused.

Obligations
1998

Lucille rang that evening to confirm midday lunch at the Living Room Café Bar and Gallery Bistro at the Batu Ferringhi Beach on the north side of the island.

"It's owned by Denny, an old family friend, and I guarantee they make the best fried chicken with their own blend of spices. The beach is also beautiful."

They met at the garden entrance. She was wearing jeans and a silky white blouse. Her dark hair with a touch of auburn highlights was loose and flowing. It was lustrous and she looked luscious.

Denny met them at the door. He bowed and clasped both hands, "*Selamat datang*, Miss Lucille."

Lucille bowed in response and clasped her hands, "*Salaam*. Denny, this is my friend from Australia, Cord."

"Welcome, Mr Cord. Please come in."

Denny was an older man, grey-haired and attired in the typical colourful Malay dress. Cord felt Denny's scrutinising eyes as he directed them to a table on the patio overlooking the beach. The scene was beautiful, the sea calm and blue, matched by the clear sky. Denny pulled out the chair for Lucille and spoke to her in Malay before leaving.

"What did he say?" Cord enquired.

"Just to remember him to Father, Mother and Rodney."

But Cord thought it might have been a little more than that.

Lucille smiled and held out her hand across the table. It was an intimate moment while their hands touched before she quickly withdrew hers.

"All right, he wanted to know if you were my boyfriend."

"What did you say?"

She looked at him, half smiling, "The meal has arrived. Enjoy."

The fried chicken lived up to expectations. They took takeaway coffee down to the shore, to a bench on a rocky headland overlooking a white sandy beach. It reminded him of Meelup Bay back home.

"What'll you do when the project is finished?" Lucille asked. "There must be only a few weeks to go."

"About three weeks. My firm wants me to go to a job up north to a station."

"Station? You're building railways too?"

"Oh, no. Not trains. At home, some farms are so big, around two thousand five hundred square kilometres, that we don't call them farms; they're called stations. They run beef cattle."

"Really! What will you be doing, Landman? Chasing cows?"

He realised she was teasing him. He brushed it off.

"No, it's something to do with a boundary dispute between two neighbouring stations. They need to have the boundary properly surveyed, but I don't know much else at the moment. I want to have a break first."

He thought, I want to have a break to take you back home with me.

He would broach the subject in the future if things went right. He didn't want to rush it.

"What are your plans?"

"I have to go back to finish my Masters in Business Administration, as well as a double major in Jurisprudence."

"Oh! MBA and Jurisprudence?"

"Jurisprudence is law."

"Where are you studying?"

"I did my Bachelor's degree at Columbia University in New York, so I continued there with the MBA. With the additional law component, Rodney wants me to specialise in commercial law for the family business."

Cord felt his lover's hopes dashed. Her life was planned. "When do you go?"

"I'll be flying back in around seven weeks."

Perhaps she could come for a short visit to Australia, then perhaps not. He blurted, "Before you go, come and visit Australia."

"I'd like that, but impossible."

They sat in silence, watching the waves curve and break as two surfers clung to the froth and foam on their ride to the shore. Cord moved closer and impulsively took her into his arms; she turned to him and melted into his embrace. They kissed. It was electrifying, and in that moment, Cord realised she was his. Why? He didn't know; she could have anyone. Why him? It didn't matter. He just wanted to soak it all in.

Lucille pulled away suddenly and wrung her hands in anguish, "This is wrong."

She paused and stood up. The words poured out of her.

"I shouldn't have come. We're different, worlds apart. What was I thinking? It can't work. I'm sorry, Cord, I don't want to hurt you. This has all been so sudden. We hardly know each other. I have to go."

Cord rose, put out his arms and tried to hug her again, but she pulled away. She was crying. All he could say was, "When can I see you again?"

She didn't reply and ran across the lawn to her car. He was dumbfounded, confused; it all happened so quickly. How could he let her go?

Denny, watching from his terrace balcony, saw the lover's embrace. He reached for the phone.

The Fight
1998

Back on the *Spree*, things turned sour because of Simon.

Day after day, the vessel ploughed through heavy seas, bucking and rolling in frantic wind gusts that buffeted them broadside on. Days had passed and Cord hadn't heard from Lucille. The violent weather contributed to his moodiness. Everyone was on edge. Even Gert, who watched their daily gains in the schedule diminish.

Simon came onto the bridge to change watch with Cord.

"Hear the Landman's got himself some Asian crumpet," he said, leering and sneering. "Nice bit of arse. Wouldn't mind that piece of tail myself. Can ya give me an intro?"

Cord took one look at the lewd face and, in a flash, landed a tight fist in the man's midriff. Simon went down screaming, "Arsehole!"

Cord landed another blow but was stopped by Brian, who had come onto the bridge. He was bigger than Cord and restrained him.

"Easy! Give it up, Cord."

Simon was writhing on the floor and called out again. "Arsehole. Fuckin' Landman. He's a maniac! He hit me. That's out of line. What's a bit of Asian crumpet?"

Brian helped Simon to his feet, the man in agony clutching his stomach.

"You're the arsehole, Simon. You're the one out of line. I've heard you whistling the tune *Dixie* when she's around and you'll be in deep shit if Gert hears you singing '*way down south in Dixie*'. Cord, take a break and get some coffee. I'll take over here. Simon, piss off back to your cabin and fuckin' stay there. You're lucky you got off so lightly; I should have let Cord give you a proper belting, so piss off. The Skipper better not hear of this."

Simon slunk off, holding his belly and muttering.

The week went by with Simon avoiding Cord as much as possible, but it wasn't easy on the small vessel. One evening, Gert called Cord to his cabin.

"Sit down. Gin and tonic?" he asked, raised his eyebrows and smiled. "Captain's privilege to have liquor on board for special occasions."

Cord nodded. This must be over his stoush with Simon. Gert filled the glass, topped it with ice and sat down opposite Cord.

"Landman, you've got your sea legs. You're a seaman now. Don't look so troubled, the gig's almost over. We'll finish in a month or so and you can go home with a wad of cash. All will be well."

Cord sat in silence. Gert went on in a more serious tone, "I hear things. Dixie tells me you've been seeing Lucille."

Cord sipped his drink and didn't comment.

Gert continued, "Look out the porthole. What do you see? It's a big ocean out there with plenty of fish in it."

Cord sat in moody silence.

"Landman, these people, they're different. They've different customs, different culture, different religion, different responsibilities. I've worked here a long time and have never really felt at ease with them. The men rule the women, so our Western expectations regarding courtship don't apply here. It's not about love; it's about business. Do you see what I mean?"

Cord thought, Lucille says we're different, Gert says we're different. I'm a man; she's a woman. That's the only difference; the rest doesn't matter.

Gert clasped his big hands together and moved forward in his chair, "Now hear this, don't get your hopes up with Lucille. She comes from a powerful family and I know first-hand that she has responsibilities. There'll be trouble ahead if you persist with this. You can take it from me, Landman, there are plenty of fish in the sea, so give it up."

Cord wasn't sure if Gert knew of the altercation between him and Simon; nothing was mentioned, but Gert's parting comment disturbed him. "Shifts need changing. We'll be a man down next week. I'll speak to the crew."

Cord was never certain as to his involvement in Simon's dismissal, but it turned out other factors contributed to his quick departure. Evidently, Simon's frequent visits to Butterworth were not only to womanise but also to gamble. He had run up a significant debt and approached Rodney for an advance, which was a bad move. Also, Mrs Brown reported that the cleaning staff had found drugs in his room. He left quietly one night.

Gert called the nav team to the galley and explained the situation.

"The problem is we're a man short. We've lost a week and still have plenty to do and we're only just ahead of schedule. It's not practicable to send for a replacement, so I'm extending shifts from eight hours to ten and reducing the four-day shore breaks to two days. These changes are immediate."

Cord was further disheartened, as the chance of seeing Lucille again was even more reduced by the shortened timeline. She still hadn't called him and hadn't answered his calls. It seemed Gert was right. Too many differences; too many other responsibilities.

The bad weather continued, yet events turned in Cord's favour when the proline drill rig fractured one day in heavy seas. Dixie advised Gert that the waters were too rough, but Gert, with a man down and under pressure, ignored the warning and went ahead in manoeuvring the *Spree* into position. The crew worked hard to lay the four anchors and the winches strained under the weight as the vessel jerked in violent protest at the surging waves. The steel ropes whined to keep the craft still as the crane dropped the drill to the ocean floor. The drill bit hadn't penetrated the bottom by more than two metres when the casing broke and the entire rig had to be retrieved.

Gert was angry; more time lost, and the crew were disappointed at the delay as they went back to port. The *Spree* was docked, waiting for the replacement rig to arrive and be fitted. Cord was the only person who was pleased; here was his opportunity to see Lucille again. Cord sent a series of messages to her that he was back in port. She finally sent a text on Thursday afternoon. His heart leapt when he read her invitation:

"Glad you are back in port. I'm going to our tea plantation in the Cameron Highlands on the mainland for a few days. Would you like to come? I will be leaving tomorrow. Let me know."

Cord texted back: "Count me in."

Tanah Rata
1998

Lucille arrived early at the manor gate. From the balcony window, Cord saw the Land Cruiser pull over and stop. He wished to leave discreetly and crept downstairs with his backpack. However, Mrs Brown was waiting in the hall, her arms folded. She shrugged, "I hope you know what you're doing. Lucille's a lovely girl, but she's Rodney's sister; don't hurt her. Don't hurt yourself. These are powerful people you're dealing with."

"I won't hurt her. I love her."

"Love?" she gestured, shrugged again and shook her head. "Love. Good luck."

He left troubled by her comment. Everyone kept warning him, but he saw Lucille waiting and all doubts vanished. But then, from a distance, he could see she had removed her sunglasses and was wiping her eyes. She appeared to be crying. At the gate, an urchin boy ran up, bucket and cloth in hand, "Hey Mr Landman, I wash your car?"

Cord recognised him as Sambo, a scrawny little fellow who hung around the gate every day touting to wash the cars for the price of one ringgit. He was persistent and efficient. The nav team had the most washed and clean cars in Penang. He thought how funny it was that the 'Landman' tag had stuck, even with this boy.

"Not today, Sambo, maybe tomorrow."

"I wash missy's car," he said, pointing to the Cruiser.

Cord shook his head.

"Why she cry, Mr Landman? I can do for half a ringgit, special price for lady. Make her happy."

Cord smiled at the skinny ragamuffin, already an adept salesman.

"Okay, make it snappy."

Lucille wound up the windows as Cord climbed into the vehicle. The boy sloshed and splashed his way around and, when finished, waved and smiled, "Good job for missy. She happy now!"

Cord wound down the window, threw him a ringgit and nodded to Lucille.

"Did that make you happy?"

She nodded and smiled, her tears drying.

Lucille was in jeans and a loose T-shirt with a Malay motif. She wore a sky-blue scarf with her hair tied back in a bun. He couldn't gauge what she was thinking. It was an awkward moment and he thought, what if she stops the vehicle and calls off the trip? Surely not, but she hadn't said a thing.

He grabbed the moment, "Lucille, I love you."

She didn't respond. She only negotiated her way through the heavy traffic down to the ferry terminal, glancing sideways at him several times.

She finally spoke, "What's love? We've only a short time together, so let's be happy, at least for now, okay?"

"How can we be happy with you crying?"

They drove in silence onto the ferry for the short voyage across the straits. Halfway across the channel, she removed her glasses, her eyes glistening with late tears. She looked so lovely, so vulnerable. He needed a miracle to make this enchanting, graceful woman stay with him. He'd never hurt her. She moved towards him and cradled herself in his arms. Sometimes, silence says everything.

The tension eased on the four-hour drive to the Cameron Highlands. They passed through Taiping and stopped at Ipoh to buy a rice meal at a street stall for lunch. Outside, it was warm and humid. Sitting on a bench by the Kinta River in the shade of a large tree, Lucille sipped a mango juice through a straw.

"This straw reminds me that this tree we're under is the *Pokok Ipoh,* which gives the city its name."

"Very interesting," Cord replied, wondering where the conversation was heading.

Pointing the straw at him, she said mischievously, "What is most interesting is that the sap is poisonous and was used by the *Orang Asli* people to tip the darts of their blowpipes for hunting, so watch out, Landman."

She brought the straw to her mouth and blew air at him.

Cord was surprised that she insisted on calling him Landman.

"I like it, it suits you."

"As I told you, Landman is just boat slang," he said.

"And, as I told you, I like it. You'll always be my Landman."

They laughed, he reached out, their eyes met and they kissed tenderly. Her eyes were closed and he fathomed as to who he was holding in his arms, this woman hiding behind those dark Asian eyes. Was she the love of his life? Yes, she had to be.

From Ipoh, they began climbing the long, winding road into the high country. It rained steadily with thunder and lightning, the vivid clash and thunderbolts sometimes rocking the vehicle. She saw his concern.

"Don't worry, it's often like this, but it'll clear when we're at the top."

"Where are we actually heading to?"

"Tanah Rata, it's where our plantation is. We have a bungalow there, but I've booked us into the Smokehouse Hotel."

How discreet, he thought, away from people who would know her. Still, he didn't know the complete arrangements and she had probably booked separate rooms anyway."

"You said you have business here."

"Yes, we'll be here for three days. Don't worry. I checked with Dixie and your boat will be out of commission beyond that. I'll have to abandon you for a day, as I'll be meeting a potential business partner. Father wants to merge our tea plantation business with a rubber processing company and they want to view our estate."

The rain eased, the sun emerged from dark clouds and Cord could see below into a deep valley, bare of trees but cultivated and covered with orderly groves of a low green shrub.

"*Camellia sinensis*, tea plant," she said, "named after a Jesuit missionary, Georg Kamel, who began cultivating them."

"Oh, why are you getting involved with rubber?"

"Father's been talking to these people for some time and we have a memorandum of understanding to join forces. Rodney says it makes sense to merge as the rubber people have a strong merchandising arm, allowing our tea to enter more markets, especially overseas. The advantage to them is they want to diversify for taxation reasons and add another string to their bow. My job here is to show the plantation and answer questions, especially regarding our financial structure."

"You're amazing."

"That's what accountants are for."

It was mid-afternoon when they reached Tanah Rata, nestled high in the mountains. The village was quiet, sheltered from the hustle and bustle of the crowded coastal lowlands. Cord stepped from the vehicle, relishing the opportunity to stretch his legs while Lucille was on her cell phone arranging the meeting for the next day. There was a noticeable change in the temperature and the environment. Above all, he noticed the abundance of roses flowering in the gardens.

"It's all set. I meet them on site at 10 am and will be away most of the day. You'll just have to amuse yourself, Landman, but I have a surprise for you the next day."

A fine mist wafted in from across the valley and brought with it a chill that prompted them to clamber back into the warmth of the vehicle. It was a short drive from the village to the hotel, which Cord described to his sister Corrine when he texted her the next day:

'It's a magnificent Tudor Mansion set in a superb garden of every species of rose you could imagine. Mum would love the place.'

Trepidation set in as he entered the foyer and insisted he would pay, but Lucille shook her head.

"It's all taken care of. It's a business trip."

Of course, he thought, it's strictly business and she's being kind to me before she lets me down.

The hotel porter set their luggage down and opened the door to a sumptuous suite. A sitting room with settee, reading chairs and tables set before an open fire already crackling away and a four-poster king-size bed with canopy and curtains. It was early afternoon. Could this really be happening? He was confused.

Lucille tipped the porter.

"Enjoy your stay, Ma'am and Sir."

The die was cast; there was no turning back. Lucille came to him with a sense of urgency that instantly aroused him. She shed her clothes and he rejoiced in her nakedness. It was a frantic union of bodies, a culmination of desire and craving, a pledge to love and commitment. For Cord, it was the greatest moment of his life and one he never wanted to end.

Later, they rose from the bed to shower together in complete, isolated intimacy.

She touched his cheek gently and whispered, "I guess you can tell this was my first time making love. I am grateful it's with you. No matter what happens, I want you to know I'll always cherish this time with you."

"Don't be fatalistic. We're right together and this is the real thing for me. I mean, I love you. I'll finish the job here, then please come home with me."

"Let's not talk about it. I wish I could, but it's not that easy, not straight away."

"What do you mean? The future is ours. I'm told you have an obligation to your family; I don't know what it is, but we can work it out. You can finish your MBA in Australia."

"Hush," she said, "let's just enjoy the moment."

There was a knock on the door.

"*Perkhidmatan*," a voice said.

"Who is that?" Cord asked, startled.

"Room service. I ordered in for seven," she said. "A seafood platter to share."

Lucille hid in the bathroom while Cord scrambled into his dressing gown and opened the door.

A porter wheeled in a table tray laden with an array of hot dishes. There was also a bottle of premium Pinot Noir, compliments of the management.

Chocolate Sailor
1998

They spent the evening in a close embrace. The initial passion was replaced by a gentle yearning to know all they could about each other. They shared snippets of their past, laughing and chatting into the early hours and woke to a knock on the door. A porter brought in their breakfast tray and laid it on the centre table.

Cord watched Lucille shower, his eyes admiring the soft curves of her body, delighting in their intimacy. She dried her hair, felt his gaze upon her and turned to face him.

"I'll call you later when I know what's happening. We could go into the village for a meal this evening. What do you think?"

"Whatever."

"What do you plan to do? You could walk into the village and have a look around. It's authentic Malay."

"I might do that."

She left wearing a grey business suit and white blouse. Lucille never needed makeup, but that morning, she had light blue shadow above her eyes and a touch of red lipstick.

"These must be important clients that you want to entertain."

"It's not what I want. It's what Father wants."

"And Rodney."

"Yes, Rodney too."

She hugged him and avoided kissing. "Lipstick!" she cried. "See you later. Have a good day."

"You too."

Cord texted his twin Corrine to tell her about Lucille and his decision to bring her home to Australia. She replied within the hour of her pleasure that he'd found someone but asked if Lucille had agreed. Being twins, he and Corrine had many of those moments that twins share where one knows what the other is thinking. Corrine married her husband Mark, a Perth stockbroker, a year before and was concerned, when they first dated, that he and Cord should get along. She arranged and insisted that Mark and Cord backpack together for a few days on the *Bibbulmun* Track, hopeful they would bond. They did and that was history. Cord admitted that he assumed Lucille would come home with him as they were in love.

She texted back: *Better ask her; don't assume anything.*

He slept again and by the time he left the hotel, it was midday. He dressed in warmer clothes for the walk to town; jeans and a polo knitwear top. He had a map of the four-kilometre walk along a stream, which included views over the highlands and the small Parit Waterfall located halfway along the narrow track.

He passed a children's playground and went onto the main road. There was a cluster of stores, houses and businesses in a haphazard ribbon development, the new mixing in with the old. Out of curiosity, he rummaged through an assortment of hand-crafted bits at a makeshift stall on the roadside. Amongst the ornaments and knick-knacks was a stack of glass-topped wooden boxes, each containing a preserved coloured butterfly. Some were up to a hands' width in wingspan and Cord was taken with their size, patterns and iridescent colours. Seeing Cord's interest, the stallholder, an old man with little teeth and a wispy beard, grinned and held up his wrinkled hand, indicating the price, but Cord couldn't bring himself to purchase a preserved insect corpse. The man fossicked through his wares and held up a box containing a brilliant blue and yellow butterfly.

"*Tuan*, for you, special price twelve ringgits," the old man said.

Cord shook his head.

"Eight ringgits," the man cried.

Cord shook his head again, but by this time, he had found a colourfully painted bamboo fan, which he purchased for his mother for the asking price of six ringgits.

The old man bowed thankfully, calling out repeatedly, "*Tuhan memberkati anda tuan.*"

Cord was pleased he'd made him happy.

He bought a mango and bananas for lunch at a small grocery store. There were backpackers everywhere, soaking up the atmosphere of this isolated mountain village. Dogs barked at the white-skinned strangers as they passed. At an open market, chicken and ducks were for sale. They were available plucked and ready for roasting or alive with their legs tied for yarding. From a fancier shop trading in jewels and silk, he bought Corrine a jade and silver bracelet and a gold necklace with a heart-shaped jade pendant for Lucille.

It was an uphill hike back to the Smokehouse and he arrived hungry, tired and footsore. He had a quick shower. There was a text from Lucille that she was delayed and wouldn't be back till the evening and to have dinner without her; that she missed him and hoped he had a great day. At a loss, he decided to have dinner in the hotel restaurant, a lone figure amongst a smattering of guests. Against his better judgement, he stopped at the cocktail bar and downed several rum and Coke doubles.

Back in the room, he ordered a bottle of red and settled on the couch by the fire, reflecting on the day. He wasn't a big drinker and soon, the alcohol kicked in. He decided to call Lucille, but the call reverted to message bank. He became irrational, angry, concerned; where was she? A few days before, she wasn't in his life; now, he couldn't bear to be without her. He tried again; there was no response. Fatigued and gazing at the embers of the dying fire, his eyelids drooped and slowly he drifted into a troubled sleep.

He woke to Lucille shaking him; it was late.

"Wake up, sleepyhead. Come on, off to bed. We've a big day tomorrow."

*****

Room service woke him with a hot coffee. He sat up, holding his head, the demons of the night before still present. He was fuzzy while Lucille was already up, dressed, bright and chirpy, "We have to get going. We're off into the jungle."

"I missed you last night."

"I know I missed you too."

"Where did you go? Where did you eat?"

"Just at the plantation. They wanted a lot of information, so I rang town and ordered in."

"Who were they?"

"Cord, this was business, don't be silly. I don't like you questioning me about this."

"Sorry, yeah, me being stupid. Where are we going?"

"Okay, we're going to meet a friend first, so wear something light, but pants and a long-sleeved shirt are best in the rainforest. Remember the mosquitoes."

Cord showered and dressed quickly, cleaning his teeth on the run. Lucille had thoughtfully ordered a lunch pack from the hotel.

"We're meeting with my childhood school friend Maisie and her husband, David. He's the Wildlife Officer here, so they're taking us somewhere special."

The district office was near the children's playground where Cord had walked the previous day. Maisie was waiting on the veranda of the building and ran to Lucille's arms as soon as they arrived. An attractive woman, she was dressed like Lucille in outdoor attire. The two women babbled away in Malay with the same melodic ring. Maisie turned to Cord, bowed and shook his hand. He knew he was being assessed; for Lucille to bring a stranger and a man to Tanah Rata had significance.

David emerged from the building. He was English, a tall man, gangly with a ruddy complexion, probably from his time spent outdoors. He greeted Cord with a firm handshake and broad smile.

"We'll go in my vehicle."

Lucille transferred the lunch pack to the back of the Nissan Patrol. "There's plenty for everyone."

They drove on gravel tracks heading eastward and upward into the thickening rainforest.

"It's good we have a fine day," David said. "Weatherman says it's okay. We get a lot of rainy days here, so you never know."

He and Cord sat in the front seats with the women in the back. David was interested in Cord's work and explained his own background in flora and fauna with a degree in Wildlife Conservation. He had been in Malaysia seven years, met Maisie two years before, they married, and at the same time, he secured his job in the Cameron Highlands. It was all he wanted. He talked about the seven hundred plant species unique to the region, the animals and the rare, almost extinct mountain pheasant.

They drove for an hour, sometimes slowly, through watercourses, over ridges and along the edge of ravines. Eventually, they descended into a deep valley where the canopies of tall Blackwood trees, all shoulder to shoulder, shaded an array of green palms and ferns on the forest floor. They stopped on the side of the track.

David said, "We'll have to walk from here. Leave your gear; just bring your camera."

They followed a narrow path that meandered through the dark, dank forest. Cord wondered where they were heading and why he needed the camera; there didn't seem much to photograph, maybe a waterfall, he thought. Suddenly, around a bend in the path, they emerged from the shadows into an opening in the tree canopy and a broad shaft of sunshine. In the ray of light, hundreds, perhaps thousands, of butterflies flew and floated. It was a breathtaking display, a kaleidoscope of colours and sizes.

Hugging Cord, Lucille said, "I told you it was a surprise."

Cord clicked away in amazement. So this was the source of supply for the old man at the wayside stall in the village.

David explained, "There's not much sunshine in the rainforest at the lower levels. Butterflies are cold-blooded and love the sun. Here, they can soak it up and keep out of the wind. This is a rich place for them as they can feed on plant nectar, lay their eggs and the emerging caterpillars are protected from predators. After lunch, we'll visit the native jungle people, the only ones allowed to trap and harvest the butterflies."

"Why?" Cord asked.

"They're the traditional owners, that's why," David explained. "They preserve and box them for the tourists. I understand butterflies have a spiritual connection regarding marriage ceremonies, but I'm not entirely sure. They catch them in nets on tall bamboo sticks and are conscious of each species' life cycle; some butterflies only live a few days, others for months. The native people know when each type has had the opportunity to propagate and has completed its lifecycle before they catch and preserve it."

The butterflies surged and cascaded around the group. Maisie cried out, "Freeze, stand still, watch this."

The group froze; butterflies swirled and settled on shoulders, arms, anywhere they could grip.

One large butterfly nestled in Lucille's hair. It had an intricate tapestry of deep chocolate brown to cream shades. It flapped its wings and Cord was able to take a quick shot of Lucille excited and laughing, waving her arms, before it sailed off unharmed. It returned and snuggled in her hair again. Once more, she shrieked as Cord clicked away till it alighted, disturbed by her flaying arms. Impulsively, he reached out, lifting her from the waist high into the air. Her laughing and screeching continued until he lowered her to the ground, where they kissed passionately and hungrily while the butterflies swirled around.

Back at the vehicle, they had a picnic lunch of chicken and salad bread rolls with slices of orange sponge cake, bananas and mango juice. The weather continued fine as they drove the few kilometres to the native village on the banks of a fast-flowing stream. They waited in the vehicle while David spoke to the headman, dressed in little more than a loincloth. He bowed and invited them into a large grass-covered hut whose open sides revealed tables covered in handmade, glass-topped wooden boxes.

Cord thought, so this is the factory, the start of the production line for the village sales. This time, he could inspect in detail the assortment of butterflies. In a corner of the hut, women were diligently preparing newly caught specimens. On a table, some men and boys were nailing together the small wooden caskets. An old man was lashing a loose round net onto a tall bamboo pole.

Lucille excitedly asked, "Which is the one that landed in my hair?"

Cord delved around the boxes on display, but the array of specimens was so huge he looked in vain. Shrugging his shoulders, he declared, "It's like looking for a needle in a haystack."

He showed the picture of Lucille and the butterfly to the headman, who eagerly nodded and went to one of the far tables. He returned with a box, grinned and asked, "Ten ringgit?"

Cord hesitated; the man dropped his price. "Eight ringgit?"

"No," said Cord, shaking his head and backing away. It wasn't the butterfly in Lucille's hair; he showed the picture to the man again. He only wanted to know its name to look it up on the Internet at home. He didn't want to buy something once vibrant and alive, now lying lifeless in a box. The man hunted around, then held up another box in sheer glee. It was the right specimen. In big, bold letters on the side of the box, it read *Chocolate Sailor* and under that, in smaller script, the Latin name, *Neptis harita harita.*

Cord was surprised. "How come they know the Latin name for the species, being jungle people?" he asked David.

"Oh, they have the butterfly researchers visiting and camping here quite often. They're called Lepidopterologists. How's that for a job description, eh?"

Cord chuckled in agreement.

The headman was keen to sell and worried Cord even more, dropping his price to four ringgit. The others watched bemused while the man ignored Cord's protest and began to wrap the box in old newspaper. Cord was reluctant but finally yielded to the man's insistence and bought it for the original price of eight ringgit. Like the old man in the village, who was probably a relative, this fellow was completely overwhelmed, bowing and thanking him profusely, *"Terima kasih tuan."*

"You've made the man happy," David said, "and you've got it for the knockdown price of eight ringgit; they're usually twelve ringgit in the village."

The day ended with goodbyes. The men shook hands, the women hugged, and Cord and Lucille were back at the Smokehouse by dusk. Cord realised that tomorrow would bring its own challenges, but tonight belonged to them. They showered together, her lips on his, their bodies moulded together in a perfect embrace. Wanting to be alone, they ordered a seafood platter and relaxed in their bathrobes, nestling on the couch before the crackling fire.

Recalling Corrine's advice, Cord said, "I'll be going home in a few weeks. Please come with me."

Lucille didn't reply immediately. She recovered from their embrace. "It's not possible. I have obligations to my family to finish my studies and help with the business. Don't make it harder for me."

"But I love you and I know you love me. You can finish your studies in Australia. We have universities there."

On reflection, he realised that she'd never said the word 'love' in all the time they were together – until then.

"Cord, if you love me, really love me, let me attend to my responsibilities. Don't be sad because we have to part. Life goes on and we'll always have the memory of these days together. No one can take that away."

Her tears flowed and Cord almost wept. They were closer that night in spirit than they'd been the night before.

In the morning, Cord gave her the Chocolate Sailor and the jade necklace. She thanked him, and beyond that, breakfast was a silent affair. The passion of the night before subsided and they faced the cold, clear light of day. So much to say, yet the silence continued from the highlands to the lowlands. For every kilometre of the descent, the distance between them grew.

Finally, Cord exclaimed, "Why are we doing this to each other? Why are you allowing others to control your life? Why?"

Lucille didn't answer but drove the vehicle faster into the twisting bends of the narrow road. Cord remained tight-lipped but could see tears rolling down her cheeks from under her sunglasses.

They completed the four-hour journey in three. At the gate to the manor, she finally turned to face him and, with a great sigh, kissed him long and meaningfully for the last time.

"Please, I have to go."

Cord was a lonely figure at the gate as he watched her drive away, his heart aching.

Sambo, the small forlorn figure with bucket and cloth in hand, approached. "Lady plenty sad Landman, tomorrow I wash her car for free."

If only that would solve the problem, he thought. But the following day, Cord would be back at sea for the last long haul.

Sweet Sorrow
1998

The project ended. It had taken just eleven weeks, a week ahead of schedule. Apart from Cord, jubilation abounded amongst the crew. Bonuses were paid and tickets booked for the team to fly home, each going their separate ways. Gert was sailing the *Spree* back to Bergen, Norway, her home port, to have her slipped, her hull cleaned and a new propeller fitted. He invited the team to visit, but Dixie was the only one who accepted.

There was a farewell banquet dinner at the Shangri-La resort where Gert presented each of them with beer steins of Selangor pewter that Dixie had arranged when she was in Kuala Lumpur. Each tankard had the name *MV Spree* on one side and underneath the names of each team member. On the reverse side of Cord's mug was his name 'Cord McCullum' and underneath it, in big letters, 'LANDMAN'. Everyone laughed.

He'd texted Lucille several times but to no avail; her phone rang out and a toneless voice message stated, 'Number not connected'. Rodney had called in all the cell phones, even hers, and Cord visited the port office personally to hand his in, hoping he might see Lucille and have a chat with Rodney about how he felt. A staff member said Rodney was away, out of town on business and not contactable. Cord tried again and again in the remaining few days, but nothing eventuated.

The day before he was to fly out, Gert invited him to meet on the *Spree* for a parting drink.

"You like a beer, Landman?"

"Sure thing, Skipper."

"We've the best beers in the world. Come to the Oktoberfest in Munich and have a real German beer. Come and stay with me. Dixie comes every year."

"I'd like that."

"Good. It was a good tour, right? I know I'm skipper, but we're mates outside these decks. That's what you Ozzie's would say, mates, right?"

Cord wondered where this was heading, "Sure, right!"

"I don't normally get involved in the crews' personal affairs, but Rodney asked me to have a word with you. He knows you've been trying to contact him. He knows it's on a personal basis and about Lucille."

This was turning awkward and Cord's face showed it.

"I only said I would because I like you as a mate, right? I said to you once before these people are different. They have different beliefs and culture. You need to know that Lucille is promised in marriage as part of a long-standing family business arrangement. Did she tell you that?"

"No," Cord frowned, shaking his head in disbelief.

"Well, she is. And I'm guessing she wouldn't have told you she met with her intended betrothed at Tanah Rata when you both visited there?"

Cord was confused; he couldn't believe what he was hearing. How come Gert knew they went to Tanah Rata? Dixie, of course. How could Lucille spend the nights with him and then see someone else? But then again, she wore makeup and returned late to the hotel on their first night. Surely she was not that deceitful. It didn't make sense.

"She said her meeting was only for business."

"Business, *ach quatsch!* Cord, leave it alone. No good can come of it. It doesn't matter what you or Lucille think, the family will never let you have her. They'll lose face and she knows that. Marriages are decided almost at birth and women in this culture have a responsibility to honour that arrangement. She'll do what they say. Look at it as an experience. Remember it's a big ocean and there are other fish. You're young, fly home, forget her and get on with your life. You can't win with these people."

They finished the beers in silence and shook hands. Gert put his arm over Cord's shoulder. "It's been nice knowing you, Landman, and by the way, Simon had that belting coming."

"Thanks."

He walked despondently along the wharf and turned to look back at the *Spree,* seeing the bright yellow bridge over the black deck for the last time. He would miss her; perhaps that's why sailors called ships 'She'. They're just steel and wood, Cord mused, but in the end, they get under your skin. The

Spree would always be real to him. Gert came out of the bridge onto the side gang and waved. Cord waved back, then turned. He never saw Gert again.

Mrs Brown stood at the manor doorway. A car was waiting to take Cord to the airport. He couldn't help but rush up the stairs and hug her. She responded with a pat on the back.

"You're a good man, Cord. There's someone for everyone, you know. Have a pleasant flight."

The 747 rose from the tarmac and banked slowly southwards on its journey home. From his window seat, Cord could see the blue water of the Penang Straits below and the myriad of criss-crossing vessels. Lucille was out there somewhere. The plane, levelled, straightened, flew through a high cloud and everything disappeared.

Responsibilities
1998

Lucille knew something was amiss when she realised Rodney had cancelled her cell phone number as soon as she had returned from Tanah Rata. He called her to his office to avoid making a scene in front of their father and mother.

He was distant and direct. It was the aggressive, ruthless Rodney.

"I've arranged for you to attend a seven-day business symposium in Singapore, then I want you in Kuala Lumpur for two weeks, that's straight away. Connie, from our KL office, will meet you to set up our new accounts. You fly out tomorrow. I'll send you a brief on the system while you're away. You will be back here for a week before returning to your studies in America. Remember, Father's counting on you. That's all; don't let him down."

Lucille knew it was a ploy masterminded to keep her and Cord apart. She was still in turmoil over their affair. She had never done anything like that before; she had never felt such feelings and her attraction to him outbalanced her usual reserve. She had never thought to disobey her father, but now it was different, and if this was love, it felt so splendid, so right. The break would be good; three weeks would give her time to think things over. She knew Cord was at sea and she had to see him again, no matter what Rodney had planned.

Time dragged before she was back in Rodney's office, mission accomplished, a few days at home before America. She'd always looked up to her big brother and they rarely fought. This time, she could feel his agitation. He didn't look up and in an offhand manner, motioned to her to sit down. She waited patiently while he attended to paperwork before he rose, came around and sat on the edge of the desk, looking down at her. It was more than agitation; it was rage.

"I spoke with Denny last month. You were at his restaurant with that Landman *bajingan*. I ignored that, but now I'm told the Australian wasn't at the manor last week. Did he go to Tanah Rata with you? What's been going on?"

His eyes were dilated and she felt a tremor through her body. Tears welled up; she took a tissue from a box on the desk.

"*Saya cintakan dia.* Yes, I love him."

He leaned towards her, his face contorted with fury. "Are you out of your mind? Love, *tahi!* What is love to these drifters? I can't believe you did this. Did you sleep with him?"

She nodded meekly.

He threw up his hands in despair. "Oh! *Tuhan!* What have you done? This can't go any further."

Shaking and distraught, he stood up and paced the room.

"This is madness. What of your responsibility to Father and Mother?"

Lucille went to speak; he cut her short, his anger rising to violence. He shook his fist, his words laced with venom, "Be careful, Lucille, be very careful. The family must not be dishonoured. You know you are promised in marriage to Kim Li's eldest son. You've always known that. How could you have done this? You know it's imperative our companies merge; your marriage will confirm the union. It's what Father and Mother want and you're jeopardising this arrangement. You'll stop this relationship immediately. You'll go to America now and complete your MBA. It's agreed you'll be married next year. It's good Kim Li's son has seen you and is quite taken with you. You'll not be a virgin bride; that matter is a problem, but it can be overcome."

Lucille responded, her blood rising as the enormity of the situation sunk in. "I find the whole situation objectionable. It's repugnant I marry a man I don't love and abandon the man I do."

Rodney moved sharply and, without warning, slapped her across the face. She recoiled in shock.

"You will do what I say. These are the thoughts and habits of Westerners; they have no morals or culture. Do you think that cornball Landman really cares for you? He just used you. He's already left without a word; he didn't even have the decency to speak to me. It's common knowledge he's been with other women while he's been here. You're a naive fool."

He lied that Cord hadn't tried to meet with him, but it was for the good of the business, for Father and Mother, and for honour.

"They're all alike that crew. Look at Gert and Dixie shacking up and that Simon we had to get rid of. They all sleep around. Good riddance to them all."

Lucille reeled from the slap and had no answer to this tirade, nor did she want to respond. It just couldn't be true about Cord, but he had left without saying goodbye. She sobbed, sniffled and wiped away a tear. How could her brother have hit her? Without a further word, she rose and left. Perhaps Dixie might know something.

She got in the car. "Drive to the manor, Edward."

The Cadillac stopped outside the gate. Edward spoke into a speaker box, the gate opened and they drove into the grounds. She didn't see Sambo running towards them as the gate shut.

Mrs Brown opened the front door and offered Lucille her hand.

"Come in, my dear. Come and have a cup of tea."

Lucille nodded, holding a tissue to her eyes.

"Come now, child."

"I've come to see Dixie."

"Unfortunately, Dixie is gone. They've all left now."

"Oh, well then," Lucille rose to leave, "I guess that's it."

"Is this to do with Cord?"

Lucille nodded.

"I thought so, but he's left too, so you've missed him. Fine man that. We all liked Cord. I know he was desperate to see you before he left. Did you know he tried to see your brother but couldn't? Cord said Rodney was out of town."

"Why? Rodney was here."

"Perhaps I shouldn't say this, but between you and me, I'm sure Rodney avoided him and oh, by the way," she paused and reached into her apron pocket and handed Lucille a card, "I'm sorry I don't have a personal address for Cord, but I have this business card for JKSurvey Group, which you can have."

Lucille took the card, thanked her, impulsively hugged her and left.

"Edward, back to the office, please."

As the car pulled through the gate, she saw Sambo standing there with his bucket and cloth. She wound down the window and his face lit up with a smile when he recognised her.

"Mr Landman gone. I wash your car for free."

She shook her head, "No, another time," and handed him five ringgits.

He was surprised and delighted. "You too pretty to cry, missy. Mr Landman will come back. I know he will."

Rodney was surprised to see Lucille return. What she now knew changed everything, but she could not divulge what Mrs Brown had told her as Rodney was ruthless and would fire her if he knew what was said.

She did not sit but stood confronting him, tears still glistening in her eyes. "Okay, I'll honour my responsibility to Father and Mother. I will marry this man you've chosen, but I want you to know that for probably the only time in my life, I was intimate, cherished and slept with the only man I will ever love. For that, I am grateful. He has left me and I'll have to live with that. You can rest assured I'll not try to contact him, but I know him and don't believe a word you said. Cord's not like that."

Rodney changed his attitude. Condescendingly, he said, "I'm sorry, little sister, I was just protecting you from the pain that will come if we let the situation continue."

He tried to embrace her, but she stood back. Nevertheless, he was relieved, pleased. "I'm glad you've come to your senses. All's not lost. Believe me, it's for the best. Come on, dry your eyes. I'll make sure that it all works out. Stay and have a cup of tea."

Lucille declined and left the room.

She had only known Cord a few weeks before those magic days they spent at Tanah Rata, and now, three weeks after they had become lovers, her brother knew. She was glad it had come out; she wasn't ashamed. But what Rodney didn't know, and what she didn't know herself then, was she was about to miss her monthly period.

America
1998

Cord had been home several days before he could get time alone with Corrine. His mother, Eileen, fussed over him, which he tolerated as best he could.

"You look quite pale. Are you sure you haven't caught something? You don't seem yourself."

"Leave the man alone," Keith, Cord's father, advised her. "He's going to see Corrine."

While in Penang, Cord had texted his sister many times and she him. Her curiosity was aroused and she wanted to know more about Lucille. They met in a booth at their favourite coffee shop on the river foreshore.

"What's this Landman beer mug?' she asked.

"Landman, because the skipper reckoned I should stay on dry land. It was a joke. Gert is a great bloke with a dry sense of humour."

She laughed, "Sounds wet to me. You were never much of a sailor."

A waitress, clearly Asian, brought their coffees to the table. Cord instantly thought of Lucille and the Chocolate Sailor butterfly he gave her. He gazed over the tranquil river. The memory of those few happy days in Tanah Rata flooded back.

Corrine reached across the table to touch his hand. "Wha'cha thinking about, bruv? You look far away."

"Oh, I just remember I gave her a butterfly in a box. I have something for you, though."

He reached into his jacket and gave her the cloth pouch containing the jade and silver bracelet.

"Oh, it's lovely. Beautiful, thank you."

She examined it this way and that before putting it on her wrist.

Corrine always spoke in short, clipped sentences and from an early age, Cord realised she always wanted to get straight to the point.

She said quickly, "I hate to see you like this. You should try to see her. You've got holidays owing. Catch a plane; go to America. Don't take other people's word; face her. You're in love, bruv. I can feel it in my bones. There's no dress rehearsal in life. You've got to act now. Seize the moment; track her down if she's the one."

"I don't know where she's gone. She might be in New York, most likely Columbia University, but she mentioned Stanford, that's in California, also Princeton, and some others."

"Well, go there. Have yourself a holiday. You've been working hard. Don't die wondering."

John Keep, his boss from JKSurveys, was pleased with the outcome of the Penang project and, although keen to have Cord back on board, agreed he take a month's break. The job up north regarding the station boundary dispute was on hold due to the monsoon season, or The Wet as it was called. It was another job requiring expertise in GPS satellite operation and Cord was the man for the job.

"The station job's next year in The Dry. I'm looking at May, June, or July," John said. "If you go to Washington, check out the Smithsonian Museum. It's mind-blowing."

*****

Cord flew to New York and the weather was fine and mild. He checked into a small hotel with an antique cage lift that lurched and struggled through the three floors and basement of the building as it had done over many years. The hotel was in Manhattan, about four kilometres from Columbia University, not too far to walk to the campus. On a rainy day, there was public transport and New Yorkers were happy to help him with directions and ticketing. "You're welcome," they'd say.

It was a bewildering place to Cord. The 'Big Apple' was much bigger and busier than Penang and he had only three weeks to find Lucille in this vast metropolis. The first stop was the university, which was a city in itself with a student population of thirty thousand; tracking Lucille was going to be hard, with many doing online courses off-campus. So where was she?

He found the Business School at Uris Hall and Warren Hall in the Morningside Campus, both buildings widely separated in the overall layout.

His initial enquiries at student services and college administration yielded a blank, as personal student information was not publicly available. Stopping students and asking if they knew her brought rebuffs and strange looks. The first week was lost, wandering the avenues and paths of the campus between the two halls in the hope of seeing her.

In the second week, utterly disheartened, he turned his attention to seeing the sights of New York. He visited Broadway, Central Park, the Statue of Liberty, Wall Street, the Empire State Building and Macy's. Everything was on the move. Helicopters buzzed overhead and sirens blared from police cars. The '7-UP' stores sold everything from cooked takeaway food to firearms. He rode the subway and saw *The Lion King* at the New Amsterdam Theatre.

New York was certainly a city that never slept, but even in this city of eighteen million souls, Cord felt strangely alone. It was too far from his home on the other side of the world, twelve hours away in the southern hemisphere. He felt defeated. He would never find Lucille here; it was just too big. She was lost to him.

He bought hiking boots, walking pants, a shirt and rain jacket to walk part of the Appalachian Trail on the southern edge of New York State. He stayed at the Bear Mountain Inn, a spectacular stone and timber lodge nestled on a hillside in the State Park. He read there were over fifty walking trails in the park, but he was only interested in the sections containing the Appalachian Trail itself.

On the first day, it being fine, chilly with no wind, he walked the Loop Trail to Perkins Memorial. The forest, densely wooded and rocky in places, reminded him of his hike with Lucille to Penang Hill. The Appalachian section was marked with white blazes, reminiscent of the yellow markers on the *Bibbulmun* Track at home. He recalled that when the *Bibbulmun* was upgraded to a hiking trail of world significance, the Appalachian was used as the model.

That night, he had dinner in the restaurant, braised short ribs complemented by a Californian white blend wine. With the threat of rain the next day, he booked a bus tour to the top of the mountain, a bald rocky expanse that commanded views over the Hudson River and distant Manhattan. He wrote the time and date of his visit in the Hiking Visitors Book and if he'd glanced at the previous page, he'd have seen the entry, 'Lucille Cao' and the name of her American hiking club.

With only a week left, Cord checked back into the same Manhattan hotel and prowled the Columbia campus for another day, but there was no sign of her.

The next day, he caught a bus to Washington and checked into a hotel near the Smithsonian Museum for a two-day stay. There was so much to see and so little time to visit every exhibition. Cord spent most of the time he had at the National Museum of the American Indian. He didn't know why, but somehow, the history and culture of the Indigenous Peoples attracted and intrigued him. The history of their resistance to change was well recorded in the displays and Cord felt empathy with these people that arose from his similar sentiment for the Australian First Nations Peoples who had also been driven from their lands. Above all, he was fascinated by a full size model of a Cherokee woman's wedding dress, exquisitely made of full-length fine white leather with a woven beaded belt dyed blue and a neck laced with gold embroidery and chain. He went to see it again and again over the day, taking in the exquisite beauty of it, imagining Lucille in it. He would have purchased it if he could.

On returning to Australia, Corrine met him at the airport. They hugged.

"No, I couldn't find her. She probably doesn't want to be found."

"You tried, bruv, you tried."

He had another week's holiday before he returned to work, spending time with his father in the workshop.

"You're up north in the outback, on dry land this time," Keith said.

"Be careful of snakes," Eileen warned.

"You're a real Landman this time," Corrine smiled.

"Yep, something different this time."

John Keep stated, "The north trip's still on. Did you get to the Smithsonian?"

Cord said he did, and that was that.

Leo
1998

Across the world in America, Lucille and her friend Leo scurried through the rain, avoiding the crowds on the sidewalk and into the warmth of the Starbucks Coffee Lounge, just a few blocks from the Columbia campus. It was cold with the threat of snow, but Starbucks was always cosy and inviting, with the welcoming aroma of coffee in the air. Leo ordered a black coffee and Lucille, her favourite medium roast blend. Normally, she would meet Leo on a Thursday to discuss assignments, etcetera, but today, Sunday, she wanted to speak to him in private, away from interruption, as during the week, Starbucks was a student haven.

Leo was Singaporean and in the same situation as Lucille. They had journeyed through their undergraduate course together and were in the final year of their MBA. Leo, cheerful and good-natured, had become a valuable sounding board for Lucille over the years. He was a little on the plump side, which belied his efforts to keep fit and disguised the fact he was an experienced hiker. The pair had walked many miles on the Appalachian Trail during their semester breaks, completing most of the trail walks at Bear Mountain. They ventured far afield to backpack more remote parts of the main trail and on two occasions, Helen, Leo's partner, joined them on walks when she visited from Singapore.

Lucille and Leo realised they would never complete the entire trail length, so once, out of sheer curiosity, determination and love of the trail, they took the bus to the trailheads at Springer Mountain in Georgia and Mount Katahdin in Maine. They sat and watched with awe and admiration as trekkers came in, in dribs and drabs, shaking their fists in the air and reaching to the sky, elated at having completed the trail.

These were great moments she and Leo shared and how wonderful it would be if only, in another life, she could share them with Cord.

She sipped her coffee and Leo sensed she was downhearted.

"What's up?"

She blurted out, "I'm pregnant."

"What? Wow! Oh, my god! Wow!" he repeated, his hand covering his mouth.

Lucille sipped her coffee again and sighed.

"Wow!" he said again, then paused. "How long?" his boyish face full of concern.

"Three months."

"Wow!"

"Will you stop saying wow!"

"Sorry. Is it that Cord you keep telling me about?"

She looked at him sideways and frowned, "Of course, who else would it be."

"I'm sorry, it's such a shock. Are you okay? Does he know?"

"No, he doesn't know and not likely to."

Lucille put her cup down and Leo took a long gulp from his. Together, they gazed out the window at the crowd hurrying by, a sea of umbrellas on this dreary day.

"What are you going to do?" he said at last.

"Finish my course. At least I've time for that before I'm due."

"Do your parents know?"

"No, it's complicated. You know I have this stupid marriage arrangement over my head."

"You can't keep this a secret. Are you going to keep the baby?"

"Of course."

He reached out and held her hand.

"How are you feeling? You should ring Cord and tell him. He should know."

"I'm okay at the moment, but I guess I'll have to see a doctor soon. I can't tell Cord. I've deceived him too. How can I explain I'm betrothed to another?"

"So, your brother doesn't know either."

"He's the one I worry about. This marriage arrangement is part of his business plan."

"Wow."

Leo went to the counter and ordered another coffee. Lucille waited, oblivious to the sounds around her. Raindrops blurred the window, distorting the figures hurrying by. Her world, too, was distorted. The rain increased and individuals scampered into doorway porches and huddled under awnings. Some came into the shop shaking umbrellas.

He sipped his coffee. "Look, Lucille, I don't know what happens back home in Penang regarding family honour and all that, but this goes beyond business expectations. Responsibility is a two-edged sword; it cuts both ways with your responsibility to your family and their responsibility to you. The stakes have changed; you're having a baby and as I see it, all bets are off. You should involve the child's father in this."

Regretfully, she said, "The truth of the matter is, I've let them down. I knew I was pledged in marriage, but it never really sank in. It all seemed far away and suddenly, it's here on my doorstep. I thought I could have one fleeting chance with someone I loved before the inevitable, but now with this baby, I don't know, I must face this alone and not drag Cord into it."

"You love him, don't you?"

She nodded her head, a tear in her eye.

"When will you tell your parents, your brother?"

"There's still time before I tell Rodney. Right now, it's a secret best kept."

He nodded and then laughed, "Well, there's one thing for sure. You won't have all those guys on campus chasing you now. You only had to click your fingers and they'd come running. Seriously, if there's anything I can do, count on me. I'll get you another coffee."

"Thank you. I just had to tell someone. You're a good friend, Leo, a true friend."

Morning trade at Starbucks was picking up and booths were filling. He helped her into her jacket and gave her an affectionate hug. The rain had eased and together they went out into the grey day.

Leo was true to his word and, over the next few months, helped Lucille with assignments and generally covered for her in tutorials. She bought loose-fitting clothes to hide her developing figure. In her undergraduate years, she had shared a university two-bedroom apartment at Morningside Heights, but she wanted more privacy in her final year and thankfully had moved into her own apartment in Manhattan.

At four months, she contacted a doctor who advised everything was normal and gave her an approximate due date. Lucille declined to know the gender of the child; it seemed to take away the magic moment of birth. The doctor recommended that as she was a foreign national and alone, she seek the services of a midwife who would help her stay healthy, monitor her progress and intervene should complications arise. Lucille had medical insurance, but engaging a midwife was an additional expense that would register in her bank account, and of course, Rodney would see it. She had to tell him.

She called him directly; no emails or text messages. She just wanted to get it over with. There was a stunned silence on the line before he spoke. The old fury returned to his voice, "Oh *Tuhan,* you little fool, what've you done? Get it aborted. It's a half-caste. It's not wanted!"

It was always Rodney's frustrated, kneejerk reaction to a crisis; shouting, ranting and shaking. She ignored his tirade, "I choose to keep this child."

He yelled, "If you do, you'll have no money from me. You'll be cut off. You've disgraced the family."

It was an absurd threat, as Lucille had her own allowance from Father, independent of Rodney.

"I've my own money. It's because of Father and Mother that I'm letting you know. I've given this considerable thought, and as promised, I'll marry into the Li family, but I'll only agree to have the child adopted."

There was a prolonged silence as Rodney gathered his thoughts.

Lucille added, "I'll need you here with me at the birth to organise this; otherwise, leave me alone. I'll have no more yelling from you. Be careful, big brother, any more threats and I'll break my promise."

She hung up. Rodney rang again, but she didn't answer.

Deceit
1998-1999

Six months into the pregnancy, Lucille's midwife, Marsha, noted the baby had changed position, which could compromise the child and mother at birth. She recommended Lucille consult an obstetrician, who placed her in private care under the supervision of Marsha, who became a good friend.

In the months leading up to the birth, Lucille completed her Masters with honours, even though the pregnancy sapped her energy. Leo also completed his Masters and flew home to Singapore, to his beloved Helen and to a management position in neighbouring Johor Baru.

It was the loneliest time for Lucille and she wished Cord were with her. She often thought it was wrong to exclude him, but she had chosen a path and there was no going back. Reluctantly, she had agreed to adoption; it was the only way out since agreeing to the arranged marriage to Kim Li.

It was November and the baby was due in late December. Fortunately, Rodney arrived six weeks before the due date. He was apologetic and appeared genuinely concerned for her welfare. He took charge and arranged everything for the birth, a blessing for Lucille as she wasn't well; the baby had moved again and the pregnancy was draining.

Rodney advised, "I've arranged for the birth at a highly recommended private clinic in the valley. No visitors, no fuss. We have contacts who guarantee the adoption will be done quietly and incognito. Don't worry; I'll handle it. Just concentrate on getting better."

Her water broke five weeks early. She was in extreme pain and the ambulance rushed her to hospital, sirens blaring. In the operating ward, she barely remembered the obstetrician speaking to her or the anaesthetist whispering before she drifted off.

Lucille woke to find Rodney sitting beside her bed. She was bandaged up and in much pain. Something was wrong.

"How are you feeling?"

"My baby?"

"He's okay. Four pounds, six ounces."

"A boy! Can I see him? Bring him to me."

"Not at the moment, I can't. He's in the intensive care unit. I've seen him and the nurses say he is doing well, considering he came early. He will be in ICU for a while. You've had a caesarean section and you're not to move and need complete rest."

She was a prisoner; she tried to move, but the pain was unbearable. What had she done? She'd signed over her son and given away Cord's child; she'd never be able to face him or look at herself in the mirror. Nothing would ever be the same.

She kept asking to see her child but to no avail, until Rodney informed her the adoption was complete. It was for the best, he said, 'a clean break'.

"Father and Mother are not aware of the events, neither is Kim Li's family and everything is still on track for the merger. You will stay here in America to fully recover before you return to Kuala Lumpur," he ordered.

Lucille was devastated that she had not seen her baby and now knew she never would. She didn't even get to name him. Her mental health deteriorated rapidly, but Rodney had to fly back to Kuala Lumpur. She was alone again, with only her carer Marsha for company.

Quite inexplicably, her wounds became infected. Prescribed drugs caused bouts of delirium and disorientation and kerbed her appetite to the extent she dropped to skeleton weight. She improved under Marsha's care and eventually returned to her Manhattan apartment.

*****

Lucille spent four agonising months in recuperation at the apartment until she eventually gained weight and could tutor at Columbia to fill in the hours. She improved physically and rejoined her old hiking club. She texted Leo: 'Miss you, my friend. Walking the trail again. Bear Mountain is a picture in the Fall.'

He replied: 'Miss you too. Stay cool and keep moving. How is the baby, boy or girl?'

Lucille answered: 'Gone, adopted. A boy. I never saw him.'

'So sorry,' Leo replied.

Rodney flitted back and forth, fussing over Lucille, protecting his major business investment. Deals had been done and the wedding date was set for the coming July. Lucille had to appear as a virgin bride to her new husband. Rodney's trusted contacts in the medical field performed various procedures to reduce and disguise the caesarean scaring.

Again, she confided in Leo: 'Here's another lie I have to live with. Is business that important when you consider the human cost?'

There was an unexpected bombshell when the doctors informed Rodney that attempts to disguise her infidelity were worthless as the vertical incisions were extensive; they would fade over time but would always be evident. Rodney was frantic; the merger was in jeopardy. His rage again shone through.

He wrung his hands in despair and shouted, "It's your fault! We will lose face."

"There's a way out," Lucille interrupted. She had been thinking about this way out for quite some time. "Tell them I've been tested and I'm infertile. They need an heir for their business and won't want a daughter-in-law who can't give them one. I'll stay here in America out of harm's way."

It was a solution from the Gods, one Rodney had never thought of. The family wouldn't lose face. In fact, the Li family would thank them for their honesty and the merger could be stronger than ever. He felt confident again. Father and Mother would be disappointed at Lucille's news, but the business union was back on track. Things would turn out well after all.

He spontaneously hugged and kissed her. "Thank you! Thank you."

Lucille was relieved at being removed from the repulsive situation of marrying someone she hardly knew. Instead of a July wedding, she applied for an intern position at the Department of Commerce in Washington, D.C., which saw her posted to Geneva for six months, and from there, her career blossomed.

Lucille's and Cord's worlds were far apart and she resigned herself to a lifetime of loving him but living without him.

PART 2
Kathy

Jacana
1999

In northern Australia, amongst the Aboriginal people, January is known as the season of *Baarramirri,* where the northwest winds break *Worlmamirri,* the period of monsoonal rain and thunderstorms called the Wet. But down south in Perth, two thousand five hundred kilometres away, it was a blistering hot summer day when Ted and Joan Bell arrived at JKSurveys to discuss the survey of Jacana Creek Station, their pastoral lease in northern Australia.

A week earlier, John Keep called Cord into his office. It was the end of a long day in the field, pegging lot boundaries in a new housing estate. Cord was tired, sunburnt and not too enthralled with a late afternoon meeting.

"Ted and Joan Bell will be in town next week; I want you here to meet them."

"Who?"

"The station owners up north having a boundary dispute with their neighbour. I told you last month, remember?"

"Oh, yeah. When will that be?"

"Next Tuesday morning, 10 am."

He'd been back at work for eight months and life had fallen into a more sedentary routine than the one he had experienced on the *Spree.* He had paid a deposit on a new apartment still under construction and was living with his parents in the interim.

His father, Keith, ran a small accounting business doing taxation returns for regular clients and was on the verge of retiring. He and Cord were close, although he didn't have the same passion for sport that Cord did, but supported him with his tennis and hockey pursuits, even though he believed only swimming was important, saying, "Tennis is a sport; swimming is a lifeline."

Cord's mother, Eileen, was a perfectionist. Prim and proper, she had fixed ideas about right and wrong, although Cord sometimes thought there was a grey area where even his mother didn't know the difference between the two. She made sure that Corrine and Cord were well educated and showed her support by being on school committees, attending teacher-parent association meetings and the like. Cord thought she attended school more than he did. She read stories to the twins every night in the early years.

It was a sore point with his mother that he was christened Cordon, not Gordon. In the excitement of having twins and the similar spelling of his sister's name, Corrine, Keith wrote Cordon on his birth certificate. In his early years, his mother called him Gordon, but as the years passed and he became Cord to everyone else, she mellowed and accepted the inevitable. She would occasionally refer to Keith's mistake, roll her eyes and say, "That man." She agreed with the gibe, 'Behind every good man, there's a good woman rolling her eyes'.

His mother didn't like the Landman tag; said it was horrible. Why? Cord didn't know. Probably because she had hoped he would join his father in the accountancy business and was horrified when he chose to be a surveyor.

Cord became a man of the land as a child. He read volumes of poetry and dreamed of the far horizons, jewelled seas, stringy barks and saplings, the country others had seen and described. Tales of the swaggies and stockmen inspired him. He read of the first owners of the land and the 'Dreaming', the Aboriginal word used for the stories passed down about creation and how the world came to be.

Many times, Keith took him and his sister bush camping. A favourite was the Dryandra Woodlands with its unique animals like the echidnas and numbats. Cord remembered the elation at finding many different orchids, like the Spider, Jug, Donkey and the magnificent Queen of Sheba. Above all, he remembered the dark, dank smell of the soil after rain and the screech of the black cockatoos in the early morning, waking them from their swags.

Then there were the trees of the forest, Jarrah, Marri, Karri and in the Dryandra, the impressive Brown Mallet, its trunk so smooth to touch. The land was magnificent and vast – and it was in his blood.

Eileen said incredulously, "Surveying? There are snakes and you'll have to leave home to live in tents in the bush and cook your own meals. You can't even boil eggs. What about your washing?"

Her protests were to no avail; the die was cast. For Cord, it was an adventure, an exciting outdoor life. He'd excelled in mathematics, geometry and trigonometry at school; learning to boil an egg seemed simple by comparison.

On his return from Malaysia, his mother greeted him with, "Thank God you're home safe and not out on that ocean. You're a little pale, Cord. You could have a touch of Malaria."

He didn't dare tell her about Lucille. Cord wasn't ill; he was depressed at losing her, but the long days at work in the field helped him to forget and ease the pain.

"You're getting on, you know, son," she went on. "Corrine's married and expecting. You should get yourself a nice girl and settle down."

Cord knew his dad and Corrine would welcome Lucille. He'd like to tell his mother that he'd met a nice girl, beautiful, kind and intelligent, but he knew once his mother laid eyes on her, she would say, "Mixed marriages never work."

One night, at a family dinner with Corrine and her husband, Mark, Eileen commented, "I think Cord has a touch of Malaria. He hasn't been himself since he's been home."

Cord and Corrine exchanged glances across the table and Mark choked on his drink. They knew what Cord's ailment was and it wasn't Malaria; it was lovesickness.

*****

Cord arrived early for the Tuesday meeting. He wore tailored jeans, a white short-sleeved shirt, loose black tie and brown suede desert boots. He wanted to look business-like but still give the impression of a seasoned outdoor man.

Marie, their receptionist, ushered Ted and Joan Bell into John Keep's office. Cord was in the plan room chatting with a few survey hands when he noticed them at reception. Ted Bell was tall with a ruddy, suntanned complexion. He saw John wince when they shook hands. Joan Bell immediately reminded Cord of his mother, about the same age, taller, slim, blonde, greying hair tied back in a bun. She had a fine-boned, intelligent face, which opened into a warm, friendly smile when she took John Keep's hand. Ted was dressed in denims and a blue checked shirt, with Williams boots and a wide-brimmed Akubra hat. Joan wore a plain blue skirt and blouse with low-heeled shoes. A wedding ring and gold chain necklace were her only pieces of jewellery. They had the appearance of farming gentry.

Discussions took more than an hour. John Keep started with, "I know the timing has to be right for this work and I'm assigning my best man to it. I'll call Cord in shortly, but feel we should discuss the job and the costs in more detail."

Ted replied, "It's just something we have to do. We can help with some expenses, lodgings, vehicles, provisions and manpower to keep the overheads down."

"Good. There's also the time factor, which is my main consideration. That's where things can blow out. You need to be aware of that. I know from our past conversations that the area of concern for you is the east boundary line near your homestead. Tell me about that."

"Yes, that's right. It's the entire boundary. We need to know what waterholes are on our property, especially Apricot Springs. There's a growing concern about water supply with our neighbour. It's possible their place will be sold and we need to consider the water rights between the properties."

"Okay. To give you the bigger picture of expenditure, at the start, we're bound to comply with the government's special regulations relating to unfenced pastoral lease boundaries."

John unrolled a plan of the area. "This is the only copy of the station lease as registered."

"Yes, I have a copy too."

"Good, then we know what we're talking about. It's clear the east boundary is unsurveyed, around sixty-five kilometres in length. In layman's terms, pastoral lease boundaries follow lines of longitude and latitude on the Earth's surface. As the Earth is round, these lines are curved; therefore, the lease boundaries are curved as well. Setting out these boundaries requires a mix of astronomical observations and fixing from satellites called a Global Positioning System or GPS. Marking the boundary will be time-consuming and requires special equipment to carry it out. I'm putting Cord on the job; he's experienced with the gear and technique. You'll be in good hands."

Joan enquired, "How long will it take, do you think?"

"That's the burning question. Honestly, I don't know, not knowing the nature of the terrain, but my estimate is three months, maybe four. That's why the contract is open-ended and subject to mutual review."

He handed Ted and Joan the Contracts of Intent. Marie brought in tea and coffee while the Bells relaxed and read through the documents.

"That much?" Ted said, his eyebrows rising at the dollar figure.

"It could be less; it depends on the surveyor. Cord will document hours spent."

Joan took longer to read; she was thorough and raised a few questions relating to billing. Ted outlined his plans to keep expenditure down and explained he'd assign two of his best hands to help with the survey. Eventually, agreement was reached and documents signed.

Ted explained, "There won't be weather to worry about. It'll be in the Dry. All we need is a certificate guaranteeing the position of the boundary, especially regarding Apricot Springs, which will hopefully get this worry off our shoulders."

"Rest assured, you will have your certificate of validity. I'll call Cord in."

They shook hands; John went to the door and gestured to Cord.

"Ted and Joan meet Surveyor Cord McCullum."

John was a great one for formalities and making an impression, but Cord felt awkward with this title suddenly bestowed on him.

"Cord's only aware of the nature of the survey. I'll let you take over the explanation, Ted."

Ted's ready smile made Cord feel more comfortable. His big hand enclosed Cord's in a firm grip. "I guess we'll be seeing a lot of each other."

Cord nodded and smiled at Joan.

Ted went on, "We're here because there could be a dispute over the position of the lease boundary with our neighbour, Bert Doig. I emphasise, could, as there's no dispute now. Quite the contrary. We're on good terms with Bert and always have been. The problem is, his property, Indigo Downs, is up for sale and that relationship may change with a new owner."

He pointed to the map and traced his finger over a sketchy outline of a creek.

"The traditional boundary between our property, Jacana Creek Station, and Doig's has always been the creek itself. Their cattle and ours drink at the creek, which is no problem during the Wet 'cause the creek runs, but in the Dry, it dries into isolated waterholes, except for a thirty-two-kilometre stretch from our homestead to the coast. That stretch is fed by Apricot Springs, which is artesian groundwater and we're reasonably confident the spring is on our property. However, the junction of the spring run-off and the Jacana Creek watercourse is another matter. We're not sure if the junction is on our property or not. That's the crux of it."

Cord contemplated Ted's explanation. "There are no survey marks at all?"

"There may be one. It's an old cairn on the southeast corner. Don't know who made that, but there are no others. If there were, they're long gone. The lease was taken up in 1897, so the boundary's just a line on the map."

"So, if you're happy with the Doigs and the status quo, won't that arrangement still stand with a new owner?" Cord enquired.

"That's what we're worried about. We've heard on the grapevine that the group interested in Indigo Downs is keen to establish a Sandalwood plantation on the property. That means they'll need water for irrigation and no doubt pump water from the creek. The spring flows all year, keeping water levels constant in the upper reaches near the homestead, but who knows what would happen under sustained pumping. That's the question. Most importantly, if your survey shows the junction and permanent water is on our property, then we can fence it and deny access to the irrigators. That's why we've come to you. We need a certified deed of survey and markers put on the ground."

John broke in, "As I said, Ted, to provide the certificate, regulations stipulate that once we set foot on the land, we're required to mark the entire sixty-five kilometres of boundary and that could take longer than three months."

Cord was taken aback; three months up north! He hadn't bargained on that timeline.

The conversation moved on to a discussion on the overall logistics of the operation. Cord listened, still shocked at the revelation; three months, maybe longer!

Joan asked Cord, "Have you been up north to cattle country before?"

"Yes, but not as far north as where you are."

"Joan, call me Joan," she said. "You'll stay in the homestead with us when you're not camping."

All Cord could do was nod and half-smile.

Ted continued, "Cord, when you fly into town, Dexter will pick you up. He has a post run to the station every fortnight. I've arranged for Albert, my head stockman and Boris, my general hand, to help you with the survey. There's a Cruiser and a Patrol available. I understand your survey equipment will be flown out in the copter sometime in May. Is that right?"

John answered, "That's right, it's all been arranged."

Cord was perplexed. Three months on a cattle station up north was not what he expected. It could be another Penang.

Trouble
1999

Dexter picked Cord up at the airport. He was a wizened man in his fifties, with a stubbled chin and a grin from ear to ear showing teeth that needed attention. His khaki shorts were oil-stained, as was his checked shirt with its sleeves ripped off, and on his feet, his worn boots had no laces.

He pushed back the brim of a battered ten-gallon hat and stuck out his hand. "So, you're the cove who's gonna go out to Jacana. Dexter Timms, that's me moniker, but me mates call me Dex. Chuck your things in the back. I made room for you in the corner."

He lifted the hatch door. "What's your handle?"

Cord squeezed into the front seat of the vehicle. "Cord McCullum."

"You're the surveyor bloke come to sort out their troubles."

Cord was guarded in his reply. "Troubles, no, just to do some survey work."

"Oh! Not what I heard, but ya hear a lot of bullshit up here."

He manoeuvred the van out onto the narrow bitumen strip of road.

"Sit back and relax. We'll be calling in at a couple of places on the way to Jacana. Always get good tucker at the stops. One of the reasons I keep doin' the job. Been doin' it for twenty years. Bought this bus new in 1980. Mitsubishi Delica, four-wheel drive manual, only ever changed the oil and the tyres. Do ya like country music?"

Cord realised it was going to be a long journey.

The bitumen finally gave way to a formed gravel road. Dex kept the speed up and the brown gravel dust swirled and billowed behind the van.

"Not worth washing vehicles up here in the dust, although they do get a scrub in the Wet. Can't get in here in the Wet for a couple of months. All the stuff comes in by copter."

"Helicopter?"

"Yep! Got two copters and two pilots; Clyde, he's the chief, and Maggot."

Maggot. What a nickname, Cord thought, not wanting to ask, but Dex was going to tell him anyway.

"Maggot's just a little bloke but a top gun pilot. He got a bravery medal two years ago for rescuing some tourists trapped in a flood. You won't see much of him. You'll see a bit of Clyde. He's got his rocks off for the Bell girl. I don't like to talk behind a person's back, but I don't give him a snowball's chance in hell wiv her."

Cord wondered what he meant by 'the Bell girl'.

"That bad."

"Yep, that bad. Do ya know the Bells?" Dex asked.

"No, not really. I only met them a few months ago."

"Good bloke, Ted. Joan, his missus is great. Great cook. Their daughter Kathy mostly runs the place now. I don't like to talk behind a person's back, but she's a good looker, all right, and hard as nails. Ya need to be tough to run a good outfit up here and she's as tough as they come. But still a real jillaroo, a novice. Best ya keep out'a her way. Clyde's got Buckley's wiv her. You'll meet Boris, big bloke, the mad Spaniard. Drinks like a fish. Never mastered the King's English. Every second word is 'fuck'. He don't say it's hot today, mate. He says it's fuckin' hot today, mate. He don't say let's have a beer. It's a 'fuckin' beer. He's not a bad bastard, though."

They pulled over in a dry creek bed under the shade of the tall gums and near a huge Boab tree. Dex dug out a thermos from under the back seat.

"Time for a cuppa."

He opened a tin of biscuits and offered them to Cord. He poured the tea into two enamel mugs.

Cord was worried about Dex's comment about 'trouble'. He decided he might as well ask.

"What do you mean, trouble?"

Dex put down his tea. His gravelly voice was serious. "Doncha' know? Well, there's a stretch of Jacana Creek downstream near the coast and it's got permanent water, a good thing to have up here. If it's all in the Bell's lease, they're laughin'. They can fence it and the Doigs miss out. But if some of it's in Doig's lease, they're laughin' 'cause they can access it and the Bells lose out 'cause it can be pumped."

"So, what's the trouble?"

"Money, me boy, money. Doig's got their place on the market and there's goss' that a Sandalwood mob are looking at it. If the place has access to permanent water, up goes the price and the sale's in the bag, so everyone will be looking at you for results, if ya get my drift. I feel sorry for old Bert Doig. I know from around the traps that he doesn't want to sell; it's been in the family for years, but his son Jason does. I don't like to talk behind a person's back, but Jason's no cattleman. A bit of a wanka' if you ask me."

Cord was troubled. He didn't want to be part of a family or neighbour dispute. He wished he'd never taken the job in this strange country. He was caught between a rock and a hard place.

They trundled on through and around rocky hills burnt red in the sun and covered with stubby brown plants and ancient Boab trees. Now and then, they crossed a dry watercourse where tall gum trees clung to the edge, hoping for rain. They spotted a few feral goats and a herd of donkeys.

"We've got a lot of ferals up here. Camels, goats, brumbies, donkeys, pigs, you name 'em, we've got 'em. A few bloody feral humans, too," he laughed.

Dex drove, singing along with Slim Dusty, laughing at Kevin 'Bloody' Wilson's jokes and repeatedly playing Lacy Dalton's *Hill Billy Girl With The Blues*.

They approached each of the dozen or so creek crossings with caution. Dexter stopped at a cattle grid with a loosely chained gate and Cord had no problem opening and shutting it. A metal sign read 'Jacana Creek Station. Private Road. Authorised Entry Only. Shut The Gate'.

"It's the Dry," said Dex, "so we can take the fifty-two-kilometre shorter route to the homestead. In the Wet, you'd have to take the longer sixty-six-kilometre route."

They wound their way through a series of low ranges and rock outcrops sporting a few desert oaks and acres of low-growing Spinifex. Occasionally, livestock straddled the road, staring and barely moving as the vehicle passed. Cord noticed the van had a bull bar, obviously in case of a brief encounter.

Over the last rise, about twenty kilometres from the station, the landscape opened into a broad valley of grassland that waved in the gusty wind. Beyond that, a range of deep blue-coloured hills contrasted strikingly against the lighter blue of the sky. On their approach, Cord saw a ribbon of trees that bordered the bed of a stream that must be Jacana Creek. Closer in, he could see structures, fences, tanks, windmills and the tin roof of the homestead glistening in the sun.

It was mid-afternoon when they arrived at the outer stockyards. A breeze momentarily whipped up dust and cattle stared at the intruders. It was hot and the air conditioner in the vehicle gave Cord a sense of security that soon dissipated as he left the cab to open what seemed a never-ending series of gates, all with different configurations of opening and closing. Cord could see Dexter chuckling to himself as this green hand wrestled with the combinations. An overhead banner at the final gate was decorated with a brightly painted sign reading 'Jacana Creek Station'. Below the name was an elaborately coloured motif of a bird with long legs and an equally long beak.

Perched on a rise of land by the creek and shaded by tall trees, the homestead had an air of tranquillity and calmness. A white post and rail fence contained the house and some other buildings, isolating the residence from the station stockyards beyond. Cord wasn't prepared for how beautiful and welcoming the setting was, considering it was so far off the beaten track and the dryness of much of the country along the journey.

Cord knew the pastoral lease of six hundred and ninety thousand acres, in modern terms, two thousand six hundred square kilometres, was taken up by the Mumfords in 1896 and the house built in 1899. The Bell family acquired it in 1935.

Native Frangipani trees bordered the drive up to the residence, where a series of sprinklers clicked away on the lush green lawns and garden shrubs that encircled the entire building.

Built mainly of local stone, the walls had stood the test of time. The house was certainly big, with a string of windows opening to the veranda that hosted a maze of tables, couches and chairs. Four brick chimneys rose through a shiny new Zincalume roof, the only modern improvement evident in the impressive facade.

Dexter helped him unload his bags at the steps of the front veranda. "I'm goin' to see the cook," he said. "Watch ya back. See ya when I'm lookin' at ya."

He waved to Cord, drove the van out of the gate and around to one of the outbuildings.

There was no movement from the house. Small flies, persistent and annoying, buzzed around Cord's head. As he brushed them away, he realised he was now in cattle country and these pests would be his constant companions over the next few months. He mounted the steps; an old dog slept on a mat near the doorstep and didn't wake as Cord knocked on the door. There was no answer. He didn't expect a welcoming committee, so he decided to leave his bags at the door.

He noticed a paved path leading to the rear of the house and followed it to where it branched off towards the cattle yards. Mobs of snorting cattle were being herded and he could see horsemen and dogs in clouds of dust as they moved them through the stockyard gates. Suddenly, from behind him, a man with a booming voice and a pronounced foreign accent shouted, "You must be the fuckin' surveyor bloke!"

He could only be the mad Spaniard.

Boris
1999

Standing behind Cord was a giant of a man, at least six-and-a-half feet tall. A wide grin with a flash of white teeth peeked through a bushy black beard. A worn, faded blue singlet loosely concealed the giant's hairy chest. Work shorts battled to contain legs the size of tree trunks firmly planted in an enormous pair of leather boots. Expressive brown eyes welcomed Cord and he extended a tanned, muscular arm.

"*Bienvenido, Senor.* Welcome to Jacana."

Cord gingerly shook the leathery hand, twice the size of his, cautious of the degree of grip.

"I'm Boris. I'll take ya to the boss. He's over there at the stockyard. Got a few ringers he's working with."

"Boris. Good, glad to meet you. Ringers?" questioned Cord.

"New chums. Ya know, fuckin' rookies."

Dex was right; Boris's command of the language was mediocre at best, but Cord later found the man managed to avoid expounding expletives in the presence of females and Ted, the boss. He continued, "Not so fuckin' hot today, eh?"

Boris didn't seem to have a problem with the flies. Cord thought it must be his beard; nothing could get through that mop. They approached the stockyard where cattle snorted and stamped. There was dust, continuous whistling from stockmen on horseback and dogs prowling the mob. For Cord, it was a bewildering scene of dust and turmoil.

"I'm the general hand, drive the fuckin' grader, fix the mills," Boris explained proudly. "The boss says I'm your offsider for a while."

"Sure, he told me."

"That's the boss there. We'll have a fuckin' beer later. What da' ya say?"

"Fine."

Ted leant on a fence rail with his back to Cord. He held a two-way radio in one hand as he spoke and signalled with his free arm to the hands as they circled and reeled, guiding individual animals into separate yards.

Cord noted one rider was a woman on a piebald horse. A shock of blonde hair spilt from the back of her wide-brimmed hat. She was whistling to a Blue Heeler dog that was marshalling a young bull out of the main mob into a smaller yard. Ted spoke and signalled to her.

The bull stood off facing the dog, neither moving. The rider spun the horse around and squared up to the animal. It backed off, angry and snorting, lowered its head, turned and trotted into the enclosure. Ted gave the rider the thumbs up.

She called out "Brutus," and the dog wheeled and followed her as she galloped back to corner a few lagging strays. They tried to scatter, but she rounded them up with the dog at their heels and trotted them back to the herd.

The rider cantered up to the fence and Cord saw her more clearly. Her faded blue jeans and cotton shirt were covered in dust; hanging limply around her neck was a red bandana that obviously covered her face when mustering. Over one shoulder, a two-way radio hung in a sling. A pair of large sunglasses and the wide-brimmed hat pulled down tight over her forehead shielded her face from sun and dust.

Ted stepped down from the fence, patted the horse's neck and spoke to the rider. She looked over towards Cord, as did Ted, who waved, having now seen him. They talked again; she nodded and cantered away. Cord thought she must be Ted's daughter, the Bell girl, but she wasn't a ringer; she knew what she was doing.

Ted greeted him, a grin on his tanned face, his hand outstretched.

"Good to see you, Cord. Did you have a pleasant drive with Dex?"

"Yes, very informative."

Ted laughed, "Also entertaining, I bet. Yep! That man can talk the leg off a wooden chair. Come on up to the house. Clyde flew in your survey gear last week. It's in the main store."

They crossed the yard to the rear of the house and up the stone steps to the veranda. It was a lot cooler there and the pesky flies left them as soon as they were in the shade of the overhang.

"Got to take our boots off here; otherwise, we'll be in big trouble. House rules. You'll get used to it."

He ushered Cord through the back door into a long, tiled passage that divided the home in two. The aroma of baking bread filled the air, the smell of yeast causing Cord a pang of hunger as he hadn't eaten since breakfast, except for that biscuit from Dex.

Ted called, "Joan, Cord, the surveyor's here."

There was no response. Ted shrugged and led the way down the passage to a large lounge room. The polished stone floor was covered in places with an assortment of rugs. Several leather sofas faced an imposing natural stone fireplace. There were several tables of varying sizes containing vases and figurines. The walls were covered with paintings and photographs of people past and present. French doors with white lace curtains opened onto the veranda.

"Have a seat. I don't know what them women are doing. You just missed the annual station muster."

"Muster?"

"Yep, every year we get together with our neighbours, just after the Wet, to let our hair down, swap yarns, play cricket and have a good time. Good roll up, everyone comes; the pilots, even old Dexter and his missus."

"Sorry I missed it."

"I'll chase Joan up," Ted said, rising from his seat just as Joan entered the room.

"Ted, you should have told me Cord was here. If it weren't for Boris, I wouldn't know he'd arrived."

Ted rolled his eyes and didn't speak.

Joan came over to shake Cord's hand as he rose from the sofa.

"Sit down, you poor boy. You must have had a long journey, especially with Dexter and his music. A week before, you could have flown up with Clyde. Why didn't you arrange that, Ted?"

Ted didn't answer immediately and went to speak, but Joan cut him off, "Cord, Boris put your luggage in your room."

Cord thought his mum, Mrs Brown and now Joan had a lot in common. Somehow, he'd acquired yet another mother.

An Aboriginal woman entered the room carrying a large tray with crockery and a plate of muffins. So that's what was cooking.

"This is May. She makes the best muffins, doesn't she, Ted?"

"The best."

May nodded to Cord and he nodded back. She left the room.

"May is Albert's wife. Albert's our head stockman. He'll be working with you."

Joan offered Cord a cup of tea and a muffin, which he accepted and hoped not too greedily.

Ted said, "Bert, Jason and Sharon Doig are coming over, not tomorrow, but Tuesday. They're keen to hear about the job. I've chatted with them, but I know they'd rather hear it from you."

Joan put up her hands and interrupted. "Ted, don't bother Cord with that now. Come on, Cord, I'll show you your room. I expect you want to clean up, especially coming in Dex's old van. I expect you'll often be away camping, but the room is here whenever you need it."

She took him to the other side of the house, showing him the dining room, kitchen and general layout.

"Dinner at 6 pm and breakfast from 5 am to 7 am. Lunch is cold meat and sandwiches in the fridge, except for Sundays when we have a roast."

Cord thought, just like the manor, Mrs Brown and Penang.

His room had veranda access through French doors. There was an antique wooden cupboard with a matching dressing table and viewing mirror on a pedestal standing against a massive four-poster bed. Against one wall were a writing table and a nest of drawers. This was a plus as there'd be times when he'd be writing reports and field notes. He checked and was pleased there was a double three-point plug on the wall next to the desk for his laptop.

Joan smiled, "I'm sure you'll be comfy here. The bathroom, shower and toilet are down the hall on the left. We only ask you to keep shower times to a minimum as we're on generator power here."

She paused and added, as an afterthought, "I'll be glad when this mess is sorted out. Remember, dinner at six."

Cord felt a sense of foreboding. What mess?

Alone at last, he opened the doors to the veranda and rested on a soft leather couch. The old dog sleeping on the mat when he arrived came round and lay at his feet. Away in the distance, there was the muffled sound of thunder. The veranda felt like a safe haven to sit back and relax after a long day.

The afternoon was cooling, and the cattle sounds from the stockyard diminished as the mob settled for the night. He could hear the sprinklers ticking away. Soon, he'd have a shower before dinner; he was mighty hungry. He might meet the Bell girl, the mysterious jillaroo daughter. From his veranda perch, he had a clear view of the drive that wound through the Frangipani trees and out to hazy blue hills in the distance. He was surprised by the sound of a large motor starting up. He looked in the direction and saw a rig filled with jostling cattle slowly edging its way along a side fence.

He caught a glimpse of the driver. That must be Kathy Bell, the rider he had seen mustering in the yards. She still wore the wide-brimmed hat. The bandana was gone, but she was too far away to see her face. The truck gathered momentum and manoeuvred through a gate onto the main track. It accelerated and disappeared under a cloud of dust churned up by its huge wheels. As the dust cleared, he saw Boris shutting the gate and harnessing the chain. It was time to eat.

Hurdles
1999

Changed and refreshed, Cord greeted Ted in the dining room for dinner. The table, large enough to seat twelve people, was set with tablecloth, crockery and condiments. Ted was alone and reading the mail delivered by Dex, which he set aside when Cord entered.

"Just catching up on the mail, always bills. May's set a place for you there. Joan and I are here, and our kids, Kathy and Barry, sit over there."

"Fine. We have fixed places at home, too."

"Drink?" Ted held a carafe of iced water. "We sometimes have a red and a beer on weekends, except Boris, of course. He loves his beer but is still a good worker."

"In that case, I best order a carton; he's already invited me to have a beer. Do I see Dex to arrange that?"

"No, I'll put it on the list for Clyde next time he flies in. What do you prefer?"

"Swan Lager is okay with me."

Joan entered the room with May behind her, carrying a tray of hot food. The aroma aroused Cord's hunger and he hoped he'd contain his appetite and not embarrass himself. The meal, a chicken stew with braised potatoes, carrots and fresh garden peas, was delicious. May had made a rich trifle with custard topping. The portions were generous and Cord's hunger was finally appeased.

"We'll have our coffee and tea in the lounge," Joan said. "You can tell me about yourself. We need to get to know you as you'll be with us for a while."

Cord thought, how long is a while?

"Not much to tell."

"Mr Keep said you had been working in Penang. That must have been interesting."

They retired to the lounge and May brought in the coffees and tea. Cord spoke about Tanah Rata and the butterflies as he reckoned the survey work would have been boring to Joan, although Ted wanted to know about the *Spree*.

Later, Ted said, "I heard from Bert. They will be here on Tuesday at 10 am. Bert's all right, but his son's a bit of a hothead, so don't mind him. Sharon, his teenage daughter, will come along and Kathy will be here too. Unfortunately, our son, Barry, is at university in Perth and only makes it home on semester breaks. When he's done with his degree, he'll thankfully be back here to run the place. With my back and knee problems, a lot now falls on Kathy's shoulders."

"Kathy does too much, Ted," Joan said. "You should get some of the hands more involved."

"I've tried, but she won't let up. She brings it on herself."

"She didn't need to drive the truck today. She should have rested, met Cord and had dinner with us. I don't know about that girl."

Ted shrugged.

It was confirmed. The woman on the stock horse and driving the truck was their daughter, Kathy. He recalled Dex's comments and she certainly appeared formidable.

"She got a bee in her bonnet to run those maverick bulls over to Ludlow Hills Station to get them out of the yard and to pick up that young Brahman bull that Don Carter cornered in his south paddock. He says it's in good shape."

"So, she'll be back tonight?" asked Joan.

"Yep. I'll let Barry know about the bull. We'll have to send a photo of it."

In explanation to Cord, Ted continued, "Barry's into breeding Brahman cattle for beef export, so that's all we run on this place. The meat has to be top-grade and he's always looking for good stock."

Talking cattle was unfamiliar to Cord and he was thankful to return to his room to consider the job ahead. He had two full days before the meeting with the neighbours. Time to assemble his equipment and become more familiar with the place. He reckoned it'd be worthwhile to take a run down to the cairn on the bottom southeast corner, where he'd commence the survey and then follow the creek back to the homestead. He needed to get the lie of the land. He was in a strange new place in a strange new land and the circumstances bothered him. In Penang, Gert was in charge and with Brian and the others, he was part of a team. Here, he was in charge and alone.

*****

He slept well, actually overslept. It was the sprinklers' constant clicking that woke him. He opened the veranda doors; the air was fresh, the sky clear and blue. He just made it to breakfast at 6:30 am.

The dining room was empty. Coffee percolated in a jug on a side table, and he was pouring a mug when May entered. He gathered she was shy and tried to put her at ease with bland morning chatter.

"Dinner last night was delicious. Should be a nice day."

"Thank ya, Mr Cord. There's cereal. Would ya like bacon and eggs? Mr Ted's had breakfast and gone off with Boris. Mrs Joan is in the store writin' orders. Miss Kathy's not down yet. She got home late."

The cereal, toast with lashings of bacon and eggs, fried tomatoes and sausages, was too ample for him to finish.

As he was about to leave, May asked, "Would ya like pancakes, Mr Cord?"

He shook his head. "No thanks, I'll just have another coffee."

He was topping up his coffee mug when a husky female voice behind him said, "So, you're McCullum, our surveyor."

He turned and there she was. Dex was right; she was a good looker.

"I'm Kathy Bell."

She held out her hand, and he took it. It was not a hardened work hand; soft, elegant fingers smelt of fragrant massage oil.

"Yes, I saw you yesterday at the yards. I'm Cord."

Dex's description had not done her full justice. In a way, her presence disturbed him. He felt she was looking right through him, seeing his faults, noting his misgivings, judging his failures. It was a feeling he'd never felt with anyone and found the sensation hard to explain.

She smiled, took her hand from his and the feeling left him. She poured herself a coffee. He was flummoxed as to what to say next; if she noticed his nervousness, she didn't show it.

"Are you about to go?"

"No, no," Cord stammered.

"Good, then I'll join you for a coffee."

She was about his age. Engaging blue eyes above a slightly freckled nose, with long, blonde hair tied in a ponytail and a ready smile that completely disarmed him. She filled her blue jeans to advantage. 'Beautiful' was the only word that came to him. The fact that she was a ridgy-didge, cattle mustering, truck driving, true-blue jillaroo worried him. In her presence, he felt inferior. She was in her environment and comfortable, whereas he wasn't in his.

Her eyes searched his; her look direct and appraising.

"So, you're going to help solve our problem."

He searched for an answer. "Well, I hope it works out okay for everyone."

"Someone's got to lose."

Cord was dismayed. He wasn't there to determine riparian water rights. The survey would provide irrefutable evidence of ownership, that's all. He was a surveyor employed to do a job, not arbitrate on water disputes between neighbours. Surely, these people realised that. Maybe her remark was a forerunner, an indicator of the tone of the meeting to come. John Keep never told him about this aspect of the job. It seemed he was the meat in the sandwich.

"Do you ride?"

"Horses?"

"Yes, horses."

"No, never been on one."

"Pity, we could have gone for a ride, shown you over the place."

She finished her coffee and rose to leave. She stopped at the door and her eyes flashed. "By the way, I forgot to say welcome to Jacana Creek, Mr McCullum."

He felt she was mocking him. Mr McCullum and riding horses.

He'd fallen at the first hurdle.

Beer
1999

The survey equipment sat neatly in the corner of a massive, fully lined and insulated shed designed for multiple purposes, including large gatherings. Cord rifled through the boxes, noting the contents of each. Much of it was hired, particularly the Trimble GNNS equipment, like the one on the *Spree*, although this model was designed for portable, robust use on the land. Thankfully, John Keep purchased a Wild Leica EDM for the job, a sweet angular and distance-measuring instrument of astounding accuracy.

One box contained his personal kit of laptop, printer, stationery and field notebooks. There was a package containing an aerial photo mosaic of the entire station taken in the Dry, dated 1994, a handy navigation tool showing tracks and water features. He'd use it to compile a mud map of the station, recording natural and artificial boundaries, names of objects and other points of interest, which would help in the meeting with the owners.

There was a case of personal accessories, clothes and his faithful 'Landman' beer stein. He sorted through the garments, repacked them and left the stein on top of the case to take to his room.

The booming voice with the pronounced accent shattered his reverie. The man mountain stood there grinning, "The boss sent me to help ya. I put ya gear in the corner. Is it okay?"

"Sure, it's fine. Just unpacking to see where I am."

The man looked at him quizzically and answered with a humourless expression, "You're at Jacana."

Cord smiled woefully. So, this was one of the hands assigned to help him. He knew he had to be clear on directions.

Boris added, "It's fuckin' hot in here. What can I do?"

"You can help take some of this to my room, my case and some of that gear."

He pointed to the case and a few other boxes.

"The other stuff over there needs to go in the vehicle. You can leave it here till we go on the job. Please, it's delicate and has to be handled with care."

He hoped Boris understood as the man nodded and bent to pick up the case. He hesitated when he saw the beer stein and his face broke into a broad grin. He examined it and exclaimed, "German! Good fuckin' drop."

He looked closer at the engravings. "This your name?"

Cord wasn't fully attentive as he was sorting stationery and nodded absentmindedly.

"Landman!" Boris said at last. "We'll have a fuckin' beer later. What da' ya say, Landman?"

So, Cord was the Landman again, but this time stranded miles from the ocean.

Boris grabbed the case in one hand and two boxes under his other arm. He carried them to the veranda, leaving them at the door. Under the watchful eye of May, he and Cord repeated the process for all the boxes.

"Ya can't come in in those boots," she said.

They obliged, took off their boots and ferried the luggage to Cord's room.

"*Mandonmujer esa!*" Boris muttered, rolling his eyes when May, the 'bossy woman', was out of earshot.

"After lunch, I'd like to drive to the southeast corner. Can you arrange that?"

"No problem, Landman."

"It'll be about an eighty-kilometre round trip. Is that okay?

"No problem, Landman. I'll pack the vehicle and meet you here."

May had made corned beef and chutney sandwiches for lunch. She poured him an orange drink without asking and left the carafe on the table. She reminded him, "Dinner at six o'clock."

He waited for Boris on the veranda. Across the lawn at the post and rail fence, he could see and hear Kathy in animated conversation with a young Aboriginal stockman, gesturing and speaking in his dialect. The fellow had his head down, looking sheepishly at the ground. Cord thought, is there nothing this woman can't do? Boris drove up in the Land Cruiser Troop

Carrier. They drove through the open front gate and Cord wondered about shutting it.

"It's okay, Landman. Miss Kathy's movin' stock up from the west paddock so we can leave it open."

They veered off the main track and continued along another narrow road, wide enough for just one vehicle. The dust curled and ballooned behind them as they followed the creek on the left, its bed hidden by tall gum trees. They passed another track that veered off to the left.

"Apricot Springs that way," remarked Boris.

Ten kilometres on, another track veered to the left. They were closer to the creek here and Cord could see the bed was dry.

Boris explained the makeshift concrete crossing. "That's the crossing to Indigo Downs, thirty-five clicks from here. You can cross it most times, even in the Wet."

The track they were on deteriorated, sometimes indistinguishable to Cord. Several mobs of cattle grazed on the tall grass bordering the creek. They drove towards a distant range of ragged high hills before stopping at the first rise.

"That's the Stony Ridge Range. We'll have ta' walk from here to the corner."

Cord could see where a gorge cut through the hills and pointed to the break. "I reckon we've gone far enough. We'll walk to the corner another day. What's that break I can see in the range?"

"That's Mammoth Gorge, a sacred site. Ya need permission to go there."

"Permission?"

"Aboriginal. Don't worry, Landman. Albert can get you in there."

They arrived back at the station at dusk. Boris parked the vehicle. "How about a fuckin' beer before grub?"

Cord nodded. He thought, why not? Still time before dinner; I can't keep saying no.

Boris led him around the back of the homestead to a prefabricated dwelling. Inside, it was clean and tidy. Boris switched on a large fan and opened the windows. There was a table and a couple of chairs, a two-seater couch, single bed and a small kitchen with a stove and a gigantic fridge. He opened the fridge door, its shelves completely stacked with beer cans.

"What da' ya like, Landman? Emu or Victoria Bitter?"

"Emu, thanks."

Boris took two cans from the fridge, handed one to Cord, cracked the top of his own and took a mouthful.

"Fuckin' beautiful," he said, licking his lips. "Didn't even touch the fuckin' sides."

He grabbed another from the fridge and threw Cord one, too. Cord finished the second and left as Boris was starting on his fourth.

Cord thought, rule number one: no grog when camping.

The Meeting
1999

May had made pancakes for breakfast with the option of bacon or honey. Cord chose the bacon version. It was early and Joan was the only one at the table, finishing her breakfast with a cup of tea.

"Good morning, Cord. Big meeting today."

"Good morning, Ma'am. Yes. Is it here in the dining room?"

"Please call me Joan. I think so. Ted and Kathy will be back about nine. They'll sort it out."

The conversation was polite. She hoped he was settling in okay, but underneath, Cord gauged she was just as troubled as he was by the day ahead.

He hadn't been able to locate the charger and the backup battery for the GPS equipment. He hoped it was just an oversight, as fieldwork couldn't start without that gear. He quickly finished breakfast, took the key and opened the main shed to look again. He and Boris fossicked through boxes, but the gear was missing.

Joan called, "Cord, the Doigs are here."

He had to get an urgent message to John Keep. All he could do was quickly pen a message and have Boris email it off, but could the man be trusted to do it, and was he capable?

He and Boris walked up the rise to the house.

"Plenty of thunder today, Landman. Is there anything else I can do?"

"Email this important note to John Keep. Here's his address. It's urgent, can you do it?"

"No fuckin' problem, Landman."

Cord winced as he handed him the written note.

"Here's a list of extra equipment we'll need. Pegs, iron stakes, cement. You can make a start. I'll go through it with you tomorrow, okay?"

"No fuckin' problem, Landman."

Cord winced again and thought, I suppose I'll get used to the language.

There was an immediate pause in conversation when he entered the dining room. Ted stood at the fireplace with another man the same age, obviously Bert Doig. Another younger man was chatting with Kathy and Joan talked with a young girl of seventeen or so. Several carafes of iced water and glasses stood in the centre of the table and water boiled in a jug next to the coffee percolator.

Bert smiled through a ruddy, sunburnt face and shook hands, at the same time introducing his son, Jason, and daughter, Sharon.

The younger man took Cord's hand limply in his. Sharon smiled, her eyes bright and extended her hand in a warm handshake. Kathy nodded in his direction, her eyes distant.

He thought, that woman, she's such a cold fish, albeit an attractive one. It was the first time he had seen her with her blonde hair loose and brushed. Once again, he remembered Dex's words, 'She's a good looker but as hard as nails'. Quite different from Lucille.

Ted invited everyone to the table. Cord sat opposite Kathy, who seemed intent on ignoring him.

"Well, now that everyone knows each other, let's get started. Joan will take minutes, nothing too formal. Kathy, will you acknowledge traditional owners?"

She rose and spoke in the native dialect, then sat.

Ted spoke again. "Let's get down to business and hear what Cord has to say. Over to you."

The atmosphere was tense, bordering on unpleasant.

Cord stood, unravelling the lease plan onto the table. He was on familiar ground explaining latitude, longitude, the curvature of the earth and how those factors had to be addressed in laying out long lines, such as the sixty-five kilometres in question. He tried to make it as simple as possible but wasn't sure if he did. How do you explain to laypeople the mathematics and the technology required to achieve the accuracy necessary to mark boundaries on an oblate spheroid? The only uncertainty was the time it would take. He felt there wasn't any more to add, thanked everybody and sat down.

Jason Doig stood, his voice high-pitched and agitated. Cord noticed that throughout his address, Jason was tapping the table, distracted, annoyed at the turn of events and having to hire a surveyor.

"Why's this taking so long to sort out? We've a buyer waiting and we could lose them."

Bert ignored Jason's outburst and calmly asked, "How long do you think the survey will take?"

Cord played it on the safe side, "Twelve weeks, maybe more."

"Twelve weeks!" yelled Jason. "I could do this with a compass. Dad, we're having the bloody wool pulled over our eyes. The Bells are just playing us for fools to buy time for the deal to fall over."

Things turned ugly. Ted stood to say something, but Bert cut him short, "Jason, shut up. That's enough. Apologise to the Bells. They've got as much at stake as we have. Ted, we'll commit to paying for our share of this work as it's also to our advantage. I'm sorry, Ted, Joan, Kathy. You don't have to put up with this."

Sharon blurted out, "Jason, how can you say such a thing to the Bells?"

Ted spoke calmly and coolly, "Thanks, Bert. Jason, I'll ignore those remarks. We've always been good neighbours and our stations have supported each other over the years, so let's not let this issue come between us."

Jason sat down, mumbling an apology.

Cord was angry but knew he shouldn't lose his cool over such senseless comments. He felt like saying 'Bloody idiot' but didn't. Kathy's eyes were on him; he couldn't stumble here.

"That's my best estimate," Cord confirmed. "I haven't assessed the nature of the country yet. I'll have a better idea in a few weeks."

Bert added, "Can you give us an idea now of where the boundary is near Apricot Springs? That's what's critical."

"I'm sure an estimate is insufficient in such an important matter. I'm aware that timing is crucial, but the regulation requires me to set out the boundary in an orderly and precise manner."

He knew it sounded like, 'Do it my way or not at all,' but he had to take charge of the situation and not be dictated to.

Jason butted in, his voice quieter but his attitude still fiery, "Timing! That's right, bloody crucial, all right!"

Cord ignored the comment; he had to remain calm and impartial. In the end, it wasn't his problem. The atmosphere remained tense. Ted and Bert shuffled their papers, Joan continued writing the minutes, Jason sat fuming quietly in his chair and Sharon held her father's hand. Kathy's eyes were fixed on Cord.

Cord addressed Bert directly, "Mr Doig… err… Bert, are you aware that pastoral leases have been sold in the past without having surveyed boundaries?"

Bert shook his head. "No, I've never considered selling."

Jason went to speak, but Cord cut him off. "If that's still the case, I think it may be an option worth considering. I know contracts can be written subject to conditions. In your case, a contract could stipulate that the sale is conditional on the boundary being surveyed and that the buyer is satisfied that water is available; the contract binding for, say, four months. A realtor would be able to draft such a document. It's a possibility."

At that moment, the tone of the meeting changed, the tension lifted, and Bert sat back relaxed. He glanced at his son as if to say, why haven't you explored this possibility? Jason looked away sheepishly. Joan hastily recorded Cord's comment and Sharon smiled.

Kathy said, "I've something to add. We all know the spring supplies water that's wasted, as it continuously drains through the creek to the sea. We could hire a hydrologist to measure the water discharge and then, instead of draining into the sea, use some of the wastage for irrigation. In that case, we wouldn't be damaging the spring itself."

Ted agreed, "We've decided that if the stretch of the creek is on our property, and the spring is protected hydrologically, we'd allow it to be pumped, as Kathy says."

Ted and Bert shook hands. Joan smiled at Cord and whispered, "Thank you."

May brought in a tray of cups and fresh muffins. Cord excused himself; for him, the meeting was over. His hands were clammy and perspiration ran down the back of his shirt. In the solace of his room, he gathered his thoughts and went out onto the veranda. He sat under the gentle draught of a large fan plugging away. This wasn't what he imagined surveying would be. He bargained on the isolation of wide-open spaces, the call of the wild, the great outdoors, not contending with all these people, their moods, and aspirations.

He missed Lucille and could see her face before him. He couldn't imagine her in another man's arms; it was too horrible to contemplate.

He thought of Kathy; she was a mystery, but she had smiled at him, so it looked like he'd jumped that hurdle okay.

It was lunchtime. Cord didn't feel like eating and went back into the room, lay on the bed and quite uncharacteristically dozed off.

A knock on the door woke him. It was Ted. "Do you mind if I come in?"

"No, not at all."

They went out onto the veranda. The air was humid, the day sultry and the overhead fan slowly turned.

"I want to thank you for diffusing an awkward situation. I didn't know where the meeting would lead, but it turned out well. That Jason, he's a loose cannon. I had a chat with Bert and he'll follow up on your suggestion with the buyer and an agent. Clyde is flying in with supplies this afternoon and he'll have dinner with us. Come down about 5 pm for drinks to celebrate the start of the survey."

Cord stayed in his room all afternoon, preparing his survey notes and reading the equipment manuals. He needed to be well prepared, not only with personal gear but with all the logistics required to run a camp. Time was of the essence. He hoped he could rely on Boris, but still wasn't sure of him; communication was a problem. There was so much to do; he sat at the desk revising details. He still hadn't met Albert, the head stockman, who was at a station camp and would return the following day.

Late afternoon, the helicopter arrived, wheeling noisily overhead before setting down behind the homestead. A cloud of dust wafted into Cord's room, heralding its landing.

He dressed in his best jeans and soft blue shirt courtesy of Corrine from Christmas last. His outfit matched Clyde's, who wore jeans and a blue shirt with the motif 'AirMuster Choppers' woven on the pocket. He came forward and shook Cord's hand. Tall and tanned with sandy hair, he winked at Cord and said, "Brought your beer and some extra survey gear."

"Thanks. What do I owe you?"

"See Joan. She manages the accounts."

Ted offered Cord a drink. On a whim, he chose a rum and Coke but thought perhaps he should have chosen a beer. Kathy arrived looking spectacular, this time in a yellow floral dress. She was made up with her hair combed down around her face. He estimated Dex was probably wrong about

Kathy not being interested in Clyde; she had no doubt dressed up for him. She was happier than he had seen her so far in his short stay, but then again, the previous few days had been full of drama, with no time for humour.

Clyde held the floor during dinner. Joan had cooked a delicious pot roast, followed by fruit salad and ice cream. They shared several bottles of Shiraz, compliments of Clyde. Cord decided he'd match this hospitality and made a mental note to order a case of wine before he left for camp.

Clyde was attentive to Kathy but was also keen to tell Ted about a new copter, an Airbus AS350 he'd placed on order.

"It isn't for mustering; it's a people and cargo mover. We'll still have our small Meridian copters for mustering, but I'm finding that we need to upgrade our services since we're losing a lot of business from the mining companies. We also need another pilot." He asked Cord if he knew any pilots out of work and jested, "Do you want to become a pilot?"

Clyde poured Ted, Cord and himself another wine and they moved out to the veranda as Joan, Kathy and May cleared the table.

Kathy passed Cord with dishes in her hand, "Would you like to visit Apricot Springs tomorrow?"

Cord was surprised, as she'd only given him a few offhand comments throughout the evening.

"Sure, thanks."

"Straight after breakfast, 8 o'clock. Bring your togs for a swim."

Bemused, he joined the others; Clyde was still talking choppers. Tired and bored, he excused himself and retired to his room. There was a knock on the veranda door. It was Boris. He had two beer cans in one hand, a piece of paper in the other and a big grin on his face.

"*Senor* Keep said he already sent the gear express delivery and you should have it tomorrow."

"Clyde's just delivered it. Good man, thank you."

"No fuckin' problem, Landman."

He cracked the two beers, handed Cord one and sipped the other.

"Fuckin' good brew, eh!"

Apricot Springs
1999

Kathy snared Cord at breakfast. "You right for the springs?"

Cord nodded as he buttered his toast and sipped his coffee. She seemed ready to go. It was 7 am and he gathered she'd already eaten.

"I understood it was an 8 o'clock start."

She responded with a bland stare. "Well, when you're ready. Bring your togs."

No acknowledgement, no apology; she made it seem it was his fault he'd caused the delay.

"Clyde flew out early this morning. It's a wonder you didn't hear him."

Cord did hear the copter take off, knew it was early, rolled over and slept again. He wondered where Clyde had slept, but then it was none of his business.

She added with a hint of sarcasm, "I'll be out in the machinery shed when you can make it, Mr McCullum."

At 7:40 am, they drove out in an old Nissan Patrol tray back that had seen better days. Kathy in her jeans, checked shirt, Akubra hat and joggers; Cord in his work jeans, T-shirt and desert boots with his day pack containing togs, towel, sunscreen and camera.

Kathy explained, "This is Boris's vehicle. The dents are from cattle horns, but it's the feral buffalo you have to watch. The bastards often attack the vehicles when they're cornered. The maverick bulls are the real buggers. That hole in the door where you're sitting, that's from a bloody buffalo bull. You should ask Boris about that."

It was strange for Cord to hear a woman swearing, but it didn't seem out of place. It was a natural thing up here, in this land of flood and fire and famine.

As they drove, Kathy quizzed him about his background as a surveyor. He mentioned America.

She sighed, "I don't suppose I'll ever get overseas for a real holiday, at least not until Barry comes home. Dad needs me here. Although, I'll be going to the USA later this year. Barry and I are attending the Brahman Breeders Congress in Texas, but it's only eight days, so not much time to see the sights."

Cord asked, "Brahman? They're the ones with the hump neck?"

She rolled her eyes, "Yep, they're the ones with the hump neck."

Cord felt foolish. How else could he describe an animal he'd no experience with?

"There are other breeds, aren't there? What makes them so special?"

She didn't answer as the vehicle hit a large pothole and slewed. She spun the wheel, throwing him hard against the door.

"Sorry, bloody bulldust."

They swung off the main track and headed across a plain of Mitchell grass, retracing the path he took with Boris. Once again, Cord saw the line of gums hugging the banks of the creek. They took the track veering to the left, the one that was sign-posted 'Apricot Springs'. It was immediately more potholed and bumpier, mainly from constant cattle hooves where it crossed low swampy ground before rising steeply away from the creek bed.

"In the Wet, this floods and you can't drive here," Kathy noted. "Clyde's flown me over when it floods and it's certainly something to see."

Good old Clyde, he thought. Was it a tinge of jealousy? Probably that mixed with mild annoyance at her mentioning Clyde's deeds for the second time.

"From the air, it's great, but on the ground, you'll see, the best is yet to come."

They drove over a ridge and swerved around a rocky outcrop, where she stopped. The rock glowed and toasted under the relentless heat of the sun.

The sunburnt country, Cord thought.

"Come and look," she said excitedly, bouncing out of the vehicle and hurrying to the edge of the outcrop with Cord following. Standing on an overhang, she pointed, "What do you think?"

Cord paused and looked down. Underneath him, clear blue water bubbled out of the rock face and fell in a series of waterfalls to several pools below, filled to the brim. The overflow cascaded noisily over rapids and sent sprays of water high into the air until, finally, the torrent spilt into the bed of Jacana Creek below. Kathy clambered down the overhang and stood on the smooth, bare rock face that encircled the top pool. She beckoned Cord to follow.

She'd left her hat in the vehicle and the breeze swirled her hair across and around her face. Once more, he felt vulnerable, appreciating her natural beauty. He scrambled after her, captivated by her loveliness and the appeal of this natural phenomenon.

"Come on," she urged, her clear blue eyes matching the colour of the sparkling pool water, open and inviting.

"Well, what do you think?"

"Breathtaking." He meant the place and the pool, but especially her.

"I just love this place. I spent a lot of my childhood swimming here with our community. It's a sacred place for them and the neighbouring communities often come to the springs to share their stories. When the crowds gather, no one else can intrude."

A light breeze skipped across the water, sending a pleasant, tart aroma into the air. She added, "It's artesian water and safe to drink – and it's free! In this top pool, it's a constant forty-three degrees Celsius. The cattle don't come up here to drink. They drink way down in the creek 'cause by the time the water gets there, it's cooled to about eighteen degrees. We swim in the third pool, where it's twenty-five degrees, that's the best. It's too warm up here."

They returned to the vehicle to grab their packs. The series of pools became smaller as they descended but were just as deep and surrounded by lush palms adorned with flowering creepers. They stopped at the middle pool and Kathy stood alarmingly close to Cord. He felt her nearness.

"See over there," she said, pointing to the far bank of the next pool below them. "Can you see the plants with those brilliant pink flowers around the edge? They're Lotus plants. And can you see the birds?"

A flock of white-chested birds with spindly legs were treading on the Lotus leaf pads. He recognised these were the same as the bird painted on the entry sign to the station.

"They're Jacana birds, native to here. We named the station after them. They're also called Lotus birds or Jesus birds because they can walk on water. We don't swim down in that pool; it'd disturb everything. We swim here."

Cord took photos to send to Corrine. He knelt at the pool's edge and let the water gently flow over his fingers; it was pleasantly warm. Although only mid-morning, the heat and humidity of the day were oppressive and the sweat showed darkly on his shirt. It would be a good time for a swim.

They laid their towels out on a flat rock under a shady overhang. Kathy produced a thermos of ice-cold orange juice and two of May's famous muffins to share.

"You can see why this place is so important. It's a natural marvel. It keeps our station economically viable and has significant cultural significance for our traditional owners. The constant flow provides water for our cattle throughout the year, so we don't have to rely on the weather. It's essential we do everything in our power to preserve it. That's why the boundary position is so vital."

Cord avoided her earnest look. As much as he wanted to allay her fears, he knew only time would tell, and besides, John Keep had warned him of the politics of the situation. He thought of Jason Doig and the need to keep cool and unbiased, so he looked away.

"Why the name Apricot Springs?"

"Oh! It's for the Bush Apricots. See around the banks, that small shrub with those glossy leaves? That's the Bush Apricot. They fruit throughout the year and are great bush tucker, sweet and juicy. I'll get you one."

She jumped up, went to a shrub and tugged at a yellow cylindrical fruit.

"Try this. We put it in our salad dishes and May makes a great relish."

Cord opened the skin and tasted the fleshy inner fruit. It was delicious.

Kathy was smiling at his reaction and he thought again what a beauty she was. He thought of his lost love, Lucille, but he was undoubtedly attracted to this woman. Lucille with her beauty and elegance; Kathy with her candour and fire. Lucille with her affection and sophistication; Kathy with her allure and ability. They were women poles apart, different in every way, yet they cast the same spell on him.

She suddenly laughed, "Who needs a spa when you've got this to swim in."

Without notice, she shed her clothes, revealing her tanned figure, perfect in a bright orange bikini. She ran to the edge and dived in, surfaced and called, "It's fabulous, come on in."

Cord was more circumspect and went behind a rock to don his bathers. He came to the edge and dived in. The water was warm. It felt slightly oily and gave a sheen to his skin. He swam to the far edge and back, as did Kathy. After a half hour, they clambered out.

"Throw me my towel, please."

Cord obliged, trying to avoid looking at her. She caught him staring and candidly stared back. She dried her hair and went behind the rock to change, while Cord went in the opposite direction to do the same.

He wasn't sure if Kathy had tried to taunt him, but he wouldn't be tormented by any woman again; the wounds Lucille had left still cut deep. He wasn't going to let Kathy get under his skin; he'd only just arrived.

They sat by the pool in silence for a while, and once again, Kathy produced the thermos, two Vegemite rolls and bananas from her kit.

"You think of everything."

"You should come up here. Remember, you can swim anytime you like, but not when the community is here."

"Sure," he said but thought, not likely. I won't be here that long.

"Tomorrow, I start fieldwork and won't be around much, but if I'm in the vicinity on the job, I might drop in for a swim."

Kathy smiled.

Back at the Patrol, she said, "On the south boundary, there's the Stony Ridge Range, which has spectacular gorges, particularly Mammoth Gorge. It's got heaps of fabulous rock paintings. Clyde and I are flying down there next time he's here. Would you like to come? He'd have room."

The third time she'd mentioned Clyde. It irritated him.

"Thanks, but I'll probably be working. I'll have to give it a miss."

She nodded.

The day had gone beautifully, but things changed. At Clyde's name, he was prickly and asked, "Clyde spends a lot of time here."

"He comes with mail and supplies every alternate fortnight to Dexter. It works out well."

"I thought he was just coming to see you."

She looked at him sideways and he winced. What a stupid thing to say. They drove on and then she spoke tersely, "What makes you say that? Quite an observation since you've only been here a few days."

"I apologise. I saw he stayed overnight."

What was he thinking? Another stupid remark! He was digging a deep hole for himself.

Her voice rose in anger, "What are you implying?"

"I thought you may be a unit." Yet another thoughtless comment.

"Well, you're wrong, Mr McCullum."

They drove uncomfortably and Kathy dropped him at the homestead steps without a word.

He didn't see her at dinner. He wanted to apologise again, somehow make it up to her; it'd been a grand day and he'd spoiled it.

Joan said Kathy wouldn't be at dinner, that she was at a barbeque at the 'hash house' where the hands and ringers gathered for meals and drinks.

Later, in his room, Cord opened his camera gallery and looked at a photo. He took comfort and it relieved his tension; Lucille was laughing with the butterflies.

Camping
1999

Boris waited for Cord to inspect the equipment and supplies he'd loaded into the box trailer. The list given him was now indecipherable as the big man had pawed and scrunched it into tatters.

Cord examined the remnants.

"I got everything, Landman, just as you said. Coupla' fuckin' things I don't know. We don't have a Jerry at Jacana. We've got Jimmy and Johnny, but no Jerry. What can Jerry do I can't do?"

He scratched his mop of thick black hair while Cord thought a moment, then chuckled. He realised on the list he'd written 'Jerry Can'.

"Sorry, I meant a tin can for diesel fuel."

He demonstrated, mimicking pouring fuel into the vehicle.

Boris responded, throwing his hands into the air, "Ah! *Recipiente de estano contenido*. Tin can. Sorry, my English, sorry. I'll get two from the store, Landman."

"One will be enough."

"I'll get two, Landman, no problems."

Cord shook his head and smiled as Boris hurried off to make up for his confusion. He returned dejected.

"Sorry, Landman. Chuck, the storeman, says he's only got one can left and if he gives it to me, he won't have one can left. He'll order us one."

It wasn't essential, but Cord could see Chuck was playing with Boris. He'd have a word with Ted about the can.

The morning went on with Cord double-checking and Boris responding with cheerful enthusiasm.

Cord hoped to see Kathy at lunch. May had prepared cold meat and salad, but he sat alone at the table. She told him Miss Kathy was down at Bore 12 with some of the ringers. He hoped he'd see her at dinner in the evening, his last in the homestead for a while.

After lunch, he met Ted in the main store to verify arrangements. Even with insulation, it was stiflingly hot under the tin roof, which creaked and groaned as the sun scorched the metal. Thankfully, Ted suggested they adjourn to the house and Kathy's air-conditioned office.

The office, a corner room in the homestead, had wide windows and French doors to the veranda overlooking the side garden. A magnificent crimson-coloured Bougainvillea vine shaded a hammock that swung between the veranda posts. Inside, a laptop computer sat in the centre of a massive antique mahogany desk with a baby blue swivel chair and blue and yellow floral drapes shielding the windows. Behind the desk stood a bookshelf crammed with books of every description ranging from the academic to popular literature. Several navy blue scatter rugs lay across the polished wooden floor.

A sky blue fabric couch in the middle of the room with matching loafer chairs faced a mahogany coffee table holding a few magazines. A small bright green filing cabinet stood in one corner. Arranged on the cabinet were four silver trophies for swimming achievements and a selection of framed certificates on the wall above, one for a Bachelor of Arts degree, another for a Diploma in Teaching and one for First Prize in an equestrian event.

Around the walls were several photos, Kathy and Barry swimming, the family and a large picture of a Brahman bull with a purple scarf and a medallion hanging around its neck engraved 'Wild Bill'. Everything was neat, in its proper place.

They sat on the sofas, Ted obviously comfortable in his daughter's office, but Cord felt decidedly awkward, as if he was invading her space without an invite. The surroundings revealed a softer, feminine side of Kathy than he'd sensed before, making him even more regretful of his foolish and reckless remarks the day before. This woman amazed him. He romanticised; was he falling in love? That couldn't be. It was just an aberration of loneliness and yearning for a woman's touch. He loved Lucille.

His thoughts were interrupted by Ted. "So, you'll be off in the morning. Is everything going all right? Boris's been packing, unpacking, and repacking the trailer. He's a real worker and always wants to please."

"Yep, it's all good. I've left the spare battery packs here on charge."

"Sure, I'll get 'em to you when they're charged up. Albert will be here later today. He and Boris know what the job's about, but I reckon they'll need some coaching to be really helpful. Albert will swap every couple of weeks with his son Davy; he's a good bushman, too. If you need any more manpower, call on the radio."

"Okay, thanks. I'm looking forward to meeting Albert. Boris sure is willing and eager to get started."

"That's Boris all right. Albert's my best hand, top stockman and first-class bushman. His people are the traditional owners and he's an Elder, a man to be respected. I'll send him over when he gets in."

Late in the afternoon, Albert rode in from the south paddock. Cord was on the veranda, checking the rewritten supply list again when he saw him walking his horse up the drive. May came running out of the house, down the steps and into his arms. They kissed and walked back together, Albert with one arm around her waist, the other holding the horse's bridle. Cord decided not to intrude.

Cord never got to speak with Kathy before they left. Boris invited him to the hash house that night to meet Albert, Davy and the rest of the station hands and ringers. The camp cook, Trudy, sat him at the table between Billy, the mechanic and part-time welder who looked after the machinery shed and Chuck, the storeman. The meal was quite a spread. Pea and bacon soup, corned beef, cabbage, oven-baked crusty bread and rice pudding; satisfying and delicious. The experienced hands poked good-natured fun at the new ringers, highlighting their lack of riding skills. Cord found that Billy, an ex-navy mechanic, had worked on workboats like the *Spree* and knew of Gert and his exploits.

Cameron, nicknamed Chuck, oversaw the storeroom. He sat back, shaking his head when Johnny said, "Does everyone know why we call Cameron Chuck? 'Cause Dex and Clyde says, when they deliver stuff to the store, Chuck says, chuck it here, chuck it up there, chuck it over there, chuck it in the corner, or I'll chuck it out."

Cord thought again of the missing diesel can.

Things took a more serious turn when the survey job crept into the conversation. Questions were asked and there was silence when Cord replied. He felt a reverence from them and their anxious faces confirmed that a great deal rested on his shoulders.

The conversation ended in good-natured banter when Old Bluey, the stable hand, cheekily asked, "If we all dob in a quid or two, what's the damage, Landman, to move the boundary our way?"

"Too much damage," Cord said.

Everyone laughed.

*****

It was daybreak, the air clean and crisp; cattle snorted in the yards as they jostled for the feeder trough. A cock crowed in the fowl yard, answered by another. The Kelpies and Blue Heelers yelped and barked around Davy as he tossed meat to them. The noises of the awakening station grew until the sounds blended, heralding one of those bright sunny mornings so typical of the Dry.

The commotion woke Cord. Rising, he went out onto the veranda. Kathy was sitting at the end of the porch with her back to him, sipping a cup of coffee. He wanted to say something but turned away; the damage had been done.

He had risen later than planned and could see Boris and Albert near the main store, already loading and hitching up vehicles; it wasn't a good start. He dressed quickly and carried his plans and equipment towards Davy, who was helping pack. Kathy had moved from the porch and was there, talking to Albert, but quickly left when she saw Cord coming. He hoped to catch her at breakfast, but she wasn't there. Breakfast was a scant affair of cereal and buttered toast washed down with a mug of coffee. He was anxious to be off and forget about the woman.

Joan entered the dining room, "Take care, Cord. When do you think you'll be back?"

"A week or so, I'll see how it goes. It all depends on the lie of the land."

"Well, we'll see you then. Ted and Kathy plan to ride down to see you if the muster starts well."

"Good."

Boris approached the house to collect the last of Cord's personal gear.

"We're ready when you are, Landman."

It was late, 8:30 am and there was no one around when they drove out, except for May, who waved to Albert. He and Cord were out front in the Cruiser, followed by Boris in the Patrol. Both vehicles were packed tight, the

Cruiser with the fragile gear, towing the horse float with two horses named Ginger and Smack.

"You never know when ya need 'em," Albert said. "Sometimes these things break down. Vehicles can't go everywhere, but horses can."

Cord noted the wisdom of this advice.

The Patrol, laden with the camping kit, towed a dual wheel trailer carrying the heavy gear, bags of cement, steel pickets, generator, battery pack, fuel drums and a full water tank.

The previous day, Chuck had said to Boris, "I suppose ya takin' the kitchen sink too?"

Boris desperately approached Cord, "Landman, do ya want a kitchen sink? Chuck don't have one."

Smiling at the misinterpretation, Cord wondered at Chuck's cynicism.

"No, we'll be okay this time."

Cord liked Albert from the moment they met at the hash house spread. There was an air of quiet confidence about him. He was stocky, of muscular build and Cord guessed around forty years of age. A silver-grey beard covered a dark furrowed face, with riveting brown eyes and a ready smile. As Ted had said, he was a man to be respected, calm and softly spoken.

They took the route Cord had first travelled with Boris and then with Kathy. It was slow going with the heavy trailers. They stopped several times to exercise the horses and for them to drink at the waterholes and bore troughs. They crossed several gullies and watercourses as they slowly made their way to the southeast corner of the lease. Eventually, the distant Stony Ridge Range came into view, its spiky battlements blazing white in the afternoon sun. At a broad platform of rock near a large billabong, Albert stopped the Cruiser.

"We're not far from the corner, but we'll set up camp here. Good water and grass for the horses."

Cord examined the photo mosaic. The creek traced a white line against the dark grassland and bush of the surrounding country. He estimated the distance to the corner was not more than five kilometres. As most equipment would be stockpiled at camp, towing the trailer with only a light load shouldn't be difficult.

Boris and Albert quickly erected five various-sized tents and positioned them under the shade of the tall river gums. A small willy-willy stirred up a dust cloud as it spiralled close to the camp. Cord busied himself unpacking and storing some of the extra survey gear not required for the next day. Boris arranged a ring of stones and he and Albert gathered wood for a campfire. Cord was surprised at how well-organised they were and remembered Ted's remark about competent bushmen.

Boris arranged the metal tripod for the camp pot to hang over the fire and stated confidently, "Fire keeps the fuckin' dingoes away, as well as the fuckin' flies."

Albert arranged a makeshift shower and bush toilet in the smallest tent. He unloaded, fed, watered and tethered the horses, patting them and speaking softly, settling them down.

Cord watched as Ginger pushed Albert in the back with his nose.

Boris laughed. "Ginger's jealous. Albert's givin' too much luv to Smack."

The day cooled and night descended. The sounds of the nocturnal bush creatures began; insects chirped, frogs croaked, and from the distant range, a dingo howled. The fire crackled and spat cinders as the three men settled to one side, avoiding the smoke. The orange and purple flames flickered and twirled, casting an occasional glow and shadows across their faces. They were here; now, it was all up to Cord.

Albert filled the camp oven with the stew May had prepared and Boris placed a billy of water on the side of the flames to boil for tea and washing up. They ate a hearty main meal and opened a tin of home-cooked shortbread biscuits to accompany the billy tea.

Each man had a tent equipped with a stretcher, folding stool, small table, portable LED lighting, insect netting and most importantly, a can of spray to ward off mosquitoes. The remaining tents were bigger, one being Cord's office and the other a makeshift kitchen in case of bad weather. Albert would run the camp and agist the horses while Cord and Boris attended to the survey work.

The fire dropped to a few embers, with each man deep in reverie. It was Cord's first night in the outback, in this remote and uninhabited place – and he slept soundly.

The Corner
1999

Cord woke to the hum of the generator and the aroma of bacon and eggs wafting into his tent. It was 5 am and a new day in the sunburnt country had dawned. The rising sun cast shades of gold and red over the cloud crests on the eastern horizon. At this hour, the chill in the air belied the coming heat of the day.

Outside, Albert bent over a frying pan perched on a hotplate over the open fire. He had a cup of tea in one hand and a spatula in the other and manoeuvred the sizzling food around the pan with utmost dexterity. Boris sat nearby in a camp chair, sipping hot tea and occasionally waving a fly from his face. Cord dressed quickly; he resolved there and then to be the first to rise in the morning. It should be expected of the leader.

Boris rose from his chair as Cord emerged from his tent.

"*Buenos dias*, Landman. It's goin' to be a fuckin' scorcher today."

Albert looked up from his task and nodded in Cord's direction. He waved the spatula at a fly.

"How da' ya like ya eggs, Mr Landman? Sunnyside up or down?"

"Whatever, I'm not fussed. Come on, Albert, call me Cord."

Albert nodded and from then on, he occasionally lapsed into Mr Cord and Landman, but mostly Cord.

Boris oversaw making toast and brewing tea. He spread the bread with lashings of butter and covered his giant-sized enamel plate with three eggs, four sausages, two tomatoes and spoonfuls of fried onion. Even with a mouth full of food, he chatted away. "Landman, we only work to lunchtime, okay? After that, too fuckin' hot, then *siesta, bien?*"

Cord liked this huge man who was larger-than-life. Despite the sometimes spattering of Spanish, he knew what he meant and agreed. Cord thanked Albert, who waved them away from the morning chores and urged them to get going.

"Ya can move cattle riding ya horse, but ya can't walk ya self in this heat. Get sick pretty quick."

With only the survey gear loaded, the trailer was much lighter and they were able to cross the rugged off-track country easily. The five-kilometre journey to the southeast corner cairn became rockier as they approached the site and there were several deep washouts before they encountered an extensive rock face. With skill, Boris eased the Patrol up the face and stopped near the old cairn. Cord was impressed with the man.

"All fuckin' rock in this country. No cattle Landman, only fuckin' camels and goats. Well, we're here."

The cairn, perched in the centre of an expansive rock slab, stood tall and firm. It was skilfully assembled from rock fragments driven tightly into wedges arranged on a circular base that Cord guessed measured some three metres wide and two metres high.

Ted had said it was there when the family bought the property and was probably a hundred years old. It stood as a sentinel. Cord decided he'd leave it undisturbed as a grand historical reminder of the past, even if it turned out not to be in the actual corner position.

The day warmed and the flies swarmed as the men retrieved the survey equipment from the vehicle. It was quickly assembled and the first pass from the five satellites picked up by the GPS receiver showed the cairn was roughly four metres northwest of the true corner position. Cord thought, not bad for a hundred years ago using antique equipment.

Further satellite passes narrowed the position further, and by mid-morning, Cord had established the precise corner position. Boris collected rocks and placed them in a wide circle around where the marker was to be placed. The two men sweated and toiled, drank copious amounts of water and swatted and cursed the persistent flies as the day heated up under the relentless rays of the sun. After rock collecting, Boris stood idly by, ready to help but unable to do much except keep Cord supplied with water as he marked crosses on the rock for reference pins. Boris pottered about the old cairn till he let out a yelp and leapt back.

"Maldito! Serpiennte!"

A large snake about three metres long emerged from a hole in the cairn. The skin was a striking mosaic of green and fawn colourings with a creamy underbelly. It slithered slowly across the rock face, ignoring the two men and disappeared into low scrub. On describing the snake to Albert at camp that night, he found it was an Olive Python, Australia's heaviest snake, a non-venomous constrictor.

Boris still shook with fright as Cord commented, "Keep out of the way of the Joe Blakes."

"Joe Blakes?"

"Yeah, snakes."

Finally, everything was in place and pointing to each cross on the rock face, Cord said, "Here's the corner. Here are the reference marks."

Boris eagerly jumped to the task and, within a short time, had drilled holes in the rock with the impact drill, driven in a galvanised pole at the corner marker and sealed it with quick-acting cement. He did likewise for the reference spikes and rested, satisfied with his job.

Cord wiped his brow and nodded in approval. It was a start; just sixty-five more kilometres to go.

"We'll call it a day," he said, sighing wearily as they packed up the equipment and returned to the Patrol.

"*Gracias a Dios,*" said Boris, taking off his hat, also wiping his forehead and crossing himself, looking towards the sky.

Tired and hot, it was past noon when they arrived back at camp.

Albert had been busy tidying up the campsite. He repositioned and rebuilt the open-topped shower under a shady white gum. He constructed a star picket and wire fence with a large perimeter to keep feral and straying livestock out and the horses in. It was large enough for the horses to roam around untethered.

"The cows are the worst. If they get in, they're so bloody curious they'll rip up the whole shebang. We had a visit from dingoes in the night. I can see their tracks, but the fire keeps 'em off."

Boris agreed, "Fuckin' dingoes."

Albert made corned beef sandwiches for lunch. Cord took an apple and went to the office tent to set up his laptop and attend to his field notes. The following day, he'd commence laying out the lease boundary, which required astronomical observations using the theodolite telescope. In the afternoon, he prepared a program for daylight star observations, which required precalculation. Boris went to his tent for a *siesta* and Albert sat under a gum tree smoking. Cord grew tired and eventually dozed off, slumping over his laptop, thankfully away from the tenacious flies.

It was late afternoon when Boris poked his head in the tent, "Landman, do ya want a cuppa?"

Cord shook his head on awakening and rubbed his hands across his face, "Yep, thanks."

As soon as Cord appeared outside, Boris handed him a mug of tea, then went off to a far corner of the enclosure to crank up the generator. Albert was sorting through supplies in the two portable Engel fridges for the night's meal.

He turned to Cord and grinned, "What'd ya like? Steak and potatoes or potatoes and steak?"

"I'm in your hands," Cord replied.

Boris called from afar, "Steak and potatoes with fries."

Albert was a good cook. The steaks were grilled to perfection, and with jacket potatoes, fried onions and a fresh garden salad, the rigours of the day faded away. The evening cooled, more logs were thrown on the fire and the men dossed down early.

*****

Cord rose early to load the theodolite and the program calculations in a safe place in the Cruiser. Albert and Boris were already up and about; so much for his resolution to be the first to rise in the morning.

Albert would stay at the camp, although he planned to ride over to Bore 9 during the day to check the windmill about four kilometres northwest. He would take both horses, riding Ginger first, then Smack on the way back. Boris and Cord were away at 6 am with a cut lunch Albert had prepared the night before, as he wouldn't be at the campsite himself until later in the afternoon.

Back at the site, Cord showed Boris how to set the tripod over the survey mark before he attached the jigger to the base plate. Cord planned to observe several daylight stars for a True North bearing and had difficulty explaining the process to Boris. He showed the prism attachment for distance measurement and could see the man was bewildered. It was going to be a long haul.

"Azimuth. Bearing." he pointed to the sun.

"*Sol?*" questioned Boris. "Sun? True North. Ah! *Si, si,* of course," Boris pointed in the air above his head.

Cord shook his head. It didn't matter that Boris couldn't completely understand, only that he could carry out the rudiments of the job. Patiently and carefully, he explained how he would direct Boris, using the two-way radio, to a position to hammer a steel spike into the ground. Boris nodded and listened attentively. Cord continued to explain, in the simplest of terms, the distance-measuring capacity of the instrument so permanent markers could be placed on the boundary. Boris was dumbfounded when he realised the device could measure distances up to ten kilometres to within a millimetre accuracy.

"Fuckin' incredible, Landman!" he said incredulously, scratching his mop of hair.

The survey routine was to be repeated many times over the coming weeks. It was important Boris got it right and Cord questioned whether the man was capable and dependable; only time would tell. Cord delayed his azimuth observation to the following day as the training took up the entire morning. In surveying, there can be no mistakes. Cord recognised Boris's redeeming feature was that he was a keen and enthusiastic pupil.

"Above all," Cord said, "no expletives on the radio."

Boris was bewildered, "What's this expletive?"

"Swearing. Using the 'F' word."

"I know, *Terrateniente.* Mr Ted told me same," Boris grinned at having loosely translated 'Landman' into Spanish.

Visitors
1999

It was the third week of the job. Cord and Boris were setting out the fifteen-kilometre marker when they heard a vehicle approaching. The Chevy Ram pulled up in a cloud of dirt and dust.

"It's the Doigs," Boris said.

The fragments settled. The truck towed a horse float with a sign emblazoned on the side, 'Indigo Downs Stables' and underneath, 'Breeder of Thoroughbred Quarter Horses'.

Bert and Sharon emerged, with Bert grinning and reaching to shake Cord's hand.

"We're on our way to Jacana, deliver some horses. Thought we'd just drop by, have a look an' see how you're goin'."

Cord liked the man and didn't mind his intrusion. "Sure, it's okay so far. We're getting there."

Bert nodded, "Good. You remember Sharon?"

"Of course."

Cord shook hands with the pretty teenager, who had sat at her dad's side at the meeting weeks ago. He remembered Ted commenting how Sharon was making her mark with breeding quarter horses and Bert confirming, "She's a natural at it just like her mum was. It'd be a shame to sell up and take that away from her."

"Any idea when you'll be finished?"

"Looks like another ten weeks or so."

"How about you come to the homestead next week, say Tuesday, and have some lunch? We'll show you around, have a chat."

Cord accepted; Tuesday would fit the schedule.

*****

It was time to move camp closer to the job and towards the Doig homestead. Boris and Davy could see to the shift while he went for lunch with Bert. He took the Cruiser, leaving them with the Patrol and a quad bike. It'd be okay; they had a whole day to shift the gear.

It was thirty-eight kilometres on the trip meter across undulating country following the northern flank of the Stony Ridge Range. There were windmills and troughs every five kilometres or so. The cattle staring at Cord passing were Brown Angus and a few Shorthorns, all with shaggy coats from running in the wild. There were mobs of large red kangaroos and grey wallabies at several scooped-out waterholes. At a dry water crossing, he disturbed a flock of brilliant green and yellow budgerigars, sending them shimmering and squawking into the bright blue sky. The occasional ancient Boab stood in the fields of Flinders and Bluegrass pasture.

The track approached a buttress in the range and around a bend, the Indigo Downs station homestead came into view, nestled close to a craggy cliff face. Like Jacana, it was a brick and stone building with high chimneys and a surrounding veranda, entirely encircled by magnificent Poinciana trees in full crimson bloom. The rock wall was the backdrop to the stockyards. On one side of the house were clusters of outbuildings, a huge, galvanised tin building, probably the main store, other smaller sheds holding tractors and trail bikes, the hash house set in a square of lawn and clusters of staff quarters. On the other side was a string of a dozen or more stables and a fenced paddock where more than twenty horses were grazing.

Cord thought, what a grand place, orderly, stately, serene. What was Jason thinking, wanting to sell? If it were his, he'd never leave.

Sharon showed Cord into the cool lounge room, away from the ever-present flies. The floor was polished slate covered in fluffy rugs and a huge crystal chandelier hung overhead. Around the room were pieces of dated mahogany furniture and the main feature was a massive open fireplace in sculptured red stone.

There were photographs dotted around, several of a smiling woman with Bert and other frames of Jason and Sharon when they were children. Cord later discovered the woman was Tracy Doig, the wife and mother, who died in a fall from a horse when Sharon was ten.

Jason joined them at lunch dressed in designer label jeans with frayed hems and knees and a black T-shirt with the motif 'CRUD – Muzik Worx'. Cord hadn't noticed that Jason had two earrings in one earlobe and various strange tattoos on one arm. He certainly looked out of place in this environment, in stark contrast to his father and sister.

He hardly acknowledged Cord, only murmuring a faint greeting before he suddenly launched into another tirade berating the need for a surveyor for such a simple task and the damage that'd been done to the proposed sale.

Cord felt disdain, not insult, at Jason's rantings.

Bert softly said, "Leave it, Jason. Cord's a guest in the house."

Jason angrily grabbed a sandwich and left the table.

"I apologise again for his behaviour. He's upset because the buyers have baulked on making a conditional offer and said they'll wait to see the survey results before deciding."

Bert looked across at Sharon, who'd been sitting quietly through the outburst. He went on, "Fortunately, it's given us time to think things over. We'd like your opinion on damming the minor creek tributary at Big Rock Gorge or even at one of the bigger billabongs in the watercourse, just in case things don't turn out our way with the springs."

Sharon spoke, "Dad's right. What if the creek and Apricot Springs junction is on Bell's property? We'd be reliant on their goodwill more than ever, wouldn't we? They're great neighbours, but if they sold down the track, the problem could resurface with new owners."

Cord was once again brought into the issue of ownership, an issue outside his province and one he really didn't want to address. He didn't answer Sharon's question but addressed Bert's request, "Constructing concrete dams? You need advice from a civil engineer, but I know from experience that major cement structures are expensive."

"I guess it's best just to wait and see what happens with the survey."

Cord nodded his head and changed the subject. "I'd like to see your horses if that's okay?"

"Sure, I'll show you over the place. The Montgomerys took up the lease in 1897 and my family bought it in 1923. They'd an old, dilapidated shack right here. My grandfather tore it down and started on this place and my father finished it in the '50s. We've always had cattle, but Tracy started breeding quarter horses for other stations and Sharon's followed in her footsteps."

Cord enjoyed the visit and thanked his hosts. He realised that as much as he wanted to stay detached from the dilemma facing the two families, he could now understand their comment, 'Water is everything out here'.

*****

The weeks passed and one morning, when Cord and Boris were heading home, a helicopter flew low over their vehicle towards camp. Cord had just placed the twenty-six-kilometre marker in position; the survey was on time and continued to go well. The boundary criss-crossed the creek in several places, sometimes on the Jacana lease, sometimes on Indigo Downs. He confided in Boris about Bert's proposal to dam Big Rock Gorge.

"He knows his community better than I do, but I can't imagine the traditional owners allowing the gorge to be disturbed."

"Too fuckin' right, Landman. It's just Jason, his son's stupid idea. Mr Doig's talkin' about it just to keep him off his back, that's all. It won't happen."

"Yeah, I reckon Sharon will have a big say when the time comes. I saw the magnificent horses she's breeding; the station's her life."

"Too fuckin' right."

The chopper was on the ground when they arrived at the campsite. Albert was changing camp boss with Davy and they were sitting with Ted and Clyde in the meshed gazebo away from the pesky flies. Lunch was spread on the table; sandwiches, salad and orange juice.

Cord noticed the Land Cruiser was gone. Ted explained, "We're waiting for Kathy to get back before we have lunch. We've got a visitor. They went over to Mammoth to have a squiz at the rock art."

"Visitor?"

"Yeah, a lady geologist doin' a seismic survey in the area."

"She's all right too," Clyde added with a wink. "A Yankee Sheila. She'll be around with her crew for a coupla' weeks. I don't mind. Plenty of work for me and they pay well."

"Lookin' for gas," Ted explained.

The sound of a motor neared. The Cruiser came into view and pulled over under the shade of the big white gum. Kathy and her passenger alighted.

For a moment, Cord was baffled as the passenger ran towards him, calling out, 'Landman'. Then he recognised her; it was Dixie. She was quickly in his arms, hugging him.

"What are ya doin' here, Landman, away from the sea?"

"You too."

It was good to see her lovely, cheerful face, those twinkling brown eyes, enjoy her bright, breezy nature, and, best of all, hear her drawling Yankee twang again. Memories of the *Spree,* with Gert and her, came flooding back.

Kathy caught up. "You two know each other?"

"Sure do, shipmates from way back," Dixie replied.

Over lunch, Dixie volunteered exaggerated stories of life on the waves and of Cord's bout with Simon, which sounded like a major boxing tournament.

"What or who did you fight over?" Kathy asked.

Dixie quickly replied, "Me and my honour, of course."

Cord felt sheepish, but what could he say? It was Dixie's way. He silently thanked her for not telling the truth.

Kathy was satisfied; this woman would easily be ten years older than Cord, clearly just a friend and colleague.

There was still time after lunch and Boris gave up his precious *siesta* to take Ted and Kathy to proudly show them the new corner marker on the southeast corner. Clyde tinkered with a skid light on the chopper while Albert and Ted moved around the camp discussing the takeover.

Alone with Cord, Dixie disclosed she and Gert were getting hitched; they bought a villa in Tuscany with a small vineyard. "*Spumante* country," she said smugly. They hired a new skipper for the *Spree* and decided to keep it in northern waters near its home port.

"The new catamarans at Penang are spectacular and fast. They've cut the journey into a half hour. Remember Mrs Brown? She's set up a home sitting business in Singapore. I bet she's pleased to be rid of Rodney."

Cord didn't want to mention Lucille but asked, "What's Rodney doing?"

"Oh, he's in Kuala Lumpur now. Runs his business from there."

She looked at him quizzically to gauge his reaction to what she was about to say.

"I heard on the grapevine he had a fallout with Lucille and she's stayed on in America. I'm told she's not married and has a high-flying job in the US government."

Cord did his best to maintain a poker face, but she saw through his facade.

"Still smitten, eh? Well, it's like Gert said, there's plenty of fish in the sea," she winked. "From what I see, this Kathy here's one hell'ava' fish."

Cord shook his head and changed the subject to his planned visit to Machu Picchu with Corrine.

"Well, what do ya know! So, you've got a twin sister? That's another thing we've got in common. I've got a twin brother, Hank. He's got a 7-UP store in Detroit, plus a wife and three kids. Not as adventurous as me."

When Boris returned, it was time for the copter to leave. They said their goodbyes and Clyde dropped Kathy, Dixie, Ted and Albert back at the homestead.

Before she left to fly out with Clyde the next day, Dixie handed Kathy a note to give to Cord.

"It's got Gert and my new address in Italy, cell phone and contact email. Thanks for the wonderful day yesterday. The rock art's mind-blowing."

"Sure, you're welcome."

Before Kathy placed the note in Cord's mailbox, she peeked at the message. Below the address and contact particulars, it read: 'Great if you can make our wedding. Gert will be stoked to see you and bring Corrine. I'd love to meet her. Take care, Landman. Luv Dixie.'

Joan came into the room. "Is that a message for Cord?"

Kathy replied bitterly, "Yes! And his girlfriend, Corrine."

The Wrap Up
1999

By the second month, Cord and his team finally neared the junction of Jacana Creek and the Apricot Springs run-off, where the fate of ownership of the two stations' water supply rested.

Occasional thunderstorms punctuated their everyday work program, but lightning in one particular storm ignited a fire in the parched grassland. Animals ran through their camp to escape the flames, disrupting the survey routine. Another storm two days later drenched the area, extinguishing the blaze.

Davy replaced Albert periodically as planned and one afternoon, Cord was in his tent attending to field notes when Davy shouted, "Watch out!"

The tent canvas lifted and filled with dust; a violent wind scattered his papers into the air. Dashing outside, he saw Boris's tent lift and flatten to the ground; pots and pans flew in all directions. Amongst the debris, struggling through the canvas of the flattened tent, Boris emerged, his *siesta* broken. Rubbing his eyes, covered in brown dust and through his caked lips, he spat and spluttered, "Fuckin' willy-willy."

"Big cock-eyed bob," Davy declared, laughing and pointing." Look at ya. Call ya cock-eyed Boris now."

The short, violent storm had torn through the temporary fence, spooking the horses, which ran off. They radioed the homestead to help retrieve them. Ted brought the ringers, Barney, Sofie and Charlotte, to round them up and help the men clean the camp.

That night, around the fire, Davy shrewdly told Cord, "Sofie said Miss Kathy wants to know how you go in the bush. In our culture, woman don't ask another woman to ask another man that, unless they have ownership."

"Come on! She's more interested in the survey outcome than me. That's where she's got ownership."

Davy's eyes twinkled in the firelight as he stirred the coals with a stick and whispered to Boris, "Bullshit."

Boris responded with a wink.

*****

In the weeks before and around the campfire, Cord engaged Albert about native culture, particularly the Aboriginal concept of 'the dreaming'. Albert was at first reticent to speak, but as time passed and their relationship grew, he became more open.

"The dreamin's when the spirits created the land. Us people have been here from the beginnin'. There is no time in the dreamin', everythin' the same time."

He told rich stories about the spiritual ancestors creating the natural world, the hills, the plants, the rivers and waterholes. Cord especially liked Albert's account of the creation of Stony Ridge Range, "This young Mountain Devil Lizard went looking for his *yorga*. He was heartbroken she had run away after a fight. He looked everywhere and went too far into bad *Boodja-Dooga* country, where he got lost and died of thirst. All 'em craggy spikes ya see is what's left of him."

Cord reckoned that Albert's account had more relationship, reverence, romance and relevance to Mother Earth as a living entity than the dull geologic textbook description, stating the range was 'a heavily eroded, uplifted slab of metamorphosed sandstone'.

The campfires every night brought the three men closer together. They'd often sit silently, deep in their own thoughts, as the flames crackled and spat, flickered orange and blue. Smoke lazily drifted upward with its warm, stale smell. Cord felt at home in a place he never knew existed until now. To him, this was the real world.

That night, Boris, with a tear in his eye, reminisced about his family. "My family in Barcelona. One more year," he said, pulling a photo from his battered wallet. He passed it to the others. It was a photograph of a dark-haired woman, smiling with two young girls by her side.

Albert didn't comment; Cord nodded and said, "Beautiful. You must miss them."

122

"I save up, one more year." He took back the photo, kissed it three times and said, "*Te amo* my wife Emilia, and Isla and Elena."

Albert rose and placed another log on the fire.

Boris's melancholic mood changed. He put the photo back in his wallet and said brightly, "A fuckin' beer would be good right now, Landman."

He sighed and smacked his lips, but he knew a beer was a long way away; there was no alcohol at camp.

Boris had surpassed Cord's expectations as an assistant, quickly picking up the technicalities and survey routine. It wasn't long into the journey that Cord realised the overall talents of the gentle giant. He was a larger-than-life figure, always affable, enthusiastic, loyal, with a positive work commitment and humility.

Cord didn't let anyone know that the following day, he would place a post on the boundary in proximity to the creek and Apricot Springs junction. He didn't want a crowd or a ceremony; he wanted the event to be apolitical. They had changed camp three times to get to this position. Forty-five kilometres of the boundary had been marked with another twenty to go. This was the last outdoor campsite before they'd reach the Doig homestead itself.

It was an important occasion as they laid the marker post, clearly showing the creek and spring junction was one hundred and sixty metres within the Jacana Creek Station lease. Boris jumped with joy as he realised Indigo Downs Station had no intrinsic rights to the water.

Cord swore Boris and Albert to secrecy. He didn't want the result to be common knowledge at the station hash house before he advised both owners of the outcome. After his evening meal, he drove alone to the homestead. He wanted Ted to know the result as quickly as possible and to email John Keep on the progress of the survey.

It was a surprise visit. He hadn't been at the homestead for a month, but on his arrival, Ted and Joan embraced him as a long-lost son. He found them in the lounge and Joan gave him a hug, something he'd never expect from Kathy if she were there, but she wasn't.

"Would you like a drink, a cup of tea or coffee?" Joan asked.

"A beer?" said Ted.

He shook his head. It wasn't time for chit-chat. "No thanks. I called in to advise the creek and run-off junction is well within the Jacana Creek lease."

Ted was silent for a moment, then shook Cord's hand, relief on his face. Joan hugged him again.

"Are you sure?" Ted said.

"One hundred and sixty metres sure."

"Oh, my," Joan exclaimed happily, her hands cupping her face.

Cord nodded. "Whenever you like, I'll take you and the Doigs to the marker post on the boundary and you can see for yourselves. I still have to lay out the remaining section to the north. That'll take another two to three weeks and then that'll be it."

Ted shook his hand again. "You've done a mighty job and we thank you. I'll let Bert know straight away."

"You can stay the night if you like. I'll make up a bed," Joan said.

Cord declined, having to get back to start out early the next day.

"Tomorrow," Ted said, "we'll have a barbeque dinner. Bring the boys, I insist. Have a breather, celebrate with us."

"You have to come," Joan said emphatically and Cord accepted.

"By the way," she said. "An email came for you yesterday. Kathy took a copy. I have it in the office. I'll get it."

It was from Corrine and read: 'Hi Landman (ha, ha). Hope everything is going okay. Just to let you know, we are all set for the trip. Got our passports, the plane tickets, booked the tour for February next year. Bought 2 Manypeaks backpacks, yours 18kg and mine 15kg. Can't wait! Looking forward to it. See you soon. Take care. Luv, Corrine.'

He brightened up with the message from Corrine. It was the trip of a lifetime that he and his sister had planned since they were teenagers; to walk the Inca Trail in Peru to the ruins of Machu Picchu. February was going to be fine.

When Kathy read it, her first impulse was to tear it up.

*****

Albert and Boris were pleased to have an evening off closer to home. Albert to be with May, although he had been back at the homestead several times over the months when swapping with Davy. Boris looked forward to consuming a beer or two in the privacy of his cabin. Cord reminded them again not to divulge the outcome of the boundary survey and that they'd only be staying overnight at the homestead; it was another early start in the morning.

It was dusk when Cord drove into the homestead grounds. Clyde's chopper was parked in the side yard. Boris rushed to his cabin to get a beer while Cord and Albert took the stone path to the back of the house. It was dim and shadowy, except for the soft glow from the distant sunset. Suddenly, a blaze of lights lit up the trees, illuminating the lawn area and the station crew, waiting in silence, erupted with whooping and cheering before rushing forward to pat him on the back and shake his hand. It wasn't a reception he envisaged but one he cheerfully accepted.

Cord brightened up again when he saw Kathy standing on the periphery, waiting for the commotion to cease before she came to him. She didn't shake his hand and said, rather matter-of-factly, "Well done. Dad and Mum are pleased. Congratulations."

It was the second time Cord had seen her in a dress; she was usually in jeans, but standing there in a yellow floral cotton dress, tanned legs, her blonde hair flowing over her shoulders, she was stunning. This was a different Kathy; he melted under the gaze of her piercing blue eyes. In her presence, he was nervous and afraid. He wanted to apologise for his comments at Apricot Springs, but before he could speak, she cut him short, "Can you pop into my office for a minute?"

She led him into the house and he followed, sensing a trace of willowy perfume. She sat at the desk, opened the drawer and produced a cheque book and pen.

"Dad and Mum are pleased with your work. They'd like you to accept a gift of five hundred dollars."

Cord stopped her, holding his hands up in protest, "Wait! Wait a minute. I can't accept that. I was doing my job, that's all. Professionally, that was what I was contracted to do. No, please, thank you. Thank your dad and mum, but no."

She looked at him sceptically and with a hint of sarcasm, "Look on it as a bonus to help with your trip."

"No, Kathy, I can't accept it, that's all."

Why did she emphasise 'trip', he wondered.

Clyde knocked and poked his head round the door, "There you are, you two." He came into the room with his hand out to shake Cord's, "Congratulations. I suppose you'll be finishing up pretty soon."

"About two to three weeks."

Kathy put the cheque book back in the drawer and rose from the desk. "I'll let Dad and Mum know." She abruptly turned to Clyde, "Let's have a drink to celebrate our good fortune, thanks to Landman here."

She clearly stressed 'thanks' and 'trip' as if dismissing him, but did she swish her skirt for his benefit as they left? Perhaps he was wrong.

It was like Penang all over again, but at the same time, different. Lucille, beautiful and serene; Kathy, beautiful and spirited. He was alone and bewildered again.

*****

The final camp was established on the east side of the creek, on Indigo Downs Station. It saved valuable time, avoiding having to track across the creek at Apricot Springs each day.

The mustering program was in full swing. All hands were occupied at the outstation camps sorting calves from the main mobs. Over the last campfire, before he left, Albert explained that Sofie, a second-season ringer, would be the camp boss for the remainder of the job. She was twenty and already a respected hand. Her main penchant in cooking camp tucker was spicy Indian fare, and sometimes, a too-generous spoonful of curry in the pot sent Cord and Boris scurrying to the ablution tent.

Cord knew she would have preferred to be part of the muster action, but as Ted said, "We expect our ringers to be able to turn their hand to anything and, above all, never to complain. We've got our eye on Sofie for the future."

Sofie certainly didn't complain and fitted in well with Cord's timetable. She was a nurse and spent much of her time at the camp reading and studying for a veterinary qualification. Bright and boisterous, she regarded it as her life's work to rid Boris of the overuse of the dreadful expletive he used so often. She fined him a dollar every time she heard it, the funds destined for the Children's Cancer Foundation. She made forty dollars over the course of the camp stay; Boris paid, but it still didn't cure him.

The last marker post was established on the mangrove shoreline fifteen days later. It was just like any other day. Sofie arrived on her horse just as Boris etched Cord's and his initials in the cement base as a final touch.

"What'd ya think, Sofie, fuckin' good, eh?"

"Dollar, please," she grinned.

So, the job was over. A few days were spent at the homestead tidying up loose ends with only Joan and May present as the muster continued in

126

earnest. The night before, Cord had an expletive beer or two with Boris, who gave Cord a tight bear hug, so tight he could hardly breathe.

"We are *amigos especial*," Boris said, with a tear in his eye.

Boris had a list of repair jobs at several of the bores and was sadly not there when Cord left; neither was Kathy. Joan had arranged for Clyde to fly Cord to the airport to catch his plane home. She, too, hugged him and that morning, May cooked the most lavish breakfast and stood by to serve him, something she had never done before.

Joan said, "Ted's sorry he couldn't be here. As for Kathy, I really don't know about that girl. She was here not that long ago, but she told me to tell you she hopes you have a great trip.

There's that word 'trip' again, he thought.

Cord was pleased he didn't have to make the return journey with Dex and endure his entertainment repertoire. Clyde ferried him to the airport.

"I don't suppose you'll be back this way in a hurry?"

"No, the job's done, all wrapped up. How's it going with your new chopper?"

"Great. Should be delivered after Christmas, when me and Melinda get married. Good wedding present, eh?"

Cord was astonished.

"Melinda? I thought you and Kathy were, well, uhm, together."

"No, shit, fuck no, she gave me the short shift a long time ago. Pity, but she's married to the station. Can't see anyone makin' it with her except…"

He didn't finish the sentence as the airport control tower interrupted. He replied and swung the chopper low over the tarmac before descending and landing it softly on the ground.

As they unpacked Cord's bags, Clyde looked shrewdly at him, winked, smiled and said, "You never know, Landman, you might have some luck there."

Brahman Breed
1999

Lucille resettled in Washington and bought an apartment near Stanton Park, a few kilometres from the Department of Commerce and an easy ride by bus. In addition to her Degrees in Business and Jurisprudence, she had the attributes of languages, being fluent in Malay, Cantonese, Mandarin and Keja. As a child, she spent many hours in the tea plantations with the Indian workers, where she also gained an understanding of Hindi. It was understandable that she was posted to Beijing for six months as part of her government internship.

The pain of losing the child was still with Lucille and she also carried the burden of letting the family down, but she loved a man; she couldn't help it. She didn't regret it and though he was elsewhere in the world, the thought of him endured. Her beauty hadn't faded; indeed, glamour came with maturity. Occasional dinners and dates with admirers never developed any further. Her commercial career flourished and was enough.

On her return from China, she was assigned to the office of the Under Secretary for International Trade and the section covering global marketing. Her initial appointment was to a task force examining the financial implications on the billion-dollar US cattle market due to the alleged infiltration of the domestic market by other countries, specifically Canada and Mexico.

There were seven members in the team and at a roundtable briefing, the Task Manager, Jerome Black, advised, "We're interested because there's currently a case before the Court of International Trade, brought by the Ranchers-Cattlemen Action Legal Foundation USA, against our own government for allowing a trading agreement to operate between us and the two countries cited. The foundation alleges the arrangement is threatening the viability of the domestic industry."

John, a senior member of the team, responded, "Jesus! Cattlemen's Foundation! These mobs are always squealing like stuck pigs. What's the heads-up on our defence? What are our top gun legal eagles doing? And why are we always involved in pickin' up the pieces?"

Lucille moved uncomfortably in her chair, hoping she didn't have to collaborate closely with uncouth John. She knew from experience he was talented but a hothead subject to tantrums.

Jerome ignored the outburst. "Here's the heads-up. Our legal gurus argue that the trade financial figures don't support the ranchers' claims and that the two countries cited don't have overlapping interests saturating supply. On the one hand, Canada supplies mature cattle for slaughter; on the other, Mexico supplies calves, which are grass-fed before they reach maturity. In fact, agisting calves is a lucrative industry for some of our ranchers who endorse the trade arrangement. Our brief is to examine the Trade Practices Act in detail, that's all."

John blurted, "That'd be fuckin' right! Commercial creeps dig a hole for themselves and we've gotta get 'em out."

Jerome reacted angrily, "Keep focused, stay sharp, do your job and John, that's enough. Cut out the gutter language when you come in here. Have some respect."

Later that day, Jerome informed Lucille she was to attend a Brahman Breeders Congress in Houston, Texas. It was an eight-day event and her task was to examine the market strategies of the various participants regarding competition between Brahman cattle and other breeds in both the domestic and international markets.

Jerome said, "The Brahman people have an excellent track record, so the information you gather will be worthwhile. It's just a small part of a very big picture, but an important one. Major exporters from Mexico will be there, particularly one Jaz Marinza. Get close to him, see what his views are, anything you can pick up."

The weather in Houston in September is warm to hot and Lucille was fortunate to have Rex, one of the congress organisers, show her around to meet registered breeders. She met families in their homes, interviewed cowhands at corrals, veterinarians in the field, buyers and sellers at cattle sales, slaughterers at abattoirs, butchers, retailers, marketers and consumers.

She reported a wide and varied response to the question regarding the influx of cattle from other countries. Jerome agreed her report would significantly impact the court's decision. For Lucille, it presented the opportunity to converse with people at grassroots level whose economy depended on government protection and also introduced her to the interesting and varied world of tariffs.

On the last evening, she was invited to the Breeders Valedictory dinner, a lavish affair with breeders and delegates from all over the world. Jerome had carefully arranged for her to be seated alongside Jaz Marinza, the prominent Mexican exporter of Brahman calves. Jerome reminded her the brief was to gauge his opinion on the current court case.

He was a handsome, olive-skinned man in his thirties. For the occasion, she wore a sleeveless royal red chiffon dress with a deep V-neck, revealing her full figure and flawless skin. With just a hint of eye shadow, red lipstick and her ebony hair tied back in a bow, she made quite an impression.

Jaz took Lucille's hand and kissed it. *"Buenas noches.* Welcome."

Lucille was cordial, polite and introduced herself as a freelance journalist commissioned to write an article on the dilemma facing importers and exporters. Jaz was charming but evasive; his reaction was to be expected. He'd abide by the court's decision but was hopeful the status quo would remain. The conversation round the table for the evening was spent in pleasantries.

Jaz invited her to a party in his hotel room afterwards with just a few other guests. Lucille realised he was more interested in his own breeding program than that of the livestock he owned and she respectfully declined.

*****

Kathy and her brother arrived in Houston exhausted after a twenty-hour journey full of delays and other frustrations. Barry didn't delay in making contact with referrals on his list. He had boundless energy, was a born cattleman and had one overriding ambition to improve the herd by introducing new strains. The Jacana Creek cattle herd was exclusively Brahman, noted for their many attributes that suited the northern tropics. Barry planned to experiment with genetics by importing either young bulls or stock semen from international producers.

They arranged tours of the ranches, taking notes of breeding lines that emphasised body weight gain for foraging cattle, not hay-fed beasts, and strains noted for quietness and sensitivity, an essential element when mustering. Barry was anxious to meet with the Mexican producers in town for the congress, particularly Jaz Marinza. They had met the Marinza Group at a ranch tour, but Barry hoped he'd be able to meet the man himself at the congress dinner.

Kathy had a limited 'fashionable' wardrobe and dressed as best she could for the occasion, wearing a dark grey business pantsuit with a red blouse. With her blonde hair cascading around her face, she looked stunning as usual. After much harassment before they left, Kathy persuaded Barry to pack his grey slacks and blue reefer jacket to wear on social occasions if the need arose. Thankfully, on the day of the dinner, they stopped at a shopping centre to buy a white shirt and red tie.

"You can't wear a fleecy checked shirt, a denim jacket and jeans to a smart dinner, even if it is for cattlemen," she said. "You don't need to look like a cowboy about to feed the cows."

Barry was still busy with his university science degree and Kathy knew that in a few more years, he'd return to run the station, probably bring a wife and everything would change. She'd be relegated to a support role like the unmarried older sister, Laura Carter, at Ludlow Hills Station and spend her time in the background as an old maid. She was only interested in one guy and he was on a trip somewhere with that Corrine.

Barry argued for a budget for their trip to purchase breeding stock, to which Ted finally agreed since he knew that the breeding traits of his station herd could be improved. He was in competition with other producers who continually refined their breeding programs. Purchasers looked for weight consistency, so any improvement there ensured long-term supply contracts. He had every confidence in his son to succeed. Yet, it was Kathy who negotiated permission from the various Australian authorities, subject to conditions, to import quarantined livestock into the country.

A few years before, Barry, then a teenager, rescued a calf, near death, bogged in a drying waterhole and hand-reared her to where she won the Champion Lightweight Carcass award at the local show. He kept her in the breeding paddock, gave her the name 'Muddy' and when he was at home on semester breaks, she would follow him around all day if he let her. This confirmed for Ted his son's natural talent as a cattleman. Yet, it was Kathy who cared for Muddy when Barry was away. It confirmed for Kathy that her father might only ever see her as the temporary minder of Jacana Creek.

The dinner party was breaking up when Barry and Kathy approached Jaz and introduced themselves. He was sitting with an Asian woman who Kathy assumed to be his wife or partner. However, the woman rose from the table, shook hands with Jaz and mumbled a thank you. She nodded a greeting to Kathy and Barry before she smiled and left. She was gorgeous, elegant and exquisitely dressed, leaving Kathy feeling dull and quite the opposite. Barry sat next to Jaz, introduced himself and launched into his aspirations to access a breeding sire. Jaz concentrated his attention more on Kathy sitting opposite than on Barry's needs.

As she left Jaz's table, Lucille recognised the Australian twang in Barry's accent. She looked back at the woman with him, an Australian beauty. She was striking with her long blonde hair, tanned skin and bright, intelligent features. Their eyes met, and both quickly looked away.

Caught in the moment, memories flooded back. Lucille thought of Cord. Where was he?

Machu Picchu
2000

It had been Cord and Corrine's dream as teenagers to hike the Inca Trail across the Andes Mountains to Machu Picchu, the historic sanctuary of the Inca people.

It was a long journey from Perth to Lima, Peru. The capital city hung on the edge of South America, facing west across the Pacific Ocean and was much like Perth itself, hanging on the edge of Australia, facing west across the Indian Ocean. To Cord and Corrine, apart from the familiar scene of the sun setting over the ocean, this place on the other side of the world, with its language and people, was exotic and unknown.

It was a city of contrasts. The Lima coastline was dull and forbidding, the beaches pebbly and the seawater murky, so different to the crystal blue water and white sandy surf beaches at home. Perth was a new and contemporary city, a quiet place, not even two hundred years old and hardly a million and a half people. Lima was archaic but alive, with seven million souls in seemingly endless movement that spanned day and night. Its history and tradition date back almost five hundred years.

Corrine basked in its charm and relished the range of architecture and gastronomic experiences available. It was filled with colonial treasures, museums and fountains; a bustling, cultured city, colourful and vibrant. They were caught up in the desire to see everything, and eventually, the emotional challenges and disappointment that troubled Cord waned.

They flew to Cusco, once the capital of the Inca Empire on the western side of the Andes Mountains, to begin their trek and meet Alain, their tour guide.

Alain was a nuggety, olive-skinned man in his thirties of Portuguese descent, with a ready smile and a melodic grasp of English. He had taken many travellers along the trail in his seven years as a guide and told Cord and

Corrine that Australians were his favourite people. Cord guessed he made similar comments to all the other nationalities he guided. He spoke the local Quechua Indian language, a necessity, as the other members of the party, two porters and a cook, were Quechua people. Alain was primarily concerned with the pair's fitness to undertake the trek, their walk gear, their reaction to the elevation of Cusco and the likelihood of altitude sickness. He always addressed them as *Senhor* Cord and *Senhora* Corrine.

They boarded a rusted ramshackle bus, which rattled along corrugated tracks for several hours through barren sandy country dotted with stands of Yucca plants. The dusty road, the swaying bus and the chatter evoked memories of Dexter and his yarns. Other walk groups were assembling at the remote trailhead, everyone excited, nervous and some grim-faced, as the distant Andes Mountains loomed ahead, formidable, alluring and blanketed in snow.

The guides were in a separate group exchanging information before Alain broke away to introduce their party of two porters and a cook. They were brown-skinned, stocky men, small in stature but strong of limb. In later years, Cord remembered their footwear was cut from old car tyres, and yet they would run past the pair carrying their large packs to the next camp while he and Corrine struggled ever upward in their designer label hiking boots and day packs. These were mighty mountain men, adapted to their native environment, as were Albert and his community back home.

The cook bought fresh food from the South American Indians along the trail and caught fish in the streams. Cord wondered how the man could accomplish so much in the short time he had between packing, running and preparing meals. At the end of the second day, the porters fashioned walking sticks for them from a hard light wood, which were presented in a formal ceremony.

Alain explained, "The men can see your struggle and believe that as you walk, the sticks will recognise your battle and absorb your spirit. Then you'll be one with *Pachamama*."

"*Pachamama?*"

"Mother Earth, their goddess who sustains life, the landscape and all things."

The ascent had begun on the dry western flank of the mountain range, where the sparse groves of Yucca plants gave way to temperate woodland. They climbed the first gentle slopes, passing stone edifices and terraced structures along the way. The trail was wide and cobblestoned in places and every so often, there was a one-room structure in which the ancient Incas would have lit fires to make smoke for communication.

They emerged into dense jungle on the third day. The terraced slopes created a complete four-seasonal environment for cool and temperate crops on the lower slopes to other produce on the wet and humid summit. Cord was intrigued by the design and concept; these were not primitive people.

On the fourth day, they reached the top ridge. Then began the descent to Machu Picchu, eventually arriving at *Inti Punku*, the spectacular Sun Gate overlooking the ruins of the ancient sanctuary.

Over the next two days, they explored the stone temples, the high terraces, palaces and the maze of aqueducts that provided water to the citadel.

The tour was at an end and Cord and Corrine would travel to Cusco by train while Alain and the porters were to return along the trail to their mountain homes. They gave the men gifts of American dollars, each bowing with thanks, but the porters huddled together in animated, earnest conversation and did not leave.

Cord and Corrine were puzzled; perhaps the extra money was not enough? It was here that Cord came closer to appreciating the deep-seated culture of these indigenous people.

Alain intervened. "*Senhor* and *Senhora*, we have a domestic problem. It's your walking sticks."

"We left them at our camp."

"Yes. The men are concerned that if you abandon your sticks, your souls will suffer."

"We can't take them with us."

"I know, I have told them that. The solution is to take them to the river and let them drift away. They say the water will absorb your spirit and you will always be protected and welcomed back."

On the banks of the fast-flowing *Rio Vilcanota*, presided over by the porters, Cord and Corrine reverently floated their sticks into the water. As the sticks drifted out of sight, Cord pondered these indigenous people and their connection with the land. He remembered each morning at camp, how they would prepare breakfast, scoop a hole in the ground and bury a serving of the meal, chanting with hands clasped in prayer. Alain explained, "It's an offering they make daily to *Pachamama*."

These people had a timeless, intrinsic relationship with the land and Cord thought of Albert.

Second Chance
2001

Another year had gone by and 2000 became 2001. Cord's life had become a familiar pattern and the adventures of the previous few years faded. John Keep invited him into partnership as the business expanded to take advantage of the mining boom. Several young surveyors were hired and Cord became mostly office-bound, sharing the administration of the practice with John. JKSurveys became KMSurveys and Cord assumed the title of Director of Operations, a glorified role he wasn't keen on but one that made his mother proud and excited. Cord now lived in his apartment on the riverfront, still close enough for her to visit regularly.

"You deserve the position," his mum said, "after all that hard work and long time in the bush. Living outback, for goodness sake, with all those dingoes and snakes."

"I came back alive and it wasn't a long time, Mother."

"And then the Malaria before that, on the ocean and in the jungle in that foreign country. No wonder you caught the disease."

"I didn't have Malaria."

"Yes, you did, and to please me, have a check-up and get yourself a nice girl."

Several months before he left for Jacana Creek, Cord began a relationship with Sandra, a workmate of Corrine's. He was still apprehensive of relationships, and while Sandra was intelligent, attractive and outgoing, their friendship was empathetic, convenient and platonic. Sure, there was sex; perfunctory, abstract, condom-covered raw mechanics and gratification without the bells and whistles, but Sandra moved interstate and the relationship ended, much to the disappointment of Eileen.

"You should be married," she said. I don't know what's wrong with you. Sandra was such a nice girl and a friend of your sister's. I don't care what anyone says, I'm your mother, and as I said before, I still think you have that touch of Malaria. You should see our doctor."

He'd confided in Corrine how he felt about Kathy and she was pleased that he'd moved on from Sandra. Then he showed her the photo of Lucille with the butterfly, and she attested to her beauty but said, "Bruv, you've got to step back and see it as it really is; a cultural difference. Sometimes, the ethos and way of life of people are too far apart even for love to encompass. Now, with Kathy, it's only the tyranny of distance that keeps you apart. If you want her, you'll have to let her know and that means face to face."

But how would he do that? He couldn't just rock up to the station one day and say, hi, I was just in the neighbourhood, thought I'd just drop in and say hello. By the way, what are you doing tonight?

When John approached him regarding a new job at Jacana Creek Station, he was surprised and elated. It was too good to be true.

"I thought of sending Rory," he said, "but they asked for you, actually insisted. You don't have to go, but it's good money. They want the southern boundary of the station surveyed. We can spare you for a month or so. Anyway, think about it."

Two years had passed since the job finished and Clyde had flown him out of the station. Cord remembered the conversation concerning Kathy and Clyde's parting words, "You never know, you might have some luck there." Corrine was right; he had to face her, but the thought of doing so both thrilled and daunted him.

There was no doubt Cord was drawn to Jacana Creek; the very mention of the name brought back vibrant images of that immense space, the outback. He had so many memories of iconic places like Apricot Springs, the rugged mountain country, cattle country where nature rules, the Dry, the Wet and the people, Ted and Joan, Boris, the gentle giant, Albert with the stories of the dreaming, characters like Dexter, Clyde, Maggot and his chopper and most of all, Kathy.

For several days, he hesitated to accept the job; after all, it could be awkward. Kathy might be married or not even be there. What then? How could he tell her he missed her when he hadn't contacted her over the years? Then again, she hadn't contacted him either.

His mother was aghast, "The bush again! Are you mad?"

Perhaps he was mad to go, and it was a forlorn hope, but in the end, as Corrine said, "Getting this job, Bruv, it's your lucky day. You've got a second chance now. You've got to go or die forever wondering."

Cord confirmed with John Keep that he would take the job at Jacana Creek.

*****

Dexter was at the airport waiting. "Ya back," was all he said.

He loaded the baggage into the near-new troop carrier full of packages and boxes. Cord felt as if he'd never been away. They drove out of town and were soon on the dusty gravel road on the long journey to the station.

Fearful that Dex may turn on his brand of musical entertainment, Cord used a delay tactic and asked, "Got a new vehicle?"

"Yeah, the old bugger gave up the ghost, shat itself at Palm Tree Gully last year. Did four hundred and eighty thou', though. Not bad for a bus in this country. Gave it to the community and they use it for a chicken coop. We don't waste anythin' out here."

"How are things out at the station?"

"Which one?"

"Jacana."

"Oh, much the same. Barry brought in a new bull calf from America or somewhere. He's a real goer, that boy. Got his head screwed on right. I'm not one to talk behind a person's back, but that Jason Doig at Indigo is bloody useless. A bit of a wanka', I reckon. He's still shitty over the land deal, does nothin' around the station and leaves ol' Bert in the lurch. Looks like the daughter, young Sharon, will come good though and run the station. She's still a young'un but a dinky-di jillaroo. Bloody good at breedin' horses, knows how to handle 'em."

"Well, I hope it works out for them."

"Ya did a good job, ya know. They're all proud a' ya."

"Thanks."

They lapsed into silence, broken only by the crunching sound of tyres on the worn gravel track. Dex reached for the CD button, so Cord quickly said, "Any other news?"

Dex thought for a while. "Clyde got his new chopper and he's gonna buy another one. Maggot's the main man ferryin' stuff to the station now. Thought Clyde might cut me out of me business, but choppers are too

138

pricey. He's into the big boys, mining. Lots'a miners round here lately; everyone's a bloody miner. They'll bugger up this country."

To test the waters, he said, "I suppose Clyde and Kathy got together?"

Dex looked at him sideways, frowned, then quickly looked back at the road as they negotiated another pothole.

"Nah! Nah, no. Didn't ya know he got hitched to Melinda Carmody? They got married last year, real ding-dong affair. Doreen and I went along."

Cord remained silent, knowing Dex had more to say.

"The Carmodys are sheep farmers down south. She's up here wiv Clyde, though. Nice lass that Melinda," he paused. "I told ya that before, didn't I? Clyde and Kathy Bell? Cripes! No, he didn't stand a chance with her. She's too much woman for him, too much for anyone if ya ask me. I'm not one to talk behind a person's back, but as I said before, she's a hard-nosed woman, smart but too choosy. Probably finish up an old maid. Pity, 'cause she's a bloody corker, isn't she? The miners and them geology boys are droolin' over her. Every time I call in, there's a bunch of 'em there, jostlin' for position, like bees round a honey pot."

"What are they mining?"

"Gas, me boy. They say there's lots of it. They get it out of the dirt with somethin' called frackin'. Funny name that. Calvin's the bossman. Between you and me, and as you know, I don't like to talk behind a person's back, but I reckon he's a sly bugger, I wouldn't trust him as far as I could throw him. From what I can see, he's got the inside runnin' with Kathy Bell, though."

Dex chuckled. "Boris got stymied, couldn't figure out the difference between frackin' and fuckin'."

Cord finally succumbed to the familiar sound of Lacy Dalton's *Hill Billy Girl with the Blues*, accompanied by the raucous, gravelly voice of Dexter. Eventually, the music and the rhythm of the vehicle induced him to close his eyes and sleep. He was on his way home.

Dexter let him sleep and opened and shut the station gates by himself as he usually did.

Cord woke to the sound of a booming voice. *"Bienvenido*, Landman, you're fuckin' back."

The door pulled open, and a huge hand dragged him from the vehicle; big arms embraced him in a giant bear hug.

"Good to be back," he gasped, detaching himself from the giant's grip.

It was good to see that familiar smiling bearded face again. Over Boris's shoulder, he could see Ted and Joan waiting in the shade of the veranda, and in the background, he could hear the familiar click-click of the sprinklers on the green lawn.

It was as if he'd never left. He was drawn to the country, the land, the outback; drawn to this sacred place. There was comfort in the heat and the dust, the constant bellowing of cattle, the station hands moving about, mustering, the Frangipani trees shading the drive, the homestead solid and welcoming. The place was alive, in perpetual motion and he was back, part of it again.

"Welcome back," Ted said with a broad smile, extending his hand and taking Cord's in a firm grip.

Joan hugged him and said tearfully, "It's good to have you back. We missed you and what you did for us."

Cord wanted to say any surveyor would do the same but just nodded and said again, "Thanks, it's good to be back."

The flyscreen door opened and Kathy appeared. Their eyes met and with a half-smile, she spoke. "Hello, Cord."

What was it with her? Did he expect too much? Her presence overwhelmed him. Here she was, the woman he wanted. Lucille was gone, his long search for her over; she was a delusion. Kathy, however, was standing right before him, within arm's reach and all he could say was, "Hi, Kathy."

Even in her run-of-the-mill, ordinary, everyday station clothes, she was breathtakingly lovely. Faded checked shirt, jeans that followed the curve of her thighs, crystal blue eyes with a smidge of freckles around her nose and her blonde hair tied in a ponytail, it was all Cord could do not to reach out and hold her. Kathy smiled again, but it was a distant, brief smile. There was still a chasm between them. She added, "Welcome back."

Then she turned to Ted. "I'm going up to the breeding paddock with Davy to check on the horses."

"Fine, you could also check the trough in the west holding yard on your way. Cyril said it looked only a quarter full yesterday."

"Okay."

She donned her Akubra and left.

Joan raised her eyebrows, shook her head a little and gestured with open hands, "Sorry, Cord, it seems it's business as usual. I am sure you'll want to wash up and have a bite to eat. You're in your old room at the end of the hall. When you're settled, May's made sandwiches. This evening, we'll be having a barbeque. Ted's cooking."

"I'll let you go. Relax and we'll talk about the job tomorrow," Ted said.

It didn't take him long to unpack. The afternoon loomed hot and humid and from the yard, he could hear a motor. He opened the French doors and went outside to the familiar sight of the Frangipani trees lining the drive. The sprinklers were silent, but the sound he heard was from the lawn mower. Boris was riding backwards and forwards in a symmetrical pattern that required his full attention. Cord sat in the shade of the veranda, watching the big man on the tiny mower, the big Spaniard who had become a special friend. He mused on Joan's words, 'Your old room'. He was home again.

*****

Fresh, showered and dressed in jeans and a cotton shirt, he found Ted out on the lawn firing up the converted forty-four-gallon drum that had been cut and converted into a makeshift but efficient barbeque, able to handle a multitude of steaks and sausages. Later, with the grilling plate removed and as the evening cooled, it would be stoked with logs and lit for a warming fire. Everyone would sit in their camper chairs, swapping yarns, watching the flames dance, warming themselves, moving closer as the air chilled. Coloured night-lights hanging from the trees added brightness and festivity. The inviting aroma of steak cooking and onions frying filled the air.

The crowd gathered and station hands and ringers stood in groups, laughing and joking. Cord was welcomed with handshakes and slaps on the back. He recognised Sofie, the young ringer who'd tried to tame Boris. She smiled, came over and unexpectedly hugged him, saying, "I'm back, like you, for my next stint."

"Yeah, I couldn't stay away either."

"This time, I've cut Boris's fine to fifty cents an expletive; otherwise, he'll go bankrupt. Got twenty bucks so far."

"He's a regular gold mine."

"Sure is. Say, if you need an extra hand at the camp, let the boss know. I'm available, that's if you want to."

"You'll be the first to know."

Cord noticed Albert standing alone on the fringe of the crowd. He excused himself. Albert was a non-drinker, so Cord grabbed a Coke from the Esky and crossed the lawn to join him. He handed Albert the can and looked into that fine black face, a face of strength and wisdom. Their eyes met, they nodded and half-smiled at each other. Nothing was said; it was a silent greeting more meaningful and more profound than the casual handshake. They stood together for some time before Boris found Cord.

"The boss wants you, Landman."

He'd forgotten he was Landman again.

At the barbeque, Ted handed him an apron and tongs. "Help me here, mate. I've got a lot of hungry mouths to feed."

Boris returned with a couple of cans of cold beer. "Smells fuckin' good, Landman."

He winked at Cord, then went back to join the station hands. He turned to see Sofie waiting, reached into his pocket and flipped her a fifty-cent coin.

"You know, he's been looking forward to you coming back, been talking about it for weeks," Ted smiled and added, "I don't eat sausages much. I'm more of a steak man, especially when you've got your own cattle. Pity Barry couldn't be here. He'll be back in a couple of years. It'll be good to have him running the place. It's getting a bit hard for Kathy alone."

Cord finished his beer and turned the sausages. "Yeah, I suppose it is."

Boris brought another two cans and Cord slipped him a sausage.

Boris left and Ted chuckled, "That Boris, he's a bloody character. You'll have to see what he's done to the old Patrol."

Cord raised his eyebrows.

"You'll see tomorrow."

Sipping their beers, they turned the browning meat. The party crowd was in two groups; the station hands and nine employees from the mining company.

"We've got a few of these mining exploration guys with us tonight. Calvin, the tall guy there talking to Kathy, is the boss of the outfit. They're after gas. There's that woman geologist you know, Dixie, is it? She's not here tonight. It's a bit of a bind, but if we're hospitable to them, we're kept in the loop, you know what I mean. Their caravans are behind the stockyards and they're drilling in the west paddock."

"Yeah, I saw the drill rig when I came in. They make a bit of a mess."

"Had some surveying guys here a few weeks ago who didn't know you. They heard about the southern boundary job from someone, Boris, I suppose. He talks to everyone. Said they could do it, but, well, we preferred you, and when John Keep said you may not be available, and he could send someone else, Kathy insisted it had to be you."

Cord gasped and choked on his beer.

"You all right?"

Cord regained his composure, "Yeah, went down the wrong way."

Extra tables were set up on the veranda. Joan and May were bringing out food and Kathy came across from the group to help. There was a variety of salads, crusty bread straight from the oven, home-brewed sauces and pickles, mangoes and May's special Bush Apricot relish. Eventually, the tables were laden with the food.

Watching from afar, Cord had one eye on the sausages and one eye on Kathy, effervescent, energetic, attending to the bush banquet. Wearing a pleated tartan mini skirt, showing her tanned shapely legs and a ruffled red blouse top, she looked dazzling. He remembered Dex's words, 'Too much woman for any man', and reluctantly agreed.

Joan came over to the barbeque with Kathy, both holding trays for the meat.

In her pleasant way, Joan had already ascertained Cord hadn't married.

"The apron suits you," Kathy said mischievously.

"It'd look better on you," Cord grinned.

It was meant to be a compliment but didn't come across that way. It had a chauvinist edge to it and wasn't what he meant.

Kathy glared at him.

"Come on, you guys," Joan said, "Everyone's starving."

Ted loaded the steaks onto Joan's tray and Cord heaped the sausages onto Kathy's. He wanted to say something to put it right, something light and witty, but nothing came to mind; instead, he fumbled a sausage and it fell to the ground.

"Sorry," he reached down to pick it up.

"Don't bother," she said sharply. "I'll give it to the dogs later."

Cord followed behind, perplexed at how easy it was to upset her. He knew she took his comment the wrong way. Surely, she could see he was smitten. It'll be good to get to the camp tomorrow, away from this woman and this confusion.

The evening wore on, the log fire ablaze. Flames leapt high, spattering and twirling, sending out a smoke haze that kept the ever-active mosquitoes quiet. Cord was chatting with a group of hands when Kathy joined them.

"How was your trip, Mr Landman?" she asked.

He was about to reply when Calvin arrived, drinks in hand with a glass for Kathy. She took the glass and moved away, ignoring Cord, not waiting for his response.

Cord sat alone, despondent, on the edge of the crowd when a booming voice said, "Come on, Landman. Let's give these fuckin' mozzies a miss and down a few fuckin' tubes."

From afar, Sofie called, "That's a dollar, please!"

Cord looked towards Kathy on the other side of the fire, sipping her wine and laughing with Calvin, her new admirer. Clearly, she didn't miss him.

"Okay, why not. What the hell?"

Boris and Cord crossed the yard and passed the holding paddock, where cattle shuffled at their approach. The smell of dung and dust filled the air.

They entered the cabin and Boris opened the well-stocked fridge. "How about a Carlton Dry."

"Sounds good."

Cord relaxed on the old sofa.

He finished his third beer and vowed it wouldn't be his last.

Stony Ridge
2001

Cord woke, cramped on the old sofa, his head fuzzy. The room and his clothes reeked of stale beer. His mouth and throat were parched. He wasn't used to binge drinking. On the lone bed across from him, Boris chortled away, his beard lifting and falling with each breath. It was early, just daylight; everyone, even Boris, would soon be up and about. He had to get back to his room unnoticed.

During the night, he'd woken to relieve himself and staggered into the darkness, but without moonlight and even under the myriad of southern stars, it was still too dark to cross the cattle yard to the house and the dogs would definitely have started barking. It was best to stay put till he could see and returned to the sofa. He berated himself for falling asleep on the couch in the first place. His first day back; this was a bad start and it was Kathy's fault.

A heap of empty cans littered the floor, with some half-empty on the table. Cord winced at the sight and left the cottage quietly, quickly crossed the yard and managed to avoid two station hands saddling horses. He skirted around the veranda and tried the French doors to his room. Luckily, they were unlocked. Back in his haven, he resolved this wouldn't happen again. The fuzziness left him as he showered and shaved. Promptly, at 6 am, he was seated at the breakfast table alone. May served him scrambled eggs and pancakes.

"Mr Ted's over at the yards. When ya ready, call him on the two-way and he'll meet ya at the store."

The main store had a large high table with enough space to layout maps and high stools with adequate room to move around. Ted had already unrolled the rough mud map of the station layout on the table and was mulling over it when Cord arrived.

"How did you pull up last night? Saw you go off with Boris."

Cord decided honesty was the best policy, "Not good."

"Thought so," Ted grinned, then pointed to a pencil line on the plan. "It's only an estimate of the position of the southern boundary. I haven't worried much about that boundary in the past. The Stony Ridge Range has been a sufficient barrier between Charcoal Flats and us, but the internal fences have deteriorated since that station was abandoned three years ago. Over this Dry, we've been invaded by animals coming through the gorges to our water."

"Animals?"

"Ferals, all sorts, mainly camels. Water buffalo, they're the worst. I'd like to get the boundary fenced as soon as possible before this Wet. It's rugged country through the range, so the contract's a bit open-ended, but I know you'll do the right thing. Albert and Boris will be with you again if that's okay. Oh, and while I think of it, we decided not to fence the east boundary. The Doig's deal fell through, so they're welcome to water their cattle in the creek as usual. It's good that it's marked if we need it in future."

"That's good."

"Maggot flew in your equipment last week. It's here in the store. Chuck stacked it carefully under Boris's watchful eye as well as Sofie's."

"Maggot, not Clyde?"

"No, haven't seen much of Clyde since his marriage. With his new fancy chopper, he's been mostly involved with the mining companies."

Albert and Boris were well ahead with preparations for the trip. Nothing was left to chance, with Albert in charge of camping gear and Boris relishing overseeing ancillaries, an occupation he flaunted before the other station hands, although they probably didn't care anyway.

Ted stated again they would be using the old Patrol, which was now virtually Boris's personal vehicle. It was unlicensed for the road and the history of its use for hard mustering was stamped in the unwashed red dust that clung to its rusted frame and the large hole in the passenger door, the legacy of the horn of the buffalo bull he was trying to cut from the mob. Boris reported to all who would listen how the buffalo horn missed him by mere inches and how he was lucky to be alive.

Ted quietly explained with a wry smile, "It's a good story; however, the hole's in the passenger door, not the driver's, but then again, you never let the truth get in the way of a good story."

Cord was packing his equipment and laptop when Boris came in, wiping his hands on a dirty cloth. He was excited, "Have a look at this, Landman."

Cord followed him to the Patrol, where Boris proudly gestured to the side door panel. Printed in large black letters was a sign that read 'Landman Team'.

"What da' ya think? Pretty fuckin' good, eh?"

"Brilliant."

They stood admiring the handy work when the cattle truck, laden with a mob of snorting steers, came out of the home paddock and passed just near enough to shed a blanket of dust over the pair. Kathy was driving. Boris waved, but she didn't look across.

"Miss Kathy's drivin' fast. Must be mad at somethin'."

The evening meal was a quiet one with only Ted and Joan, as Kathy was away down south for a few days. Joan cleared the dishes as Cord commented to Ted, "I plan to be out two weeks at first. I'll send Boris back if we need anything urgent. I gauge from the map that the boundary runs through the edge of the range. It's about forty kilometres in length, twenty-five kilometres shorter than the east boundary, so we'll see how we go."

"Okay, a few of the hands were down that way last week. Seems there are a few dingoes around, but they shouldn't bother you much. Just don't leave anything loose around the camp when you're out and Albert's not there. Bloody dingoes, they're sly buggers. Keep the fire going. There's a few goats, too, and they get into everything. Also, the boys saw camels and brumbies at a gorge waterhole. The horses are okay, but you have to watch the camels, especially a bull with a cow and calf. Don't get between him and them. Albert and Boris have their rifles. I'll come down when you get further into the job. I want to know what I'm fencing in and fencing out."

*****

The men left in the early morning for the slow drive to the southeast boundary corner, as they had done before. Albert and Cord in the Cruiser with the survey equipment, towing the horse float with Ginger and Smack and Boris following in the Patrol with the big trailer and the camping gear. They passed the Apricot Springs turnoff and Cord thought of Kathy and the magnificent day they'd spent there together. It was a sacred place to the Aboriginal people and now a special place to him.

They stopped several times to rest, release the horses from their tie straps and have something to eat. May had prepared roast beef sandwiches along with slices of apple pie, bananas and a flask of apple juice for the journey. They sat on the banks of a broad, deep billabong, a remnant of the last Wet. The white bark and shapely trunks of the river gums had sturdy boughs draping over the calm water, providing shade and welcome to the weary traveller. On the opposite side of the creek, a mob of cattle drifted in to drink.

"They're Doig's herd," said Albert.

"How do you know?" asked Cord.

"Easy, they're mainly Shorthorn and some Angus. Ours are Brahman breed. They're different."

He remembered Kathy laughing at him.

"The ones with the hump."

Albert chuckled, "That's right. There's lots of beef breeds and there's a lot to breedin' cattle. Can take a lifetime to get it right and then ya probably have to start again. Now young Mr Barry's a gun at it."

It was early afternoon when they reached the old campsite they'd set up years before. The fire pit that Boris made, ringed with rocks, was still intact; nothing had changed.

Boris was pleased. "What do ya think of that, Landman?"

"Excellent."

Albert and Boris pitched the tents and before long, a fire was crackling away. With the horses set and the billy boiling, all was normal again. Albert placed a pot of stew in the embers and night descended. A dingo howled in the distance.

In the morning, Cord and Boris drove to the corner cairn. Boris was elated that the first marker post he'd cemented in place was still standing upright. "Pretty fuckin' good, eh."

"As it should be."

The men followed the same routine as they had previously, with Cord and Boris attending to the surveying and Albert managing the camp. The survey headed west towards the first ridge of the range. It was a gentle slope through broken shale and sand, so the first markers were easy to place and trench.

After a few days in the Spinifex plain, the land rose more steeply and the sandy country became interspersed with large boulders. The survey slowed and Cord realised the magnitude of the task as the main range with its rock ramparts and barriers was still three kilometres away. It was even more daunting when Cord used the theodolite telescope and discovered that the boundary was deeper into the range than indicated by the pencil line drawn on Ted's mud map. If so, their progress through the high country would be even slower. The terrain was much more challenging than he'd bargained for, but the pair stuck to it.

Camp life was routine and well-organised. In the afternoon, the men would return to camp early to avoid the crushing heat of the day but also to soak under the cool water in the open-topped shower tent Albert had rigged up. Then Cord would attend to office tasks while Boris enjoyed his traditional *siesta*. The heat didn't seem to bother Albert as he moved around, quiet and easy-going, cooking the evening meal, fuelling the generator and provisioning the horses.

Sunsets at the range were often spectacular events. In the distance, the ridge crests turned golden and fleecy clouds reflected brilliant fiery patterns of crimson to the watchers around the campfire below. Slowly, as night descended, the colour display faded. The moon rose and bathed the chilling land in a ghostly glow as dingoes howled.

One late afternoon, the clouds became jagged, dark and ominous. The wind picked up, lightning flashed and thunder rolled in across the windswept plain, scaring the horses. From deep in the gorge, a pack of dingoes howled in chorus. These events added to the diverse nature and spectacular beauty of the country. Cord was in love with the spaciousness, the mystery and the overwhelming isolation of this secret outback land; it was spellbinding.

Albert stirred and added another log to the fire. "Better check on the horses."

Boris went with him, leaving Cord alone, deep in thought, to watch the embers flirting with the new log before it suddenly burst into flames of red and blue; it startled him. He fingered the warm mug of tea in his hand, took a sip and his thoughts turned away from Kathy and how she teased him to an earlier conversation with Albert about Aboriginal culture.

"Don't we all have a connection to country?" Cord had asked.

Albert replied, "Perhaps. Us people are custodians of the land. We keep it and it keeps us."

Cord told Albert of the Quechua people of the Amazon and their *Pachamama*, Mother Earth. He spoke of the Native American Indians of America when he visited the Smithsonian, their struggle and the Great Earth Spirit.

Albert nodded, his face bowed and his reaction indecipherable.

Cord yearned to have a deeper understanding of the Aboriginal culture than what had come from Albert's previous short, sharp, measured replies. He began to wonder how Albert viewed his role as an Elder and Cord's role in setting boundaries and dividing land into parcels.

Albert explained, "In our culture, we don't own land; the land owns us. The land is one entity. Each generation's purpose is to preserve and maintain the land for future generations. We have the rite of passage across country to follow the seasons."

Cord told Albert of Robert Frost's metaphorical poem, *Mending Wall*, where two neighbours meet each year to mend their crumbling dividing wall. One man cannot see the purpose of having the wall as he reasons his forest won't invade the neighbour's plot; however, the other maintains that 'good fences make good neighbours'.

"Which one are you?" he asked, hoping to draw Albert into further discussion on the subject.

Albert shrugged and shook his head. "Aboriginal people don't disturb the land. There's no boundaries, only those in our mind."

"People call me Landman as a joke. Does that bother you?"

"That's just a name. You've got to be of the land, be part of it, not separate from it."

"I don't understand."

Albert stroked his beard; the conversation was closed. He smiled, "That's understandable, Landman. Welcome to Country."

Camels
2001

By the end of the third week, they'd progressed to Mammoth Gorge. Albert showed Cord rock art on the walls and in the caves; paintings and engravings etched in the soft sandstone. He explained the meaning of the circles, dots, the animals and their tracks. There were silhouettes of hands and outlines of the human form, with all sorts of variations reflecting the culture of the people. Deep in the gorge, majestic river gums, centuries old, framed a series of dark green pools set within the high ramparts. Brilliant green native fig trees clung to cracks and fissures in the rock. Small rock wallabies peered from sheltered crevices, curious at the strangers passing and Jacana birds skipped over the floating Lotus leaves.

"We get ochre from the creek bank," Albert said, "mix it with water and mark the rock with fingers or sticks. You can see splinters in the caves, which are bits of the hard rock the people brought in to make the carvings. See that big mound there? That's a midden, heaps of campfires over the years. It's our dreamin' place. Our job's to keep everthin' safe."

"You've kept everything safe for over sixty thousand years, haven't you?"

"Yeah, but there's always tomorrow, wiv all them minin' buggers runnin' round."

Davy replaced Albert and moved the camp to the foot of the gorge. The men swam in the cool, fresh water at the end of each day; for Cord, it was another memorable time.

It was slow and tedious work. Stony Ridge Range was rugged country. Giant craggy sentinels of rock criss-crossed the boundary line. Cord radioed the station, highlighted the difficulty of the terrain and added an opinion that fencing would be a challenging task. He advised Ted that progress was slow and costs may blow out. However, his job was to mark the boundary; fencing and budgets were Ted and John Keep's problem.

Boris used his expletive vocabulary to the full as he lugged cement and water up the rock faces and ledges to place the marker posts in position. They reached Little Rock Gorge by the fourth week. It was spectacular but narrower than Mammoth Gorge. The pools were shallow and drying, but the sandy banks provided easy access for the many animals that came there to drink.

One morning, Cord advanced to the far side of the gorge, leaving Boris behind to place a post in position, when a train of camels trotted round the rocky spur to drink. Cord was between them and the water and they hesitated when they saw him. A calf, anxious to drink, ran ahead and its mother quickly followed. A large bull camel broke away from the main train and galloped towards Cord, bearing its teeth and snorting wildly. Cord faltered momentarily, then grabbed the tripod and instrument to retreat but tripped and fell, hitting his head on a rock. Dazed, he lay in the dirt and saw the bull camel looming close, ready to kick and bite. He heard a rifle shot; then all went blank.

When he came to, he was groggy and tried to stand. The camel train had disappeared, except for one, the giant beast now lying at his feet. Boris was running towards him, rifle in hand.

"*Bastardo*! I saw 'em coming. Camels can hurt, even kill you! Are ya all right, Landman?"

Cord fingered his head. There was blood and a large egg-shaped lump under his hair. Boris picked him up like a sack of potatoes, carried and laid him on a rock ledge in the shade of an overhang.

"I'll go get the Patrol. Be back in ten minutes."

Cord was in a daze and didn't hear the vehicle approach.

Boris lifted him again and laid him on a tarpaulin in the utility tray.

"The instrument?" Cord questioned.

"Looks like it's fuckin' buggered."

The big man roped the legs of the dead camel to the tow hitch of the vehicle.

"Landman, are ya okay?"

"Sure. A bit shaky, that's all."

"I'll get ya back to camp. Just want to get the fuckin' brute away from the water."

He dragged the animal out into the open plain, untied the rope and left the carcass there.

Cord held a cloth to his head. "Is that a good idea? Won't it just rot leaving it there? Shouldn't we dig a hole and bury it?"

"No need in this country. It won't get a fuckin' chance to rot. The eagles and dingoes will make short work of it. There'll be clean bones in a week. Just lay back and relax."

Back at camp, Davy attended to his wound. Cord lay on the stretcher in shock and even in the hot confines of the tent, fell asleep and slept well into the next day.

*****

He woke to hear muffled voices using words such as 'concussed', 'stitches' and 'bull camel'. There was a woman's voice. He drifted into sleep again and finally woke with Kathy sitting on a stool beside him.

She touched his dressed wound and said, "You gave us quite a scare, Cord. You're going to have a decent bruise. You shouldn't chase camels, you know."

Cord nodded, smiled weakly, his head still pounding, and gingerly sat up in bed. It was good to have her near him. He could smell sweet perfume as she handed him a glass of water and a Panadol. Didn't she know she was the tonic he most needed?

"Dad's outside. We're pulling down the camp and moving you back to the homestead."

"I haven't finished the survey," he replied, wincing at the same time.

"Well, you can't finish it with smashed equipment. Besides, Dad wants you back home."

Ted came into the tent. "How ya goin', young fella?"

Cord felt better. "A bit of a sore head, that's all. You were right about the camels. Hadn't been for Boris, I don't know what would've happened."

"Yeah, they're angry beasts, mainly keep to themselves out in the desert country. Sometimes they need culling. The government blokes come in and do that."

Changing the subject, Ted continued, "Anyway, I've looked at the boundary work; it's bloody goat country. You're right. I can't put a fence through the range, so I'll fence around it and put in a few gates for access to the gorges. So, I'll pull the pin on the survey work. Can't see the point of it now that you've shown me how deep the boundary is in the range."

Cord was unprepared for the job to terminate this way, but Ted was the paying client; his distance-measuring instrument was smashed and from what he remembered, a repair would take months.

He nodded, "Just as you like. I'll let John Keep know."

"I've spoken to John. It's all settled. How about staying on for a couple of weeks? You're part of the woodwork now. I mentioned before, we have a shindig every year before the muster. Have a chinwag about cattle, the weather, have a game of cricket and the like, and let our hair down. It's just for immediate neighbours, friends and station hands, but this time, because of the mining, I invited Calvin, the boss geologist. While we're all together, Kathy thought it'd be a good idea to have him talk about this gas fracking stuff. It's our turn to host this year, so stay here, get over your injury, relax and have a beer before heading home."

Cord thought, that's right, Kathy's idea; bloody Calvin's the flavour of the moment. What chance did he have? But he agreed to stay on, only because he wanted to tell Kathy of his feelings, even if she laughed at him. Also, he didn't want to face his mother sporting a head wound. He was such a coward with women, except Corrine.

He was at a loss to keep himself occupied in the week that followed, apart from a brief exchange of emails with John Keep, who understood the situation and adjusted the account accordingly. Cord examined the distance-measuring device; the casing was badly damaged and it was inoperable. John advised it was insured and probably a write-off. Unfortunately, the prism accessory for the instrument had been left behind in the gorge. A station hand, sent to pick it up a few days later, found it knocked over and trampled by goats; another write-off.

Cord kept a low profile, as he didn't want to be a burden around the place. Occasionally, in the first few days, he followed Boris and Kathy about as they attended to farm duties. The more he saw of her, the more she overwhelmed him. She could ride a horse better than any other, replace a horseshoe, drive a tractor and a rig, climb a windmill to adjust the sails, mend broken fence wire and be up to her waist pulling a stranded calf out of boggy soak. She supervised the changing of the cattle truck tyres and praised the ringer's work efforts, yet at the same time admonished one-and-all for sloppy performance. She sat for ages conversing with the Aboriginal women and their children. Her pet Brahman bull, Wild Bill, followed her around the yards and the dogs skipped and pranced at her feet.

There wasn't a moment when he was able to see her alone. She was always busy, and as it happened, she was away mustering at an outcamp for the remainder of that week. Nevertheless, he resolved to say something, even though he felt there was still some mysterious, unfathomable distance between them. Time was running out, but there was still next week.

He texted Corrine of his dilemma; she replied: 'Bruv, if you don't say something, I will. Don't worry, just joking'.

*****

It was the final week of his stay with the Bells and on the Friday, neighbours began arriving in their trucks and vans for the weekend talkfest and the big cricket match, the Jackaroos versus the Jillaroos. The station women were busy cooking and the hands tidying up the grounds and preparing the dirt pitch. Cord followed Ted around as he selected some of his best breeding cattle for showing. Boris was in his element arranging lights and a dance floor for the evening activities and setting up the stereo equipment as the self-appointed disc jockey for the match and drinks waiter.

The game was twenty overs per team, but Cord soon found there were rules for the boys and others for the girls. May was the umpire and obviously knew little about the refinements of the game as she gave Cord out, caught behind when his bat was nowhere near the ball, but she knew enough to call 'No ball' if one of the Jillaroos was clean bowled or caught.

Kathy was at the crease. Wild Bill was grazing on the adjacent gateless commonage and saw his beloved mistress, Kathy, close by. Abruptly, he and a dozen heifers wandered onto the pitch. The game was poised at a crucial stage when Kathy downed bat, gloves and pad to lead the errant beast and his harem off the field. It took some time to remove the cow pats the mob had left behind before the game could resume. There were soon shrieks when a fielder inadvertently trod on an unrecovered pat. Sharon Doig hit a ball squarely into fresh cow dung, a bullseye, and there it rested. No one volunteered to retrieve the ball from its smelly resting place. Sharon was given four runs to add to her score, another ball recouped from the kit and the game went on.

Every time a batter was dismissed, Boris opened the stereo to full pitch, blasting and blaring out the Sherbet hit *Howzat*, to which spectator and player alike joined in with great enthusiasm.

Kathy was the last batter dismissed, bowled by Cord with an inswinger and before May could bark out 'No ball', Kathy walked. Later, she told him she walked because she didn't want to hear his moaning and grizzling afterwards. Kathy, Sofie and Sharon Doig scored most for the Jillaroos and Davy made a flurry of runs for the Jackaroos. Much to Cord's annoyance, Calvin was a competent cricketer and received pats on the back and congratulations.

At the end of the game, the score was eighty runs to fifty in favour of the Jackaroos and Cord was well pleased. His pleasure was short-lived as May declared the Jillaroos as winners at the presentation ceremony. Kathy accepted the battered enamel cup containing the sweet-smelling ashes of a burnt Sandalwood bough and held it high for all to see.

Confused, Cord asked Dex, standing nearby watching the ceremony with can in hand, "How can that be?"

"Oh, it's tradition. Jacks haven't won a game for years. Ya see, the final scores are doubled for the Jills and halved for the Jacks. So, it's one hundred for the Jills and forty for the Jacks. Another whitewash." Dex sighed and continued his rant. "Bloody cricket! Never played the game and I don't understand it. 'Bowled a maiden over', what does that mean? 'Silly point, deep third man, square leg', lotta crap if ya ask me. I only put in an appearance to be sociable. Come on, Landman, have a beer an' drown your sorrows. Boris's kept a few coldies for us."

*****

Cord retreated to his room before the evening event began. He sat alone on the homestead veranda, still smarting from the loss. He sipped another cold draught, escaping the last heat of the day, thankful to be away from the noisy milling crowd in the garden. Kathy came out of her room onto the porch wearing a soft blue pastel cocktail dress that clung to the curves of her trim figure.

She spied him out of the corner of her eye, approached, pirouetted and said, "What do you think? Should I wear this or not?"

It was an intimate question, which dumbfounded him. He wanted to say, 'Beautiful, please be mine', but Joan emerged from Kathy's room. "Come on, love. Calvin's here and Dad's waiting."

Kathy asked Cord again, "Well, what do you think?"

All he could say was, "Nice."

She stared at him blankly, frowned, said, "Thanks, I think I'll change," and left.

The evening's festivities got underway and Boris played requests from the crowd, mainly country music. He enjoyed himself, downing many 'fuckin' beers' which Sofie was slyly counting for settlement later. Cord was glad the station crew had forgotten his injury now that the bandage had been removed.

Sofie caught him alone, "My donation money box is empty since you've had Boris away surveying. I've told him I'm now counting beer cans and expletives; fifty cents each, a dollar for them both."

"That should bring a fortune," Cord chuckled.

Kathy had changed into an iridescent green short-sleeved V-neck blouse, revealing the smooth, tanned skin of her neckline. Her blonde hair hung loosely over her shoulders and several gold chains swung loosely around her neck. A pair of black polished cotton slacks and black-heeled shoes complemented the outfit. Cord found the outfit stunning.

She spoke privately to Calvin, who took the floor and indicated to Boris to cut the music. Immediately, he began informing the audience of the fortune to be made if a gas field was discovered. He was confident the sandstone underlay contained vast amounts of gas and hydraulic fracturing, or fracking as it was called, was the method used to extract it from the shale. He was in full flight and emphasised it was a safe, tried and true method. Calvin added that it was early days in the drilling program, so it was a wait-and-see situation. Questions flowed from the floor and Cord, standing back on the edge of the crowd, saw Albert walk sadly away. He too had his doubts.

Afterwards, he joined Ted and Joan at their table.

"Have a beer," Ted said. "What do ya think of all that?"

Cord took a sip of his drink. He thought of Apricot Springs and what fracking might do. "What do I think? I hope it doesn't happen."

"Good, so do I."

There were couples dancing and Cord noticed Calvin and Kathy together on the floor; she was laughing. Would he ever get the chance to tell her? He knew time was running out.

Joan woke the two men from their gloom and changed the subject, "Well, it hasn't happened, so there. Cord. It's a good, manly name. I've wondered, is it a family name?"

Cord took his eyes off the dancing couple. "No, it's a mistake. It was supposed to be Gordon, but my birth certificate says Cordon. My mother blames my father, but it could have been anyone, really. The nurse, the doctor, the registrar. I think the mistake was just a flick of the pen error, as my sister's and my name both start with C, O and R. That's Cord and Corrine."

He thought of when they were teenagers. Corrine had bantered, "What if they got it the other way round? You'd be Gordon and I'd be Gorrine. How horrible, I'd have to change it."

He remembered laughing and joking, "Then you'd be Gory; I'd call you Really Gory." She'd punched him on the arm.

Joan's eyes widened, bringing him back from his reverie, "Oh, so Corrine's your sister?"

"My twin sister."

"Twin? She's the one you went overseas with?"

"Yes, that's right."

Joan raised her eyebrows even more, now very interested. "Where did you go? Tell us about it."

Cord spoke about the Inca Trail, Machu Picchu and the Quechua people.

The music stopped as Boris abandoned the hi-fi to get another beer. Kathy came to the table and sat on the opposite side to Cord. Calvin went to get drinks.

Joan smiled and slyly addressed Kathy, "Kathy, it's interesting. Cord was just talking about his overseas trip to South America with Corrine."

Kathy responded off-handedly, "Do tell."

Cord was aloof; he didn't feel like repeating himself anyway.

Joan butted in with her eyes firmly on Kathy. "Corrine is Cord's twin sister."

Kathy turned sharply to him, bewildered. "What! You have a twin sister?"

Cord nodded. He noted an immediate change in her manner and facial expression; she mellowed. Boris returned to his disc jockey post and played Neil Young's wistful rendering of *Harvest Moon*.

Kathy held out her hand to Cord invitingly. "You haven't asked me to dance."

Cord went to the floor, mesmerized, unbelieving, as he held this magnificent woman in his arms. At last, he could tell her how he felt. They danced close to the sultry music, the lyrics warm and evocative, her perfume heady. She rested her head on his shoulder; their bodies touched intimately and Cord couldn't control his arousal. Kathy pulled back from the embrace and looked down to see the bulge in his jeans.

"Sorry, so sorry," he pleaded, stepping away.

The music stopped and he tried to hide his shame. Fortunately, the desire subsided quickly. Embarrassed, he escorted Kathy back to the table. Calvin returned with drinks.

Cord apologised, "I guess I'll call it a night."

Kathy didn't look at him and thankfully, no one noticed his dilemma.

"Stay. It's still early," said Joan.

"Need a rest, Cord? Cricket too much for you, old man?" laughed Calvin.

Cord ignored him. "Please excuse me."

He crossed the makeshift dance floor, almost running, seeking the safety of his room.

Boris called, "Hey Landman, come an' have a beer."

Cord slammed his room door behind him and leant against it, his body shaking, anguished about what had happened. How embarrassing, how stupid; she'd never forgive him. He couldn't speak or look her in the face again. He ripped at his clothes. He had to leave Jacana as quickly as possible, the next day, if he could.

There was a knock on the veranda door. Bloody Boris, he thought.

The knock was louder; he went to the door and flung it open. Choking with desperate anger, he cried, "Boris, I'm going to bed."

But it was Kathy standing there. "You said you were calling it a night?"

He nodded. "Kathy, I'm so sorry. I apologise. It was unforgivable."

She brushed past him into the room and Cord blurted out, "Kathy, I love you." There, he'd said it at last.

She put a finger to his lips and smiled.

"Hush," she whispered. "The night's just begun."

She walked towards him, slowly unbuttoning her blouse.

Images
2002

Cord and Kathy spent as much time together as possible. Since that magic night, their relationship blossomed. They held hands, hugged and kissed often, made love on a blanket at Apricot Springs and tried to start the day with breakfast together.

Kathy and Cord discussed the future path of their relationship, where they would live and how they would manage. It wasn't an easy conversation, but it became patently clear Kathy couldn't leave the station before her brother returned, nor did she really want to. On the other hand, Cord could approach John Keep to do his consulting and administrative duties at a distance, only going back to the office intermittently. Then, he could stay at the station to help out. John agreed.

"I can't quite see you as a ringer," she said. "You can't even ride a horse."

"You'll have to teach me."

She smiled wickedly, "I don't have enough hours, but then I could let you ride Old Moses. He's retired and been put out to pasture. You could ride him around the top paddock. He can't gallop or even trot, so you shouldn't fall off. Should suit you."

"Thanks," Cord grinned.

The news of their courtship travelled fast around the station. Ted and Joan were pleasantly concerned; they had never seen Kathy this way. She was always in control, focused and determined, but she was different, not in her work around the station, but in her demeanour. She was supremely joyful. Cord seemed the same and stayed at the station, occasionally returning to the KMSurveys offices.

When Kathy was away mustering, Ted and Joan faced him with the time-old question, "What are your intentions towards our daughter?"

Cord's response was the time-old formal request, "Ted, Joan, I seek your blessing to take Kathy's hand in marriage."

It was easily settled with a slap on the back, a handshake and a motherly hug from Joan, "I knew he was the one for her, didn't I, Ted?"

The marriage of Cordon Heath McCullum to Kathryn Joy Bell was celebrated just seven months after the night she first came to him. It would be a gala event held at the station and attended by just about everyone in the outback.

The months leading up to the occasion were a flurry of activity, including a trip to Perth for Kathy to meet Cord's family and shop for a wedding dress. Eileen approved. How could she not accept and admire this beautiful, intelligent woman who unexpectedly appeared in her home to be her daughter-in-law?

"You never told me she's the reason you've been going bush," she said. "I can see why now."

Cord's father was smitten and anxious to drive Kathy and Corrine wherever they wanted to go in search of the elusive wedding dress. Barry, still finishing his degree, came to dinner twice and joined Cord and Kathy for morning coffee at the Dome a few times. Corrine took Kathy under her wing, introduced her to friends and generally fussed over her.

"Oh, Cord, she's lovely," Corrine said. "I'm so happy for you, Bruv. Now I have a sister."

Kathy confided in Corrine that for a long time, she was jealous of her, not knowing that the 'Corrine' of Machu Picchu was Cord's sister. She also said that she fell in love with Cord at a place called Apricot Springs.

"I'll take you there when you come up. I remember him on the edge of the pool, just touching the water with his fingers. A strange feeling came over me and something inside said, that's your man, but I never thought it would happen."

"Oh, don't you worry! I know he loved you from the start, but that's our shy Cord."

The day before the wedding, Clyde, in his new fourteen-seat helicopter, flew in Margaret, the wedding celebrant, his wife, Melinda, the McCullum family, Barry and a giant wedding cake.

Joan was on hand to personally welcome the McCullums and make them comfortable. It was the first time she had met them in person and she was pleased they were wonderful people. Ted took Keith on a tour of the yards and Joan showed Eileen over the homestead.

Later, Eileen said to Keith, "It's quite a nice place. Cord always made it seem that it was in the bush. I like it, even though it's hot and muggy."

Keith rolled his eyes and agreed.

*****

It was a perfect wedding day; it didn't rain. The sun rose in pink wisps of cloud and in the early afternoon, the happy congregation gathered, spilling out onto the newly mowed lawn.

Because of the unpredictability of the Wet, the ceremony was held in the main store, cleared and decorated with fronds of Fan Palm that Boris and Sofie spent hours gathering.

Presents flowed in. Their parents combined resources and presented the couple with a fly-and-cruise honeymoon holiday from Singapore to Hong Kong. Boris hand-crafted a two-seater lounge chair from polished native Sandalwood. The Doigs gifted a thoroughbred quarter horse gelding that Sharon had raised by hand.

John Keep couldn't attend but gifted five hundred shares in a flourishing rural company. The accompanying card read: 'To my friend, colleague and top gun surveyor, congratulations on your wedding. This is a small gift for you and your good lady, Kathryn, to help in your pastoral pursuits. All the best and take care, JK'.

Kathy had chosen an A-Line knee-length and backless white chiffon dress with open-strap high-heeled shoes. For her hair, May wove a headband of native flora, including flowers from the Bush Apricot. Cord wore cream cotton slacks and a pale blue shirt and tie. Ironically, even though they had all just met, Corrine was Kathy's bridesmaid and Barry was Cord's best man. Cord was spellbound as his wife-to-be walked down the aisle towards him.

Vows were exchanged and champagne flowed. Cord only caught an occasional glimpse of his wife, perpetually surrounded by well-wishers. When he did, their eyes met and chemistry sparked.

Over two hundred guests attended the reception, including Maggot, Dexter and his wife, Doreen. The women of the neighbouring stations clubbed together for the catering, giving Joan a welcome break. The community women hunted turtles and mangrove crabs and speared sea fish as they'd always done as young girls. They harvested edible plants and prepared them for tasting by the guests. All the while, they sang traditional songs of courtship and danced in private ceremony to ensure the couple would be joined forever.

Dexter pulled Keith aside. "Cord and me are great mates. I knew he an' Kathy would get together the moment I met him. I'm not one to talk behind a person's back, but I can tell ya, a few of those other station guys who chased her are bloody trash, not a touch on your boy. Take Jack Jackson. I knew he was keen on Kathy. He puts on the dog but's turns out he's a real wanker. Like I said, I'm not one to talk behind a person's back, but you've gotta call a spade a spade, don't ya? Yeah, like I said, me and Cord are great mates. What say we find Boris and down a tube?"

Everyone feasted and made merry and speeches and toasts to the happy couple were long and meaningful. Night descended; the moon drifted in and out of high clouds and the muffled and sporadic sound of thunder in the distance sent the jubilant revellers back under roof to the main store. The storm drew closer, lightning flashed, thunder clapped and the pounding of heavy rain on the tin roof all but drowned out the laughter and music.

At a break in the storm, Cord and Kathy departed the noisy throng, not without catcalls, meaningful looks, hugs and handshakes. They crossed the lawn and hastened to their room. What a moment to share, what exquisite ecstasy, what heavenly bliss. It all came together for Cord that day, that night. He finally had Kathy; they were one.

After they'd showered, Cord lay back on the bed admiring Kathy's figure in the mirror as she combed her shining hair in long, broad sweeps and carefully removed traces of makeup from around her eyes.

A thought came to him unexpectedly; he reached for his phone and opened the photo gallery. He flicked through images till he found Lucille, laughing with the butterflies, the Chocolate Sailor in her hair. He pressed the delete button.

Kathy saw him reflected in the mirror. "What was that?" she asked warmly.

"Nothing. Just getting rid of some old stuff."

Singapore
2002

Singapore was a delight to Kathy. They had three days to taste the culture and explore the city sights, from shopping on Orchard Road to the Sentosa Island Aquarium to the Gardens by the Bay and much more. It all became an intermingled, exhausting, frenetic adventure. It was almost a relief to board the cruise ship at the end of each day to relax and make love in the sanctuary of their balcony stateroom. The vessel visited ports where there was more sightseeing, but the land tours were more orderly and stress-free.

When they berthed at Penang, there were three full days to explore the island, but Kathy was keen to wander the streets of George Town and the port area where Cord had worked.

The old ferries running between George Town and Butterworth had been replaced by faster, sleek catamarans that ran from the new berths a few kilometres to the south. Two old ferries were docked at the old terminal, tied up, repainted and refurbished as museum pieces acknowledging the historical past.

Cord looked out across the murky water of the harbour and memories came flooding back, sharp and vivid. The bouncing of the *Spree* as she pushed her broad bow into the swell with Gert shouting orders. The whine of the GPS as it tracked and the cursing of the loss of a satellite fix in bad weather. The pervading aroma of baked beans rising through the galley air duct and the endless black nights on a relentless race against time. He thought of Dixie, his mate Brian, Sachin and even that arsehole Simon. He thought of Rodney but tried not to think of Lucille.

The first morning ashore, Kathy and Cord walked from the quay to Lebuh Downing and down the side alley past the manor. Cord was half expecting to see Sambo at the gate with his bucket of water and cloth, but the gates were locked, and the house closed and empty. It was hard to imagine the hustle, bustle and urgency that existed there just a few short years before. He remembered Mrs Brown, smiled and recollected how she ran a tight ship; you either shaped up or shipped out, just like his mother. He knew that in the years ahead, Kathy would be the same.

"What were you thinking, my love?" Kathy said, linking an arm with his.

"Oh, it's strange to be back here again. It's the same, yet it isn't."

"It's so hot and humid here I must get an umbrella. Look at those clouds. It could rain any minute."

She tugged on Cord's arm to hurry. They could hear muffled thunder; rain wasn't far away. They quickly darted through side alleys to the main Lebuh Chulia, chock-full of busy, tooting taxis, overladen motorbikes, tandem bicycles, rickshaws and hand carts, all dodging and weaving their way amongst the dense mass of pedestrians. Nothing had diminished; Penang had become even more hectic. The streets and alleys were full of the same hawkers trading trinkets and the ever-present food stalls, with the vendors calling out for them to come and try as they passed. Cord was pleased to find the Curry Mee hawker on the same street corner as before.

"Probably his son, but try this," Cord urged.

Kathy laughed and squirmed when he raised the spoon to her mouth to taste, but instead, he quickly pulled it away, stooped and kissed her.

"That tastes better, much hotter and more delicious than the curry," she smiled and elbowed him.

The overhead lanterns strung from shop to shop were plentiful, bigger and more colourful than he remembered.

"The Malays like colour," he explained. "Both sexes adorn themselves in bright, colourful clothes. We'll come back tonight when the lanterns are lit. The place will be alive with people. Only problem is more crowds means more pickpockets."

He insisted on buying her a gift to remember this colourful place. In the main clothing bazaar on a side alley, she settled on an elegant sarong and matching jacket in glossy red taffeta with gold embroidery and braid. The ensemble complemented her tanned complexion and lustrous blonde hair.

Although he was cheerful, Cord felt uneasy in this place. The distant connection with Lucille still existed and no matter how beautiful his wife looked in the ethnic dress, he didn't need a reminder of all that had gone before. He wondered what he would say and do if he saw Lucille, but it was unlikely to happen in this teeming city.

"I'll wear it tonight, only for you, Landman," she said, smiling coyly.

Kathy had booked an afternoon tour on the funicular railway to Penang Hill, the hill he'd climbed with Lucille, but this time it was a sedentary and tourist-orientated journey. They passed hikers crossing the track at various places and he envied them their freedom tramping in the great outdoors; it was splendid but not as splendid as his beloved Jacana Creek and Apricot Springs. The train reached the top terminus and the passengers spilt out onto the viewing platform, already overcrowded with sightseers.

*****

On their last day, Kathy booked a guided tour to the Penang butterfly farm at Teluk Bahang. The ship's bursar promoted it as a must-see destination. It was not in Cord's mind to visit a butterfly farm; he had seen the natural menagerie of wild butterflies in the rainforest at Tanah Rata, but Kathy wanted to go, so they went. The bursar was right; the park lived up to expectations, but the photos Cord took of Kathy laughing and surrounded by a whirling mass of butterflies reminded him of a past that continued to haunt him. This really wasn't the right place to come on his honeymoon.

Part of the tour was a banquet lunch at a seaside bistro, with the afternoon free to shop or walk the coastline. The coach group were ushered to tables already prepared and overlooking the bay. Cord recognised it as the place where he and Lucille had met. They sat at a table for four with an American couple from Texas who introduced themselves as Rex and Trudy.

"Where you folks from?" Rex asked.

"Australia," said Cord.

"Aussies, eh! Never been there, but it's on our bucket list, eh Trudy? Where in Australia? Sydney?'

"No, Perth. Three thousand kilometres on the other side of the country."

"Ya don't say. What's that in miles?"

"About two thousand."

"Ya don't say."

"Are there kangaroos and snakes there?" Trudy asked.

"Not any longer," Cord teased.

"Ya don't say. Have you been to the US?" Rex asked.

Kathy replied, "I've been to Houston, to a Brahman Breeders Congress, just last year."

"Well, ya don't say. Did ya hear that, Trudy? That's where we come from. And you're a real Aussie cow gal?"

Rex was in the motor trade; heavy haulage sales of Mack and Kenworth was his game. He was impressed when he heard that Kathy drove a rig, a 1994 Western Star and further impressed to find she and Cord were honeymooners.

"Join us at our table back at the ship tonight. Meet some of our other Texans. Sherman's in the cattle trade and so's his missus, Shirl. She rides broncs at rodeos. Should be able to swap yarns with her."

"I don't know what to eat in these places," Trudy remarked, "I truly don't."

She was a short, dumpy woman with a ready smile. A waiter came to their table, an elderly man dressed in Malay attire. He bowed, clasped his hands together and said, "*Selamat petang*. Would you like to order?"

"What do you recommend, Cord? You've lived here before," Kathy said.

"Fried chicken," he said automatically.

The waiter turned to look at Cord and mutual recognition dawned; it was Denny. He smiled broadly, "Ah, Mr Cord. You have come back."

He then looked across at Kathy. Rex butted in, "They're on their honeymoon. Let's have an Anchor brew to celebrate. Not as good as a Buddy, but okay."

Denny nodded, lowered his eyes, looked back at Cord and then away.

The food and beverages came, served by a different waiter, and Cord never saw Denny again.

They took leave of Rex and Trudy and strolled to the beach. A light breeze flicked at the sails of a yacht gliding across the bay; a flotilla of sailboats was already at anchorage. For a while, Cord and Kathy sat on a bench under the shade of a tall palm, watching another small vessel tacking and jibbing its way through the fleet to a mooring closer to the shore.

Cord went to put his arm around Kathy and kiss her, but she pulled away. "Who was she?" she said.

"Who was who?"

"There was someone, I know. You've been distracted all day and even yesterday on the railway like you don't want to be here. And that man, that waiter, the way he looked at you, at first smiling and then looking away.

Disappointed somehow when that Rex guy mentioned our honeymoon. He knew you. You must have been here with someone else. Who was she?"

Cord was flummoxed and didn't know what to say. She was right, of course; it had affected him. He didn't answer immediately, and the question hung in the air, awkward and arcane.

Kathy stood up. "I'm going back to the coach."

Cord watched her walk away from the same beach, the same restaurant Lucille had fled from all those years ago. It was déjà vu. He followed, dejected and dazed, and they didn't speak again till much later in the evening. It was their first real disagreement and it brought home to him the commitment made in marriage. He had to tell her everything.

There was a smart dress code for dinner on the cruise. Kathy chose her new Malay ensemble and Cord wore his cream wedding suit, pale blue shirt and tie. Rex, Trudy and their dinner party welcomed them with open arms. Champagne was ordered for the newlyweds and the main meal of veal scaloppini marinated in red wine was superb. Kathy mellowed as the evening wore on and the male Texans, all of them old enough to be her father, were enchanted by this amazing, authentic cowgirl from down under.

In their cabin afterwards, showered and in her nightdress, Kathy asked for the third time, "Who was she?"

"Sweetheart, that was a long time ago. Yes, I was at that restaurant. She was the sister of one of the guys and it was only a few dates. She showed me around the island, that's all. I wasn't here for long and she went back to finish her studies in America. Her brother told me she was promised in marriage to someone here. That's their custom and that's all I know. I haven't heard from her since. The whole place seems strange to me now; everything is blurred. What can I say, except I'm here with you and I love you."

Silently, Kathy slipped into bed and turned away from him. He slid in behind her, put his arms around her and pulled her to him, fitting his body to the curve of hers. The ship heaved in the ocean swell as they lay together, two lovebirds in a nest. She turned to him, her blue eyes misty and tender.

"I love you, Cord," she said.

Homecoming
2002

Lucille gazed in the mirror, her fingers softly tracing the caesarean scar still prominent across her abdomen. Sure, the outline was slowly fading, but she knew it would never diminish enough to allow her to wear a bikini. Although, that was something she'd never have the opportunity to wear anyway.

She thought of her lost son, who sadly didn't have a name, and wondered about the child's father, who had left her without a word. Sometimes, she thought of throwing away the photograph with the butterflies and the Chocolate Sailor keepsake, but she could never quite do it because she had to admit, it was one of the happiest days of her life.

It was Saturday morning on a free weekend and it was cold out. She dressed casually in a warm light grey hoody with matching track pants. She brushed her hair, rolled it in a bun and donned a black embossed Nike cap. It was good to slip into a comfy pair of joggers and out of the heeled shoes she wore all week. She checked that her leather shoulder bag had everything required for a day's outing, especially her Polaroid sunglasses.

As she left the building, Sam, the elderly, uniformed security guard, said, "Good morning, Miss Lucille. It's going to be cold out, but fine."

"Good morning, Sam. Yes, it looks like a lovely day."

The last few years had been good to her and she worked at keeping a trim and taut figure with regular workouts at the gym. Any spare time, which wasn't much, was spent in hiking segments of the Appalachian Trail with the local walking clubs. She didn't have a man in her life and actually avoided lasting relationships, regarding herself as a one-man woman. Social activities revolved around art exhibitions, collecting small sculpture pieces, research writing, live shows, musicals and opera.

Lucille had taken an interest in the history of Indigenous people and, on some Saturdays like this one, would catch a bus across town to the Smithsonian Museum complex to spend the day there, mainly at the Freer and Sackler Art Galleries. Of late, Lucille also enjoyed the artefacts and library in the National Museum of the American Indian.

She'd hit the big league in the Department of Commerce and had risen to a senior position in the Office of Business Liaison, with several of her business papers published. She was a regular on the university circuit, conducting workshops for academic staff regarding developments in current work practices and public affairs.

The following week, she'd return to Penang for the first time since leaving under a cloud. It was a reluctant but necessary visit, not because of Rodney's insistence that she come to the banquet to be held in honour of the family leaving Penang, but for other more important reasons.

When Rodney rang several weeks before, typically smarting about business obligations, he declared, "It's essential you attend. Kim Li will be here and your presence will be noted as a sign of good faith between our families, especially after your wedding contract was cancelled."

Angrily, she replied, "Your wedding contract, not mine."

Lucille's personal reasons for accepting the invitation were to see her ageing parents and meet her three-year-old niece, Mia, for the first time. On a business trip to Geneva the year before, she bought a fluffy, cuddly cow for the child. It had large eyes, a goofy smile and let out a deep, long 'moo' when squeezed. She wanted Mia to have it while she was still young enough to enjoy it.

She arrived in Penang unannounced to surprise her parents, who were leaving soon to settle in Kuala Lumpur with Rodney. The road to Pantai Aceh wound its way through the familiar hills of her youth and memories flooded back each time the taxi crossed one of the many trails she'd hiked in the past. It was hard to believe that the grand, spacious house her father built in the jungle would soon be sold to strangers.

The taxi driver retrieved the luggage from the boot as her father and mother came onto the porch. Her mother's eyes brimmed with tears and her father approached with his arms wide. They embraced, and he welcomed her home, clutching her tightly.

They relaxed on sofas in the lounge overlooking the jungle courtyard; how she missed the familiarity of this home in the lush rainforest. The furnishings hadn't changed, the palm tree fronds still hung over the veranda, providing welcoming shade, and overhead, the same slow fans cooled the interior. A servant Lucille hadn't met brought in a tray of iced tea and sugar biscuits.

It was pleasant to speak her native Malay again, as her parents still hadn't grasped English. Even though she'd sent many emails via Rodney, they wanted her to repeat everything about her life in America and her travels. They emphasised how proud they were of her accomplishments.

The conversation became awkward when her mother, under the impression Lucille was infertile, asked, "Were you able to do anything about making babies? There must be drugs. Soong Tran's wife died and he's looking for a new wife."

Lucille recalled Soong Tran was elderly, at least sixty.

"Mother! Soong Tran! Really?"

She missed the customs and traditions of her home and past life, but arranged marriages? Never.

There was a tiredness about her parents, probably from resignation on leaving the family home. Her father was bereft of the verve and vigour she remembered so well; he'd always been confident, positive and reliable. Mother was a little stooped and greyer. A child cried somewhere in the house and Mother gestured for Lucille to follow and explained that they were looking after Mia until Rodney returned home in a few days.

Rodney had an interior decorator renovate and refurbish one of the guest bedrooms into Mia's nursery. Lucille was impressed; the cot bed, tables, chairs, chest of drawers and wardrobe were good quality rattan. The walls were a delicate shade of pink, as was a large floor rug. An overhead fan with pink teddy bears imprinted on the blades silently fluttered away. The cot was covered with a gauze-like material to thwart the intermittent mosquito. On the shelves were cushions and an array of toys, some cuddly bears and an assortment of gaily coloured plastic playthings.

The child was no longer crying but wide awake and playing with a soft plastic ball. The two women tiptoed over to the edge and looked in. A smile briefly crossed Lucille's face and then tears moistened her eyes as she looked upon this plump little figure attired in a white cotton 'onesie' pyjama suit, chortling to herself with legs and arms pumping. Her Eurasian features were apparent; an angular face and a finer-shaped nose were complemented by enchanting slanted brown eyes and full petal lips, which opened in a broad smile at the sight of the two women. She was a beautiful child; for Lucille, it was a moment of pure love and emotion. Her mother bent, lifted Mia and passed her to Lucille to hold.

"Be careful, she's heavy. She's toddling now, almost running," her mother said. "Always on the move."

Lucille was surprised at her weight. The child settled in her arms and stared at Lucille for a while. Then Mia nestled her head on her shoulder and began to suck her thumb. Lucille's anger towards her brother faded; it was no time for bitterness, even though the child in her arms brought back the memory of what she'd lost and that secret part of her life she must keep from her parents.

But resentment still lingered. It wasn't fair that she gave up the man she loved because of some draconian business arrangement; unjust that she suffered the pain and anguish of losing a son who was whisked away, only for Lucille to become an outcast in her own land of birth. All this while Rodney had a child out of wedlock with an English woman the family had never met and that was deemed acceptable? It angered her.

It was clear from correspondence that Father and Mother doted on the child, unaware they had a grandson somewhere in the world. Unknown to Rodney, Lucille used her influence in the department to trace the adoption papers, but to no avail. He'd covered it up well, as though the child had never existed.

She spent golden days with her parents, enjoying their company, but when Rodney arrived later in the week, he seemed jaded and destroyed the tranquil mood. Mother scolded him for working too hard. He spent much of his time in deep, meaningful conversations with Father in private rather than spending time with Mia; he was more inclined to pass her to his mother.

Lucille spoke to Rodney. "Mia's lovely," she declared. "I could bundle her up and take her home."

"She is home," he replied darkly.

*****

The farewell banquet was well catered for and over one hundred guests strolled the house and grounds. Kim Li and his family were there. She felt like a leper and defenceless under their quiet scrutiny, knowing they carried the false knowledge of her infertility. However, it would soon be over and she'd return to the comfort and security of her Washington apartment.

172

Standing alone on the lawn and listening to the guest speeches honouring her parents, she became aware that a man had sidled up next to her. It was Denny.

"It is good to see you home, Miss Lucille."

"Thank you, Denny. It is good to be home, but only for a short time. I won't be around when the house sells. Rodney's taking care of that."

"It's sad to see your parents leave. Everything is changing."

"Are you selling the bistro?"

"Oh no. My son Henry is taking over. I saw Mr Cord here a month ago. He was on a boat cruise."

At the mention of his name, Lucille's heart skipped a beat. Had he returned for her?

"Here?"

"Yes, he was on his honeymoon with his lady bride."

Lucille couldn't believe the sudden pain and dread that jolted through her body. She'd never contemplated that Cord would or could be married; it seemed impossible.

"Honeymoon?" her voice choked in disbelief as she questioned what was said.

Denny looked keenly at her, noting her reaction. "Yes, she's very pretty, and they were celebrating with their American friends."

A waiter came by with drinks and in the distraction of the moment, she was able to quickly excuse herself.

Broken and bewildered, she retreated to her room. She didn't cry; she just stared blankly at the walls. So, it was true what Rodney had said. Cord was a womaniser! All this time, she had lived a false hope that he'd return to her, a dream now shattered. Eventually, she curled into a tight ball on the bed and drifted into a deep, troubled sleep. Her mother came and covered her with a blanket.

The morning she left, she placed the cuddly cow next to the sleeping child, bent over the cot and kissed her softly on the cheek. Mia stirred, threw out a little hand that Lucille held briefly, then tucked it back in under the bedspread.

The taxi came after lunch. She embraced her parents, Mother crying and holding Mia, Father looking glum, standing on the porch sadly waving goodbye. She nodded to the driver and as the taxi moved down the drive, she looked back and watched the house and the people she so loved recede from view.

On the way to the airport, she asked the driver to pass by the manor in the side alley just off Lebuh Light. It was empty and bare; Lucille felt the same.

Maggot
2002

The honeymoon was over. Cord and Kathy had been back at Jacana Creek for six weeks when Kathy said, "It's time you learnt to ride. I can't have my husband remaining a greenhorn ringer."

Kathy appointed Davy to teach Cord to ride, as she'd have nothing to do with it.

"He's the only person patient enough to handle the ringers, especially the really old ones," she teased.

Davy chose Mango, a quiet, four-year-old mare, for the job.

Autumn was closing in and the mornings were chilly and dark, but Cord rose early from the marital bed. He wanted to be part of the team, not just a bystander. Working with Davy, Cord became familiar with pack saddles, the smell of leather strapping, the chink of bridles, inspecting horse hooves and shoeing. For the first few days, Kathy, Ted and Albert would perch on the yard fence, chuckling as Cord attempted the challenging task of riding a horse, something he'd never contemplated.

Boris took it seriously and offered words of support. "*Bueno*, Landman. Good, good," he cried at Cord's every success and failure.

Cord usually showered rather than bathed and confessed he'd never taken so many baths as he did that first month, just to relax and soothe his aching buttocks.

"Has my little darling got a sore bottom?" Kathy teased. "Does he want mummy to ease the pain?"

As time progressed, Cord became hardened and more comfortable in the saddle. He knew he wasn't good enough to ride lead in a full cattle round up but was confident he could ride the flanks of the herd.

The Bells kept seventy horses in the breeding paddocks under Davy's care. Kathy explained she worked each of her own five horses, Penny, Mack, Twobob, Florin and Quid, over several days in a muster. Cord stood at the stockyard fence, amazed at how they'd come to her at a full gallop from the far reaches of the paddock as soon as they saw her.

Davy broke in a new mare for Cord. She showed good disposition and was a piebald, like Kathy's horse Penny. Cord named her Dollar, in keeping with names with a monetary theme. He watered her, fed her, brushed her, washed her down and under the tuition of Clarrie, the blacksmith, managed to shoe her. It was the first animal he'd ever cared for and he relished the bond that grew between him and the mare.

*****

The sun peeped over the brim of the eastern wall as the chopper threaded its way through the twists and turns of Mammoth Gorge. The highest thorny spikes of ancient rock glowed red and gold, and below, in the clefts and crevasses, deep shadows were retreating in the early morning light.

Maggot slowed the machine for Cord to see more easily the course of the creek meandering through the deep ravine.

"Have ya seen anythin'?" Maggot asked.

"Nothing yet. It's still too dark down there."

They flew through the canyon till it petered out into flat, swampy channel country beyond. As the copter passed overhead, a train of camels and a small herd of donkeys out in the open cantered away. A colourful flock of Jabiru storks flapped their wings and lifted from the reedy wetland.

Maggot swung the copter around. "Better avoid 'em. We'll head over to Little Rock Gorge and have a squizzy there."

The narrower Little Rock Gorge was shorter in length than Mammoth. It was brighter now and Cord pointed to a herd of brumbies grazing on the edge of a large waterhole. The craft flew lower; the horses stirred at the noise and wind draft, then broke into smaller groups.

Maggot explained, "See that white stallion leading that bunch out. Bugger escaped from Charcoal Flats when it was abandoned. He was tamed, broke, a bloody good quarter horse. Now the bugger's gone wild. Ted has his eye on him, but your missus says he's too old to geld and too unpredictable to handle. She'd know. The bastard would probably try to break out all the time and take a few mares with him."

Cord reflected on 'your missus'. He was now at Jacana Creek permanently, at least until Barry returned the following year. John Keep was accommodating in the arrangement for Cord to work at a distance from the station, as Rory, Cord's survey assistant, was experienced and able. Cord and his missus were grateful for John's generosity.

Cord watched the brumbies move out of the gorge and into the open plain. Maggot hovered the machine briefly, then remarked, "Nothing here. Back to Mammoth and have a look again. Ya know they could be in Big Rock Gorge on the Doig's place, out of our spread."

"Yeah, I suppose so."

The chopper turned, lifted and headed back to Mammoth Gorge, this time a little lower and slower than before. The day had brightened and halfway into the reaches, Cord saw the four feral buffalo standing in the main waterhole.

He cried out, "That's them there at ten o'clock."

Maggot spun the craft to view the beasts, saying into his headset, "Mike, Romeo, Sierra, Chopper to Jacana Base, are ya reading? Over."

Ted's crackly voice came back, "Jacana Base reading. Go ahead. Over."

"Yeah, we've got 'em. A bull and three cows. They're in Mammoth, a few k's in. Over."

"Roger that, Chopper. Albert and Boris are on their way. Should be half an hour. Over."

"Okay, Jacana. I'll settle the bus down and wait. When they're here, I'll go back in and flush 'em out. Over."

"Good-oh, Chopper. Keep me posted. Over and out."

Maggot set the craft down in a flurry of dust near the gorge entrance.

"Pity I couldn't put her down in the shade under them white gums. Ya can get out and stretch ya legs if ya want."

He took off his helmet and turned the radio on full volume so he could hear it at a distance. Cord removed his helmet and joined Maggot on a log in the shade.

Maggot's given name was Remo Magotti. He was of Australian-Italian descent, older than Cord, in his thirties. He was a short man, not more than five-foot-five tall, of thin, stringy build with golden skin that seemed stretched tight over his tiny frame. His angular face was clean-shaven, serious, not partial to smiling and had the darkest eyes. As a helicopter pilot, there was none better; Clyde said he was the best pilot he'd ever seen and called him the Michael Schumacher of Choppers.

Maggot was generally a man of few words, so Cord asked, "You been flying long?"

"Commercially, about ten years."

"Before that?"

"Air force. I was in the RAAF, aero mechanic. Worked on choppers, big ones, Bristows, Chinooks, military ones, but never flew 'em. Got me license when I got out."

Cord looked across at the sleek machine sitting low on its skids, a two-seater, bright red Robinson R22, with the words 'The Missus' painted neatly in scroll font on the canopy.

"I like the name."

Maggot brightened. "Yeah, it's me missus, all right. She's me lady. I put her to bed every night and make sure she's serviced regularly," he winked. "I look after her; she looks after me. Ya know, I went to California to the works to pick her up new before she got shipped here. It was love at first sight."

He stared at the chopper and grinned. "She's my third bird in the business and a real beauty. Go back to California every two years for a refresher course and look at the new babes. They're always younger and prettier."

Cord also grinned. "What made you choose mustering?"

Maggot looked at him quizzically. "Who wouldn't? The country, the freedom, the people. I like that song *Great Southern Land* and I feel part of it out here."

"Ted says the buffalo are a menace destroying wetlands and a threat to the cattle because they have diseases, especially respiratory sickness and diarrhoea. He calls them vermin."

"That's right. They're bloody vermin, all right, full of ticks. Those buggers get in and run with the cattle and hurt 'em too. It's hard to get buffalo out of the herd, so bloody big and dangerous with their horns, 'specially the buffalo bulls. This feral bull injured a breedin' Brahman last week, so Ted wants these four that've come in from Charcoal Flats shot and burnt. It's the only way to get rid of any ticks and diseases they're carrying. The cattle just come to drink, but these bastards come and take over the waterhole. They stand in it, shit in it, piss in it, drink it, no wonder they're diseased. Foul it up in no time. Even the camels won't drink the water."

In the distance, they could hear the roar of a vehicle approaching and then saw the dust billowing behind it as it came over the last hill.

"You've got 'em?" enquired Albert, alighting from the vehicle.

"Yep, they're a couple of k's in, so I'll go back and flush 'em out. There's a good shooting spot over on those rocks. I'll bring 'em out as slowly as I can."

Albert instructed Boris, who already had his rifle out, checking the cartridges. "We both target the bull first, then the cows, okay? When he falls, they'll stop running."

"Come on, let's get goin'." Maggot gestured to Cord.

They flew in a wide arc around the gorge to come in behind the buffalo. Cord's heart was in his mouth as Maggot dropped the chopper to just above tree height and made slow, patient progress along the gorge with the cliff faces remarkably close to the whirling blades. Around a sharp turn, they eventually confronted the animals, which began trotting then galloping in front of the machine. For what seemed a long time to Cord, but what was only a few minutes, they pursued the buffalo till they emerged from the Gorge proper. Immediately, shots rang out, the bull collapsed and Maggot swung the craft high and fast away from the scene. From the copter bubble, looking back over his shoulder, Cord could see that the cows did stop; more shots rang out and they, too, fell to the ground.

Maggot set the copter on open ground, well away from the ensuing fire site. Boris had roped the hooves and dragged the dead animals into a heap. Albert saturated the carcasses with petrol.

"One of 'em cows in a bad way. Nothin' more than a skeleton, eyes bleedin' an' covered in ticks."

Cord thought, what if she died in the waterhole? They were swimming in it not long ago.

Albert read Cord's concern.

"Don't worry. The big Wet cleans up the land. This will all be washed away soon and become whole again."

Boris ignited the pyre, which leapt into a high, savage flame.

"Landman, we can't leave 'em here to fuckin' rot. They'd pass on sickness to dingoes, eagles an' everythin'."

Cord watched the flames leap higher and turned away from the roast, an aspect of station life that faded the romance and appeal of life on the land.

It was a raw awakening to the often harsh reality and challenges of making a life on the land.

Maggot bade farewell and left, circling once over the burning carcasses as Cord and the others crammed into the Cruiser to return to the station. It was a silent drive home, and nothing was said except for one comment from Albert. "Them fellows no good. Don't care for country. Bugger up Apricot Springs real good if ya let 'em."

Cord realised it was a necessary act, albeit a sad one.

Surprisingly, his mind strayed for a moment as he recalled Maggot's parting words, "Say hello to Kathy." The man then hesitated and corrected himself, "Err, give me regards to ya missus," and so he knew there was yet another person under her spell.

Serpiennte
2003

They had forty-five applications from hopeful ringers for the new season muster. There were eight places available, which would bring the staff level to thirty-three. Cord sat in on the interview process with Ted and Kathy and was pleased to see Sofie's application come forward for a third round. They would invite the best twelve for on-site interviews and Clyde would fly them to the station for the two-day assessment. Each applicant would be evaluated in the main store without the air conditioner running, making it hot and stuffy.

Ted said, "It's to gauge their reaction to the heat and humidity. Second-timers are the best; they're already trained. We know they can think for themselves in the midst of the muster. I'm glad to see Sofie back. That girl has what it takes to become permanent if that's what she wants."

"Do you think Boris will welcome her back?" Kathy asked with a half-smile.

Cord replied, "What do you mean?"

"She's making a fortune out of the man's swearing. At least it's for a good cause, the Children's Cancer Foundation."

Cord laughed, "The fortune will grow. All the fines in the world won't cure him."

Kathy gathered the pile of application papers. "We'll sit on this overnight and decide in the morning. Dad? What say Cord helps me with planning the muster program? Davy sorts out the new ringers with Sofie, and Clarrie concentrates on the first camp draft, leaving you and Albert with time to put all the pieces together?"

"Okay, that'll work. I want to start the muster towards the end of March, so we've only got a month to get everything right."

"I'll keep my eye on the training and make sure the new ringers are horse trained and matched to their own animals by the time the drive commences. A few other things need attention. Our new stock horses have to be broke. Albert will be running that. It's early morning work, so Cord, when you're not helping me, you can be his offsider. What do you say? And who do you think should keep the trail bikes and vehicles serviced and in good repair for later in the season?"

"Boris!" they said in unison.

The pace of life quickened. Kathy was absorbed in mapping out the mustering staff program, attending to accounts, ordering provisions with her mother and monitoring the progress of each ringer for temperament and skill level.

It was early to rise and late to bed for Cord and he felt awkward handling these new and strange tasks he was assigned. He was all at sea, something like his first days on the *Spree*. He was undoubtedly busy, but it was only in the humdrum of station life, an existence on the periphery of the main action, the muster. He longed to be working stock at outcamps, paying his way, but the months went by and he was restricted to the homestead. Kathy said it was important he be there with Joan by the radio.

He occasionally checked the horses in the breeding paddock, rode Dollar whenever he could and agisted Barry's purebred young bull, Jim Beam, that had just arrived from America.

Kathy would come home as often as she could "To check on my man and see he's not getting into any mischief," she said.

One evening, she cooked a delicious meal of lasagne and apple pie. It was an intimate setting at a table for two with starched cloth, silver setting and candles on the veranda. They relaxed afterwards on a comfy cushioned sofa and sipped a chilled Chardonnay. A soft breeze wafted the sweet scent of the Frangipani trees into the air and the moon rose big and bold, casting a silvery glow that completely encircled the homestead and the two lovers. The night was warm and sultry; she moved close to him and nestled her head on his shoulder.

"You see, I can do other things than ride horses."

"I know you can."

Kathy wanted a child and they made love every time she returned. Cord basked in her sunshine. He loved this beautiful woman sighing below him and that last fierce, exquisite moment of climax. He was a lucky man, and it wasn't for the lack of trying that they didn't conceive.

*****

It was late in the season. Over the year, cattle moved around the station in small, isolated and separate mobs, foraging for food and drinking from waterholes and bores. The breeding cows and weaners had been sorted. The remaining cattle were still to be rounded up, sorted, yarded, trucked and sold for export. When the chopper arrived with the returning crew, some of whom traded their trail bikes for horses, Cord finally got to join the final stages of the muster.

Boris was in his trusty Patrol and Cord joined him as radioman, responding to the copter's call when a mob was sighted.

Boris said, "The idea, Landman, is not to be fuckin' gung-ho but to get behind 'em and work 'em into the makeshift yards the boys set up around the place."

This was Boris's specialty; he was a skilled driver and loved the chase. He'd often told Cord of driving trucks, 'big fuckin' rigs' all over Europe, Spain, Russia and the UK.

"Why don't you drive the cattle truck here?" Cord asked.

"That's another fuckin' story," was all the big man said.

Cord saw rounding up stock was easier said than done. On one hand, it was the country itself; the dust and scrub, intoxicating heat, rocks and potholes. On the other hand, it was the cattle's nature to scatter, requiring the bikes and vehicles to dodge and weave, homing in on any animals that broke away from the mob, especially maverick bulls, which could unpredictably stop and turn on the rider.

"See that hole there, Landman." Boris pointed to the passenger's door. "Fuckin' buffalo bull almost got me last year."

It was dangerous work, exciting and satisfying. At the end of each day, with the cattle yarded but still agitated and snorting, the crew relaxed and washed up as best they could. The campfire kept the mozzies away, and eventually, the rigours of the day faded as the smell of freshly baked damper, grilled steak and onion filled the air.

Ted and Albert carefully inspected each yarding and each animal, choosing those to be cut out and released from the main mob for various reasons. They took their time, as it was necessary for the livestock to settle before they'd be moved to the homestead yards. They'd been running wild for a year, with little human contact, so they needed to be approached in a peaceful way.

Around the campfire, in the third week of the muster, Ted said to Cord, "I suppose you wonder what this is all about. What's the next step?"

"I see the chopper's left and the crew have returned to the homestead to bring up horses."

"Yep, we're in the final stage. You see, you've got to know your breed. We've been working Brahman for a long time. Compared to other breeds, they're sensitive creatures. They don't like noise and are quite jittery. The chopper and vehicles are necessary to bring them in from the bush, but from here on, we move them to the main yard with horses and dogs to cut out the noise. Our dogs are trained not to bark. Using only the vehicles, we had the mobs galloping, which made them lose weight, so now the round up is slow and easy-paced. We let them forage at will."

Cord dossed early and was awakened by his tent zipper being drawn and then a warm, perfumed figure slipped onto the mattress beside him.

"Hush, Landman," she said. "I've brought up the horses, Dollar, as well. You can ride flank with me tomorrow. Our first muster together."

"I was hoping to ride with you now," he smiled.

"You're a naughty boy. Go to sleep."

He felt her arm around him, dozed and then drifted into a deep sleep; all was right with the world.

The cattle had settled and when all the yards were cleared and dismantled, the herd was merged into a main mob totalling two thousand head. Ted and Albert had chosen 'leaders', individual animals with a quiet temperament. These would take the lead and the others would mindlessly follow. The stockmen kept the mob in a tight bunch and hardly had to work their mounts, as a good quarter horse is itself cattle savvy. The dogs kept at the mob's heels and close enough to keep them on pace to stop stringing. Dollar responded to Cord's every touch and he felt this was outback life at its absolute best.

The muster ended and life returned to normal except for the endless convoy of cattle trucks that shuttled backwards and forwards, transporting the cattle to the auction yards in town.

*****

One day, it all turned sour.

Cord was out with Kathy and Boris at a bore. The windmill sails needed adjusting and one sail had broken off in a recent storm and lay on the ground. Kathy climbed the ladder with Cord helping and winching the broken sail into position. He was also on standby to assist Boris with a leaking water trough nearby. Boris was underneath the bowl, searching for the break, when he let out a scream.

He clambered out, holding his wrist and ran towards Cord. "Fuckin' *serpiennte!*" he cried and fell to his knees just as Cord reached him.

Cord knelt and grabbed hold of him, resting his head on his knee.

"Fuckin' snake, Landman!" The big man shivered and stiffened. A tiny glob of saliva seeped from his lips, his eyes rolled back and his whole body convulsed. Suddenly, he was still.

Kathy came running. Cord cried out in anguish as the tears welled within him, "Oh, my God! Oh, my God, don't die on me, you crazy, fuckin' Spaniard."

But he did.

It was all over so quickly. It was the saddest moment in Cord's life. He cradled the big man in his arms and sobbed uncontrollably. Kathy crouched beside him, held him and wept. How could this have happened?

The following days passed in a daze. Cord slept a great deal and when he woke, the horror of it all returned. It was not a nightmare; no, it was real. He was inconsolable. The station was in mourning and people came from all over to pay their respects. Corrine flew up to be at Cord's side at the funeral.

Conversation at the dinner table, usually bubbly and breezy, was subdued and dismal. The station was forlorn. Boris was to be buried in the homestead cemetery at the breeding paddock on the cliff at the head of the creek, overlooking the ocean. Funeral arrangements had to be completed and Cord was adamant that he would pay and arrange for the headstone.

He said to Kathy, "What about his wife and children? He was saving to bring them out here. Who's going to tell them?"

"Didn't you know? His wife and children are dead. They died in a car crash; Boris was driving. He came out here, as far from Spain as he could get, to be away from it all. Why do you think he drank so much? He was lost in a dream."

Cord was astonished. "He never told me."

"He never told anyone. Dad only knew because he was able to track his passport and that was because of Albert."

"Albert?"

"Yes. Albert told Dad he could feel that man's spirit was sad and his heart broken. We found out what had happened but kept his secret."

Two weeks after the funeral, the headstone arrived and in a private ceremony with only the family, Albert, May, Davy and Sofie present, it was erected on the grave. Sofie buried a two-dollar coin in the soil and, half-laughing, half-crying, said, "I confiscated this one last week; he might need it to buy a beer."

The white marble headstone with black engraving read: In Memory of a Gentle Giant. Bonito 'Boris' Bautista. Died 12 Dec 2003. Aged 38 years.

Loving Husband to Emilia and Father to Isla and Elena. Here lies a Mighty, Mighty Man.'

For the coroner's report, the station hands dug out the trough and found the snake's nest. It was a Northern Death Adder, considered one of the most venomous snakes in the world.

Ted said, "In all my years here, there's never been a snake bite. It's just bad luck."

Cord grieved; he missed his friend. Life would never be the same and he'd curse snakes for the remainder of it.

Decisions
2003

Try as they might, Cord and Kathy couldn't erase the melancholy that began with the death of Boris, a melancholy that deepened as they tried to have a child. The invitation to join Cord's family for Christmas down south gave them the opportunity to consult a gynaecologist with their concerns.

It was unbelievable. How could this happen when they loved each other? Surely, this was no more than a temporary setback in their plans. After all, they were both healthy, active people in the prime of life. It was a private personal affair, which they shielded from the family as best they could.

Cord felt a change in Kathy as she underwent the clinical tests, unexpectedly questioning the possibility of infertility. He felt the same way; perhaps he had failed her as a man. A rift grew between them and there were long periods of awkward silence as they became engrossed in their own worlds, unable or not wanting to share their concerns with each other. Who was to blame, or was it both of them? Were their bloodlines incompatible? Consequently, it was difficult to become absorbed in the joyful atmosphere of the festive season as they anxiously awaited their results.

One morning, at breakfast, while Kathy still slept, Corrine asked, "What's wrong, Bruv? You look down."

"Nothing, just tired. Must be a touch of Malaria, like Mum says."

"Codswallop! You're not yourself and neither is Kathy. She's always so full of beans. Is there something wrong between you?"

Cord reluctantly told her of their concerns and how much it had affected Kathy's psyche, even his own.

"She's always run the show and now it looks like it's running hers. The longer we wait for our test results, the more it dulls her spirit. But I feel the same way. Perhaps I can't have children."

"Maybe, but let's face that when we come to it. Tell you what, I'll take her out for lunch tomorrow and we'll catch a film. Get her shopping for Christmas. That'll cheer her up."

Christmas was a lovely day. Eileen's roast turkey was superb; Corrine's plum pudding was mouth-watering. The oohs! and aahs! as the Christmas crackers were pulled and presents opened encouraged more waves of laughter and bubbly banter. It was a happy time and thankfully brought Kathy out of her shell. She seemed happier and that made Cord happy, too.

It was just as Keith said when carving the roast at lunch, "Happy wife, happy life."

"That man, really, what would he know?" Eileen exclaimed, rolling her eyes.

*****

In the New Year, Doctor Clifford's receptionist called to arrange an appointment to discuss the results of the tests.

"About time," Kathy said.

She was anxious to get back to the station. Barry had completed his degree and was back at Jacana permanently, and with Kathy in Perth, they hadn't seen each other over the Christmas period either.

It was a surprise that he'd brought a guest home with him. Her name was Patricia Best, a fellow student and farm girl from the Wheatbelt. It looked like she was his intended and Kathy was anxious to meet her before she left.

"Very nice lass," Joan said on the phone. "You'll like her."

Doctor Clifford was tapping at her computer when the receptionist ushered Kathy and Cord into the room. She quickly swivelled in her chair and smiled at them both.

"Please sit down. I hope you had a pleasant Christmas."

They both nodded, "Yes."

The room was decorated in soft blue tones and a large window opened onto a lush, dense indoor garden. It was a calming, peaceful environment. Doctor Clifford was a tall, elegant woman in her forties, now dressed impeccably in a grey business suit, distinct from the blue tunic and pants garb she wore during the clinical tests. As usual, her demeanour was positive, warm and comforting. She smiled again and removed her gold-rimmed reading glasses.

"Whenever I speak to partners about the issues of childbirth, I'm always aware of the impact of what I say. The question of fertility and infertility strikes at the very heart of a couple's relationship and natural expectation, but it's my hope that my patients keep on loving one another."

Kathy went to speak, but the doctor raised her hand to stop her and continued, "The facts are that while you both have no physical problems in the mechanics of sexual intercourse, the result will not be conception."

Cord and Kathy looked at each other in disbelief. Kathy shuddered as Doctor Clifford went on, "Kathy, our tests show that right now you are a healthy individual, but evidently some years ago, perhaps as a child, you contracted a streptococcal or a staphylococcal infection which resulted in acute endometritis, affecting your uterus and causing infertility. The symptoms may have been mild at the time and passed with little notice. I'm sorry to say there's no medical cure for this. I'm so sorry."

She rose from her desk, came to Kathy and put her arm around her. Kathy was in disbelief and sat there staring, tears welling in her eyes. Cord was distressed; having a child seemed such a natural event. Without ever questioning it, he assumed he would one day be a father.

Doctor Clifford returned to her desk. "I'll be contacting you again in a few weeks. I can put you in touch with other couples who've faced the same problem if you so wish and there are other options available which I'd like to discuss with you."

Kathy withdrew completely. They left the clinic like robots, not speaking, not touching and in the car park, Kathy said, "I want to go home."

"But… Doctor Clifford?"

"I want to go home. Now."

"You don't mean it."

"Now! Alone!" she shouted. "Leave me, Cord. I want to go home alone."

"I cannot let you do this, Kathy. You're my wife."

She remained silent and slumped into the passenger seat of the car. She sobbed as tears flowed readily down her cheeks. She gazed blankly out of the window. Without looking at her, Cord started the car and said, "Wherever you go, I go too."

*****

On a clear southern summer morning, they flew home to the warm, humid, tropical north and the Wet.

Maggot was flying the fortnightly delivery to the station in the two-seater chopper and could only take Kathy and some of their luggage. Dexter wouldn't be doing his deliveries till the next month, leaving Cord to arrange a lift with a rig hauling windmill parts and accessories to the station. He was a week behind Kathy in the process. The roads were quagmires, but Kell, the driver, had driven these roads many times and prided himself on getting the goods through.

"Good money in it in the Wet. Lot of the other truckies won't have a bar of it, fair-weather trucker fuckers. Leaves plenty for me."

There was no one to meet Cord at the station when he arrived. He opened the main gate to the homestead drive. The house looked the same but seemed a little sad, or perhaps it was just his mood. The Frangipani trees had lost their leaves, the drive was wet and muddy and the sprinklers weren't clicking away. There was no big man saying, "Welcome back, Landman. Let's have a fuckin' beer." And worst of all, there was no Kathy.

He went around the veranda to the back door and into the kitchen. May was preparing a beef shank and looked up, a little surprised.

"Oh, Mr Cord. Miss Kathy didn't know when to expect you. They're all over at Ludlow Hills helping clear up. They'd a big blow over there coupla days ago. Mrs Joan is here; she's in her room. Shall I fetch her?"

"No, it's okay. Do you have a cup of coffee?"

May looked at him sadly, and he knew that everyone knew.

"Yeah, can I make you a sandwich?"

He tried to be cheerful, "That would be great. Thanks, May. I'll just put my gear in the room."

He lay on Kathy's bed, the bed they had shared on their wedding night and slept, forgetting about the coffee and sandwich. He woke suddenly from a rap on the door; it was late afternoon.

Joan's voice called, "Cord, are you all right?"

"Yes, I'm sorry. I must have dozed off."

"We're having early dinner, so come down when you're ready."

He washed up and found that it was just him and Joan for dinner.

"They're still at Ludlow. Quite a bit of damage there. I don't expect them home tonight."

"Perhaps I can go over and help."

"Well, Ted suggested that when you turn up, you could help Albert with the breeding cows and horses."

"Okay."

Joan broached the awkward subject that was on both their minds.

"I don't know how she could have contracted such a thing, Endomet… something." Joan paused, baffled, and Cord felt sorrow for the mother. "Kathy's always been such a healthy girl, and they say there's nothing we can do. Ted said we should get a second opinion."

"We went to the best. I reckon a second opinion would only cause more anguish."

May came into the room and quickly cleared the dishes.

"Will you have that coffee now, Mr Cord?"

He nodded.

"In the lounge," said Joan.

They sat on the soft sofas in a fabric Kathy had chosen. Joan clasped her hands and said, "How are you coping with this, Cord?"

"How are we coping? It's been a tough time and I hope we can put it behind us. Our doctor said most couples need counselling and I'm happy to do that, but I've had no response from Kathy. I love her, but I can't get her to engage with me. I don't know what to do."

"Neither do we. We've noted a big change. She kept to her room for the first few days and we were concerned that you two had broken up. Then, she finally told me. After that, she spent three days with our community Aboriginal women and then rode to Apricot Springs for a swim with young Sofie the next day. And yesterday, right out of the blue, she joined the crew helping out at Ludlow Hills. We don't know what to expect from her."

Cord had to admit, he didn't know either.

*****

Cord breakfasted early, ready to help Albert and found him at the stable yard with the horses that needed shoeing. Albert extended his hand and held Cord's for some time, his dark eyes reflecting empathy and understanding.

"I brought Dollar over for ya. She's over there in the next yard."

Cord took two carrots from the chaff bag hanging on the stable door and went to the yard fence. The moment Dollar saw him, she cantered over and nuzzled her head on his shoulder. He patted her neck fondly and gave her the carrots.

"At least you're glad to see me."

Albert drove the Cruiser to the top breeding paddock. It was an all-day excursion and May had prepared a large picnic lunch.

"Women! She's always tellin' me I'm too fat, then she gives me this."

Cord grinned and asked what had been going on while he was away.

Albert went on, "Ted retired six horses and brought in another six, bred by Sharon Doig. I gave Ginger to me grandson, Davy's boy, and Smack to me eldest granddaughter. Ted gave the others away. Barry's breedin' cows have mated with his Yankee bull. Interestin' to see what happens there. There was a salty down at the head of the creek last week. We haven't known 'em to get up over the waterfall into the creek up here, but ya never know with those bloody crocs. He was a big bastard, four metres. He's no longer with us."

"I thought they were a protected species."

"Depends. Not with my people. We can shoot 'em, but Ted can't. Sometimes it's good to have a black fella on ya land," he chuckled. "What da' ya think, Landman?"

"You mean *your* land, don't you?"

Albert smiled and nodded his head; his white teeth glowed. "You're a good man, Landman. Better get back. Storm's brewing."

They looked at the high clouds gathering in the distance. White curling tops were unfurling over a developing dark grey underbelly that now and then glowed with the faint flicker of lightning.

"How's the livestock in this weather?" Cord questioned.

"They'll be right. Bloody storm may not get over this way. You're in the Wet now, Landman, anythin' can happen. Ludlow Hills copped it all right."

Back at the homestead, Joan said Ted had called on the radio and they hoped to be back that evening, but after the evening meal, Cord sat alone on the veranda, watching the distant flashes of light and hearing the occasional muffled sound of rolling thunder. It was humid and sultry; it hadn't rained yet.

The storm approached, and Cord retired inside. With each flash, he saw the Frangipani trees bowing and sighing as the wind swept and gusted through their bare branches. Suddenly, it was upon the house and rain pelted down. The noise on the tin roof almost cut out the crack of thunder that followed each blinding lightning bolt. Showers of water cascaded over the bursting eaves and the torrent swirled down the drive. So, this was the Wet.

Then, as quickly as it had come, it was gone. The rain eased then stopped, the lightning and thunder receded and the moon came out from behind a break in the cloud. It was just as though it had never been.

Cord couldn't sleep and went out onto the veranda to watch the retreating storm. The humid night returned and the moon glowed brightly. Drops of water dripped from post and plant; the shock of it all kept the mosquitoes buzzing. He was moved by the storm, its impact on the land and how quickly it passed. There was a message in it if only he could describe it in words. He set out to write a letter to Kathy with all he wanted to say but couldn't write a word, so he returned to the room. Despite the overhead fan, the humidity was unbearable. He stripped off his clothes and lay naked on the bed inside the mosquito net.

Sometime in the night, he woke as a warm, perfumed body slid into bed beside him. He didn't stir and feigned sleep; he was thankful Kathy was close.

In the morning, she was still beside him. Cord reached out, but she pushed his arm away.

"Don't," she said. "We have to talk."

With her back to him, she said, "I've thought this over. I don't want to hurt you, but I can't be a true wife. Not the wife you deserve. You deserve to be a father, to have children. It's not fair on you. I'm just a burden."

He pulled her to him, and this time, she didn't resist.

"If that's what you think, then you don't know me."

"Cord, let's face it. It's me. I can't have a child."

He turned her over to face him and kissed her tenderly. "So what? You've got me. I can be a child if you want."

She attempted a smile as a tear rolled down her cheek.

Bibbulmun
2003

After her conversation with Denny, Lucille returned to Washington a changed person.

She no longer lived in hope and the dream of a 'happy ever after'. She'd mistakenly believed that love naturally involved commitment, but it seemed men believed in only one kind of love. She'd misjudged Cord, even though Mrs Brown said he tried to contact her before he left Penang; obviously, he didn't try hard enough. Turns out she was just a one-night stand.

No one had even come close to replacing Cord in her heart. For a short time, there'd been Blake, an American-Chinese academic. They had a lot in common; he spoke Cantonese, lectured in Humanities at Yale and had a great love of the outdoors. They'd met through the hiking club and hit it off immediately.

After several dates, they kissed, but it did nothing for Lucille. He wanted to pursue the relationship further and begged her to go to Aspen with him for the winter skiing, but she declined. After a few more rejections, he drifted away. She concluded love was an algorithm of the brain. Only Cord had negotiated her flow chart, crossed the negatives and ticked the positives, but as before, she resolved she was a one-man woman. Unfortunately, Cord was not the same; that was that. She knew she should get on with life.

Lucille's interest in human rights grew, especially regarding the plight of the Native Americans. She keenly offered support in their effort to gain greater access to 'The Land of the People of Mother Earth'. She applauded the decision of the Inter-American Commission on Human Rights that the government had violated the rights of these people, referring unilaterally to the gradual deprivation of access to their ancestral lands. Human rights activists approached Lucille to assist their legal team in negotiating better rights for disadvantaged indigenous women across the globe and she considered accepting the invitation.

Over the years, she'd continued online contact, texts and the occasional phone call with Leo, her university classmate and confidant. Leo had married Helen and one day rang Lucille with a proposition. He worked for a Japanese manufacturer of tractors and, for the previous six months, had been in Australia negotiating franchises and marketing outlets and was in Perth, wrapping up the last leg of a contract. He and Helen planned to stay on for a month or so and hike a particular trail called the *Bibbulmun*, an ancient walking track of the *Noongar* Aboriginal people and invited her to join them on the venture.

Lucille had holidays due and agreed, partly because she knew that Perth was Cord's home town. Not that she'd try to contact him; it would be inappropriate even though easy to do, but just to see the land where he came from would be enough and also walk the track that he'd offered to take her on that time, long ago in Penang. Also, there was the added attraction of following in the footsteps of the native people and sensing their connection to land, an objective that appealed to her.

It was March and freezing in Washington. The days before departure, in the warm comfort of her apartment, she examined the world globe and began to wonder what on earth she'd done in accepting. Perth was an isolated place on the opposite side of the world to Washington, in the Southern Hemisphere. Resources on the internet stated it was one of the most remote cities on the planet.

The airport was snowbound and her flight delayed six hours. Twenty hours later and a trip via San Francisco, Honolulu and Sydney, Lucille finally arrived in Perth. Fortunately, she flew business class all the way and slept comfortably. The 747 descended over low green hills in clear blue skies. From her window, she could see the white beaches on the blue Indian Ocean before the aircraft turned on its final approach. The view changed to a city of high-rise buildings on the banks of a large lake or estuary. Business class through customs is always fast and soon she was in the baggage foyer with Leo and Helen running excitedly to meet her.

Despite his hiking ability, Leo hadn't lost his chubby look and Helen had put on a little weight too. They were dressed in shorts, T-shirts and joggers, looking completely relaxed.

"You look terrific," Helen said, hugging her and Leo gave an extra-long affectionate embrace.

Lucille walked out of the airport into a balmy, warm autumn day of twenty-eight degrees Celsius; it was the tonic she needed. From the taxi, she could see the city was modern and clean with, thankfully, not the same noisy traffic she experienced in Washington.

Helen was her bubbly self and said, "We'll go for a swim after lunch. I said to bring your bathers." She knew Lucille would want to wear a one-piece suit. "Right now, we'll go to our place and have crayfish for lunch, a glass of local Chardonnay and a chat. We need to know what you've been doing."

"Crayfish?"

"Yes," Leo, the perfectionist, explained. "Well, to be biologically correct, it's actually lobster, but here they call it crayfish. It's more flavoursome than American lobster. You'll see what I mean."

Their unit was on the beachfront and had views over the cleanest, whitest sand Lucille had ever seen. Sunbathers lay on the wide beach and a host of surfers were in the water catching the odd smooth swell that rolled in.

Lucille didn't swim that day as the lunch and wine made her drowsy. She dozed and woke at dusk. Leo and Helen were in the lounge watching the news on television. She went out onto the balcony as the sun was sinking, its golden ball disappearing into a sleepy ocean; there were still people on the beach and some in the water. Enchanting place, she thought and returned to the lounge.

"Sorry about the swim."

"No, it's fine," said Helen. "It's good you had a sleep. Plenty of time for a swim."

"It looks like California and the Pacific in July."

Leo laughed, "No, it's Australia and the Indian in March. Same climate, though, except here it's winter in July. We'll go to the tavern on the strip for dinner. Tasty food and cheap. What do you say?"

"Fine."

*****

The next few days, Leo and Helen showed her around the city and environs, and Lucille could understand why Cord would want to come home. Perth was a calm, beautiful city and she felt at home. Leo broached the subject of the lost child, but Lucille declined to comment, only to say, "That chapter of my life is well and truly over."

He left the subject alone and changed the subject to explain the logistics of the hiking trip, and when she baulked at the gear needed, he added, "Don't worry, it's all arranged. You only have to bring yourself. The entire trail would take up to three months to walk, but because of the limited time, I've chosen three short sections of around a hundred kilometres each. There will be overnight camping at different points, the first commencing at the trailhead at Kalamunda, in the rolling hills close to the city. The second point is amongst the tall Karri trees in the central temperate rainforest and the third at Albany, a provincial town at the trail terminus on the rugged coastline of the Southern Ocean."

"That's some impressive planning, Leo," Lucille interjected.

"That's not all," Leo continued. "I've also arranged transportation between the set down and pick up points with some of the walking clubs helping us. Rest easy. There are no grizzly bears, lions, or tigers. There are snakes, but they're sensitive creatures and you rarely see them. I walked a bit of the trail at college and only saw one, a Dugite, at Lucky Bay, and he skittled out of our way."

"You went to school here?"

"Yes, that's why I know the trail and want to walk more of it. Then I thought of you."

Lucille began a journal of the journey. She purchased a hard-backed pocket notebook and filled sixty pages with her adventures over the twelve days on the trail.

Excerpts from her notes read:

'The Perth hills are clustered with orchards of all varieties of fruit; the apricots and peaches are in season and on the first overnight camp, we indulged in the fruits of our labour.'

'The giant white-barked Karri trees, the third tallest in the world, are spectacular in their dense, lush green setting. Occasionally, a flock of red-tailed black cockatoos would come screeching overhead, annoyed at our trio of human intruders. The temperate rainforest has many rare species and the Peppermint tree's leaves taste like peppermint. Took lots of photos.'

'At a small village, we met Colin, a Noongar Elder who spoke of country. It was fascinating as he told of their six seasons. The season we were travelling in is Bunuru, the second summer. There are so many natural native foods, from goannas to witchetty grubs and much more. The Aboriginal culture is passed on from generation to generation in stories and songs called 'The Dreaming'. Colin said they are the custodians of the land and I sense a common connection between these people and the reverence the American Indian tribes have for Mother Earth. NB: Follow this up at home.'

'I'm confused. It's crazy. This notebook is so full of dates and images I'm forgetting what it's all about. The written word can't completely capture the splendour of the scenery we're crossing. The rocky bays, cliffs and shoreline of the wild great Southern Ocean are awe-inspiring. Leo's going out later to try to catch a fish. Tomorrow, we reach journey's end at Albany.'

'Here we are at last and we rang the bell. It's really for trail end-to-enders, but we couldn't help ourselves. Hugs and kisses all round. Nice comfy bed tonight. Bought a cuddly whale souvenir. This used to be a whaling town.'

Tired but buoyant, the three bussed back to Perth, giving Lucille a week to relax before flying home to winter. She shopped for souvenirs and special gifts for Leo and Helen, her faithful friends. The evening before she left, sitting on the balcony watching the sun set over a lazy ocean, Helen asked, "Do you have anyone special?"

"You mean a man? I did once. This is his home town."

"Really! Are you going to contact him?"

"No. He married someone else. It's all over."

Lucille said her goodbyes to Leo and Helen, and her sixteen-hour flight to Washington via Hong Kong touched down on a murky day. Rain had turned the roads to slush and the taxi crawled through the slow lanes of traffic. It was gloomy, but she was back home safe and secure.

Sam, the security guard, was at the cab door with an umbrella as she paid the driver.

"Good to see you home, Miss Lucille."

"Thank you, Sam."

"Did you have a pleasant holiday?"

"Yes, excellent."

The apartment was already warm from the central heating system the janitor had set for her homecoming. At the airport, she'd bought a few essentials for the fridge, expensive but convenient, considering the harsh weather outside. She'd shop properly the following day.

Unpacking her luggage didn't take long; the last item, her notebook, was cradled in a side sleeve of the case. She flicked through a few pages and smiled before placing it on the bookshelf near the Chocolate Sailor. She reflected, there you are, Cord McCullum. I did trek the *Bibbulmun* track, even though it wasn't with you.

There was nothing more to say.

Sofie
2004

At breakfast, Ted said, "We've put on a new general hand. Remember Cliff Mason? He was a ringer with us ten or so years ago. He'll be starting next month. Good bloke. He's been managing a run in the Tablelands in Queensland. Got a wife and two young'uns. Can't put him in Boris's old cabin, so can we tizzy up the blacksmith cottage? What do you think, Kathy?"

"I didn't know you'd interviewed anyone," Kathy replied.

"Oh, yes, Barry and I caught up with him. Didn't want to worry you, love. You've got enough on your plate."

Kathy and Cord glanced at each other across the table.

With Barry back at the station permanently, he was full of ideas to increase production. He was a tall, gangly man with a ready smile, full of energy and a cheerful disposition. Cord liked him, knew he had a cool head and would be calm in a crisis, essential qualities to run a big outfit like Jacana. Just two years Kathy's junior, Barry was a competent horseman with a flair for breeding Brahman cattle. Having been away studying, he lacked the experience Kathy had in supervising mustering and running the outcamps, but it was clear that he'd acquire these abilities in time. Ted relished the opportunity to have another man about the house and was soon heaping jobs on him that a few months before would have been Kathy's province.

Within a few weeks of Patricia visiting the station, she decided the distance between her and Barry was too great to have a meaningful relationship and they should go their separate ways. Barry was a little broken-hearted.

Joan said, "Such a nice girl, but don't worry, someone else will come along."

"When one door shuts, another one opens," Ted added, which turned out to be true because waiting in the wings was Sofie.

A few months before, Ted and Kathy offered Sofie the main store job as Chuck had thrown it in and gone east. It solved a festering problem for the station crew, as Chuck had the uncanny knack of rubbing people up the wrong way. It was a relief to see him go.

"Sofie's shaped up as our top jillaroo," Ted continued. "She prefers being out in the field, and I don't want to lose her, but we need someone competent in the store and there's no one else good enough. You know she's a nurse and studying veterinary stuff."

Kathy also knew that Sofie's parents had died; she had two older brothers, which led her to break away and take on new life experiences.

"She's doing what Boris did, not for the same reasons, but for the chance to be free. That's why they got along so well," Kathy said.

Sofie took on the job with unbridled enthusiasm. The store had never been so well organised and Joan, above all, appreciated the new bright and bubbly assistant. Sofie revamped ordering procedures to online via satellite phone. She convinced Ted to preserve and store some of the old machinery and artefacts, including Boris's old Patrol, rather than discarding them on the rubbish tip. She organised the community kids on a scavenger hunt to recover the lost artefacts and the results were rich and rewarding. Hands brought in rusted relics, old signs, bottles, sets of buffalo horns and an amazing set of goat horns, which she hung on the main shed door.

Sofie was in perpetual motion, a ball of enthusiasm and an attractive, vivacious brunette who caught Barry's eye.

"There's the next Mrs Bell," Kathy said. Cord agreed.

Cord and Kathy had stayed on at the station after the bitter pill of infertility rocked their marriage. For the time being, it was a safe haven. The news brought sadness for Joan, who blamed herself for not realising any symptoms that may have appeared in Kathy's youth.

She said, "I should never have let you swim. All that time you spent at Apricot Springs."

"Oh, Mum, you swam in the Springs all those years when Dad was courting you and Violet, our cook before May, and all her girls. They've all had babies. Even the doctor doesn't know how you get infected."

For Cord, it was a hard topic to mention, even though it affected his life as much as Kathy's. Doctor Clifford had been in touch offering support, particularly regarding surrogacy, which Kathy rejected out of hand, and adoption, but it was still too early to contemplate any of these solutions.

Doctor Clifford offered personal advice to Cord. "Sometimes it's the male who's infertile, but not in your case. I've found that being together and having mutual goals eases the pain you both feel now. I can recommend experienced counsellors, religious organisations and other similarly challenged couples you can talk to. Good luck, Cord."

*****

Barry finished his bacon and eggs and said to Kathy, "Kat, can you show me where Doig's cattle are getting across the creek and into our place? Albert thought it was at the six-mile, but I went down there yesterday, and it wasn't there. He said you'd know."

"Sure, it's at the eight-mile. It's not that evident. I should've marked it with tape for the hands to wire it off, but didn't have any tape with me. Cord and I'll ride down there and mark it."

"Oh, I'll come too. It'll be good to see what's happening upstream."

"Looks like the weather is building up for later, so best we take the horses. If we saddle up now, we should get back and miss the rain."

The three set off, keeping the horses at a canter, following the creek closely to the eight-mile, where the flow had cut deeply into the bedrock, the bank obscured by overhanging river gums and low scrub. It wasn't immediately obvious where the cattle crossed.

Kathy rode to the edge, squeezed her horse through some thick undergrowth and called, "Over here."

"Great pick up, Kat," Barry cried.

"I'll tape it," she replied.

"Tape needs to be high up; otherwise, the buggers will pull it down and eat it."

Kathy moved on, "There's another opening over here."

She was out of earshot, so Cord asked Barry, "I hear you call her Kat."

Barry grinned. "She's a cat all right. Purring one minute, clawing the next."

Cord thought perhaps her brother knew her better than he did.

A dam was to be excavated to trap more water in the thirsty, dry area near the western boundary. Kathy joined Ted and Barry to select a site and peg a grid for Cliff Mason to follow with the bulldozer. Cord was out of sorts;

setting out and banging pegs into the ground was his game, yet he wasn't invited along. It was a sign he wasn't needed.

He saddled Dollar and rode alone to the breeding paddock and on to Boris's grave at the top of the headland overlooking Jacana Creek and the ocean. It was breezy and the usually calm sea was covered in white caps that sent salt spray into the air and up the cliff into his eyes and nostrils. Cord dismounted, dropped the reins and Dollar stood quietly grazing on the tussocks of Bluegrass. He pulled two cans of beer from the saddlebag and squatted on the ground.

"Hello, my friend, I've brought you a fuckin' beer. What do you like? A VB or a Swan Lager?"

He waited. "Good choice. Okay, no problem. You'll have the lager, I'll have the VB."

He opened the cans and drank from one, pouring the other over the grave.

"Not a bad fuckin' drop, eh? I thought I'd better come and let you know I'll be leaving soon. Don't know when I'll be back, so take care. Sofie's around, so not too many expletives, or you'll go broke. See what you've done? I'm swearing myself. I'll have to give her a couple of bucks."

Back at the stables, Dollar sensed there was something amiss. Cord looked at her shoes; they were okay and gave her carrots from the chaff bag before letting her out into the paddock. She didn't want to go and Cord virtually had to push her through the gate, and even then, she hung back with her head over the fence looking at him.

He patted her nose. "See you later, old gal. You take care."

He left, his eyes moist, and didn't look back.

*****

The Wet had well and truly arrived and almost every day, the clouds peeled off the ocean and sent welcoming buckets of rain drenching the parched ground. Water cascaded and fell in elegant silver streamers over the once-dry waterfalls. The ever-reliable Apricot Springs merged with the floodwaters in a torrential onslaught, which sent the Jacana birds to shelter in the higher pools. The most savage storms, cyclones, came as swirling, violent, electrically charged cloudbursts that destroyed everything in their path, driving the livestock into the scrub and under the trees dotted around the paddocks.

Albert said, "Fortunately, these buggers don't come that often. Tomorrow night, it'll be clear. Let's drive to the jump-up at the twenty-mile. From there, you'll see the range in the distance and hear Mammoth Gorge singing."

Cord told Kathy, "I don't know how he knows it'll be a clear night, but anyway, he said it would. It's secret men's business."

"He knows all right. You shouldn't get wet."

So, they went. It was a clear night, in the dark phase of the new moon, with only twinkling light from the galaxies of stars lighting the sky. Stony Ridge Range was a black silhouette against the lighter blue heavens.

At the twenty-mile, on a crest in the track, they stopped.

"Listen, Cord," Albert whispered. "It's still. Listen. Can ya hear the song of Mammoth Gorge? Telling us stories. Can ya hear your story?"

Sure enough, far away, Cord could hear the momentous roar of water surging to escape the confines of the gorge. He reckoned that would be something to see by chopper. The two men sat there under the spell of the night, in awe of the place and overwhelmed by the tumultuous sound of the far-off music. After a while, Albert produced two sticks, which he beat together in rhythm, accompanied by a low, soft chant in a language unknown to Cord.

Cord knew the music was a song of farewell. "I heard my song," he said.

"I know, Landman, I heard it too."

Cord knew one day he'd have to leave. As much as he loved the station, he had to face it; here he was no more than a tag-along. He'd come to do a job that required his expertise; he was needed then and that was it. John Keep had been patient and accommodating, but one day, he'd have to return to his profession and do what he did best.

He'd lost touch with Kathy. Perhaps she'd choose to remain at Jacana, but the writing was on the wall; Barry had returned and Sofie was very much in the picture. It boiled down to whether Kathy would be content to remain in a diminished position or choose to go with him to a new life down south. Cord didn't know what her reaction would be, but the end was nigh. For several weeks, they slept beside each other but barely touched. She remained in a deep melancholy that hadn't abated, a malady that was slowly but surely eating away at her and isolating Cord. Finally, he broached the subject.

"Kathy, I've been in touch with John Keep and I need to go back to Perth. As a fellow Director, I can't rely on him to carry on alone. It's been a long time and the firm has a lot of work on the go."

"When will you go?"

"Soon. I'm hoping you'll come with me."

She didn't reply, but he knew enough from her silence what her answer was.

Maggot was flying in supplies the next week, so it was a good, clean time for Cord to leave the station.

At dinner, the night before leaving, he explained to the family that he needed to leave for business reasons. The news didn't come as a shock to them; they half-expected it and weren't surprised that Kathy wasn't going with him.

Joan attempted to make the best of it. "We'll take good care of her. When do you think you'll be back?"

Cord looked at Kathy, but she looked away, so he just shrugged and said, "Impossible to say when, but I'll be in touch."

Ted shook his hand and nodded, Barry looked sheepish and Sofie blinked and pursed her lips. Later, May approached him in the hallway, put out her hand to shake his, then stopped and hugged him instead. There was a tear in her eye.

"Good luck, Mr Cord."

Maggot was leaving early and Kathy was still sleeping, or perhaps feigning sleep, when Cord left. He only saw Albert over in the distant yard, standing on his cabin porch. They waved in unison as Cord climbed into the chopper. Soon, he was flying high over the homestead and as the craft swung away towards the west, he could see Apricot Springs and Mammoth Gorge in the distance before they also disappeared from view.

Emeralds
2004

The months dragged on and contact between Cord and Kathy was limited. Cord sent emails and texts that weren't returned. He was bewildered and shocked at what had happened and how deeply it affected Kathy's psyche. He confided in Corrine, "I think she hates me."

"Nonsense! Give her time, keep calling her and don't alienate yourself. I know her, Kathy's a good person. She doesn't hate you. She hates herself. I think she's giving you an excuse and enough time to bail out, but she loves you."

For once, his mother didn't comment, at least not to him.

One afternoon, Cord was in the workshop with Keith, who was turning a block of Marri timber into a fancy utility bowl. He stopped the machine and ran his fingers over the smooth surface. Cord told him of Corrine's comforting but twisted analogy about love and hate.

Keith smiled, "My boy, look at this timber. Marri has such a beautiful grain. You can admire it, work with it, lacquer it, but you can never change it. People are much the same. If you can understand women's intuition, you'll be struck a medal, erected a statue and given a permanent slot in the Guinness Book of Records."

Cord half-smiled and gave his father a friendly hug.

John Keep had taken a much-needed holiday, a three-month world trip. Rory had been acting on Cord's behalf in his absence and stepped up to fill the vacancy left by John, so there was continuity and smoothness in the handover.

Cord arrived back as the firm was branching into the mining sector. It involved training staff in the new 3D computer programs designed for volume calculation. Much of Cord's time was spent assessing software and applications that best suited their particular needs. It was fascinating work and he felt worthwhile at last. The firm had eight teams in the field and could have had more, but he and Rory decided not to take on any more work and concentrate on providing quality service to existing clients.

Cord was not personally familiar with the mining sector, and as a principal member of the business, he couldn't expect crews to operate in an environment he didn't know himself. He deemed it a priority to join one of the teams for the experience, but with only him and Rory running things, it wasn't easy to arrange. An opportunity arose when he met with Kevin Jameson, a long-term client, in his office at Mineral House. Kevin's company operated several mines in the Eastern Goldfields and was developing alternative interests elsewhere.

Kevin and Cord met in the company boardroom, furnished with photographs of mining equipment, site plans and grinning miners in hard hats. A polished mahogany table, surrounded by a dozen or so leather plush chairs, held a selection of plans and documents neatly stacked across it. Kevin was a chubby, grey-headed man whose appearance belied his reputation as a hard man to deal with in the industry. Cord knew this, but the man always paid on time. Kevin introduced Trevor, a senior company geologist.

"Cord, we're looking at developing an open-cut mine in the north and need some upfront survey work to be done urgently. We have people and equipment ready to go, but the Board needs a cost estimate for the complete project before committing."

He turned to Trevor, who drew Cord's attention to a site plan.

"You can see here, this is the area we're looking at. It's an emerald field. It's been fossicked over for many years and the site is pock-marked with trenches and tunnels. We think the deepest is about thirty metres, but there are no maps. Also, it's a fragile environment. Emeralds are found in loose material scattered randomly over the site, so our open-cut diggings will have to be strictly controlled."

Kevin added, "We can't send our machines in there without an up-to-date plan showing all the workings. It's imperative we have a proper survey done. I won't even ask you for a firm quote on this upfront, just your assurance you'll be able to do it straight away. I'd like to see a detailed plan on my desk by the end of next month. Can you do it?"

Cord patiently perused the topographical maps and the plan showing the dimensions of the mining tenement. The aerial photographs certainly showed major disturbances over the ground.

"You say the deepest shaft is thirty metres. There's only one?" Cord asked.

Trevor replied, "That's as much as we know, but there could be others. Also, they're not shafts as such. They're declines which are really walk-ins."

"More like crawl-ins," Kevin laughed.

"We can do the job, that's no problem, but the timeline you've set will be a challenge. I need to visit the site to get a feel for the extent of the underground activity before I can send in a team. I'm sorry, Kevin. I'll have to take a rain check on this one and get back to you."

*****

The following week, Cord found himself standing with Trevor and two mine employees at the mine gate.

"We've had to cordon off the tenement from amateur fossickers, not only to protect our asset but to protect them from injury."

Cord allowed himself a week to walk the site and investigate every significant digging. It was hot, dusty work in an environment resembling a moonscape, devoid of trees and covered with a maze of shallow holes surrounded by mounds of rock and clay spoil from the excavations. Three major declines were found, ranging from fifteen to thirty metres in depth.

The thirty-metre decline ended at a well, clearly dug for water in this semi-desert country. A decayed overhead wooden gantry supported a rusty iron bucket attached to a frayed steel rope. A hand winch mechanism, long since seized, operated the bucket movement. Trevor pushed the bucket and the gantry swayed, creaked and shuddered. The bucket swung backwards and forwards before it suddenly broke from its harness and plunged, banging and clanging into the darkness below, stopping with a clatter and splash at the bottom.

The two men peered over the edge into the well and Trevor laughed, "Well, we know there's water there, all right. Must be another fifteen metres or so below."

Without warning, the wooden gantry groaned and collapsed, the timber beams falling across and onto the two men below it. Cord only remembered an intense, searing pain that engulfed his left arm as he tried to get up. Trevor lay next to him, not moving, his face covered in blood and his hard hat skewed on his shoulder. Cord's left arm had disappeared under rubble and a wooden beam, which he tried to shift with his right arm, but it wouldn't move. He wondered why his left arm wasn't hurting anymore before he lapsed into unconsciousness.

He woke to the humming noise of an aeroplane engine. A medic was attending to the slow breathing of someone on a stretcher near him; it was Trevor, his head covered in bandage and a leg set in a cast raised and strapped to an overhead harness. Cord stirred and the medic turned her attention to him and said, "Doctor."

A man rose from a stool and leant over Cord. "How are you?"

"Where am I?"

"You've had an accident. You're with the Flying Doctor on your way to hospital."

The plane engines changed momentum as the craft prepared for landing.

Cord grimaced and said, "What happened? How's Trevor? I can't feel my arm."

"He's okay. You're in shock, but we'll have you in the hospital soon."

He bent over, examined Cord's eyes and nodded to the medic who twisted a knob on the drip in Cord's right arm. He drifted into sleep.

*****

Keith, Eileen and Corrine sat in the waiting room at the hospital. "Mark will be in later," Corrine said to make conversation.

Keith was glum and anxious. Eileen was tearful and wringing her hands. "I should never have let him become a surveyor. It's a dangerous job gallivanting around the world, over the ocean, what with Malaria and the like. Look at his friend, bitten by a snake and now this. I should never have allowed it. Keith, you should have supported me and got him into accounting with you."

They let her have her say without protest.

Keith was the first to be notified of the accident as next of kin after Kathy couldn't be contacted. He called Joan, who confirmed that Kathy was away with Ted, so he gave her the summary of what had happened. However, he did not repeat the content of his conversation with the surgeon, who explained, "Please advise his wife of what I am about to tell you. We don't know exactly what we're dealing with until we operate, but his left arm between the elbow and wrist has suffered major trauma. The bone's been fractured, splintered and may be crushed. I'm sorry, but we may need to amputate."

Keith was shocked and had no words.

The surgeon continued, "There's a chance we won't need to, but if he hadn't been rescued as quickly as he was, his arm would certainly have been lost."

Keith recovered and was finally able to speak. "Does my son know?"

"Not to the extent of our conversation. We've kept him sedated and the arm blocked, that is, it's in a drugged frozen state and he feels no pain. It is an extensive surgery and will involve two teams over four to five hours, so I suggest you and your family go home and get some rest. He'll need you here when he wakes. We'll keep him sedated till morning."

Keith put on a brave face to the others and said, "They're going to do surgery to fix his arm. We'll come back in the morning."

He wasn't prepared for the frantic telephone message he received from Kathy. She was sobbing as she explained Maggot had picked her up in the chopper, flown her to the airport and that she'd be in Perth that night.

Corrine picked her up; it was late and raining. Kathy was still in her working clothes; Joan had packed a bag for her, but she hadn't changed. Distraught, anxious and dishevelled, she looked nothing like the Kathy Corrine knew. She immediately wanted to go to Cord, but Corrine explained it wasn't a good idea.

Eileen had prepared coffee and Kathy sat at the table, a lonely figure holding the cup tightly and crying. She said repeatedly, "I should have been here with him."

Keith decided not to divulge the doctor's opinion. News could wait till morning; it was best to let her rest. Her whole body shuddered as her sobs increased. He rose and put his arm around her.

"What did the doctor say?" Kathy cried.

"Just to rest and come back in the morning."

"I've let him down."

"Only if you leave him."

*****

Cord woke to the friendly voice of a young nurse tucking in the bedclothes.

"Well, now! You're awake, Mr McCullum. You've had us worried. I'll make you comfy. There are visitors waiting to see you. Doctor will be along shortly. Hold still while I adjust the drip in your arm."

Cord realised the bed head had been raised, so he was reclining rather than lying. The nurse concentrated on replacing the drip fluid. He could see his left arm was immobilised, cast from shoulder to wrist and resting entirely on a narrow table, he thought, like a little ironing board attached to the main bed frame.

"There now. Would you like a cup of tea or some breakfast?"

Cord was groggy but nodded, saying, "Tea, please."

"Would you like to see your visitors now?"

He nodded again.

The surgeon was with the family in the waiting room. "It all went well. The fracture required a plate and screws, which we'll remove in due course. The main artery and blood vessels weren't as damaged as we initially thought and thankfully, his elbow is okay. He'll only have limited control over his hand for a while, but with proper therapy, it'll return to normal function."

They thanked him profusely. He nodded and smiled, "We'll keep him here for a week. It's important he doesn't move the arm and that'll apply for the first month to six weeks, then he'll be in a sling for another eight weeks. Therapy is the key to recovery."

The doctor left and Keith said, "I think we should let Kathy see him first, in private."

Everyone, even Eileen, agreed.

Cord couldn't believe his beloved Kathy was standing before him. Changed and refreshed, the word spectacular came immediately to his mind. Neither spoke as she approached the bed and lay beside him, one arm carefully reaching across his chest. She tucked her head into his shoulder and settled there silently. Eventually, she raised her head and kissed him, her blue eyes misty with tears.

"You're home," he said.

"I'm home."

PART 3
Mia

Rodney 1
2007

It had been three years since the accident and Cord had recovered well.

He was in the ground floor office poring over a mining lease plan when Marie, his personal assistant, said, "Cord, there's a Rodney Cao on the line. Will you take it down there?"

Cord was disconcerted. Rodney. What did he want?

"No, I'll come up."

He hadn't seen or heard of him since 1998, nine years ago. If it was something to do with going back to Malaysia to work, it was too late for that.

"Hello, Rodney."

The familiar lilting Malay voice came across strong and clear. "Hello, Cord. You're a hard man to track. I had to follow up with your survey firm and I believe you have a new business. They tell me you had an accident. All is well now, I hope?"

"Yep, a little different, no marine survey work. We're customising development projects now."

"You're still the Landman, though. Look, I'm in Perth for a few days and would like to catch up."

Cord didn't feel like catching up; he left Penang full of resentment towards the man but was curious about what he wanted. There was one thing for sure; Rodney wanted something.

"Sure, okay."

"Come to lunch. I'm staying at the Crown."

Cord kept the news from Kathy. Having Rodney around from a past life was too close for comfort and it was easy to say Rodney was a mining executive, for he often met and lunched with clients. He wouldn't tell Rodney about Kathy or that he was married; it was none of his business.

Cord was surprised when he arrived at the hotel bistro the following day. Rodney had aged and put on a slight paunch. Nevertheless, Cord sensed the bustling vitality and drive of the man was still there. He had a child with him, a little girl he presented as his daughter, Mia.

As was Malay customary with special friends, Rodney introduced her, "Mia, this is Uncle Cord."

Cord took her tiny hand, "Pleased to meet you, Mia."

She spoke perfect English.

"Thank you, Uncle. I am pleased to meet you."

Cord chose a light dish of steamed fish and salad; Rodney had vegetarian gnocchi and Mia, a bowl of asparagus soup with a bun. The conversation revolved around the days in Penang and the ongoing port development. The new ferries were running.

"Mia's tired and rather than talk here, let's go up to our suite for a coffee. There's a favour I want to ask of you."

Uh-oh! Cord thought, here it comes, the favour.

The suite overlooked the city block, a spacious apartment in keeping with Rodney's affluence. Mia sat patiently on a couch, her legs curled up underneath her, listening attentively to her father.

"In short, I want to buy a property here, but it's not a simple process for a foreign national. As you're probably aware, these purchases are controlled by the Australian Foreign Investment Review Board."

Cord nodded and wondered where this was heading.

Rodney chuckled, "I hesitated in dropping in on your doorstep like this, but I remembered you are the Landman. I thought, under the circumstances, you were definitely the right man to see. At home, things have changed. Father hasn't been well and we've relocated to Kuala Lumpur mainly to diversify our interests outside of tea. The point is that Australia's stable economy makes investment attractive. So, my aim is to invest in property here. Putting it bluntly, would you help me with this?"

Cord was uneasy.

"I'm sorry, Rodney, you've come to the wrong man. Arrangements for foreign nationals, the review board and investment advice, really, it's out of my field. I don't know much about these things."

"Please hear me out," Rodney persisted. "My initial preference was to buy an established residence, but this is out of the question as the aim of your government is to increase housing stock through building. However, I can buy a plot of land, subject to certain limitations, and build a dwelling on it. That's where I'm hoping you might help me."

"Again, buying and selling property in these circumstances is really out of my line."

"But you live here, you know the place. Locations to buy in, where you'd put your money, etcetera. That's why I've come to you, hoping you can point me in the right direction."

Cord sat back in his chair and looked at Mia, staring attentively at him. It wasn't such a big favour and he could possibly help.

"All right, I have a friend, Carol, who runs a realty business near me. She has her ear to the ground and is in the best position to suss out what you're looking for. I'm sure she's had experience with these applications, so you'd be in good hands. I'll have a word with her."

Rodney looked confused for a moment at Cord's broad Australian accent but smiled and said, "Okay, could you arrange that while we are here?"

"Sure, I'll get her to ring you. How long are you staying?"

"Another week."

"Also, I have some builder friends I can put you in touch with."

Rodney nodded and shook Cord's hand. "Thank you, my friend. Mia, love, I want to talk to your uncle privately for a little while. You're tired, so go to your room and have a rest, okay."

She nodded, smiled, shook Cord's hand and left.

Rodney leant forward in his chair, a growing look of concern on his face. "There's another reason I've come to you, my friend. It concerns Mia. Her mother died several years ago and she's been brought up by Mother and Father, who are now elderly."

"I'm sorry about her mother."

"Thanks. You see, it's not the same for her here in Australia as it is for her in Malaysia. Our culture, our rules, are different for women, especially those of mixed blood. We're a male-dominated society and most of our religious and legal institutions are run by men. It's difficult for women to have recourse to the court on family matters and especially to own land outright. You know, Cord, in 1965, our government took up your country's Torrens land title system, but it's an abbreviated version with limited reciprocal rights for women. A friend told me of a case in Sarawak where the bank foreclosed on a farming property when the male owner, who was aged, feeble and had been incapacitated for some time, died. They seized it even though the farm had been running successfully for many years, managed by his wife and two daughters. The bank refused to transfer the loan to the widow, so they lost their farm solely because of gender discrimination. With Mother and Father ageing, there's only my sister Lucille and me."

Cord thought, how could I not know?

Rodney added, "Lucille's now an American citizen and would be viewed as a foreigner in Malaysia if she returned. As I said, for Mia, not being an ethnic Malay, it'd be even more difficult for her should anything happen to me. If I can establish a base for her here, with your support, my friend, I will be forever grateful. She can own land here, which is most important, and I know she'll blossom in this multi-cultural society."

Cord recalled the fragile face of the little girl who sat peacefully studying him attentively with those beautiful dark eyes. Without a mother, adrift in a society that may reject her, she looked fragile and alone.

He saw Rodney through fresh eyes; the man was concerned, not for himself, but for his daughter, and Cord could understand his anguish. It was a Rodney he hadn't seen before; this man was in complete contrast to the hustling, bustling, ruthless, aggressive businessman he knew during those early days in Penang.

"Don't worry," Cord said reassuringly, "I'll arrange it."

But would it be all right? There was one thing for sure, it was easy to buy and sell land in Australia, thanks to Robert Richard Torrens.

As a licensed surveyor, Cord was quite aware of the Torrens title system. Amazingly, the system had gained international recognition and been adopted as the model for buying and selling land in many countries. Torrens pioneered land reform in Australia and introduced his legislation in South Australia in 1857. On a global basis, it had stood the test of time. Its main feature was that the title deed was guaranteed free of error by the government.

Cord agreed Rodney was smart. There'd be no problem or objection to Mia owning land in Australia and he could help make that happen.

Rodney 2
2010

July means winter in Australia.

Clouds and light rain scudded across the river. Raindrops clung to the office window, distorting the view of the high-rise buildings across the water. Below him, on the promenade, Cord watched the city ferry loading passengers scurrying along the jetty, closing umbrellas in mad haste to gain shelter in the onboard cabin.

It was Friday, the end of a busy week. Initially, he looked forward to a quiet evening meal at home and a beer with Kathy. Now this matter had arisen, it had to be attended to urgently and in the afternoon, he'd take the papers he'd received from Rodney's lawyer to his own lawyer, Harold Foy, for advice. He hoped the weather would clear before then.

Earlier in the week, he'd stood at the same window staring pensively at the familiar winter scene, sheltered from the swift rain squalls and high winds churning up the river and buffeting a ferry desperately trying to disembark passengers. He pondered the contents of the email message he'd just received. It read:

'Hello, Landman. It's been a long time since we met. I am in town and would like to catch up. I'd be delighted if you and your good wife Kathy could join me for lunch or dinner any day this week. I am staying at the Hyatt. Please call me there or leave a message. Rodney.'

After meeting with Rodney three years before and assisting him with his proposition, Cord hadn't expected to hear from him again. After all, they had little in common, and in truth, there was still a trace of resentment the years hadn't erased. He knew he'd been helpful in Rodney successfully acquiring an allotment in town and building a residence, but that was all. Carol, his realtor friend, had arranged the transactions. Cord had nothing to do with it other than the initial introduction to Carol and Steve, the builder. He wasn't even sure where the property was located. At the last moment, when Rodney was leaving, Cord changed his mind and told him about Kathy and his marriage.

Now Rodney was back.

Kathy was in her office talking to Mollie, he guessed about a conference they were arranging, but as the conversation was in the Aboriginal vernacular, he unobtrusively entered, sat on the corner couch and waited. Unlike his austere and neutral office, Kathy's office sparkled with the deep, rich brown ochres, reds and gold of the Indigenous people. Full of paintings and artefacts, it engendered excitement and culture.

He had one Aboriginal artefact hanging on his office wall. It was a gift from Albert, a *Nulla-Nulla,* a club, which Albert hand-crafted from a Bush Apricot tree from Apricot Springs. The weapon was a solid hardwood stick, debarked, saturated with natural eucalyptus river gum oil and layered at one end with successive applications of resin made from the apricot fruit. The club end was the size of an Emu egg; it was heavy.

The message from Albert, translated from the tribal dialect, said:

'Landman, tomorrow is a shadow. With this Waddy, Country will always treat you fairly and keep you safe.'

After Mollie left the room, Cord confided in Kathy he had no idea what Rodney wanted, but it'd definitely be something to do with business. Referring to him in the note as Landman was disconcerting and a lunch or dinner invite seemed too casual.

"He might want me to go back to the Penang Straits."

"You read too much into it," she said. "Be positive. It may turn out to be to your advantage."

"And pigs might fly."

She looked at her schedule on the whiteboard. "Wednesday lunch would be fine, or even Friday."

"Okay, I'll arrange it," Cord said, returning to his office.

The offices of Landman Inc. and Landwoman Inc. were located on the ground floor of a two-storey building overlooking the esplanade parkland that skirted the river. They acquired the complex two years before; Carol let them know it was up for sale and it was ideal for their purpose. The top floor was divided in half, one side being their private residence and the other containing Cord and Kathy's adjoining offices. There was a spacious central foyer with several loungers and chairs and a display area of their past business accomplishments with an alcove office for Marie, their joint personal assistant. Off to the left and overlooking the river was the boardroom, where functions were also held.

Their lives took on a new direction with Kathy's return to him after the accident. Together, they formed the two complementary enterprises.

Landman Inc. operated as a consulting firm focusing on all aspects of land development above and below the ground. The firm's mandate was to provide expert advice on matters regarding physical landforms as well as the conservation, biodiversity, and sustainability of ecosystems. It offered clients a balanced and considered approach, ensuring participation in the process by developers, state and local government entities, landowners and other stakeholders, including traditional owners. Cord also retained his position as Director of KMSurveys on the retirement of John Keep, with Rory retained as General Manager. Busy though he was, he couldn't bring himself to relinquish his preferred role as a surveyor.

Landwoman Inc. set out to establish strong relationships with other organisations already actively spreading public participation in the reconciliation process. Its mandate was developing educational systems, training consultants and establishing a marketing base for the northern communities. Kathy was a trailblazer, bringing her academic intellect and broad skills to the fore. Being of and from the land, she quickly gained respect and popularity in the new venture.

The two organisations combined resources to employ staff embracing the fields of mediation, geology, biodiversity, town planning, occupational health and safety and civil law. They overlapped their resources and formed consulting relationships with other groups where necessary. It was an immediate success and provided a pool of specialist knowledge clients wanted to access. He wondered which services Rodney wanted to meet about.

He watched the ferry leave the dock with a new load of rain-soaked passengers. Cord turned from the view; he'd enough time before his next appointment to ring Rodney at the Hyatt. A soft, delicate child's voice answered. He thought it must be Rodney's daughter, Mia. What would she be now, eleven or twelve?

He said his name and she replied, "Oh, hello, Uncle. I'll get Father."

Rodney sounded breezy and he laughed, "Great to hear from you. Thanks for calling back. Hope I didn't shock you with the Landman tag. Thought you might have forgotten me otherwise."

"No, I'm used to it. I get it all the time now, what with the business named Landman Inc."

"Yes, I saw that. Very appropriate name. You must tell me about it. How's the arm?"

It had been six years since the accident and Cord was still recovering the use of his hand the year Rodney first visited. He politely asked after Rodney's parents but avoided mentioning Lucille as well as the purpose of Rodney's visit; no doubt that would come over the lunch date, which was set for the following Wednesday.

Marie brought him a flat white coffee.

"Your appointment's running late and asked if ten fifteen would be okay. Is it?"

"Sure."

"You're free till midday after that."

"Good. Also, let Kathy know we have a lunch appointment for noon Wednesday. I'll let her know the details tonight."

"Okay."

Marie left the office and Cord swung his office chair around to take in the view.

The rain was erratic and the sun occasionally peeked through the low grey clouds that hurried in from the west. The wind whipped up waves that continued to buffet the ferries as they crossed. For some reason, the violence of the weather took him back to the time of his accident six years before. A lot had happened since then.

*****

For several weeks after the accident, Cord floated in a drug-induced haze where the reality of seeing Kathy was no more than a dream, a hope she might really be there when he woke. Sometimes, he saw Sambo with his bucket of water and Lucille crying, then Corrine standing at the Sun Gate with Machu Picchu before them. There were horses and butterflies swirling and diving and Boris's grinning face fading into a mist. He felt the comfort of Albert's quiet stare and heard Gert laughing and calling out repeatedly,

"Landman, Landman," till he woke perspiring and agitated and the nurses hurried to his bed to calm him.

The surgeon explained to Kathy, "We must keep him sedated to keep his arm absolutely still. It's best he stays another week or two. The painkillers are causing the fever, but we're easing him off them."

During the ensuing weeks of his stupor, Kathy had permanently moved into his apartment, much to the support and joy of the family. Over the previous months, she too had been in a stupor, albeit self-induced, despondent from the shock of her infertility and the realisation that her status at Jacana Creek would slowly erode as Barry assumed control and took on a wife, probably Sofie. Kathy knew it had to come but didn't know the timing of it. The one thing she certainly didn't intend was to be an old maid jillaroo like Laura Carter at Ludlow Hills.

And, of course, there was Cord. She loved him and didn't want to drag him down any further. She'd hurt him enough after he left the station.

She recalled how things took a turn when she was saddling Twobob one day and Joan came out to the yard.

"Kathy, I think you care more for your horse than your husband. You're a headstrong, foolish woman. Your dad and I want you to go to Cord. He's a good man and was here for you after you found out about your infertility. You should be at his side in his time of need. What's happened is his loss, too, so don't be so cruel. Pull yourself together. You're not the only one feeling sorrow."

She was mulling over her mother's outburst when Albert cantered in on Dollar.

"Just took Mr Cord's horse for a ride. I'll hose an' brush her down."

"No, I'll do it."

Albert looked at her quizzically, "Sure, Miss Kathy."

He paused, then added, "When'll ya see Mr Cord?"

"Soon."

"Would ya come to the cottage, please, Miss? I've somethin' for him an' May and the women mob want ta' speak ta' ya."

"Sure."

The woman mob turned out to be over fifty representatives from the surrounding communities and they met at Apricot Springs the following weekend. At first, Kathy was bewildered when invited to attend the secret women's business event as she'd never been asked before, but very soon, their intention was clear. They wanted Kathy to be their voice.

It was a frenetic time. Stories emerged of the stolen years, exploitation with drug and alcohol problems, domestic violence, every story pointing to the slow disintegration of a sixty-thousand-year-old culture. But the main message they shared with Kathy was that there was hope. Advocates for change had arisen throughout the country and the Jacana communities wanted a voice in these groups shaping the reform.

May spoke out, "Ya a true friend, Miss Kathy. Ya know our culture, ya speak our tongue, ya can help us and go places we can't go. Ya go to Perth with Mr Cord, ya can talk with 'em."

Kathy wasn't prepared for the role that was being thrust on her. Quite naively, she thought the gathering was a gesture of caring by the tribe for her own predicament, but it was much more than that. It was a plea by the women's mob for urgent help with their own identity and domestic difficulties. She didn't want to refuse them and apart from her parent's intervention, it finally took Cord's accident to shake her despondency and go to him.

Guardians
2010

Cord confirmed his appointment with Rodney. "Hello, Cord, thanks for calling back. Noon at the café is fine."

"We're not big lunch eaters, so a club sandwich would be fine."

"Me too. Club sandwich it is."

It was approaching noon when Cord and Kathy drove over the Narrows Bridge and along the Terrace to the Hyatt. The weather had cleared, but it was cold out. The arrival of clear weather brought with it a frosty morning, but in Perth, there was never snow; you just had to have an extra layer of clothes.

Kathy wasn't present when Cord met with Rodney three years before but was now curious to meet this mysterious man from the east, who was part of Cord's exotic oriental life. She often chided Cord about his sojourn in Malaysia, hoping to find out, in her guileful woman's way, more about the anonymous female who took him on excursions in the hills, but Cord remained tight-lipped, other than his nonchalant admission on their honeymoon. Intuition told Kathy it'd been a romantic affair and Rodney likely knew something about it; however, she let the matter rest.

Once, over lunch, she'd asked Corrine about Cord's life in Penang, to which Corrine replied, "We hardly ever heard from him."

Even Corrine was tight-lipped and Kathy thought, what did it really matter? After all, he was now hers.

Cord noticed Kathy wasn't dressed in her standard business apparel but casually attired in a purple midi dress with a neck shirt collar, low-heeled shoes and a matching shoulder strap handbag to complete her outfit. The colour of the ensemble complemented her shoulder-length hair, which she'd brushed out and left naturally curled. Kathy didn't often wear jewellery but wore a nest of silver bracelets on one arm for the occasion. With just a slight touch of makeup, she looked her beautiful feminine best.

"Won't you be cold out?"

"I've got my thermal underneath. I'll meet this friend of yours as your wife, not as a feisty businesswoman."

Cord smiled, shook his head and thought, women!

There were only a few diners in the café when they arrived. Cord saw Rodney sitting alone at a table by the window overlooking the Terrace. He rose to greet them, a broad smile on his chubby face, bowed to Kathy and shook Cord's hand carefully.

"I remember your injury and wasn't sure which hand it was."

"The left, but it's all okay now."

"Please sit. Would you like a drink?"

A waitress came to the table; they ordered. Rodney smiled at Kathy, his eyes scrutinising her. He took her hand and kissed it.

"It's a great pleasure to meet you at last. I was sorry I missed you previously."

"Yes. It's good to meet one of Cord's friends from Penang."

"Oh, they were good days on the *Spree* with Cord, Gert and the crew."

Cord was dumbfounded, as he doubted whether Rodney had ever been on the *Spree*, let alone mixed with the crew. Good days? Most of the time, Rodney and Gert were at loggerheads over payments and progress.

"Mia's not with us?" Cord asked.

"No, she's upstairs in our room. I'll call her down later after we eat."

"I'm looking forward to seeing her again. She must have grown."

"Me too," Kathy said.

"That's right, you haven't met her, have you? Well, she's grown all right; she'll be twelve in November, going on twenty, of course. Naturally, I'm very proud of her. She's academic and as I said to Cord, she loves her sports, clothes, games and music. Plays the guitar."

Rodney showed interest in Kathy's background, about Jacana Creek Station, mustering and the size of the property. Cord thought he was almost interviewing her.

Rodney was astonished. "You drive for sixty kilometres from your front gate to your house and helicopters fly in your shopping?"

Kathy, too, engaged Rodney with questions about life in Penang.

"Cord doesn't talk much about it."

"Oh, he had a key role in the project. You know, tight budgets and timelines and all that time at sea, so there wasn't much time for anything else."

Cord was thankful for Rodney's reluctance to detail. Kathy gauged he was being evasive but let the matter lie.

Eventually, having eaten and sitting back, Kathy with a green tea, Cord with a cappuccino and Rodney with an apple juice, Rodney said, "I've got to thank you, Cord, for your help. The property here's going well. The government guidelines are that I can't rent it out for seven years, but when those restrictions are lifted, it can be rented or sold. The rule is, right now, I have to reside in it, but I let it out rent-free to friends, usually to their children studying over here. I really bought it as a base for Mia. I'm here, though, to ask another favour. A big favour."

Cord winced. He thought so.

"It concerns Mia. I'd like her to remain in Australia for schooling. She needs to be with her peers. Father and mother have aged and can't attend to her needs in KL and I'm too often away on business."

He paused and gathered his thoughts, "Frankly, I'd like to place her in your care as a legitimate ward."

Cord shifted uneasily in his chair, gobsmacked, and Kathy stared blankly ahead, showing no reaction or emotion.

Rodney continued, his gaze directly on her, "Please, before you say anything, there's one big consideration and it's in an area I am not well equipped."

He paused again before he said a little awkwardly, "That is, she needs someone to take her through her womanhood. Her time is approaching. Cord, you know my partner Ruby died. Mia has no one and she needs a woman, a mother figure."

He clasped his hands together and looked directly at Kathy. "I wouldn't trust her with anyone, but I know you, Cord, you make good choices."

Kathy was startled and wondered what he meant by good choices.

There was a prolonged silence before Cord spoke, knowing it was a lame reply, "I don't know what to say, other than that we're not prepared for such a situation. I'm flattered, but we have businesses to run. We don't have children ourselves."

Kathy remained silent. Cord realised he'd unwittingly touched a raw nerve with her.

He had to ask, even though he didn't want to, "And there's no one else?"

Rodney showed surprise at the question; however, recovered his composure and spoke with less emotion. "Well, there's my sister in America, Lucille. She's unmarried, has a high-powered government job, travels a lot more than I do and lives in a high-rise apartment in the city. Mia would be disadvantaged there and would have to be placed in a boarding school. She'd be even more isolated than ever. It's not an option. All I ask is that you consider this. I know it is a big ask with great responsibility. Bobbi Hahn, my lawyer, has prepared documentation for you to consider. I'd like you to read it. Rest assured, I'll place unlimited funds for her every need at your disposal. She'll be well catered for. Please give it some thought."

Kathy hadn't spoken and Cord asked, "Does Mia know of this plan?"

"Yes, to some extent. She'd like to go to school here but doesn't know the logistics of it all. She's very popular, well-adjusted, flexible and a happy child. She reads a lot about the courses and sporting opportunities. She thinks she'd come and board each term and then return home to Kuala Lumpur for the holidays. I've gone along with it till now but know the situation wouldn't work for Father, Mother and me with travelling. We're looking at something more permanent. I'll call her down. No, better than that. Please finish your drinks and come up to our room."

His suite was on the fifth floor, a two-bedroom apartment with a comfortable lounge and a spacious balcony overlooking the river from which Cord could see their office building on the far shore.

Mia was lying on a recliner on the balcony reading; their voices surprised her. She stirred, stood up, straightened her clothes and came into the room. She was much taller than when Cord saw her last; to be expected since she was three years older. She wore faded blue jeans, sneakers and a dark green T-shirt embossed with lighter green palm leaves and a motif that read: 'MOONGATE – Like to Hike – PENANG'.

Cord immediately thought of Lucille and the Penang Hills as she came towards him, offering her hand. "Hello, Uncle."

She smiled as he took it. Her deep brown eyes penetrated his, jerking a memory of the same eyes and presence Lucille had. She turned to Kathy.

"This is Aunty Kathy," Rodney said and Mia bowed, holding out her hand. "I'm pleased to meet you, Aunty."

Kathy's first impression was of a slender, pretty girl, not yet adolescent, quiet and well educated. She had a delicate, beautiful Eurasian face, golden skin tones and a shock of thick, glossy black hair tossed in a ponytail. A typical modern emerging teenager.

Cord and Kathy sat on the sofa while Rodney and Mia sat opposite on lounge chairs. Mia tucked her legs under her.

Kathy broke the silence, "I like your T-shirt. Do you go bushwalking?"

Mia looked puzzled.

"Sorry, I mean hiking."

Mia's voice was soft and warm and Kathy was pleased that she took a moment to think about what she was about to say before replying.

"Yes, and camping. I joined our school botany club to hike, go camping and collect specimens."

Happy to expand on the subject, the spontaneity of youth emerged, "I'd like to trek the Himalayas and go skiing."

"Oh, she'd like to do everything," Rodney added lightly, "but school first. Did you know Mia has her own business in KL?"

"Business?" Cord asked.

"Tell Uncle and Aunty."

Mia spoke, her confidence growing. She tossed back her hair, her hands now animated with expression. "With Grandmother's help, we made some T-shirts for the street markets, something to do on holidays and guess what? We sold them all. Would you like to see my designs?"

Before Kathy could reply, Mia went to her room and came out with a satchel. She sat by Kathy's side on the couch and proudly pulled out sheets of paper. Kathy took her time looking at each one while Mia spoke enthusiastically.

"This one's Moon Beam, this is Moon Light and this is Moon Shadow. My favourite is Moon Glow. Grandmother's favourite is Harvest Moon." She rolled her eyes. "Naturally, Father likes Blue Moon. Which one do you like?"

"I like the one you're wearing, Moongate."

"It's the first one we made. Moongate Trail. That's the track I hike with my club."

Kathy looked at Cord, "You've been there, haven't you?"

"I think so." He quickly changed the subject. "What will you do when you run out of moons?"

Mia smiled and shook her head, "Oh! I won't run out of moons, Uncle. There are other moons. There are two hundred and nineteen moons around our planets. Poor old Mercury and Venus don't have any moons. Mars has *Deimos* and *Phobos*. Jupiter has ninety-two and Saturn has eighty-three moons. I could do a T-shirt for each one and also for windcheaters, Father said."

"You can see she's done her research," Rodney said proudly.

Cord nodded and smiled in approval.

Mia jumped up excitedly, "Aunty, come to my room. I've got my laptop set up and I'll show you a photo of *Deimos*. It's a funny shape, ugly looking, not very big and named after the Greek God of Dread and Terror. I like my moons, but I don't know if I'd do a design for that one. What do you think, Aunty?"

While they were away, Rodney called room service and ordered fresh juices for everyone. He asked Cord again to seriously consider the request.

"You can see her intelligence, her love of natural things and her enthusiasm for learning. She needs the opportunity to be with her peer group and live in a homely, stable situation. It's something I can't provide."

Cord, bewildered and recovering from the proposal, realised even though it was a short encounter, he'd warmed to Mia just as he had done when they'd first met. Hope rose in Rodney's eyes when Cord shrugged and said, "It's really up to Kathy."

It was clear from the moment they came back from Mia's room there was a marked change in Kathy's thinking. Here was the perfect gift; a child, a daughter she had always hoped for but was cruelly denied. They had looked at adoption, but nothing eventuated. Here was Mia, vibrant, intelligent, on the verge of womanhood and there was no doubt Kathy could help her. They knew her background and it'd be good for their marriage to have someone else to care for. It wasn't anyone else's decision, only Cord and hers. Then again, what if Mia baulked at the proposal? She may not want to live in Australia with relative strangers. It had to be sorted out there and then. Kathy was committed.

"How are the moon maidens?" Rodney said flippantly as Kathy and Mia emerged.

"Aunty has ordered a Moon Glow T-shirt in blue and silver, size ten, cotton V-neck. It's at cost, Father."

"All right, if you say so, but what say we give it to Aunty as a gift."

"Okay, great."

"Thank you. I hope to get it when school starts next year," Kathy said, then looked at Cord and added, "Your proposition, it's a possibility for us to consider."

Rodney took the cue, "Good. Mia, now you've clinched a business deal with Aunty, would you perhaps like to go to school here and stay with Aunty and Uncle?"

Mia frowned, "For the whole year?"

"Why not? You could go surfing and I could visit when you have your holidays."

"What about Grandfather and Grandmother?"

"Mia, you know they can't drive anymore and I'm not home much. This would be a wonderful opportunity for you."

"I can take you to Jacana Creek and teach you to ride," said Kathy.

"Ride a horse? Sensational!"

It was a *fait accompli*. Cord was surprised that a matter of such great consequence could be settled so quickly and relatively easily. Cord remembered his father's comment on understanding women; it seemed he really didn't have a say in the decision, but he supposed he could have objected if he'd wanted to.

Transitions
2010

In the days following, apprehension set in. Kathy and Cord had second thoughts and the consequences of their action loomed large and foreboding. Rodney rang and emailed several times, adding another layer of frustration to the situation.

Two weeks after their lunch and meeting with Rodney and Mia, Cord and Kathy met at Harold Foy's office. He had taken that time to appraise the brief from Rodney's lawyer regarding the wardship. Foy rose from his desk when they entered and ushered them to the lounge suite adjacent to the window with river views.

"Please, make yourselves comfortable. Would you like a coffee, tea, juice?"

They declined.

He returned to his desk, on which lay a manila file containing the brief and research notes on the proposal. He brought it to the occasional table and said, "I've assigned Sonya Mitchell to your case. She's conferred with lawyer Bobbi Hahn. I've read her report and her conclusions are sound."

Carefully, he thumbed through the pages, stopped at one that was tagged, removed his glasses and wiped them with a handkerchief he took from his pocket. Foy was a methodical, calm man and always spoke in a relaxed, informal manner.

"You're absolutely keen to establish a relationship with this child?" he asked, his eyes searching theirs.

"We've thought it over and know we can offer her a family environment," Cord replied nervously.

"And you, Kathy? You're prepared to take on this responsibility?"

"Yes."

"Well, firstly, let me fill in the background of our laws on childcare. The law in Malaysia regarding these matters is different to ours. In our case, wards are wards of the State. That is, children left homeless or removed from delinquent parents and taken into state care. The aim then is to arrange foster parents where possible. Now, this is not your case. The father, being the only parent, has requested you be involved with the child's upbringing in an important and trustworthy way. Over here, there are opportunities for overseas students to reside alone within a student visa system. These are self-sufficient mature students, which, of course, is not the case with Mia, being a minor. On the face of it, my initial view was that the proposal could well violate immigration laws regarding a foreign national wishing to enter the country permanently."

Cord and Kathy looked at each other with concern. Foy paused, replaced his glasses, rummaged quickly through the file and opened the page he had tagged before. He put up his hand to continue.

"Do I have the right pronunciation for Mia's surname? *Chow*, is that correct?"

"Yes, it's a little more like *T'sow* in Mandarin," Cord replied.

"Good. *Chow* will do."

Cord went to speak, but Foy waved his hand again and continued, "Now, on the other hand, Mr Cao has property here, which is held in a family trust. I believe you're aware of that."

"Yes," Cord replied.

"I have here an email from Mr Cao's lawyer stating Amir Afsah Cao, that's Rodney, and Aisyah Latipah Cao, that's Mia, are the sole parties to the trust, registered as the Moongate Family Trust. Now, this allows Mr Cao to visit and live at his property occasionally and indirectly gives Mia the same right to reside there. This circumstance makes the matter much easier for you. Mr Cao can simply appoint you as housekeepers."

"Housekeepers!" Kathy remarked, moving to the edge of her chair. Cord was confused and rubbed the back of his neck.

"It's just a name," Foy said. "As housekeepers, Mr Cao can appoint you to carry out a multitude of duties, all connected to Mia's needs. Driving, meals, schooling, whatever."

"Would we have to live at his property?" Cord asked.

"No, no, no. Just a token duty to look after it."

He reached for his office phone. "Sonya, will you come up and bring the reworked McCullum-Cao contract? Thank you."

He continued, "Sonya has reworked the brief to remove the elements referring to custodianship, introduced a clause allowing mutual cancellation of the agreement and tightened up the sections covering financial issues. Basically, it's a contract for services, renewable annually."

Sonya was in her late twenties, smartly dressed in a grey business suit, complete with designer glasses and her auburn hair tied back in a bun. An attractive businesswoman, Kathy thought. She greeted them briefly, handed Foy the contract file and left the room.

"I gather this means Mia's not our ward?" Cord observed.

"Technically, she's not, but surely it's what you make of your relationship with her that counts."

He handed the file to Cord. "Take your time to read it and for any questions, please contact Sonya directly. I'm pleased with it, so once you're satisfied, you can authorise her to send it on to lawyer Hahn."

Cord couldn't believe that by the end of the month, the matter had been settled and Mia would be with them for the commencement of the school year. Messages went back and forth between Rodney, his lawyer, Sonya and themselves as the necessary arrangements involving applications for school, uniforms, and the outfitting of a room were addressed.

Kathy took on the task with great gusto and Cord sensed in her a resolve that had been missing for some time. This was her chance to be a mother and no doubt, she'd give the role her best and full attention. He savoured this change in her as she set about converting the large storeroom, where they only kept bits and pieces, into a bedsit. Fortunately, there was a window and a glass door, which opened onto a small balcony with river glimpses across to the city skyline. Kathy spent hours mulling over decorating possibilities and often conferred with Corrine for an opinion. He was never asked, just kept in the loop, more content to accept arrangements than be involved in them.

He overheard Kathy tell Corrine, "I want this to be a haven for her if she wants to be alone. Teenage girls need that. But it must also be spacious and airy if she wants to have friends over. No one uses the toilet and shower opposite her room in the hall, so it'll be private for her."

Rodney scanned an image of the green Moongate T-shirt and forwarded it to Kathy, who had a signwriter copy it onto the wall above the queen size bed as a surprise for Mia. The grey concrete floor was sanded and painted in soft beige with several striped coloured rugs straddling it. It was an ideal setting for the Sandalwood two-seater lounge chair Boris had made for their wedding and Kathy had cushions made in green fabric, which complemented the primary colour of the wall painting.

A student desk with bookshelves, office chair, several wardrobes and a mirrored drawer cupboard, all in white, completed the furnishings. On one wall was a large clock with a clear dial, large numerals and below it, a full-length mirror.

She told Corrine, "The clock will keep her on time in the morning while she's getting dressed. I've left the other walls clear so she can hang her own paintings, photos, etcetera. You know, girl's stuff."

"It's great what you've done. You've thought of everything. I know she'll love it."

Keith acquired a section of mature, richly grained Marri timber and, on the lathe, turned it into an ornate stand, a single twisted stem on a solid base with an array of hooks for hats, coats, bags, scarves and an umbrella.

"I'll give it to her when we meet."

"I hope she'll appreciate what you're doing for her," Eileen commented to Cord.

"You'll like her Mother."

"I hope so, but that remains to be seen."

September arrived and winter became spring. Kathy and Cord sat on the balcony. It was twilight and everything was still, one of those beautiful evenings so common in Australia. Across the water, two small yachts drifted lazily, their white sails fading, becoming fainter and fainter in the gathering dusk. Kathy sat close to him, her head on his shoulder.

She sipped the glass of Mateus Rosé he'd poured. "Do you think we've done the right thing?" she asked, tilting her face towards him.

They briefly kissed and he felt her closeness, relishing the aroma of her perfume. He couldn't be happier.

"Sure, but only time will tell."

*****

Rodney kept the news of Mia's impending move to Australia from Lucille. He saw no need to involve her in the process; it was his business. Lucille learnt of the decision from Mother, who said it was for the best as she and Father were finding it difficult to cope with Mia's needs, especially schooling. Initially, she accepted that it was a good thing to broaden Mia's horizons in a new country, but her mild acceptance quickly turned into anger and then fury. It all began with a simple email she sent to Mia wishing her the best on her new adventure and the reply she received.

It read: 'Thank you, Aunt Lucille. I've met the family I'll be staying with and they're very nice. I met Uncle Cord a few years ago when Father took me to Australia and last month, I met Aunty Kathy, who is lovely and kind. She loved my T-shirts and has ordered one for herself. Did you get the Moon River one Father sent you? I hope it fits.'

Lucille was in shock and immediately emailed Rodney: 'How could you? Mia billeted with Cord, of all people, and his wife! You called him an Australian hayseed. Now he has my niece. How can this be? What have you done?'

He replied: 'This is not about you or me; it's about what's right for Mia. Time heels all wounds and I turned to Cord because Australia is the best place for Mia to be. I did this for her and I hope you can accept that. Remember, she's still your niece.'

There was an undeniable truth in his words. On the surface, it was reasonable to place Mia in a caring environment, but the circumstances were offensive and intolerable. Lucille knew she wasn't in a position to care for Mia, but she had to admit Cord was a good man; she knew that much.

She left her apartment in her lycras and joggers with dark glasses and a cap pulled well down to cover her swollen tear-filled eyes. Every Sunday, when at home, she ran the six-mile loop to Capitol Hill and back.

Sam opened the swinging door for her, "Aren't you feeling well, Miss?"

"Just a sniffle, that's all."

She needed to get away and be by herself to fully absorb what had happened; she needed time to think it through.

Life wasn't fair. There was Rodney, who basically never wanted children but fathered a beautiful daughter whose mother abandoned her and died. Lucille had a son somewhere in the world, a son she never got to name, by a man who abandoned her and who now had her niece. It was a script from a soap opera.

She shuddered at the thought of Cord's wife being involved in Mia's upbringing. It added salt to an already deep wound. She sobbed as she ran on, fighting back the tears. Why was it that destiny decreed that Mia and her son, blood cousins and close in age, would never know each other? On top of that, what hurt most of all was that she'd lost the man she loved. It all pointed back to Rodney's business ethic and his intrusive meddling in their lives. She never wanted to see her brother again.

Brakes screeched and a horn blared as she crossed the road. The shock brought her back to stark reality. The angry motorist leant from his window, his face red, shaking his fist, yelling, "Ya dumb bitch! Wanna get yourself fuckin' killed?" With tyres screaming, he took off again.

Upon returning to her apartment, Lucille replied to Mia: 'That's good news. Enjoy school. The T-shirt is great and does fit. I'm going away for a short while, so I won't be in contact for some time. Take care. Love Aunt Lucille."

It was all too much to absorb; she wasn't going away, but it had to be a clean break from the past. She had to leave it all behind. Get on with life. Sadly and regretfully, she'd lied to Mia. Everything was in transition.

Missing Person
2011

The Department of Justice canvassed for seasoned recruits to focus on emerging issues regarding Land Rights for Indigenous people and the sensitive matter of violence against women. With her business and law degree, experience and financial background, Lucille was head-hunted to head up the new unit.

She recruited a team to tour the tribal communities, sponsoring events supporting Native American sovereignty and also oversaw a funding program providing relief services to female victims of criminal and domestic violence. She quickly gained a reputation as a mover and shaker for disadvantaged groups and her fame spread to recognition in both the public and private sector.

She became involved in a search for a missing backpacker on the Appalachian Trail. It so happened that the hiker went missing in an area in the Harriman State Park that she'd hiked several times with her club. The trail section is heavily wooded with steep terrain and picturesque lake scenery; it is real bear and elk country and easy to get lost. Her club, amongst others, was called in to assist in searching the area for several days, but apart from the hiker's backpack found abandoned just off the trail, the search became another unsolved cold case.

Unexpectedly, Chenoa Chavos, the mother of the missing hiker, Jessica Chavos, approached Lucille to look into the matter. Lucille had had many business meetings with Chenoa, an active member of the First Nation Committee examining reservation treaties. While Lucille felt there was little she could contribute to the situation, the location of the incident and knowing the mother induced her to become involved.

"I know Jessica was angry with me. She's such a headstrong girl and I never liked the friends she hiked with. I was told she was seeing a boy outside the tribe and thought perhaps she ran away with him." Not wanting to face what might be a grim reality, she added hopefully, "She might just be lost out there?"

The newspapers reported the story in the middle pages, headlining 'Another Hiker Missing' and the county sheriff gave only a few details about the case. Lucille had access to the US Marshals office in the same building as hers and raised the matter with Marshal Herman De Luca at the bi-monthly interdepartmental meetings. He was a big man in his early fifties, brash and over-confident, but boasted a network of contacts that went all the way to top government. At the meeting, he was anxious to sit opposite her and try to establish eye contract. Lucille never encouraged the man but knew he was smitten.

Consequently, he welcomed her request with a smile and a wink. "It's a situation out of my jurisdiction, but I'll have a chat with the county sheriff and see what I can do." He added suggestively, "Especially for a colleague."

*****

A week later, Lucille asked Chenoa to come to her office to share the information she'd gleaned.

"I've talked with the Marshals office. As you know, Jessica's backpack was found abandoned on the trail and I'm sorry to say that's as far as the investigation has gone."

"What do you mean gone?"

"The sheriff called the search off pending further information, whatever that means. I managed to obtain a transcript of his report, which is confidential. I can't copy it for you, but I can read it to you, okay?"

"Okay."

"Good. The two friends she commenced the hike with are two girls from her workplace who have been cleared. Firstly, there's a statement from these two companions, followed by an independent report from the sheriff."

Lucille began reading the transcript and Chenoa listened intently.

The transcript read as follows:

'We parked our car at Elk Pen trailhead at about 10 am and took the Long Path towards Silver Lake, where we proposed to camp for the night. A couple of miles along the trail, Jessica rolled her ankle and said she was okay

239

to walk back to the parking area and call her mother as there was mobile reception there. At that time, a group of six hikers coming back from Silver Lake met us and offered to walk with Jessica as they were heading back to the trailhead. We left, understanding that's what would happen. It was before lunch and we never saw Jessica again.'

"Are you okay, Chenoa?" Lucille asked.

She answered yes, so Lucille continued with the sheriff's report:

'The area is a heavily trafficked trail section. Twelve other walkers were on the trail that day and at the times stated, no one saw the subject, Jessica Chavos, between where she left her companions and the Elk Pen parking area. The six hikers were interviewed individually and all confirmed the subject declined to walk with them as she said she would slow them down.

Her pack was found forty-eight hours later complete and apparently untouched, about five metres off the trail on the eastern side, approximately a mile further along the track. This is not in the direction of Elk Pen Trail parking but towards Silver Lake, where her two companions were heading. Three other hikers coming from Silver Lake passed her two companions in the afternoon, continued to Elk Pen and never saw the subject. There have been bear attacks in Harriman Park, but rangers advise there have been no bears in that section of the park in the past three months.

Indications are the subject changed her mind. Planning to catch up with her friends, it appears the subject wandered off the trail and got lost, or a third party was involved in her disappearance. The Trail Log, which is not compulsory to complete, recorded no other hikers on the trail that day.

Signed: Dalby Clemmons. County Sheriff's Office."

"There you have it," Lucille paused, put the report down on her desk, rubbed her eyes, and reached out to hold Chenoa's hands. "It's all there. I'm not sure what else I can do to help."

Chenoa held a tissue to her face and wept.

"She always talked about running away and the morning she left, she said, 'Good riddance; it'll be good to see the last of you'. Doesn't that seem a strange and prophetic thing to say on the day she disappeared?"

Lucille admitted it did and that afternoon, she called in on Herman De Luca again.

"To what do I owe this pleasure?" he leered.

"Any further results? Leads?"

"Do you know how many people go missing on the trail?" he said laconically. "Heaps! And for all sorts of reasons."

"It's just I've close contact with the mother who reckons she's run away."

"Tell me about it. The sheriff says his office is full of these people looking for runaways."

Lucille didn't flaunt her beauty, but she knew that with most men, including Herman, if she asked for a favour, within reason, they'd comply.

"Let's suppose she ran away, staged her own disappearance to put her mother off. What better way to do it than on the trail, throw away your backpack and create a mystery?"

"So?" Herman said, rolling his eyes as he lay back in his chair and smiled. "Okay! What do you want?"

"There are only a few major roads in the area. Could you check videos, security monitors, gas stations and diners in the area? See if she turns up on any of them."

"Well, that's the sheriff's domain. He won't like me muscling in."

He paused thoughtfully, tapping his fingers on his desk. "But he owes me. You'll owe me for this one. I'll see what I can do. It'll take a couple of days."

Herman handed the request to Kevin, his deputy. Kevin smirked, "You're married. She's quite a dish. You could steer her in my direction."

"She's out of your league, man, way out."

Six days later, Herman called Lucille to his office.

"We got her at Arden, at a gas station that afternoon and traced the vehicle to Crooked Creek. She's shacked up with a young guy, Seth Mudge. He's got a potato farm there. It was all arranged. You were right, she hadn't rolled her ankle. When her friends left, she continued towards Silver Creek, threw away the backpack to confuse everyone, got to Fingerboard Mountain, turned on to the Pine Swamp Track and met Seth, who was waiting where the track joins Seven Lakes Drive. Neat plan, eh!"

"Where do we go from here?"

"That's it. It's in the sheriff's hands and there's nothing more they'll do. The case is solved," he laughed. "They might charge her for littering, abandoning her pack in a national park. The girl's nineteen, has no record and is entitled to leave home if she wishes. The sheriff's contacted the mother with all the details since she put in a formal missing person request."

It was another feather in Herman's cap and he was elated. To all and sundry, it appeared he'd solved the case by his own initiative. He was interviewed on local radio and television and basked in his newfound glory.

He called Lucille. "You and I should celebrate, go and have dinner. What do you say?"

"Thanks, that'd be good, but only if your wife comes. It's Daisy, isn't it? She should be part of the celebration."

She knew she wouldn't hear from him again and didn't.

*****

Chenoa brought Lucille a cornflower in a fancy clay pot and a handmade boho Native American headpiece in braided leather decorated with an array of woven coloured cotton ties. Lucille placed it away for safekeeping with Mia in mind.

Chenoa hugged Lucille. "I'm so grateful. I went to Crooked Creek to see Jessica. We made up, she's happy and Seth seems a nice enough boy, umm, man. He's twenty-four, a hard worker and has his own farm. Their place is neat and tidy. They plan to get married. What more could I want? I'm happy she was found, thanks to you."

Lucille's reputation as a champion for the underprivileged grew to the extent she was recognised on the international circuit. She was appointed to the International Commission at the World Congress for Rights in Canada, with a specific portfolio inquiring into missing Indigenous women globally. Her busy life became busier and busier and her past personal hurt slowly faded.

At the next World Congress in Sydney, she was invited to speak on recent innovations in the World Movement. It was to be a glittering affair, held over five days at the stylish Pier One Venue on Sydney Harbour and one of the four hundred delegates attending was Kathy McCullum.

*****

On the third afternoon at 3 pm, Kathy made her way to Function Room 5. She'd hastily booked into Lucille's session when she received the conference program at home several weeks before, which read: 'Innovations and Trends in the World Movement – Speaker – Lucille Cao (MBA, LLB) – Member – International Human Rights Commission.'

She kept the secret from Cord and Mia that this could be, no, must be, Rodney's sister and Mia's Aunt Lucille. She also reasoned this might be the mysterious companion to Cord in Penang, the subject he always avoided. She sat in the front row and her presumption was confirmed when one of the most beautiful women she had ever seen entered the room and walked up to the dais.

She was familiar; Kathy had seen her before. At the Brahman Breeders Congress, she recalled. So this was Lucille Cao.

Lucille spoke emotively and succinctly. Elegant as always, in a light grey pantsuit with her hair tied back and just a trace of makeup around her eyes and lips, she held the attention of everyone in the packed room. Her paper highlighted the emerging studies pointing to marked commonalities between atrocities against Indigenous women in Australia and those in the US and Canada. She spoke of the grassroots movement at home in the US and the support coming from the United Nations Organisation Conference on the Status of Ethnic Women. The message embraced the sadness of the past and gave hope for the future as the tide turned against the perpetrators of the violence. The cries of ethnic women were now being heard across the globe.

Kathy was impressed by both Lucille's eloquence and beauty. While there was a half hour of question time, she chose not to participate but just sat and stared, surprised at her own timidity to introduce herself. Later, she reflected, where was the fearless horsewoman who led a muster and headed seasoned jackaroos at the outcamps?

There was a gala dinner for delegates on the last evening, but Kathy and Mollie were flying home that night and couldn't attend. Kathy had brought Mollie with her so they could participate in as many sessions as possible, as most sessions ran concurrently. They'd brought artefacts and artwork from the Jacana Creek community for sale and display in the main hall and were packing up that afternoon when Lucille passed by browsing. Kathy had just bought Mia a T-shirt with a purpose. It was black cotton fabric with a white circular moon blazoned across the chest. The Aboriginal word *Meeka* was inscribed on the moon face in black jagged letters. Kathy thought it an appropriate present for her moon girl.

Lucille stopped at the display and smiled at the T-shirt Kathy was holding. "Cute. What does it say?"

Kathy was surprised at Lucille's broad American accent.

"It's the *Noongar* Aboriginal word for moon."

"Oh, good. Thank you."

She went to move on, but the casual nature of the chance meeting prompted Kathy to stop her. "I attended your talk."

"I hope it was helpful."

"Oh, yes. It's satisfying to hear that the sisters of the world are banding together."

"Thank you. Yes, it's taken so long to be heard. Now we need action."

"I was wondering, are you related to Rodney Cao?"

Lucille was taken aback, surprise written on her face. She hesitated, "Yes, he's my brother."

Now confident that all she had guessed and thought was true, Kathy extended her hand. "I thought you might be. Pleased to meet you. I'm Kathy, Mia's guardian."

There was a pregnant silence as Lucille digested what she'd just heard. So, this blonde, blue-eyed, attractive woman shaking her hand and smiling was Cord's wife, the woman he'd chosen over her. She fought back a sudden wave of loss and disappointment; it took all her fortitude and strength of mind to answer calmly, without choking emotion.

"Oh, yes, Rodney told me he'd schooled Mia in Australia. I would have liked to have seen her, but as she's over on the other side of Australia, it wasn't possible this time."

It was such a lame comment and for once, she'd lost control of the situation. Not knowing what else to say, she half-laughed, "Well, that's a good buy. The moon T-shirt is very appropriate for her."

They searched each other's eyes.

"Nice to meet you."

"You too."

And they parted.

*****

Cord, Kathy and Mia had breakfast on the balcony; it was still chilly but a fine day. Mia wore her school uniform and munched away on cereal. Kathy had cooked Cord's favourite, bacon and eggs and was preparing her own meal, a yoghurt and fruit smoothie.

"Thanks, Mum, the T-shirt's great. I might do a design for guys as well. Must be so many foreign words for moon. I did one for Pa, *Titan*. It's a moon of Saturn and means immortal in Greek mythology. Suits Pa, don't you think?"

Mia was in her second term at a private girls' school and had one day, quite casually announced she'd like to call Kathy 'Mum' and Cord 'Pa.' It stemmed from their many appearances at school and sports functions and she didn't want always to be saying 'Aunt Kathy' and 'Uncle Cord' to her friends. Her teenage view was, it's so embarrassing, with emphasis on the 'so'.

Kathy was thrilled and Cord said, "If your father agrees, then it's okay." Rodney agreed and it became definite, although Eileen thought it inappropriate.

Looking sideways at Cord to gauge his reaction, Kathy said, "Mia, I met your Aunt Lucille at the conference."

"What! Really, did you, Mum? That's fantastic. What did she say?"

"She said to say hi and she'd visit another time. She's quite a highflyer."

"I know she's always busy, same as Father."

Kathy looked across at Cord.

"You've met her, haven't you, Cord?"

He'd paused in eating and was thoughtfully sipping his coffee.

"Lucille? Yeah, a long time ago."

"She's beautiful, I mean, really beautiful and intelligent. I was most impressed with her talk."

Cord rose from the table, "No doubt a career woman. *Titan,* you say, immortal. That's me! Can't wait to see it. Come on, I'll drop you at school."

Tuppence
2012

Clyde swung the helicopter low over the terrain so that everyone, especially Mia sitting in the cockpit, could see the mosaic of rivers and creeks cutting through the ranges and wetlands, dividing the land into segments, creating a jigsaw of coloured landforms. They were soon flying along the rugged coastline with its bays and white beaches fringed with crisp green mangroves. The blue ocean, silky, lazy, serene, caressed the shoreline and in one final swoop, the chopper lifted and crested the coastal cliffs, revealing beyond a vast expanse of lush tall grass that stretched to the far horizon. The craft slowed as the welcoming site of the homestead and yards came into view before Clyde sat it down gently in a flurry of dust at the backdoor.

It was the start of the Dry and the mustering season and apart from Kathy, Mia and Cord, the other passengers were four new ringers just as excited as Mia to be at the station. People came running; Joan enveloped Kathy in a bear hug, and Ted quickly shook Cord's hand and uttered welcome phrases. Albert and May stood back, smiling, waiting to help with the luggage. Davy helped Clyde unload supplies.

Cord felt at home amongst the hustle and bustle. He could hear the ticking of the sprinklers on the lawn and see the delicate pink flowers on the Frangipani trees that bordered the driveway. A feeling of nostalgia came over him as he saw a man perched on a ride-on mower, criss-crossing the side lawn. For a moment, he pictured Boris, but it was an unfamiliar stock hand and the moment passed.

Barry and Sofie were on the veranda at a table, hustling the bush flies away from May's famous muffins. Mia was the centre of attention, but the shy teenager stayed close to Kathy.

Joan embraced her. "Hello, Mia. We have a surprise for you, sweetheart, but first, we'll settle you all in your rooms. You'll have Kathy's, oops, your mum's old room. How would you like that? But we have a bigger surprise later."

The women and Mia retreated into the house while the men sat on the veranda under the slow flapping fan. Clouds billowed, showing their grey underbellies; the day was turning sultry. May brought a flask of chilled water and iced glasses with lemon slices.

Ted spoke, "You're looking well, Cord. Joan says it's been almost two years since you were here last. I can't keep track."

"You're looking well yourself."

Ted chuckled, "Woke up this morning. That's the main thing. How's the arm?"

"Oh, I'm lucky the arm's healed, but it's taken time, all right. Yeah, we've been busy, what with setting up the business and with Mia at school. Time just goes. Everything in place for the muster?"

Barry answered, "We're hiring our ringers now. We've got eight returning and the four new ones who came with you. It'd be great to have Kat back, but I bet you've got other plans for her."

"This son of mine's a bloody taskmaster, almost broke my back," Ted remarked.

Barry continued, "Keep twelve September open in your calendar. Sofie and I are tying the knot and before Kat pipes in, we'd like you and her to be in the bridal party. Sofie's brother Mike is the best man and she's set it in the school holidays, 'cause she'd like Mia to be her flower girl. Is that okay?"

"We'd be honoured. It's a date. Is it here at Jacana?"

"Too right! A real bush wedding."

Barry was in his element and spoke enthusiastically about the new breeding program while Ted looked on with pride. He'd introduced cow strains from Mexico to increase the herd's productivity rate and imported a Simbrah bull from the USA, a variety known for muscle weight and quality beef.

"Have a look at him later. He's a brute but a softy; wouldn't hurt a fly. Sofie's almost finished her vet's nurse course, which'll be a big help around the place. You know she's already a registered hospital nurse!"

Cord was back; he wanted to embrace and open his arms to this land he loved. The Stony Ridge Range beckoned with its memories of cragged ramparts, the spectacular Mammoth Gorge, camels, buffalo and the haunting howl of the dingo at night. He and Kathy would take Mia to Apricot Springs for a swim to taste apricots fresh from the bush and see the Jacana birds treading lightly on the lily pads. In time, he'd chat with Albert; often, it was not a chat, just a sitting together in a mutually enjoyable silence. He hoped Albert would sing for Mia and tap his sticks, but it was always up to him whether he did or not; it wasn't something you requested.

They were here for the two-week term break and it was Mia's first time on holiday with Cord and Kathy since commencing school. At home, she'd quickly won the hearts of Corrine, Mark, her new cousins, as well as Keith, who right from the start said, "Call me Gramps, but don't call me late for dinner."

It was an old joke that Mia thought hilarious and repeated it with explanation to Cord and Kathy. Eileen did her best but found it taxing to have a child in the family who looked racially different; beautiful, but still different. Mia's intelligence and obvious skill at hockey went some way to easing Eileen's initial discomfort, although the term Gran, which Keith insisted Mia use, sat awkwardly with her, but it was better than Mia calling her by her first name, a situation Eileen just couldn't tolerate.

Joan and Sofie had pulled out all the stops for dinner, a sumptuous beef stroganoff with mashed potatoes and broccoli. May made a jelly containing Bush Apricot pieces and vanilla ice cream from a secret home recipe. Mia was unusually quiet and ate sparingly except for the vegetables and dessert.

"She's a partial vegetarian," Kathy said. "Sorry, Mum, I forgot to tell you. I think it comes from her Malay upbringing. She'll eat meat in a curry, though."

"So, we have an enemy in our midst," Ted chuckled. "Does she eat fish, seafood?"

"Yes, loves it stir-fried."

"I'll get Davy to go to the creek tomorrow to catch a Barra and a couple of mangrove crabs."

"Great, Dad."

*****

Kathy and Cord relaxed on the swing lounge on the veranda, watching the morning sun breaking through distant clouds. Mia came with a cup of coffee for Cord. "May says she's bringing your tea. She says I should call her May. Will I call her that, Mum?"

"Yes, that's okay. Today's your big surprise. Put on your jeans, long-sleeved shirt, joggers and that brimmed hat I bought."

Mia had just left when Kathy abruptly stood up, "On second thoughts, I'd better organise her with her new bra. She's coming of age, you know."

With everyone ready for the surprise, they walked to the first yard with Ted and Joan. Mia ran ahead to see the horses standing quietly, munching hay Davy had thrown them.

Ted rested one foot on the lowest fence bar and said, "I didn't want to worry you, Kathy, but we put Penny out to pasture last year with a fetlock injury and she never recovered, but Twobob is still working the muster. Come on, we've a surprise for you both. Have a look here!"

Davy led two young mares into the yard. Joan came to the fence and held Mia's hand. "They've just been broke. Albert says they're as gentle as lambs. Now, which one would you like, sweetheart?"

Mia gasped and held her hand to her mouth in astonishment. She looked the complete jillaroo in the wide-brimmed hat and clothes Kathy had chosen for her. She pointed to the grey, leaving Kathy with the golden brown.

Mia jumped excitedly, "Oh! Mum! What's her name?"

"You can call her what you like."

Cord had taken a bunch of carrots from the stable, walked to the far paddock boundary and leant on the top rail. A horse broke away from the herd grazing in the far corner and galloped towards him. Dollar arrived snorting and nudged Cord powerfully, pushing him backwards off the rail. He recovered and stepped forward to stroke her softly across the nose. Her big eyes were upon him as he reached under the crossbars to pat her belly, which he knew she liked and always stood docile.

"It's good to see you too. How about a ride later?"

Dollar nodded her head in agreement. He fed her the carrots as the herd slowly moved towards them. He noticed Twobob amongst them, as well as Old Moses. Kathy said she'd teach Mia to ride on Old Moses, the most patient and quietest horse they'd ever had, a true quarter horse.

That afternoon, after much discussion, they decided to retain the monetary theme and Kathy's brown became Copper and Mia's grey Tuppence.

The first few days, Kathy spent most of the time with Joan, with Mia always close by. Each day for two hours, Kathy gave Mia riding lessons and allowed her to pet Tuppence under Davy's supervision. Mia was a natural at sports and quickly took to riding so that by the end of the first week, she could saddle up, ride at a canter and brush the horse down. She spent as much time as she could with Tuppence.

In the meantime, Cord was able to catch up with Albert, who agreed to drive him and Mia to Mammoth Gorge in the next week.

"Waterfalls still drop down. Swimming no good. Plenty swirlys," Albert said.

*****

During the first week, a truck with a fully enclosed back canopy and lettering on the side reading 'Dexters Deliveries' drove in and parked at the homestead steps.

Dexter emerged from the cab in his worn khaki shorts and shirt, pushing back the brim of his tattered Akubra as he made his way up the steps onto the veranda. His eyes lit up when he saw Cord sitting there and his craggy, sunburnt face burst into a wide grin.

He held out his leathery hand. "Crikey, you're a sight for tired eyes, Landman. Where've ya been hidin'?"

Cord shook his hand. "Here and there. Good to see you, Dex. How've you been?"

"Up ta' mud. Same-old-same-old, but I can't complain. No bugger listens anyway. Heard you broke your arm. Hope it wasn't your beer arm."

"Nah, lucky it wasn't. See you've got a new vehicle."

"Yep, an Isuzu four-wheel drive. Can kip in the truck cab when I want. Had to get it, as I do a lot now for Aussie Post and take some bigger stuff the choppers can't handle. Yeah, she's a beauty, all right."

At that moment, Mia came out of the house and Dexter smiled. "Well, what've we got here? You're a cutie."

With no better explanation, Cord simply said, "This is Mia, our daughter."

Dexter removed his hat and scratched his head. "Well, I never. Yeah, she looks…" he hesitated, then said, "She looks nice."

He was still entranced by the child when Cord asked, "We flew in with Clyde. How's Maggot going? Is he still around?"

"Maggot! He's contract musterin' in the Territory. Got himself married to a Yankee Sheila he brought back when he got his new chopper. A real beauty."

"The wife or the chopper?"

Dexter ignored the comment and continued, with a wink and a nudge, "Her name's Marylou, a real bonza lass. She's a qualified copter mechanic. He's got his head screwed on right, that boy."

He chuckled again, "Mixes business with pleasure if ya know what I mean."

He paused and rubbed his bristled chin.

"Charlie Cox at Minindi Wells reckons Maggot's too dear, but we've all got our overheads. He should grizzle! Everyone knows he charges like a wounded bull for his weaners. Makes every post a winner, that prick. I tell ya, he was goin' on and on about Maggot bein' a thief with his charges. Now, ya know me, bein' a person who don't like to talk behind another person's back, I told him I'd clobber him if he didn't shut up. Maggot's a good bloke, not a wanka' like Charlie."

He gave Mia a wink, scratched his head and said to Cord, "Ya know Laura Carter at Ludlow?"

"Yeah, sure."

"She ran off with that cocky bastard Bluey Giles, another bloody wanka'. The Carters are pissed off, ya can't blame 'em. It's not like the old days round here. The country's full of wanka's, especially those minin' pricks, but they pay on time, that's the main thing. Well, I'd better see Sofie and get these supplies unloaded. I'm stayin' for tea. How about a beer later?"

He smiled at Mia, showing his yellowed teeth. "See ya later, cutie."

Mia had been sitting, listening in silence. After he left, she said incredulously, "Pa, what's a wanker?"

Cord was dumbfounded for a moment, gathered his senses and answered, "It's a man you wouldn't trust."

"So, it's gender-specific?"

Cord thought, really? At thirteen, where did she get these terms?

"Yes, gender-specific, but it's a swear word. Don't let your mum hear you use it, okay?"

"Okay, but who was that?"

"That was Dexter." Then, with a mischievous smile and a wink, he added, "Unaccustomed as I am to talk behind a person's back, Dexter is a fair dinkum, true-blue, dyed in the wool, ridgy-didge, Aussie battler. A rare and dying breed."

*****

On a cooler day, Cord, Kathy and Mia saddled their horses and headed to the high ground, to the small graveyard overlooking the sea. The tide was out and the narrow beach with its fringe of mangroves was exposed to the cliff edge. A light and warm tropical breeze floated across the water, swirling and tossing, keeping the flies at bay. They dismounted near the greying tombstone containing the inscription for Boris.

"Is this your friend who died from a snake bite?" Mia asked.

Cord nodded, knelt and pulled long grass from the grave.

Kathy and Mia strolled to the cliff edge to watch a flock of storks patrolling the tidal flat below.

"Some people call them Jabirus," Kathy said, "but they're actually Black-necked storks. Why they're called Black-necked when their neck plumage is iridescent blue is a mystery. Can you see their long, bright red legs?"

Mia nodded, completely fascinated with the splendour of it all.

Cord pulled a satchel from his saddlebag and removed three bright red beer cans. He was out of earshot of Kathy and Mia.

"Here you are, you crazy Spaniard. Let's have a fuckin' beer. I tried to keep 'em cold. You'd recognise 'em. They're *Ambar Cerveza* from your home town, Barcelona. A craft shop got 'em for me."

He twisted the ring tabs on two cans, took a swig from one, poured the other over the grave and then sat back on his haunches. A tear came to his eye. "I hope there's a heaven and you're up there with your wife and kids. Miss you, man."

He drained his can, put the two empties in the satchel and put it back in the saddlebag. He scraped a hole in the grave and buried the full can.

"That's for later. Not a bad brew, eh?"

Kathy and Mia were already mounted and standing someway off. Cord mounted Dollar, looked back sadly at the grave and slowly rode away.

*****

The trip to Mammoth Gorge with Albert was initially disappointing. Jacana Creek was running full and the vehicle track to the gorge itself was unpassable. They couldn't get close enough, even on high ground, to see the stream gushing from the gorge mouth and had to be content with hearing the booming and thundering as the torrent cascaded through the ravine.

However, their disappointment soon abated when Albert said, "Stop here, Landman. Listen to the song of country, remember, like before. The land's singing from the Wet."

He hummed to himself, produced his tapping sticks and then began to chant. Cord and Mia listened, transfixed by the wailing cry of the gorge and the magic of his ancient song. He stopped abruptly, "Come on, storms coming."

Cord and Mia were inspired by what they had just witnessed and heard. Back in the vehicle, Cord said, "Tomorrow it's Apricot Springs. We'll ride the horses there."

*****

It was sultry but hadn't reached the sapping humidity that came with the later months. The ground was wet and boggy in places, but in these conditions, the horses held their own. May had packed a light lunch, green salads, cracker biscuits with lashings of Vegemite, cheese cubes and two flasks of chilled orange juice. After leaving their picnic gear at the top pool, they tethered the horses under the shade of river gums by the creek where they could graze and access water. Mia was enchanted as they climbed to the top, touching the water at each pool.

"It's so warm and feels tingly. Which one will we swim in, Mum?"

"Down at the third pool, it's cooler."

Mia raced ahead.

"Don't you slip," Kathy called.

"Do you remember this?" Kathy said as she emerged from under the rock overhang in her orange bikini, her figure trim and curvaceous.

"Lives in my memory," Cord replied.

Mia was below them with binoculars, spying on the Jacana birds. She was in a two-piece suit of deep green and Cord noticed her figure was beginning to show the allure of approaching womanhood, but she was still a child at heart and would always be a child to him.

She continued to astound him. Last evening, after spending some time researching 'stuff' on Kathy's laptop, she said, "Pa, I've decided to be an Analytical Veterinarian."

"Why? Do you want to study cattle?"

"No, snakes, Pa! Your friend would be alive if there was anti-venom. You know some animals can resist snakebite. They found that chimps in Africa, where there are snakes, have venom resistance receptors in their body, but the same chimps in Madagascar, where there are no snakes, don't have resistance receptors. You know, some snakes inject three toxins, but the Australian Inland Taipan injects nine toxins. It's the deadliest snake in the world and it lives up here where we are. There's enough toxin in a single bite to kill a hundred humans. How about that! There are therapeutic drugs made from venom for heart disorders. I'd like to know all about their poisons and invent a cure."

Cord was amazed at her verve and intelligence. "That'd be good."

"Could we take Tuppence home, back to Perth?"

"No, that wouldn't be fair. Tuppence is a quarter horse and she belongs up here."

The water in the lower pool was much cooler and the Bush Apricots bordering the edge were in full bloom. Kathy laid out a large blanket under a rocky outcrop and the three swam and frolicked in the pool till lunchtime. They accompanied the picnic fare May had prepared, with the mouth-watering taste of fresh fleshy apricots and there were enough on the boughs to pick a bagful for Sofie. It was a day whiled away in complete solitude. Cord dozed in the shade of the overhang while Kathy told Mia tales of the traditional owners and the sacredness of this special place.

Mia said, "It's so beautiful, I never want to leave."

But they had to and it was late afternoon when they rode into the yards. The day had cooled by the time they finished attending the horses and Mia was ready for bed. May made her a toasted sandwich, she had a quick shower and she was soon in bed, fast asleep.

Cord lay in bed listening to the quiet breathing of Kathy sleeping beside him. It was a full moon and an hour before, they danced in close embrace on the veranda to the romantic voice of Neil Young crooning their favourite song, *Harvest Moon*. Half an hour earlier, they'd made gentle, exquisite love. A slight breeze tickled the curtains of the open French door. He could hear the faint ticking of the lawn sprinklers and occasionally a snort and a bellow from the cattle in the yards. He turned over to gaze at his slumbering wife. How beautiful she looked. He couldn't be happier and eventually drifted into a peaceful sleep.

Hoon
2013

Mia hadn't seen her father for a year, so was overjoyed when he arranged for her to fly to Kuala Lumpur to be with the family on her fourteenth birthday. She needed a week off school to coincide with the date and Kathy arranged it with the principal.

For the occasion, Rodney booked tickets for a tour-meal package at the Bird Park but unfortunately chose the package themed for children with balloons, face painting and a clown for the guided tour, not quite suitable for a teenage girl. On a call to Cord, Mia mentioned that her father was worried and distracted with business concerns.

"Grandfather told me Father had to sell the tea plantation at Tanah Rata to pay off debts and Aunt Lucille is taking time off work to help out. Grandfather and Grandmother aren't well. I should be there to help as well."

Cord contacted Rodney, hoping to gain further information, but Rodney brushed his concern aside. "Yes, we sold one of our plantations merely to consolidate our financial position. We needed to expand our portfolio in other directions to keep up with market trends. Other than that, it's business as usual."

Cord told Kathy, "Typical Rodney, he's a mystery man. I often think his right hand doesn't know what his left hand's doing."

"Just as long as Mia's safe."

"Oh, I'm sure she is."

After her birthday week in Kuala Lumpur, Mia returned to school to finish the school year.

She was among the top students and, with her sporting ability, was popular at school. During the year, Kathy arranged sleepovers for Mia with school friends and there was always something happening at the McCullum house. Kathy was pleased when Rodney proposed Mia stay in Australia over the holiday. He was arranging retirement accommodation for his parents and promised to visit when he could. Mia didn't seem to mind staying on. The holiday was six weeks and Mia said, "It'll be time to chill out."

Cord gave her the opportunity in December to learn to surf. "If you want to surf, now's the right time. You'll have to go to classes to get the Bronze Medallion like I had to. Surfing is exciting, but it can be dangerous, especially if you're not trained."

Mia enthusiastically responded to the challenge. Classes were arranged with a coastal surf club and she and Kathy became regulars at meetings and carnivals. Kathy wanted to devote as much time as possible to Mia and was pleased that Mollie could now step up as the primary go-to person for Landwoman Inc.

On the other hand, Cord had his own challenges. He'd always maintained a hands-on approach to Landman Inc. and one client, in particular, had a lease to mine iron occurring in banded ore formations termed 'BIF' country. The lease was located in ranges riddled with caves containing paintings of spiritual significance to the traditional owners, as well as artefacts and middens of archaeological importance to the nation. It was a complex matter from a political and economic perspective; the weight of the mining fraternity with the benefit of royalties and large-scale employment was pitted against the growing swell of public opinion opposing the destruction of Aboriginal sites and unique flora and fauna species. The input of Kathy and the Landwoman Inc. team was a bonus. It was a sensitive issue and Cord briefed his team that it was essential the report be impartial and free of bias.

"Remember, our mission at Landman Inc. is, first and foremost, to protect Mother Earth. In this case, our brief is simply to advise our clients where on their lease they can mine with impunity and subject to the challenges we've detailed. We'll advise on where they cannot mine, and most importantly, where they do get permission to mine, there's a comprehensive rehabilitation program in place."

Consequently, Cord oversaw the final recommendations and faced meetings with the stakeholders. It was a busy and trying time; business was booming and in the midst of it, Kathy developed a cold that quickly turned into full-blown influenza.

"You're taking on too much," Cord said. "We need a break and have a window. What say we take a trip to Jacana and have Christmas there with your family? It'll give Mia time with us and the chance to see the country during the Wet?"

So, they went.

The Wet lived up to expectations and almost every day rain cascaded down from massive black thunderclouds. Lightning struck the ground, sparking brief fires in the remaining dry grass, which the rain quickly extinguished. The creek rose in flood, with rapids and waterfalls everywhere as the torrent surged to the sea. Horse riding was limited to some extent, but Cord rode with Mia every time there was a break in the weather.

Christmas Day dawned, sultry and muggy. The homestead fans were at full tempo; the delicious aroma of roast turkey and pot roast filled the air. People came from the surrounding communities with presents of hand-woven baskets and paintings. The children sang *Silent Night*, a little out of tune but with great gusto. Ted flicked on the outside yard speaker system for everyone to hear *Gurrumul* singing *Amazing Grace*. Even the cattle stood silently in the yard. It was a time for presents; beer and wine flowed freely, and Ted kept his eye on the young ones.

Mia received an array of RM Williams riding gear from the family and a painting of Tuppence from Davy, who had a flair for drawing. Kathy brought along a package for Mia she'd received the month before. It contained a cheque for three hundred dollars from Rodney and a braided leather Native American headband from Lucille with a finely hand-crafted pair of soft leather riding boots stamped *Apache Nation*.

Kathy's flu persisted, keeping her inside with Joan and May for most of the time as they applied various tried and true homemade bush remedies to break the malady.

Mia loved to stand out on the lawn laughing and excited in the warm rain that drenched her, while Cord sat on the veranda smiling, cuddling his wife as her cough persisted. It was a relaxing time, but Cord noticed Kathy was listless, far from her normal self. She tried to put on a brave face, but as the malaise persevered, Cord resolved that she see a doctor on their return home.

Eventually, the rain ceased and Clyde flew in medicine, a course of antibiotics from the town clinic, and over the next week, Kathy's condition improved; she began to feel like her own self again. She rode with Mia every day before they sadly departed Jacana and headed home.

*****

In the south, the weather was unpredictable, with no set pattern. The days see-sawed between fine, still, sunny days without cloud to fierce rainstorms that quickly abated.

It was a fine day and Mia had already left for school. Kathy made Cord a cappuccino and they looked forward to a quiet time to discuss the day's events in the privacy of their lounge room and enjoy the tranquil river scene through the bay window. Kathy's mobile phone rang.

"Yes, it is she."

Cord couldn't make out the gist of the conversation filled with yeses, ohs and a final thank you.

Kathy seemed taken aback and bewildered. "It was Doctor Roberts. He said the results of my blood tests are through and he's referred me to a Doctor Chang who specialises in blood prognosis."

"What does that mean?"

"He didn't say, just that I have an appointment next week. He insisted, so I'll have to change my schedule."

Cord was worried, but to allay her concerns, said, "These cold wogs can hang around. It's good the doctors are on to these things."

"But I'm feeling okay now."

"Yeah, you've turned the corner, but it's best we go and sort it out."

Doctor Michael Chang's rooms were at a private hospital on the north side of the river. Kathy was nervous as they drove through the heavy morning traffic to the first appointment and Cord tried to hide his concerns with idle chit-chat. Doctor Roberts was non-committal when Cord followed up on the telephone conversation Roberts had with Kathy, except to say that her immune system was down, and Chang was a haematologist specialising in this area.

After a half-hour wait, the receptionist ushered them into Chang's office. It was a stark white room with the barest of furniture; a desk, two visitors' chairs and a stretcher bed. There was electronic equipment with flickering lights standing in one corner. Chang was a short middle-aged man with an earnest, concerned look that his ready smile couldn't hide when they shook hands. He gave the impression of aloofness, which Cord surmised was part of the nature of the job, not to get too close and personally involved with patients needing his specialist care.

"Tell me, how are you feeling today?" Chang began.

"I feel better now than a few weeks ago when I had that dreadful flu."

"On a scale of ten, how would you rate today on how you would normally feel?"

Kathy thought for a while, "Six to seven. No, definitely seven."

"The tests you've had show evidence of a blood disorder, disrupting your immune system. We need to conduct further tests over the next few weeks to get to the root of the problem."

And so it went. Kathy began weeks of tests and treatment, driving to the clinic twice a week through the city traffic. She said to Cord, "I hate driving here. It's a rat race. There's no courtesy and everyone's speeding."

"I'll drive you."

"No, you won't. You've got lots to do here."

"You'll get used to the traffic. The trouble is you're so used to driving up north where neighbours, truckies, tourists and even strangers wave as they pass. Some often stop to have a bit of a chat. Outback people are on a different timeline to your city cousins."

"These people are not my cousins," she said indignantly.

*****

Hubert 'Hughie' Riley was at home on leave from the navy. He grew up on a government housing estate in the outer suburbs and left school at fifteen to work in a takeaway pizza shop. His lazy mother quickly seized any money he made to supplement her cigarette supply, even though she was on full government benefits. His father left home when Hughie was seven and no one knew where he was.

"Good riddance," his mother said, "I never want to see that bastard again."

Now, his married sister, separated with two kids, lived with his mother. Hughie didn't relish coming home, but it was all the family he had and now he arrived home as a man, not a kid.

At seventeen, Hughie joined the navy to get away from it all. From the start, he loved being in uniform and forming friendships with his peer group. He liked the discipline, the schedules and the sense of duty. For once, he felt a sense of belonging.

Now he was twenty, halfway through his tour of duty, and while his sense of purpose hadn't changed, he knew his dream to become a commissioned officer and wear a uniform of rank would never be realised. It took all that time and effort to rise from his intake rank of Leading Seaman to his existing rank of Able Seaman and there he'd probably plateau. If he hadn't progressed at the end of his stint, he thought he might try the merchant ships; they might give him a rank and a uniform.

He would probably need to take that route since one senior officer rated Hughie as: 'Competent Seaman, but scatterbrained, irrational, given to spontaneous rash decisions. Not suitable for a combat role. Recommend ship maintenance duties'.

Navy personnel were entitled to free travel to and from their home State each year and Hughie qualified for this entitlement. He had money in his pocket from years of saving and his mother and sister took advantage of this windfall, ingratiating themselves using loving words and gestures, but they didn't even cook him a meal and food was still takeaway. He didn't mind paying for shopping sprees for their cheap clothes, toys and cinema for the kids; after all, it was only for a few weeks. It made him feel wanted and important.

"There's a nice new Thai restaurant over in the shopping centre, sweetheart. They do takeaways. We could try that. The kids want fish and chips and there's a fish shop there too. Let me just finish watching my TV show. We can drive over after that if you like, lovey?"

"Sure, Mum."

His sister was outside on the back patio painting her toenails and having a fag; the kids were playing in the sand pit. She cried out, "Make sure ya get extra noodles!"

Hughie indulged himself by renting a newly released Commodore Super Sports V6 sedan in glossy lime green paintwork and was pleased to exhibit it in the front driveway for neighbours and all to see. It was another mark of importance and success, which no one could deny.

He drove on his own to isolated spots on the suburb outskirts where he could hoon, put his foot down and test the turbo on this baby. It was going to be a hot day, so that morning, Hughie decided to drive to the beach to check out the chicks in their bikinis.

Traffic was heavy and a big rig he was following in the right lane slowed and showed no indication of moving to the inside left lane to let him pass. He was impatient. Bugger this, he thought, planted his foot and swung into the vacant left lane, not realising that the truck was slowing to let a small car turn right across traffic into the driveway of a medical practice.

The Commodore surged forward. He saw the turning car and braked hard, but it was too late; he slammed into the vehicle, catapulting it into a lamppost. Hughie's car rolled, skidded on its hood and was dragged under the rig's wheels. The lone driver of the small car and Hughie died at the scene.

The other driver was Kathryn Joy McCullum.

Moving On
2013

Kathy's burial was in the small graveyard on the high ground by the cliff overlooking the clear blue sea. The station homestead could be seen in the distance and the site overlooked the horse paddock where the Bluegrass pasture was sprouting. Twobob stood by the graveyard fence for days.

They say horses don't grieve, but Albert said, "Twobob's not himself. He knows somethin's wrong."

It was supposed to be a private funeral, but up north, such an event doesn't exclude anyone who wants to pay their respects. People came from everywhere; some drove hundreds of kilometres to be at the homestead overnight. Maggot and Marylou flew in, as did Clyde and Melinda, who also brought Reverend White. Laura Carter came out of hiding without Bluey Giles, and Dexter came with Doreen. There were the Millers, the new owners of Charcoal Flats, a busload from Ludlow Hills, Bert and Sharon Doig with a large complement from Indigo Downs except Jason, who was overseas. Sharon came early to help the family, Joan, Sofie, May, Eileen and Corrine, cope with managing the gathering crowd.

The community mobs had been drifting in over the days before and the women's wailing penetrated the nights. Rodney was contacted in South America and sent his condolences. The closed coffin rested in the living room and mourners in silent tribute paraded past the casket, layering it with heaps of flowery wreaths.

Sofie and Mia brought fruit and blossoms from Apricot Springs for the burial, which was to be a private affair, family and selected guests only, to be held the day following the funeral ceremony and wake.

Cord was numb. Now two weeks after the accident, he still hadn't recovered from the shock to even eat or dress. Keith stayed with him while

Eileen and Corrine cared for Mia. There are degrees to mourning and the depth of grief is an isolated personal experience. Cord sank to the lowest level as his mind wandered, bordering on the brink of deep depression. The drugs his doctor prescribed allowed him to sleep in short, sharp bursts until he woke suddenly bathed in sweat, recalling images of the two women he loved, teasing him, taunting him. There would never be another woman; it was too late. Why was it so? He lost Lucille without so much as a goodbye. He couldn't believe her callous deception, selling herself for commercial interests, and his Kathy who left him so suddenly, so quickly, without the chance to say goodbye. Now, there was nothing; he was doomed. Then he thought of Mia; she needed him. He couldn't lose her.

The day after the massed congregation had departed the station, the family gathered and conveyed the casket, on a buggy drawn by Twobob and Dollar, to the family graveyard overlooking the bay where the waters of Jacana Creek flowed quietly into the sea. The station community followed in procession. The grave was dug in the deep, black, fertile soil close to Kathy's grandparents. In the distance, white fluffy clouds gathered. A swirling breeze stirred the budding Bluegrass, ruffling clothes and sending hats flying. A flight of Curlew Sandpipers swooped overhead, squawking in protest at the intruders close to their cliff nests. May said the Earth was paying a final tribute to a life well lived. The women wept and howled.

Mia held Cord's hand tightly, tears streaming down her cheeks as Reverend White read the last prayers. Chairs were brought, but Cord stood erect. He couldn't cry. With dry eyes, he stared blankly across the inland plain to the faint smudge of the distant Stony Ridge Range on the horizon.

Barry delivered the final eulogy as the casket was lowered to rest. The women were now silent, but softly, in the background, Albert began tapping his sticks, chanting a song of Aboriginal farewell.

Head bowed, Barry spoke sorrowfully and with aplomb.

"My big sister was, and still is, my inspiration in life. I can't imagine this life without her here looking over my shoulder. She approached life full-on and taught me not to be afraid. I remember when I was five and Dad had isolated a young maverick bull in the muster for future breeding. It was wild and angry, alone in a side yard. Every day, Sis would take a sheaf of corncobs to the yard and place it inside the fence. After a week, Sis opened the gate, went into the yard and placed the sheaf in front of the bull. He didn't move. After another week, and I know Dad and Mum were angry when they found out, she was able to hand-feed him and pat his nose. She called him Wild Bill. Those weeks, I stood in awe at the rails, watching her. Weren't you scared, I asked. She said she was but sympathised with what Bill had been through. He was young and confused. Being caught and yarded in the muster and then left alone in a yard without the protection of the herd, he was probably more scared of her than she was of him. I guess I just wanted to calm him, she said, he was so frightened. That was her way in life with everyone she met. Calm, dignified, beautiful and effervescent. We all know Wild Bill became one of our best Brahman breeders and followed Sis everywhere she went. And so it went with her. She had that way with animals; the horses, the dogs all flocked to her side. As a champion equestrian, she could have trained for the Olympic team, but her heart was here at Jacana. How many things do you touch in life? Sis touched so many and accomplished so much. She conversed and knew the language of our traditional owners, which came from a profound love of the land we share with them."

He paused and choked a little, wiping a tear from his eye with his fist. "Kathy, now that you're gone, life will never be the same for me or for any of us at the station, but I know that because of you, I will never be afraid. Rest in peace, my sister."

Slowly, the mourners came and individually dropped the apricot sprigs onto the lowered coffin. Ted held Joan tightly, both sobbing as the family followed. Albert sang while Davy played the didgeridoo. The haunting sounds of the ancient instrument echoed across the land as it had done for thousands of years.

Cord didn't leave the grave till nightfall. He watched the station hands slowly, silently, shovelling the last clods of soil until it was a neat, sculptured mound before they downed tools and walked away. A sultry half-moon rose in the sky and the rain held off. He was a lone figure, except for Albert and May, whom he didn't see, squatting away in the shadows, quietly waiting and watching.

The homestead lights were twinkling below when Sofie and Corrine drove up in the Cruiser. "It's going to rain later tonight," Sofie said as an explanation to leave.

Corrine wrapped her arms around her brother. "Come on, Bruv, Mia's waiting for you. It's time to go."

He stood and then the tears flowed. His body rocked with paroxysms of anguish and he bellowed into the night louder than any dingo howl. The two women cradled him in their arms, they too crying as he clutched at them for comfort. "Why?" he cried.

Kathy was gone and there was nothing he could do.

Albert and May waited until the vehicle had gone and came out of the shadows. May took a handful of soil and wrapped it in a cloth; Albert broke his singing sticks in half and placed them on the grave.

*****

Sofie was the bright light in the darkness of despair. Her presence and positive outlook shone through in the stressful days following the troubled time. As Barry's wife, she'd taken on the role of daughter to Joan and Ted and brought new and refreshing ideas to station life. She set up a veterinary clinic for ailing animals, available to all the neighbours.

Sharon Doig took advantage of Sofie's professional status with her quarter horse breeding program. Sofie endorsed a certificate of progeny and a health profile for each animal, which enabled Sharon to gain registration as a qualified breeder of thoroughbred horses. They became firm friends.

On the banks of the creek in the black alluvial soil, Sofie established an extensive garden of vegetables and herbs fully protected with a solid fence and mesh against marauding birds and cattle. Davy was given the job of catching a few nanny goats.

She explained, "When they're tamed, I want to try goats' milk and making cheese."

Sofie's museum for station artefacts was well established but not open to the public yet. Boris's old Patrol with the hole in the door from the buffalo was highlighted. The surrounding stations supplied objects, rusted, broken and discarded; it didn't matter for her enterprise. Cliff, who replaced Boris as a general hand, was sent methodically to the station rubbish tip with the bobcat to carefully excavate the contents. The treasure trove grew; it was a bonanza.

Barry was reluctantly involved in supervising the restoration of the pieces. Initially, he complained, "What do ya want with this old junk?"

"You never know," Sofie said. "We might have tourists here one day. Everyone in the city wants to experience the great outdoors, so we best be prepared. We can even jar and sell May's Bush Apricot relish."

She was dynamic and full of ideas. Barry nodded, succumbing to his woman's indisputable logic.

Cord's responsibility to Mia brought him out of the doldrums. Mia and Sofie bonded from the moment Mia was engaged as a flower girl at Barry and Sofie's wedding. Cord realised that his trips to Jacana would be limited in the future, but he was pleased that Mia could visit regularly. He stayed on at the station for several weeks before returning to Perth.

One evening, he and Corrine sat on the veranda overlooking the drive and the Frangipani trees that had, just that afternoon, begun to shed their delicate pink bloom onto the green lawn.

"This really is a lovely place," Corrine said. "I can see why you love it here."

Cord leant forward in his chair, bowed his head and covered his face with his hands. Eventually, he said, "If I hadn't taken Kathy down south, away from here and doing the things she loved, she'd still be alive amongst us. I'm to blame."

"That isn't true. She loved you and wanted to be with you. You and I both know; in fact, we are the only ones who know about her diagnosis of acute Leukaemia and that her time was limited. She started her treatment, but even with that, she knew it was six months at best. It was a secret she wanted kept from Mia and her parents till later, so let's keep it in our hearts, honour her wish and move on. You still have Mia to care for. The accident was a rotten fate. Don't beat yourself up on this."

"Mia! But for how long will she stay with me? What will Rodney do now that Kathy's gone?"

"Don't worry, let's take each day as it comes."

When it was time to go, he confessed to Sofie that he had cracked two cans for Boris on his previous trip and buried a full one in his grave. "I figure I owe you three bucks in fines."

Sofie smiled and hugged him, "Don't worry, Landman," she said. "With Boris, it's now on the house."

Fraud
2013

It had been three months since Kathy's death. Autumn had come and gone; the sun rose and set later as winter arrived, the days were clear and the nights chilly. It was a dark time for Cord and the changing season reflected his mood. It was only his obligation to Mia that kept him from floundering. Life moved on.

Mollie acquired Landwoman Inc. with the help of a government grant and shifted the venture to a new purpose-built building in the city. Landman Inc. continued as usual. Cord and Kathy had built an accomplished, dedicated team able to operate independently. With Kathy gone, Cord altered the company management structure and appointed Geoffrey and Simone, with their individual geological and biological expertise, to head up the organisation. He formed a Board of six members, which included Mollie, with her Indigenous background. Outside of that, he continued as a Director and owner of the KMSurvey group with Rory as Principal.

He planned the change to spend more time with Mia. It was hard for her, virtually abandoned by a work-alcoholic father and losing Kathy, she withdrew into her shell. Her grades slipped and her competitive spirit lagged.

Cord confided in Corrine, "I don't know what to do. She wants me to hug her all the time. It's just that I'm her guardian and without Kathy, I'm at a loss. Rodney's disappointed her. She doesn't hear from him much as he trips around the world and we never know where he is. He's true to form, though; business is more important to him than his daughter. I would never let her know I think that, of course."

Corrine could only hold his hand and listen. She knew he just needed to get it all off his chest.

"After Kathy's death, I thought he'd come and claim her but only emailed saying he'd like things to continue as they are. That she was settled at school and he'd continue to support her, that's all. I tell you, if I had a say and she was my daughter, I would want her with me. But I suppose it's worked in my favour. I love having her around, but I feel I'm failing her."

"Yes, being her guardian and a man, it's best you not hug her too much and she's growing up. It's okay for a father, but I've read enough crime novels and seen too many movies to know these things get misconstrued. She'll get over it. It's a natural grieving process being alone in this big world without ever knowing her birth mother, a father on the other side of the earth and losing Kathy. Naturally, she's in shock. Just hang in there for her. She'll realise she's got a ready-made family. Dad dotes on her and I know Mum's always popping in to see you both and getting her girly things. Tell you what, I'll get her back into hockey and involved in the off-season surf club programs."

"You know, Sis, you're the best."

*****

One evening after dinner, Mia was in her room studying while Cord was watching the TV news when his phone rang; it was Rodney. He was distraught and babbled in his thick accent about coming over and something about selling the Australian property. The conversation was broken, but Cord realised it was important and Rodney would arrive tomorrow.

Cord said, "Stay here with us. Mia will love to see you," but Rodney had already hung up, so Cord could only wait and ponder, not realising the calamity about to descend on him.

Mia was at school when Rodney arrived. Cord was taken aback at his appearance. How long was it since he had seen Rodney? Perhaps several years. The smooth, well-dressed, confident businessman image was gone. Rodney was unkempt and agitated and almost fell into Cord's arms when they met. He had put on weight, had a pudgy, unshaven face and long, greasy hair. The creased, drab clothes completed his uncharacteristic, dishevelled appearance.

He was highly distracted and blurted out emotive conversation in bursts of language that combined English with Mandarin. For the most part, it was incoherent gibberish to Cord's ears. Cord brought him aspirin and water and slowly, he calmed, flopping back on the lounge sofa, exhausted.

268

It took some time and questioning before Cord could comprehend Rodney's dilemma. The property bought for Mia had been sold without Rodney's knowledge. "It's fraud!" he cried. "How can this be? I've been cheated."

He was inconsolable and drifted in and out of the conservation. Tears ran down his cheeks, his face contorted in bitter disappointment. The only way out Cord could see was to contact his solicitor; it was a legal issue and Harold Foy would know what to do. He dialled the number, believing it must be a mistake; it couldn't happen in Australia. Foy wasn't available, so he left a message with the receptionist. Rodney was still sitting, sobbing and distraught on the sofa.

"Come on, let's get you showered. Have a rest and a change of clothes. Mia'll be home in a few hours and wants to see you."

While Rodney rested, Foy rang back and Cord relayed to him the sparse information he had. Foy responded, "I really can't help you here, Cord. Commercial fraud is a serious matter requiring expertise in a sphere of criminal law outside the realm of our practice. I suggest you contact Manx Mooney Attorneys. They specialise in property law, sale and management. Ask for Miriam Manx."

After an hour, Rodney emerged fresh and changed but clearly still disturbed.

"I have a contact for you, a lawyer specialising in the property arena. I suggest you make an appointment. If you like, I'll come with you. It could just be a giant mistake."

Rodney's hands were shaking, "It's no mistake. Pok Yang, my tenant, told me he had to leave. An agent came and put up a for sale sign."

"Which agent was that?"

"I don't know and Pok doesn't remember the name."

"Mia will be home soon. Make the call. We don't want to alarm her."

It was mid-afternoon, a bit early to imbibe, but Cord poured them a gin and tonic to ease matters. Despite Rodney's religious adversity, he took the glass, swallowed the contents in one swift movement and held out his glass for another, which he swallowed equally as quickly. He made the call and hung up just before Mia ran into the room and flew into his arms.

Cord stood and watched. Mia's joy knew no bounds as she hugged her father tightly. Perhaps the seriousness of Rodney's situation distracted him, so his response wasn't as warm as hers; he just patted her briefly on the shoulder. Cord thought, Rodney, you're a cold fish. He couldn't see that his daughter craved his affection. Mia hadn't seen him in so long, yet he was indifferent. Cord had to give him the benefit of the doubt; he was under considerable pressure.

Cord piped up, "Tell you what! We won't cook tonight and rather than go out for dinner, I'll leave you two alone and pop out to the Chinese takeaway. I'll be back soon."

Dinner was a quiet affair and Rodney retired early. Cord and Mia put on warm jackets. Mia made coffee, the aroma pleasant, the mugs warm and comforting in their hands. Silently, in the chill, they sat on the balcony, watching the city lights dancing on the rippling river.

Eventually, Cord spoke, "No homework tonight?"

She answered despondently, "No, I did it last night. I wanted to see Father."

"I'm sure he wants to be with you, but he's got a major business problem to address. Give him a few days to sort things out and everything will be all right. You'll see."

*****

The following day, Cord and Rodney were on the ferry. There was a chance of rain and the ride across the river was bumpy. Workers travelling to their jobs were rugged up for the wintry weather. It was a solemn journey judging by their concerned faces, buried in newspapers, thumbing mobiles, or numbly listening to radio, music or whatever on their earphones. Cord also felt depressed, sitting next to a silent and sombre Rodney on their way to meet Miriam Manx.

Manx Mooney Attorneys was in the Terrace near Harold Foy's practice. Miriam saw them straight away. She had a short stance and plumpish figure, dressed in a grey tweed trouser suit. A short, black and blonde streaked haircut and a noticeably large wristwatch gave her an overall macho appearance, but her voice was calm and soft as velvet. Cord guessed her to be in her late thirties.

They sat in a spacious, high-roofed office with black leather lounge seating for a dozen bodies at least. One wall held a massive green tapestry drape depicting a forest scene. Paintings on other walls were abstract pieces in subdued colours. A high window let some daylight into the room, but the primary illumination, except for one low-hanging central pendant, was from free-standing lamps set on and around low casual tables. The intention, by design, was to create an overall sense of peace and calmness and Cord thought it worked well.

Miriam introduced herself and Chelsea, her assistant. Chelsea was younger, a shapely brunette in her twenties wearing large horn-rimmed glasses and subdued business clothes, clearly not wanting to outshine her dowdy boss.

"Mr Cao, following our conversation last evening, I must tell you I've never had or seen a case like this before. This morning, we'll tape an interview with you. We want to know details from when you purchased the property to the last time you had access to and received information as owner. If fraud has occurred, and at the moment, we don't know that for sure, it has the momentum to disrupt the real estate profession on a major scale. It will involve the Real Estate Institute, which oversees agents acting in the industry, the government title registration body and the criminal law court itself. Before we proceed, Chelsea will explain our costs in accepting the brief."

Cord sat in while Rodney answered the questions from the two lawyers. It took several hours with a morning tea break. At lunchtime, Miriam said, "We've enough to go on for now. We'll research the title documents. Finding the agent involved shouldn't be too hard. In the meantime, don't go near the property. We don't want to alarm anyone and avoid conversing with others about the matter. In a few days, we'll meet again to discuss our findings and how we'll proceed if there's been fraud."

They had sandwiches at a food hall in the central city. Rodney was still upset but more relaxed and positive in his manner following the morning interview.

"Come on," said Cord. "Let's have a look."

Despite Miriam's directive, he took a chance and slowly drove by the property. It was clearly occupied, with cars in the driveway. Garden pot plants and hanging baskets decorated the veranda.

"Look at that. There are people there I don't know. There's been a fraud," Rodney cried and Cord reluctantly agreed.

"Well, I thought your tenant may have got it wrong. The agent may have put the sign on the wrong property and then realised their mistake. It still could be just a series of innocent mistakes. You never know. The lawyers will sort it out. I'm sure Miriam knows what she's doing."

The days were lonely for Mia as she realised the depth of Rodney's preoccupation with his business problem. Corrine took him to Mia's hockey game on the weekend, but he showed little interest in the outcome, even though she scored a goal and was nominated the best player. Likewise, although in lockdown for winter, a tour of her surf club didn't gain his attention. Seeing Mia's disappointment, Cord felt he should say something but tried to alleviate the situation by arranging more activities and events for them to attend.

*****

It was a week before Miriam Manx rang and invited them back to her office. Cord liked her; she was a straight-to-the-point, no-fuss type of person. There was no beating about the bush and when she talked, you listened. They relaxed in the leather lounge chairs while she explained her findings over coffee.

"Our opinion is that fraud has occurred. We've been in preliminary talks with the Real Estate Institute and have the name of the selling agent, Really Ready Realty. The property settled ten weeks ago and transferred to a D. K. and M. L. Parry for the sum of 2.3 million dollars, which was deposited into an overseas bank account, we believe in India."

Rodney uttered, "India?" and moved forward in his chair to speak. Miriam cut him off and continued, "The implications are massive. The State and Federal Police will be involved, and you will be questioned, as will you, Mr McCullum, being a close friend of Mr Cao. The fraudster must have had the most intimate personal details of Mr Cao, including passports, licences, details of the property, etcetera, which appeared bona fide to the agent. But they, too, are not out of the woods, as they could have been involved in the deceit. Also, the Parrys and yourself are initially under suspicion."

Rodney and Cord were shocked and silent at being implicated.

"The investigation will be extensive and thorough," Miriam continued. "You will need to stay here in Australia, perhaps for a month, to make yourself available to authorities. In the meantime, I need you to provide me with the names and contacts of every tenant you have had, especially those who've rented the property several times and of anyone close to you, business associates, agents, everyone. You will need to brace yourself. The media will sensationalise this."

"My friends never paid rent," blurted Rodney. "To keep within the Foreign Investment Board constraints, I only made loose arrangements with friends and business associates to occupy the property. It was all casual, the only condition being they paid service costs, water, electricity, you know."

Miriam emphasised, "We want the names of these people. Think deeply and prepare a list for Chelsea."

Rodney's upset continued, his agitation returned and he yelled, "2.3 million dollars! I never wanted to sell. It's for my daughter and I want my property back. Someone's responsible. What about the agent? Aren't they responsible? Shouldn't they pay? What about those people, the Parrys, they could be the cheats?"

To stop Rodney's rant, Cord asked, "Will the property be returned to Rodney? He's the rightful owner."

"I don't know yet. Maybe or maybe not."

Rodney gasped in disbelief. Miriam raised her hand and added, "Our method of land tenure, known as the Torrens system, has an inbuilt safety mechanism known as Title Indefeasibility. On registration of the title deed, the government agrees to its authenticity. That is, it provides protection for the owner and buyer against fraud. Now, if the Parrys are an innocent party, they will retain ownership and if you are innocent, as I'm assured you are, you will be compensated the full amount through the government's indemnity fund."

Cord enquired, "What happens then?"

"The Federal Police will pull out all stops to track down the perpetrator."

"But I want my property back." cried Rodney.

Miriam shrugged. "I'm sorry, Mr Cao, but we'll have to wait and see."

*****

The investigation continued and at the end of the second month, Rodney was able to fly home. Lucille met him at his townhouse on the busy Jalan 2, in the central restaurant precinct. Lucille had arrived earlier, juggling the joint responsibility of managing the family business as well as supporting her parents, now residing in the Tempat Terbaik Retirement Village across town.

The news of the sudden sale of the family tea plantation at Tanah Rata shocked her, and despite Rodney's offhand response about needing to diversify and that it was business as usual, she took two months off work to assess the situation and ensure that the family's assets were safe and secure.

It was a plush apartment. The brother and sister sat upstairs on the balcony, overlooking the lush green palms in the parkland opposite, a plate glass balustrade shielding them from the noise of the busy road below. Rodney was clearly agitated and spoke little. The sale of the plantation and the anticipated compensation from the government for the Australian property would alleviate the burden, but he still seemed troubled.

In an effort to ease the situation, Lucille prepared his favourite dish, stir-fried garlic prawns with soy sauce and corn on the cob.

"How's Mia?"

"Growing up."

"Two months? You were away a long time."

"It took that long to come to terms with what happened. The investigation's ongoing and I'm yet to receive approval for the compensation money, which could take months, even a year."

"It's good it's being sorted, though. You can now move on. Father told me Mia's guardian had died. He said she was in a traffic accident."

"Kathy, yes, earlier in the year."

"So sorry. How is Cord taking it?"

"Badly, but he's there for Mia."

"What are you going to do now? With Mia, I mean."

"Firstly, I'm going to start again and try to buy another property for her in Australia when business improves. Under the circumstances, the Foreign Investment Board has granted me permission to buy a residence outright rather than having to build again. Mia's all right for the time being. She's happy at school and I'll see what happens after she graduates."

"Is it wise to leave a man as sole guardian?"

He raised his eyebrows, "Why? Didn't you love him once? Sorry, Lucille. I shouldn't have said that."

She was surprised; it was out of character for Rodney to apologise.

"She's with good people in a good family, has made good friends and loves the place. Cord's a good man; he's helped me a lot. She's had enough disruption in her life."

It hurt when she heard him say 'good man' after all these years, after all that had gone before, but now that her brother was on the back foot, she broached the subject. "I've been going through the accounts."

Rodney winced. She went on, "When you entered into the agreement with Kim Li, our Tanah Rata plantation was valued at five million dollars, carrying a bank mortgage of three million dollars, and at that time, Kim Li guaranteed a personal loan of two million dollars to you. What was that for?"

"Plant and equipment for modern processing. We had to update or be left behind."

"Until I examined the records, I couldn't believe that the property was sold for three million dollars, only just covering our bank account debt, and now Kim Li wants his loan of two million dollars repaid. Why weren't you watching? How could you let this happen?"

Rodney waved his hands wildly. "We needed the equipment! It's just that our share of the rubber market dried up. Thailand began producing greater volumes of natural rubber and the United States increased production of synthetic rubber by thirty per cent. It's something none of us could have foreseen." Then, as an afterthought, he added, "But we've kept our plantation in Penang."

"Thank God it's in Father's name, or Kim Li would be after that, too. So, this two million dollar debt to him will be satisfied with the compensation money from the sale of the Australian property?"

"Yes, Kim Li's aware of the situation. It's been agreed. We'll be debt-free."

"Is there still money for Mia's living, etcetera?"

"Yes. I told Cord the compensation money would pay off a business debt and Mia would be okay."

"That Kim Li! Goodness, such money wasted. We need to break all ties with him and I've already put the process in place. I can't imagine what a mess I'd be in now if I'd married into that family as you wanted me to. It's too horrible to contemplate. You don't have any more tricks up your sleeve I'm not aware of?"

Rodney shook his head, smarting that his little sister had gotten the better of him, but he didn't want to tell her more.

Jillaroo
2015

The real estate swindle was a sensational case; it rocked the establishment and took a year to resolve. The real estate agent and the Parrys were exonerated. The contacts Rodney provided were patiently investigated and cleared. It was a trying time for Cord, and he was glad it was over. Cord and a subdued Rodney met with Miriam for the last time. Beforehand, they had coffee at a shop in the Terrace with a pretty Asian waitress serving.

"It's all over and you're sure to get your compensation. You must be pleased with Miriam."

"Her fees were steep. I can't recover them and they aren't covered in the compensation funds."

Cord thought, typical Rodney, every post a winner.

In her office, Miriam explained, "It was an extremely well-planned scheme. The fraudsters studied your situation, noting you lived overseas, remote from the property and rarely visited. They were obviously aware of the informal arrangements you had with your various tenants, everything on a casual and a first-name basis. I believe loose talk by these people triggered the idea with the imposters, but that's only an opinion. The realty agent had never met you in person, so the forged documents with photos of a person chosen at random and other credentials were accepted as bona fide. The money was transferred to an account in India and I understand from reliable sources the money trail now ends at the Cayman Islands."

"What happens now?" Rodney asked.

"As I explained, under the Torrens system, the Parrys keep the property and you will receive full compensation. Chelsea has that process in hand and it shouldn't take long, now that the investigation is complete. You should have the money in a few months. The Feds are pulling out all the stops to trace the perpetrator, but they only have the money trail to go on, and as I said, that's dried up."

"Months!" Rodney exclaimed.

Miriam shrugged her shoulders.

*****

Three months later, the money was deposited into Rodney's account, and he immediately began the process of purchasing another property for the Moongate Family Trust. He returned to Australia and his old form, the polished businessman, brighter, but his tone was still bitter.

"It's not what I wanted, but it's something," he told Cord. "This whole thing has been a distraction and it's cost me business. It's been a job picking up the pieces and then Miriam's fees as well."

Something didn't seem quite right to Cord and he was troubled. How could Rodney be buying another property in Australia with the compensation money when he said the money was to pay out an outstanding business debt? Perhaps he'd got it wrong. Maybe Lucille was involved; she was an accountant, but then it really was none of his business.

That week was a happy time for Mia. Rodney was attentive and involved her in the property purchase. Mia wanted a horse property in the hills for Tuppence, but Cord convinced her and Rodney that wasn't the best prospect for a thoroughbred stock horse. Under Carol's realtor guidance, they chose a townhouse near Fremantle with harbour views.

"Come and have a look, Pa. You can see the ships."

"That should interest you, Landman," Rodney said laconically and then seriously. "It cost a couple of million with it being on the river, but it's worth it. A good location. Tonight, we're dining out on me. My friends recommend the Chinese restaurant across the street from here."

They shared an array of dishes selected by Rodney from a menu that boasted the best authentic Chinese cuisine. Mia was entranced by her father's stories about the house her grandfather built in the jungle, especially the stories involving Cord in Penang. He added, "When you finish your studies, we'll consider setting up the Moon Shirts as a proper business venture. What do you think?"

Mia was buoyant. He took her to Kuala Lumpur in the term holidays to visit her grandparents and promised to take her to Penang, to their family home at Pantai Aceh in the jungle. She was only four years old when they sold; he knew the new owners and would organise a visit.

Cord could see trouble looming. At the end of her schooling, Rodney would take her and he couldn't do anything about it. He'd send her to live with her aunt and attend university in America as the family did with Lucille.

Cord brooded on this possibility, confessing to Corrine, "She's all I've got. Kathy and I raised her and she wants to be here. We had her future all planned. It's not fair that it might all end."

"She's his daughter. You took on the responsibility knowing that and surely understood it might happen one day. Ultimately, it's up to Mia what she intends to do with her life and that day, Bruv, is fast approaching for you and Rodney."

The school holidays were lonely for Cord. His businesses ran themselves and even his passion for surveying dissipated. He spent more time with Keith in his workshop turning toys on the lathe for the children's shelter, than in the office. Corrine's advice haunted him and his mind raced. He couldn't let Mia go, not without a fight. She was he and Kathy's lost child, the child they were meant to have. He reckoned Rodney was tempting her with new possibilities in Malaysia and America. Lucille was probably in the plot, too. She was adept at deception and an accomplished manipulator.

*****

It was autumn and the night was cold with the threat of rain. Cord waited at the airport with Mia's jacket and an umbrella for her incoming flight, which was already delayed. It was ominous that she'd stayed two days extra in Kuala Lumpur, cutting it fine and spending only one day at home with Cord before school commenced. They had texted every day, mainly at his instigation, and he could tell Rodney was lavishing her with attention.

He glimpsed her in the distance coming through customs, and for a moment, he thought, Lucille. She seemed taller, sporting new clothes, probably designer label, and a bobbed haircut. Her eyes lit up with a broad smile when she saw him.

She raced into his open arms and said the words that brought immediate joy to his heart.

"Hi, Pa. I'm home."

"Hi, sweetheart. My oh my, your haircut."

"Do you like it? It's the rage in KL. I'll probably let it grow again."

"Looks good. I missed you."

The chill of the night air hit as they exited the airport foyer. Mia snuggled into her jacket, lifted the hood and hooked her arm in his as they crossed the car park. As he opened the car door, she turned and lightly kissed his cheek.

"It's good to be home, Pa. I missed you too."

It was her final year at high school. The following year was university and her grades had picked up to where she could be selective on career courses. Her interest was in the pharmaceutical area, particularly Enzymology. To Cord, the language was baffling, not to mention the meaning.

"What does this Enzy stuff mean?" he asked jokingly when she mentioned her choice.

"Snake venom."

*****

The mid-term holiday was in the Dry at Jacana and for a break from studies, Cord and Mia took advantage of the chance to visit. It was unfortunate that Clyde and his copters were involved elsewhere and the only transport to the station was with Dexters Deliveries. Mia relished the opportunity to see the intervening country on the road to the station. The cabin in the truck was spacious and the three sat comfortably for the day-long journey. The vehicle bounced through creek crossings, skirted around high red rock bluffs, kangaroos scattered and at the March River, they stopped for lunch, parking in the shade of a white barked Ghost Gum. Dex arranged a rickety table and camper chairs by a remnant pool where stock had been drinking.

"Bloody crossin' got wiped out last Wet. Took me all me time to get across. Had me missus with me an' while I'm up to me armpits tryin' to get this bugger out of the bog, Doreen's sittin' there whingin' about getting' her feet wet. Women!"

They drove on through stands of Boab trees. At one monster, Dex stopped and, clambering out of the truck, called to Mia, "Have a Captain Cook at this, sweetie."

The tree had a blaze in its bark, very old but clear, which read: 'Crampton 1856'.

"One of the early explorers. He was a surveyor like ya dad."

Both Cord and Mia chuckled at the word dad.

Thankfully, Dex played only country music as they drove and not Kevin 'Bloody' Wilson. A willy-willy crossed the road ahead, sending Spinifex and whirls of dust into the air. Mia was fascinated, aware and absorbed in the natural environment while Cord dozed beside her. Dex prattled on, enjoying the company of the young, attractive teenager.

"You'll be here for the start of the muster?"

"I hope so."

"Sofie's havin' a bub by Christmas, I think. They'll have ta' get in extra help. She's a goer that Sofie. They can't do without her now that your..." He paused and changed the subject. "Ya dad's okay now?"

"Yes."

"What ya learnin' at school? Never went past infants meself. Taught meself to read an' write to make a quid. It just depends on what ya good at. Now I can drive a truck. Tell ya somethin', just between us, I've never rode a horse. I don't like 'em. It's our secret, okay? Got enough horsepower in this bugger. Tell ya what, I only ever read one book called The Sentimental Bloke. Read it a coupla times. Have ya read It?"

Mia shook her head.

"Aw, should have a squizzy. It's got my Doreen in it," he laughed, "Doreen reckons I'm The Kid."

He winked, "One day, sweetie, you'll be some bloke's Doreen."

Mia rolled her eyes.

Cord woke from dozing in time to open the first gate. Dex chuckled, "We've been talkin' about schoolin'. Went to the school of hard knocks meself."

"Did Mia tell you she wants to study snake venom?"

"Snake venom! You've come to the right place, sweetie. Plenty snakes in the grass up here, 'specially them wiv two legs."

The entry gate and posts to the homestead had been freshly painted, as well as the Jacana Bird motif on the arch overhead, obviously Sofie's doing. The building stood solid, serene and welcoming at the end of the drive, bordered by the Frangipani trees in full pink bloom. As usual, sprinklers ticked away, sending spray out and across the newly mowed lawn, which always reminded him of Boris. Joan and Sofie came to the door to greet them, fussing over Mia. Joan was now 'Nan' and Ted was 'Pop'.

"Ted and Barry are out at the breeding paddocks; they'll be back for dinner."

Cord sorrowfully entered the room that he and Kathy first shared. Everything was the same. Her growing up photos with Ted, Joan and Barry, another in school uniform, another older with head back, eyes flashing and laughing, golden air blowing in the wind. More photos of her riding Penny at a muster at eighteen, campfire photos and a large frame of her and him at their wedding, signing the register book with everyone holding glasses and smiling in the background. It was hard to believe a person so full of life was gone. He loved her so much and now wished he hadn't come for a visit. She was the second love he'd lost; the wounds of losing her still cut deep and now he was likely to lose Mia. He wondered if there was an end to this tragedy.

The atmosphere around the dinner table was subdued that first night. Sofie did her best to keep the conversation flowing with details about the latest ringer intake and a new building she planned for staff amenities.

Ted was angry that a ringer left a gate open, two horses had bolted and it was lucky Davy was able to round them up. He fumed two seasons ago when Poppy, one of the thoroughbred breeding fillies with fine black and grey markings, had escaped through a gate left open by a ringer and joined that bloody white brumby stallion he wanted caught. The ringers needed to know to shut the gates.

Barry expounded on a cattle-breeding program he was working on, something to do with Bovine Agrigenomics, extracting molecular samples from animals, tracing characteristics and scientifically selecting the best breeders.

The years hadn't erased the sense that Kathy was missing from the table. Cord could picture her sitting opposite, their eyes meeting and the beautiful splash of her smile. How lucky he was to have been her chosen one, even for that short time.

*****

Cord stood sullen and Mia wept openly when they visited Kathy's grave, neatly kept by Joan and adorned with a cluster of flowers. A marble tombstone engraved with the family names was now in place. The land was timeless; overhead, the sun shone brightly in the azure sky and the distant blue ocean beckoned. They stood on the edge of the cliff line, looking down to where Jacana Creek spilt into the sea. It was a spiritual place. A place where the earth itself was alive. Cord could feel it calling him. He was now, and always would be, one with the land; Kathy and Albert had made sure of that. At that moment, he expected to see her ride over the hill and into his arms.

Nearby, Boris's plot had been claimed by the Bluegrass pasture; the land was hugging him tightly. Cord thought, Mother Earth claims everybody, in the end, even me and Mia.

They rode Dollar and Tuppence to Apricot Springs on a cloudy day; the top pool was shrouded in a warm, dank-smelling vapour and at the bottom pool, Mia saw her first dingoes. Two brown dogs lying under a rock overhang rose immediately, both tall and lanky, showing their scrawny frames. There was a brief silent confrontation between man and dingo. Slowly, the dogs turned, slinking away and disappearing without trace into the low scrub.

Albert and Davy were preparing the outcamp for the first muster and Mia was excited to be part of the action. There was makeshift fencing to arrange, tents for the hands, the camp kitchen, water for the horses and so on. Mia assisted with unbridled enthusiasm. It was the Dry and there were deep green remnant pools in the gorge full of waterfowl and the majestic Jabiru. Davy showed Mia and Cord the ancient cave paintings high up on the ridge above flood level.

Around the campfire one night, with the flickering, crackling flames keeping the mosquitoes away, Mia asked Albert about dingoes. A crescent moon cast eerie shadows on the ground and a dingo howling in the gorge set the scene for the answer. The long moaning howl sent chills up and down her spine. Another dog took up the cry till the gorge incessantly echoed as others joined in the wailing. Then suddenly, it was quiet.

"Many names for 'em, but we call the old ones that follow us on walkabout *Dinju* and the young savage ones like you hear out there *Warrigal*. They're sly buggers, ya can't trust 'em. They take the tucker rite outta ya mouth if ya let 'em."

"So, you hate wild dingoes?" asked Cord.

Albert didn't answer immediately. "No, they're part of the dreamin'. To us people, we don't have wild, we don't have wilderness. To us, everythin' here's tame and the same, even dingoes and snakes. We all got a place an' a part to play. In our dreamin', we have kinship with everythin' that lives. Ya only have to grab a handful of soil to be part of the earth and our ancestors.

We all go back to dust. The land's what keeps all livin' things together. It's more valuable than money."

Cord nodded in agreement. Mia sat back thoughtfully, then rose, went over to Albert and hugged him. Albert picked up his music sticks, closed his eyes and sang a song of the dreaming. Davy joined in.

*****

Davy and a new ringer, Connie, had driven a herd of stock horses down to the new makeshift yard. Dollar and Tuppence were amongst them. Cord and Mia decided to ride to Little Rock Gorge. It was narrower than Mammoth Gorge, with stands of tall Cabbage Tree Palms and mosaics of creepers clinging to the grey-bleached walls. Cord saddled the horses while Albert and Mia prepared a bush lunch.

Davy advised, "Ya can swim in the pool, no crocs up there. Could be cattle, but they'll move on. You'll see a big Ghost Gum at the entrance. A sacred tree to our people."

The tributary to the main Jacana Creek had sliced a thin channel through the weathered sandstone, so only a little sunlight ever entered the gorge and then only at midday. In the shade, through fissures and caves high on the rock walls, a colony of rock wallabies peered at the two visitors riding slowly into the ravine. Cord remembered the buffalo Maggot and he chased from Mammoth Gorge all those years ago and hoped there were no buffalo trespassing here as they rode deeper into the shadows. A flock of Long-tailed Finch with their striking orange beaks scattered overhead, chirping angrily at having been disturbed at the waterhole.

"It's so special here, Pa. I just love this country, this place."

"Just like your mum. Welcome to country."

A flat rock provided a pleasant seat for lunch. They tethered the horses to a palm tree with enough rope to move about, to graze and drink from the pool. They sat for a while in silence. There was no wind and the water was deep, green and calm. It was a place of solitude.

"Are there crocodiles here, Pa?" Mia asked.

"Yep, freshwater ones. Not salties. They're the dangerous ones. The freshies usually keep out of your way."

They lapsed into silence again and eventually, Mia spoke. "Pa, why does everyone call you Landman? Even Father does sometimes. Is it just because you're a surveyor? Albert says land is more valuable than money. What is it?"

Cord laughed, "Too many questions. I got the name Landman because I wasn't a good sailor and got seasick a few times. It was a bit of a joke, but that's okay. When we get home, I'll show you the mug I got when I went to sea. Albert is right. Land is more valuable than money. It's a commodity you can't replace."

"Father thinks so, too. That's why he bought the unit here, but he also needed money to pay off a business debt. Aunt Lucille was so angry at Father. It's all good now, though."

"Business debt?"

"I heard Grandfather on the phone telling Aunt Lucille it was two million dollars. Our new property cost two million dollars as well. Both Father and Grandfather are happy."

Cord was puzzled. The doubt he'd mulled over previously returned to worry him, but then he thought Mia must have got it wrong. There weren't two lots of two million dollars.

He remarked, "That's good it's all settled."

The horses snorted and pulled back on their ropes, backing away from the water; something had disturbed them. They heard a whinny and a grey horse with black markings trotted out of the shadowy depths and nuzzled into Dollar and Tuppence. The mare had a colt with her, a striking chestnut, which stood off at some distance, shy of humans.

"That's Poppy!" Mia exclaimed. "Remember, Pa, it's the mare Pop lost when the gate was left open. She recognises Tuppence and Dollar."

"Be careful, she's wild now."

The three horses stood head-to-head. Mia didn't hesitate and slowly took a spare bridle from the saddlebag. Without fear, she approached Poppy; the horse didn't move. Deftly and murmuring softly, she patted the noses of Dollar and Tuppence and then Poppy.

"Hush," she said.

Tuppence nuzzled her, a little annoyed at the attention to Poppy. Cord didn't move.

"Be careful, she's wild," he said again.

"No, she's not, Pa."

Mia patted Poppy and gently drew the bridle over the mare's head. It was over in a flash and the prize mare was back in the fold. Poppy didn't protest as Mia continued to stroke and assure her that all was well. She roped and trailed her back to camp with the young colt following at a distance, unsure and untethered.

"What've we got here?" Albert exclaimed, taking off his hat and scratching his head. "Well, well, well, if it ain't Poppy. Boss'll be pleased. He'll have to put ya on the payroll. You're a real jillaroo."

Poppy and the colt were yarded with the other horses; the colt stood quietly close to his mother.

"He's a good'un," exclaimed Davy. "I reckon a yearling. Quarter horse, all right and proper chestnut coat, too. You caught him, ya name him."

Mia rested her arms on the fence top rail, pleased at the honour. "He's got a fine glossy coat, Davy. What do you think, Pa?"

"Looks like a million dollars."

"You're right, Pa. I'll call him Crown."

On their return to the homestead, there was a banquet for Mia. Ted was elated at the return of his valuable breeding mare and the bonus chestnut colt. There was a further bonanza later that week, as Sofie confirmed Poppy was in foal again. Ted couldn't be happier; it appeared the wild white stallion had paid him back in triplicate.

On invitation, Sharon Doig visited from Indigo Downs to assess the colt.

"He's pure quarter horse. Excellent conformity, good disposition. I wouldn't geld him. I'd keep him for breeding. He should make a top stallion."

Ted's joy knew no bounds. Mia blushed as Cord related many times how she'd calmly and confidently approached the horses.

"A true jillaroo like your mum," Sofie said excitedly, hugging Mia.

Albert said quietly to May and Davy, "More than that. A horse whisperer."

*****

Later that week, Clyde was at the station and able to fly them to the airport for the trip home. He remarked, "Well, young lady, you've become a legend in these parts."

Once more, Mia blushed.

Clyde started the chopper blades rotating with a slow swoosh before they increased their momentum. Standing at the bottom of the homestead steps, Albert called to Cord, his big dark eyes searching as his gnarled, rubbery hand showed a thumbs up.

Albert murmured, "Take care, Landman. Keep your Waddy with you. Find your life again."

As the chopper rose from the ground, he looked back and wondered if he would ever return to Jacana.

The break left Cord relaxed, happy and contented, but his elation was short-lived as the misfortunes of the past returned to haunt him with one final twist.

Business Before Pleasure
2015

The more Cord thought about it, the more certain he was. The remarks Mia made at Jacana began to raise his doubts. Sometimes, on reflection, he felt he was wrong, overreacting and reading too much into what was probably an ordinary matter. Then again, the overwhelming distressing possibility he was right came flooding back to trouble him.

How could Rodney buy a replacement property in Australia for two million dollars and simultaneously pay off an overseas business debt of two million dollars? Was it a coincidence, or more than that, was he in cahoots with someone else to commit fraud? Could it be Lucille?

Cord surmised if it was fraud, it was larceny of epic proportion and Rodney was the perpetrator. Many times, over coffee in the galley on the *Spree*, the crew would beef off, maligning Rodney for being two-faced and sly. Perhaps they were right. From a personal viewpoint, he saw Rodney as an efficient, determined and accomplished manager with a dark, ruthless streak and a certain disregard for others. He recalled Mrs Brown, the housekeeper's warning not to let Rodney know about his growing relationship with Lucille. Also, Dixie whispered to him, "He's a shifty dude. Keep out of his way."

He overheard the frequent volatile arguments between Gert and Rodney over supplies and finances, with Gert slamming down the two-way receiver and swearing loudly in German, "*Schuft.*" Rodney openly boasted his creed of business before pleasure, which Brian, Cord's compatriot surveyor, interpreted as "the prick wants to make every post a winner."

If Rodney had committed fraud, then he was the greatest actor of all time and a liar on a grand scale. Cord recalled the frustration, despair and anguish

Rodney displayed when he came to him with the news of the property loss. It was a convincing performance and it fooled him and everyone else.

The doubt persisted. It was preposterous; surely, Cord was wrong. There was probably a simple explanation and it was all a coincidence. But then, pocketing two million dollars from the house sale and another two million dollars in compensation from the Torrens Assurance Fund yielded a tidy sum of four million dollars, enough money to make a desperate man do desperate things. But why risk everything on a gamble of not being found out? There had to be a good reason. If it was fraud, was Lucille a party to the deception? He couldn't imagine that to be so. And what of Mia? She was an innocent party but implicated through the Family Trust Deed.

What should he do? What could he do? How could he broach the subject without causing alarm? There was only one option. Cord had to go to Malaysia and confront Rodney face to face.

He told no one of his dilemma, announcing to Mia, "I'll be away for a few days. Nan and Gramps are coming over to stay with you."

"Where are you going, Pa?"

"To KL. I've got business to attend to there. It's good. I'll be able to catch up with your father."

"Great. Ask him about the Moon Shirts and when he's coming over."

He declined Rodney's invitation to stay with him at his apartment; he didn't want to alarm him and used a meeting with a fictitious client to stay in a hotel.

*****

A few days after Cord arrived, they had lunch on the balcony terrace of a café on Jalan Ampang. The day was humid and sticky. Cord had dressed casually in slacks and an open-neck shirt but could feel the wet sensation of sweat clinging to his back. Rodney was in shorts and a loose top and appeared happy and relaxed.

Cord was bombarded with questions.

"Have you been to Kuala Lumpur before? It's great to see you over here. How long are you staying? I'll show you around. I recommend the garlic shrimp. I see Mia's doing well with her studies."

"No, it's my first time. I'll be here a day or so. The shrimp's fine. Yes, we're all proud of her. Next year, university. What are your plans for her?'

Rodney was non-committal. "We will see how she goes."

Cord noted the emphasis on 'we'. Was Lucille involved in Mia's well-being now? Was he really about to lose her?

The waiter fussed around serving the food. Cord drank the cup of iced lemon water, but the sweat still trickled down his back. They sat in silence till the waiter had left.

Cord felt a nervous dread flood through his body, as what he was about to say could likely end his relationship with Rodney and confirm the loss of Mia. He desperately hoped he was wrong, but the figures just didn't add up. Perhaps someone more skilled than he would be able to extract a response without offence, but Cord only knew the direct approach.

"The Torrens fund has worked well for you."

"Yes, it put us back on an even keel being able to replace the property. I still prefer our original holding, though."

"And pay off that two million dollar debt."

Rodney replied spontaneously, "Yes, that as well. The sale got us out of a bad situation."

He bent his head, suddenly realising and regretting the admission he'd just made. He stopped eating and sat upright. Cord saw a frown of concern and then a flash of fright in his eyes. So it was true; Rodney had committed significant fraud. He had double-dipped. Rodney wiped his face with a serviette, looking sheepish.

Cord sat upright in his chair and placed his napkin on the table. "Rodney, I know what you've done. It's something we can't discuss here. Come on back to my hotel and we'll talk this through."

A contrite, humble Rodney sat in the lounge chair in the dark of the hotel room, his head down and Cord sat opposite.

"How could you do this? The consequences are tremendous. Unbelievable! Four million dollars with two million scammed."

Rodney wiped his sweating brow. Distraught and pleading for understanding, he explained quickly, almost babbling, wringing his hands.

"I didn't want this to happen, but there was no other way out. We had a major debt to Kim Li; he bled us dry. We were in a bad place and he was closing in on Father. I had to sell our Tanah Rata plantation at a loss and it still wasn't enough. It only cleared our bank debt and we still owed him two million. I didn't know what to do, so Kim suggested the scam."

Rodney took a breath and Cord stared at him, waiting for more.

"Selling the Australian property for two million Aussie dollars wouldn't be sufficient to pay the debt. You see, transferring the money through normal channels would involve a significant loss of cash with transfer tax to pay and that wasn't acceptable to him. He lent us two million US and wanted the full amount back, paid directly, no overheads or taxes. He'd be able to launder the money through an overseas account. Untraceable, he said."

"And what happened next?" Cord probed.

"He suggested the Torrens System could be manipulated and be the vehicle to sell the Australian property without trace," Rodney continued. "It was the only way out for the family to clear the debt, or he would send us bankrupt. It allowed him to avoid the mandatory Malaysian financial requirements, as he was already in trouble there and had already relocated to South America to escape prosecution. I only had to provide my personal particulars, where the duplicate title deed was kept and so on. He masterminded it all. The sale, the Indian bank account, everything. I didn't even know the property had been sold and settled until he sent me a note that the money had come through. Then, I applied for the compensation."

Rodney sensed Cord's disbelief and disappointment. "I did this for Father and Mother and Mia," he wailed, "otherwise they'd have been destitute. You can understand that, can't you, Cord?"

"I'm worried about Mia's involvement in this."

"It won't affect her."

"She's in the family trust. It must affect her."

"I tell you, it won't affect her."

"Did Lucille have anything to do with this?"

"Of course not, Lucille detests Kim Li. You, of all people, should know Lucille wouldn't be involved in something like this."

Cord was surprised at his comment, 'You of all people'.

"She still cares for you, you know."

"Bullshit." Cord wrung his hands, "For fuck's sake, Rodney, you defrauded the Australian government! If they finally trace the paper trail, and there's any connection to you at all, they'll crucify you and that will absolutely involve Mia. I think you should talk to Miriam Manx urgently."

"Cord, believe me, I didn't want to do this. I had to for Father and Mother. Give me time to think. I'll work something out."

Cord left Kuala Lumpur wondering what Rodney planned to work out. What was to be the outcome? It didn't appear he had any option but to admit to the scam. All Cord could do was wait to see what action, if any, Rodney would take. What if he didn't come clean? Would Cord take the matter further with the authorities?

He didn't have to wait long for the outcome. Three weeks later, he received a message from Miriam Manx. It was a copy of a text sent to Rodney:

'Mr Rodney Cao. I have been advised that following an anonymous tip-off, the Australian Federal Police are in the process of recovering the stolen funds. The funds have been traced to a person in Suriname, South America, who has assets in Sydney and the Gold Coast. These have been seized and the court is seeking that person's extradition to Australia. I understand the perpetrator is Kim Li of Tropki Trading Co., a long-time business associate of yours. As such, he was in your confidence and would have been in a position to extract your personal details to effect the fraud. Sincerely, Miriam.'

There was no word from Rodney, but Cord guessed the identity of the anonymous tipster. There'd no doubt be repercussions from the Kim Li family if they ever found out who the tipster was, but one thing was sure, Rodney would be amongst the list of suspects. From a follow-up conversation with Miriam, Cord understood Kim Li had made many business enemies, the main reason he fled Malaysia.

*****

The year passed slowly with still no word from Rodney. November was a significant month on two counts, as Mia completed her exams with high grades and celebrated her seventeenth birthday.

Cord texted and rang Rodney but received no response. It was Lucille who responded, telephoning Cord at work. It was 10 am, morning teatime. He was downstairs in the plan room with Greg and Simone when Marie called on the intercom, "Phone for you, boss. Shall I transfer it?"

"Who is it?"

"It's a Lucille Cao."

Marie was surprised at his reaction. There was a long pause before he replied. He sounded flustered, not like her boss. "Um. Okay, I'll take it upstairs in my office."

Marie waited for him to go upstairs, then said, "Putting you through now."

Cord's heart raced; ten in the morning in Perth meant ten at night in Washington. After his confrontation with Rodney, was this the reply he had been expecting and did it mean Lucille was involved in the deception? The moment he heard her voice, his heart jumped. How long had it been since they'd last met and talked? It must be going on twenty years, he guessed.

"Hello, Cord, it's Lucille." Her melodic Malay had given way to a soft American accent. It sent another chill through him.

All he could say was, "Hello."

"I hope you're well. Sorry to disturb you, but I didn't want to worry Mia with the news her father is in a rehabilitation clinic here in the US. He's had a mental episode and was admitted three weeks ago. I know it's her birthday and she's passed her exams, but he's in no condition to talk to her right now. I know he's thinking of her. Please pass on my best wishes to her, and tell her I'll be in contact on her birthday. It'd be great if you'd send me a photo of her. I don't have a recent one."

Cord reflected there was still no explanation or solution to the matter.

He recovered his composure, "Okay, sure, I'll arrange one. It's good to hear your voice." A stupid thing to say. He quickly added, "A mental episode?"

"Yes, he's been under a lot of pressure in the business, stress-related. Father and Mother aren't well and he feels he's let them down. Not the case, of course. He's always been there for them."

"Yes, he has."

"Thank you. Tell Mia I'll be in touch." She paused, then added, "It's good to hear your voice too."

With that, she hung up and was gone from his life again.

The conversation had been stilted, without emotion, belying the undercurrent that had been reawakened. There was so much to say, yet neither could say it.

Cord thought, how could this woman just speak and touch his life once again, so deeply, so easily? It was good she was on the other side of the world and couldn't harm him from there.

Lucille sat back on the lounge, drained. It had taken all her courage to make the phone call and to hear his voice again. Too many years had passed between them, but the old feeling was still there. Why did this man touch her when she knew she could have any other? Why this mystery? She couldn't dwell on it. She needed to get some rest.

Rodney was discharged from the clinic and immediately flew home to Kuala Lumpur. Lucille dropped him at the airport. He briefly hugged her.

"Thanks, Lucy, I can't stay longer. You know I must get home to Father and Mother." She was taken aback. Lucy, a loving word he hadn't used since they were children.

Upon landing, Rodney checked in at the retirement village, made sure all payments were up to date and extended the cover to provide nursing assistance when required. Back in his apartment, he wrote a joint letter to Lucille and Cord and an individual letter to Mia.

The following day, he visited his lawyer, Bobbi Hahn, with instructions that the sealed letters only be opened in the event of his death. The joint letter was to be read by his lawyer in the presence of Lucille and Cord, and Mia's letter was to be read independently.

He waited until his office was closed for the day and staff had left before he entered and left a note on his secretary's desk with his lawyer's and Lucille's contact details.

It was evening when Rodney returned to his apartment and sat silently in the darkened room for some time. On his way home, he had bought a bottle of gin, and although he wasn't a big drinker, he guzzled a few mouthfuls. It seared his throat. Eventually, he slid off his shoes, lay on the bed, relaxed and closed his eyes.

He thought of Penang and the house his parents built in the jungle. They were happy days, following his father around the tea plantations. He half-smiled, remembering his words, "This will be yours someday. Remember to be the boss and don't fraternise with the workers. It's business before pleasure. Always keep that in mind."

His father was building an empire and he wanted to be part of it and make him proud. Unlike Lucille, he didn't have time to play, make friends and walk in the jungle. Rodney saw Lucille's growing beauty as an asset, something that could be exploited and it was he who brought the idea of her betrothal for business advantage to his father. He now regretted that because of him, she'd been promised to a stranger before her sixteenth birthday and without her knowledge. But it was too late for regrets. He never wanted children. Father and Mother were his children, but now there was Mia to consider.

He retrieved the prescription sleeping pills he was given on discharge from the rehabilitation clinic, resting on the bedside cabinet. He guzzled mouthfuls of the gin, opened the pill bottle, consumed a handful and drank more of the liquid. He did so until the pills and gin were finished. The bottle slipped from his grasp and fell to the floor, spilling the last dregs.

Rodney was content; all was in place. Father would be proud of him that they were protected and secure. He would be out of the grip of Kim Li, and Mia was in a safe haven. Only one more thing remained and Bobbi Hahn would do that. Kim Li couldn't touch him; nothing could touch a dead man.

He felt an unreal peace. He was once again a young boy running to his father's arms, being hugged and lifted high on his shoulders, as they watched the workers building their house in the jungle.

Tears drifted down his cheeks as he took his last long breath.

Disclosure
2016

The news of Rodney's untimely and controversial death rocked the McCullum household. It was an outcome Cord never foresaw that evidently resulted from their confrontation in Kuala Lumpur. Cord felt a sad responsibility for Rodney's death, the death of Mia's father. Christmas was a bleak, solemn affair, with Mia reclusive, sullen and distraught.

Cord had to tell someone, and it was Corrine, who was astounded and sat for a while, comprehending the gravity of the situation.

"You did the right thing, Cord. Rodney got himself into this mess and if it had been let go, you, Mia and the entire family would have been caught up in a whirlpool of deceit if the matter came to light later. It's a terrible thing to say, but Rodney did the right and brave thing in his final act to remove the taint of complicity in the fraud from you and Mia."

Cord felt more at peace, but it still hung over him that with Rodney out of the picture, Lucille might demand that she take Mia. He went to see Harold Foy in early February for some clarity.

Bobbi Hahn reached Perth a few days later, just before Lucille arrived from the US.

He called Cord once he had settled into his hotel. His voice was distinguished, polished with only a hint of accent. "Good morning, Mr Cord, it's Bobbi Hahn. I believe you're expecting me."

"Yes, of course. How are you?"

"A little jet-lagged, flying at night. Just to let you know, Miss Lucille will be here the day after tomorrow. Can we meet the following day, Friday?"

"Sure, would you like to meet at my place?"

He gave the lawyer his address.

"Would ten, ten-thirty be okay?"

"Ten-thirty will be fine," Cord confirmed.

It was a short conversation, to the point; no need for small talk. So Friday, the big day, had arrived.

*****

Mia's final results came through and she'd graduated with distinction, ensuring a place in her chosen field at university. She hadn't yet fully emerged from her grief when, over breakfast one morning, she raised a topic she'd spoken about before.

"Pa, I'd like to have a gap year away from study. I want to be a real ringer at Jacana, not just a visitor. Sofie says I can. I can work here with you during the Wet and go to Jacana for the Dry."

Cord thought it had merit to shake the shackles of dismay of the last months. It would give her a fresh start.

"So, you've been hatching something with Sofie," he smiled. "I would like you to be here for your eighteenth."

"I'll be home by then. The muster is from May to October. So, you agree?"

"You know it's not only up to me. Your aunt may have a say in this. You're not of age until November, so if it's your father's dying wish that you become her ward, our lawyer advises there's nothing I can do. Perhaps she might agree with what you want. Who knows? It's all in the melting pot."

"Can't you talk to her? It's only nine months to my birthday?"

"She may not listen to me."

"Don't you like her?"

Cord was stunned for a moment. "Why do you say that?"

"I know you know her, but you always seem so negative when she's mentioned. It's as though you've had an argument or something."

Cord ignored her candid observation; the subject of his feelings about Lucille was best left alone.

"Anyway," Mia continued, "it's a strange arrangement with this lawyer from KL. If I've got it right, the lawyer will read a letter to Aunty and you in private and I'll have a letter that I should read by myself. Why's that?"

"I don't know, it's your father's wish. That's the way it is. Stay around the office on Friday morning. I'm sure your aunt will want to see you."

"Of course, Pa! I want to see her too, but please talk to her, okay?"

Cord took his coffee onto the balcony. The radio blared the latest sad news and the talkback discussion that followed bored him. At least the monotony of it took his mind off the coming confrontation with Lucille and the bad news that was sure to descend on him.

It was a calm, cloudless day. Across the river, the distant Kings Park, a weathered limestone buttress covered in native bush, towered over the adjacent city block. The water lapped at its edge, blue, unperturbed and serene, a scene that always pacified him, but not with all the uncertainty around Mia.

In truth, it was not only about Mia but also about Lucille. It was a long time, back in 1998, when he last saw her. What would he say now when they met? Would he be able to contain himself and not fly off the handle? Oh, how he would like to challenge her about the arranged marriage that didn't eventuate, the sham of their lovemaking at the Smokehouse and her deception. She'd used him. They were bitter memories, issues that should have been resolved there and then. It was too late to fix them now. Best he remained focused on Mia's situation. He had to fight to keep her, even if it meant hiding his injured pride.

*****

Lucille felt desperately alone. Rodney's death, so unexpected, left her in shock. He was always a larger-than-life figure and it didn't seem real he'd gone. Had he really taken his own life, or was it a mistake? If he had, why? That she couldn't fathom. And then to leave Mia alone? She didn't have the answer and now she'd be confronting Cord; she didn't want to face the entire ordeal.

She arrived in Perth annoyed, harassed but on time. Her busy itinerary was rearranged to comply with Rodney's extraordinary request to meet with Mia and Cord in Australia. It was cruel of him to do so; he knew how she felt, but the overriding factor of the guardianship induced her to attend. The long flight in business class from New York, with a short stopover in Sydney, allowed her to sleep comfortably, but the twelve-hour time difference between Washington and Perth affected her body clock.

Though she had been to Perth many years ago to walk the *Bibbulmun* Track with Leo, she wasn't prepared for the bright, hot day that greeted her after leaving home in the snow. She waited till the cool of the evening before taking a short walk from the hotel to the grassy banks of the river. Traffic was light here compared to back home. She watched a small ferry crossing the river; it gave the impression of a city at peace with itself. She decided to rest for the evening and contact Bobbi Hahn in the morning.

Dinner was a light chicken stew and a bottle of spring water via room service. Her mind strayed to Cord and the secret she'd kept from him. He was a father and they had a son she'd given away, lost forever. What would he do if he knew? She would have to tell him and shuddered at the thought of the dreaded confrontation that was to come. What would he think of her? All she knew was that she still loved him, but it was all too late.

Wrapped in a decorative package was the box with the Chocolate Sailor butterfly, intended as a gift, a peace offering, a reminder of a happier time, that's all.

Bobbi Hahn briefed Lucille over breakfast on Thursday regarding meeting arrangements. She spent the morning browsing in the city, buying Mia a stylish, soft leather shoulder bag. In the afternoon, she toured the Indian Ocean surf beaches before stopping in Fremantle town, with its authentic English colonial buildings, for an early dinner of delicious ravioli at an Italian restaurant the earnest cab driver recommended.

She retired early. She would see Cord the following day. She wondered if he'd changed character, appearance, whatever. What would happen when their eyes met?

This was the opportunity, face to face, to tell him they had a son somewhere in the world; he'd be around the same age as Mia and she had given him away. It was always something she intended to do. She could never have told him such bombshell news by email or text, which would have been a vindictive and callous thing to do. She'd be honest and face him, no matter the consequences.

*****

Friday morning arrived and Mia called Cord to the balcony for a cup of his favourite coffee blend.

"Sit here, Pa. I'm cooking bacon and eggs for you. You've got to be strong with Aunty for me."

"I will, sweetheart. I'm sure your aunt will be reasonable. You can talk to her, too."

He dressed in office attire; a beige cotton shirt with the motif 'Landman Inc.' embroidered on the pocket and brown slacks. He reckoned the outfit would give a business air to the meeting. He wanted the meeting to be as formal as possible and not emotive, which no doubt it could be. He arranged for Marie to provide a light lunch in the boardroom and ensure the air conditioning was switched on at least an hour before the meeting. He knew that at least one person at the gathering would not welcome the Australian summer heat.

Lucille felt the hot summer day looming. It was already warm at eight in the morning and a quick swim in the hotel pool, followed by a cereal and fruit breakfast in her room, refreshed her for the day. In the shower mirror, she fingered the still evident caesarean scars that lingered across her middle; time hadn't erased them.

She chose a burgundy-toned business suit with a fitted skirt and long-sleeved blazer with a matching cloth belt pulled tight to emphasise the slim waist of the wearer. Her hair was razor cut and styled at shoulder length to hang loosely around her ears and above her shoulders. Her favourite jewellery piece, the jade heart strung on the gold necklace Cord had given her at Tanah Rata, hung from her neck. Would he recognise it? A light smudge of burgundy-based lipstick was her only makeup.

Bobbi Hahn tried to keep the conversation light and bright on the taxi ride to the meeting, but the awkwardness of the situation wasn't easy to ignore. He eventually lapsed into silence.

Lucille expected to see Mia on her arrival, but Marie ushered the pair upstairs to the boardroom, offered them coffee or tea and advised Cord would be with them shortly.

Bobbi Hahn was arranging the contents of his briefcase on the boardroom table when Cord arrived. Lucille stood at the window overlooking the river with her back to him, watching a few people waiting on the jetty for the approaching ferry. It was much like home, only smaller.

"Hello, Lucille."

She turned; their eyes met.

For him, that exquisite feeling of when they first met cascaded back; time hadn't removed the spell she had and could still cast. He was once again hypnotised. How could he remain distant and angry at this beautiful woman who once made love to him?

For her, he was still handsome, his manly eyes alert and compelling, while she lowered hers to hide their mistiness.

"Hello, Cord."

She offered her tiny hand and he held it in his; it belonged there. He felt its soft smoothness, then reluctantly let it go.

Bobbi Hahn shuffled the papers, anxious to proceed.

"Would you like coffee, tea, water?" Cord asked.

"Not for me. I'd like to get started."

Lucille also declined.

They sat at the table, chairs apart and opposite the lawyer. Bobbi Hahn was in his fifties, dressed immaculately in a tailored grey suit, button-necked shirt and red tie. He was of Indian-Malay descent with fingers covered in gold rings. He had the air of a no-nonsense, skilled legal practitioner and had been the Cao's family lawyer for some time. He passed the sealed envelope to them to view. It was endorsed: 'To be opened in the event of my death' and signed by Rodney.

He took the envelope, broke the seal and opened it.

"At the outset, I must inform you I have no idea as to the contents of this letter. Mr Cao did not confide in me in this regard. Nor to the letter to be given to Miss Mia."

Cord felt a sense of unease as to what was coming. Lucille was troubled. As was her habit in such situations, her hands were clasped tightly together and resting on the edge of the table. The lawyer began reading the letter:

'My Dear Sister Lucille and Good Friend Cord,

I want you to know, first and foremost, I have tried to be a good father to Mia, a position I am not worthy of.

Looking back, I regret choosing a path in life where I valued business success above moral ethics and believed that the pursuit of commercial interests was more important than the basic principles of honesty and decency. How many times, Lucy, did you ask me to walk the Moongate Trail with you and I didn't have time? I never did walk it. I am sorry I missed those opportunities. I believed what I did and the decisions I made were always in Father and Mother's best interest, but I realise, too late now, that I used them as scapegoats in pursuing my vanity and self-centeredness.

Cord, I purposely stood between you and my sister and, quite wrongly, lied to you both and interfered to keep you apart. I am sorry. This leads me to something which should have been said a long time ago and for which I am ashamed. Lucy bore you a child…'

Cord jumped from his chair, his brow contorted in disbelief and anger. "What, what's this? Bore a child?"

Lucille slumped forward in the chair and sobbed into her hands. The news of her deceit was revealed before she had time to tell him herself.

Bobbi Hahn removed his spectacles and wiped his brow, disturbed and in disbelief at what he was reading.

Cord recovered and looked desperately at Lucille. "We had a child?"

Lucille turned away, afraid to face him.

"Please, please," Hahn raised his hand, let us continue."

The lawyer read once more:

'I convinced you, Lucille, that Cord had other women in Penang and had abandoned you. Also, I persuaded you it was in the best interest of Father and Mother that the birth remained a secret, as it would damage an arranged business deal. It was unforgivable, I am sorry.

Lucy, you were not well. I said you had a son, an ailing child that required nursing care and, in your fragile state, arranged for adoption…'

Cord choked and cried out, "Adoption! A son! I can't believe this. How could you?"

"Please, please," Hahn responded. He went on, anxious to finish the letter:

The truth is, Lucille, you had a healthy girl, a daughter, and I named her Mia. You two, Cord and Lucille, are Mia's paternal parents.'

Bobbi Hahn stumbled at this revelation. Lucille looked directly at Cord, her eyes swollen, trying to grasp what she had just heard; this couldn't be true.

Thoughts flooded Cord's mind. What was this? The child was a girl, not a boy. Was Mia really his daughter and Lucille, her mother? What had Rodney done? Was this a dream?

Bobbi Hahn was floundering, "I repeat to you, Miss Lucille and Mr Cord, I knew nothing of this." He didn't wait for their reply and continued to read:

'I registered myself as the father, hired a wet nurse, Ruby, and spirited Mia back to Penang as my illegitimate child into the loving arms of Father and Mother. I brought her to you, Cord, when she was nine, hoping to set matters straight and to advise Lucille at the same time, but found you were married. When she was twelve, with her grandparents' failing health, I brought Mia to you again, knowing that Kathy could take her through womanhood and she would be with her rightful father in Australia. I failed you both, but I never thought it would come to this.

I do not expect forgiveness for my atrocity; the only consolation is I know that in my passing, the way is clear for Mia to have a good life, a life she deserves, hopefully with her true parents.

Yours in Sorrow,

Rodney Cao.'

Bobbi Hahn shuffled his papers, wiped his brow and rose from his chair, muttering that he had to deliver Mia's letter to her.

Numbly, Cord said, "She's downstairs in the office."

"Good. I'll leave it with her and, in the circumstances, give you some time to digest this. I'll see you again before I leave."

He left clearly shaken.

Lucille hurried to the bathroom, leaving Cord perplexed, alone and bewildered. Where to now?

Recovery
2016

Bobbi Hahn was mystified at what he'd just heard and witnessed. The event added another bizarre chapter to his relationship with Rodney as their family lawyer. Over the years, he thought he'd established a relationship, more as a friend and confidant, but it now appeared that wasn't the case. He was at Rodney's side when the Cao company teetered on the brink of insolvency and again when Rodney was a suspect in the fraud investigation. That had been resolved and now there was this; family deception on a significant scale, playing with people's lives.

Hahn wondered how money came through to satisfy the business debt to Kim Li and then Kim Li's extradition back to Malaysia from Suriname to a hefty jail sentence for tax evasion. It had occurred to him that Rodney may have been party to Kim Li's fall, but dismissed the thought when Rodney's suicide ended it all. It was baffling.

Mia waited nervously in a small office downstairs for lawyer Hahn, puzzling over the content of the letter she was about to read. She'd just come from the gym, was still in her lycras and planned to change before the meeting, but he called to say he was on the way down.

She'd already resolved that if her father appointed Aunt Lucille as her guardian, she'd plead to be allowed to stay here with Pa and the family she'd grown to love. Surely, it wasn't too much to ask as she'd be of age to run her own affairs in November.

Bobbi Hahn now saw Mia in a new light. She was Eurasian; he knew that since Ruby, whom he'd never met, was her mother, but Ruby, too, was an illusion, a fabrication. Now it was revealed who her real parents were.

Mia rose when he came into the room. With his mind refreshed, Hahn could see Lucille's intrinsic beauty and the intelligence of Cord in the girl's silky green eyes. How she'd react to the news, he didn't know, but it was important he read the letter aloud for them both to comprehend and then for her to read it silently alone. He jotted on his notepad to have the original letters signed by the parties and to leave them a copy when he left.

"Hello, Mia. I'm terribly sorry about your father…"

His voice trailed off and he hesitated, knowing, at that moment, he'd made a mistake; he should have said Uncle, but how could he? It was too premature to say that; he'd wait till she read the letter.

"I hope you remember me. I met you a few years ago. Rodney and I were good friends."

Mia nodded.

"I have here a sealed letter which I want you to open. I'll read it to you. I have no knowledge of its contents."

Mia nodded, took the envelope, broke the seal and handed it back to the lawyer.

Bobbi Hahn cleared his throat and read:

'Mia, my dear child,

I have much to account for in shaping your life, and I pray that with my passing, the road ahead will be brighter and easier for you. Of all people, you made me realise that responsibility to family transcends all other considerations in life. A long time ago, I chose to pursue a business goal, ignoring and overriding the basic rights and interests of others, especially you, your Aunt Lucille and Uncle Cord. My self-interest deceived everyone, including your grandparents, to the extent that as the years rolled by, the love and enjoyment you all should have shared as a family was denied by my greed. It is time to set things right. The truth I concealed from everyone is that Lucille had a child, a beautiful daughter, whom I took from her with lies and deceit and the father was my friend, Cord.

The child was you, Mia. You are their legitimate daughter. I know this is a great shock and I do not expect forgiveness, but hope I have finally done the right thing. I do love you.

Enjoy your life with your parents.

In sorrow, your Uncle Rodney.'

Mia sat for a long while, her head low. The letter hung limply in her hand before it fell loosely to the floor. Bobbi Hahn reached down, picked it up and placed it in his briefcase. What more could he say?

"No doubt you'd like to go upstairs." He couldn't add, "to see your parents." It was still such a strange thing to say.

Mia shook her head, "No, I'm all right."

*****

Light rain fell as Mia ran from the building and along the river foreshore. She ran hard, passing other joggers and on through the parkland till she crossed the river at the causeway to the esplanade pathway on the city side. She stopped, out of breath. There was her home beckoning on the far shore, the building she had just run from. Even on this autumn day, with wisps of drizzle in the air, the river, dimpled by the droplets, remained calm and serene. Her mother and father would be waiting. What could she say?

She remembered Gramps telling one of his humorous stories about a Prophet sitting on the bank of a river when a man called to him from across the stream, "How can I get to the other side?" The Prophet replied, "You are on the other side."

Gramps said, "Remember to look at things both ways. See the other point of view before you make major decisions."

She'd been on the other side all her life; now it was time to move over.

Two ferries crossing in opposite directions caught her eye. They converged on each other as if they might collide but passed without incident.

She thought of those on the ferries, individuals coming close together for a moment, then passing, never having met. Is this what life's about? She thought. Ships passing in the night? I don't want things to pass me by. I want to be part of a real family. Is it true I have a living father and mother?

She thought of Rodney; all this time, he was her uncle. He'd provided a good life for her, never involving her in his personal anguish and trouble. It wasn't in her heart to resent him; she felt sorrow at his loss.

She thought of Cord, her real father. Perhaps there was a being within her who knew she was his daughter all along. In panic or sad moments, she would turn to Cord for comfort rather than Rodney and sometimes she felt ashamed of the feeling.

She thought of Kathy, her mum, the only mother she'd ever known, who showered her with love and affection. The tragedy of her loss was still with her. Mum? Could there ever be another?

She thought of Lucille, her distant aunt, now her mother. It was unbelievable. Would she be able to turn to Lucille and receive the same

305

warmth and care? She'd try her best to overcome the barrier the years had placed between them.

She sprinted over the Narrows Bridge and onto the foreshore reserve, stopping outside the apartment entrance, panting heavily. She paused, gathering her thoughts, preparing herself and bracing for the coming encounter before she pushed open the door and entered. No matter what, it was time to move on.

*****

Cord waited, but Lucille stayed locked in the bathroom. Soon, Mia would arrive. What then? What would be the outcome of this day?

He went onto the balcony and sat alone, overlooking the river. The surface was shrouded in a light mist. It was a grey, sullen scene and through the murkiness, two ferries converged till they passed without incident. For a moment, he saw the flash of a person running hard along the foreshore. It looked like Mia, but too far away to know. He guessed it couldn't be.

His mind wandered, recalling the Penang ferries and the Moongate Trail. They were good times on the *Spree*. He thought of Lucille so near yet so far away, and now, with her so close, the fireworks in his head returned, just like the first time he saw her. They were born on opposite shores and like the Penang ferries, their youthfulness was bright and colourful. For one brief moment, their courses converged, collided and here was Mia, the innocent survivor of the impact.

He felt a numbness at Rodney's revelation; it was typical of Rodney's mantra, 'business before pleasure', but he never thought he'd gone this far. The man was a charlatan, a swindler, a faker, sacrificing integrity for cash and love for money, yet he felt sorrow at Rodney's demise. His final act of truthfulness at least gave them all the chance to move on. He resolved that's what he would do, no matter the consequences.

*****

Lucille sat on the pedestal in the bathroom, not wishing to emerge and confront the overwhelming situation that had sent her senses reeling. How could she look Mia in the eye and see her as a daughter? How could she face Cord, knowing she'd kept the secret of his child from him? What was she thinking in those days? Was she like her brother, a callous individual who saw no wrong in manipulating other people's lives?

306

She was alone in this strange country, away from the comfort of her apartment and the security of her job. Her only intimate relations were in addressing staff and casually greeting Sam, the apartment doorman. Is that a life fulfilled? She had hidden herself in her work, hoping one day, quite hopelessly, that her true love would come to her, but that was dashed a long time ago. Now, he was in the same building but still so far away. There was nothing she could do.

She had to move on; she must go home. There, she could sit and think, but there was still the here and now.

*****

Lucille came back into the room, and Cord, sitting on the balcony, noted her return. She clasped her hands together and sat upright in a chair.

Neither spoke until Cord said, "Would you like coffee or tea?"

She nodded absentmindedly, "Yes, please. Coffee."

He called Marie and ordered.

"We have to talk. You know I came to America looking for you."

Lucille was astounded; his admission stirred her. She rose and stood facing him.

"I thought you'd abandoned me!"

With a rush, she vented the deep feelings that troubled her. "I shouldn't have believed Rodney. I shouldn't have kept the news of my pregnancy from you. I meant to tell you today. I thought I'd lost a son, but today, miraculously, I've gained a daughter."

The door opened and Mia came running into the room, into Cord's arms.

"Oh, Pa, is this true? I can't believe it!"

Her bright eyes shone with tears. Lucille stood quietly by as the pair hugged. Finally, Mia turned and went to her. She fell to her knees, clasped Lucille around the waist and buried her head in her lap.

"Mother!" she sobbed.

Lucille looked down tearfully and stroked her daughter's hair.

Cord remained transfixed by the two women. He felt a sense of ownership, but were they his, or was he theirs? He went to them as Mia stood and the three embraced. Cord hoped there'd never be another parting.

Reconciled
2016

It was a difficult time. Rodney's admission didn't have the desired bonding effect that he had planned. Instead, it created three strangers confused and bewildered at the prospect of what lay ahead. The world was completely different and no one knew what to say or do.

An awkward silence prevailed until Lucille broke free of the embrace. In the flick of a finger, she'd found her niece was her daughter and Cord was the father. She needed time to think this through; this, too, was a script from a soap opera. Lucille needed solitude. It was all too much.

There was a strangeness in the word 'Mother' that Mia whispered repeatedly. How often she wished to have Cord's arms around her and now that they were, it felt strange. Rodney's revelation had broken through her comfort zone and brought a new responsibility that frightened her.

Cord sensed her withdrawal. He was also confounded. Being Mia's father changed everything in legal terms but added nothing to the natural love he already had in his heart. It was not a great shift for him, but what of this new situation with Lucille? It took their relationship to a new level and cast a shroud over Kathy's memory. Cord noticed Mia sobbed the word 'Mother' and not 'Mum' as she did for Kathy. For her, too, it was a paradigm shift in affection. As her father, he could now fight for possession; he was on firmer ground.

Mia's joy shone through. She was no longer an orphan; she had real flesh-and-blood parents. Still dismayed, not knowing what to do next, she exclaimed, "Mother, you'll stay with us now!"

Lucille looked away, trying to remain cool. "Thank you, *sayang manis*, but there's business I must attend to. I'll call later, darling, I will."

Anxious to leave, Lucille smiled briefly and picked up her bag. Cord hadn't recovered from the shock. All he could say was, "I'll see you out. I'll drive you."

Lucille reneged. "A cab will do. I need to see Bobbi Hahn and check in with my office. I'll call later."

He noted her withdrawal. "Suit yourself. Marie will call you a taxi."

She turned and walked away. What was she doing, losing him again? She needed time to think. She had a daughter; her joy should show no bounds, but shock and deflation consumed her.

Dumbfounded, Cord watched her go. She was on the run again and it was history repeating itself. Mia stood silent, confused at her mother's response.

Bobbi Hahn was busy. He needed Harold Foy's advice as soon as possible to convert the Moongate Family Trust from Rodney as Trustee to Cord and Lucille's Trusteeship and settle other matters of Rodney's Estate. Then, there was Mia's identity and nationality to consider. He advised Lucille to extend her stay for at least a week. Despite all the emotion, he felt the three had to be DNA tested to confirm the family bond.

That night, Lucille texted Cord, apologising for leaving abruptly. She had a headache and would call Mia in the morning, and that she'd be staying another week. Cord texted back. He wanted his response to be conciliatory and bland; she mustn't know how vulnerable he was to her charm, even though she'd chosen a course of betrayal and kept the knowledge of the baby from him. It read: 'Sorry, we can catch up when you feel better. It's been a shock for us all. You being here and being her mother means everything to Mia. For me, having been with her now for five years, I've been the lucky one. I can understand the burden this places on you and you need your space. Mia understands this, too. She already wants to know how we met, what happened between us and so on. I can't do this alone. Sometime soon, you and I need to talk this through with her. Would you please have lunch with us the day after tomorrow? Let me know, Cord.'

*****

They picked Lucille up at the hotel at midday. 'Casual dining wear', Cord said when they made arrangements, so she wore summer wear, a light green frock, hair in a bun, sandals, sunglasses, and no makeup. Mia was excited and anxious to see her mother. She wore jeans and a Moon Beam T-shirt she'd designed and made.

"Do you think Mother will notice my Moon top?"

"I'm sure she will."

Cord wore blue jeans and a Country Road pale blue cotton shirt. They looked like a regular family on a typical outing. There was a brief awkward moment on greeting. Lucille longed for Cord's embrace but held back; it was a new experience. He opened the door and took her hand; it felt good.

Kings Park restaurant enjoyed excellent views over the city and river. People strolled through the gardens; some had blankets and picnic baskets on the lawn. Children played on swings and the setting was calm and relaxing. With the sky blue and the day warm, Lucille felt at ease.

The night before, she thought of Mia, her birth and the years she'd been denied. She woke thinking it was a dream. It was incredulous this bubbly teenager by her side was her creation and belonged to her.

Mia took her hand as they walked the paved path to the restaurant steps and pointed excitedly, anxious to please. "See, Mother, my old school's over there and the university I'll be going to is that way, on the edge of the park."

Other people were at the restaurant table who stood when they arrived. Lucille was caught off-guard. Her anxiety returned, the calmness evaporated and the air was charged with emotion and anticipation.

Cord spoke, "Lucille, please meet my, umm, our family."

The group were smiling, their eyes fixed on her, taking in the natural beauty of this exotic woman who had borne Cord a child. It was a shock for them. Overnight, Mia had become blood family and here was this stranger, this woman from the other side of the world, intimately connected to them forever.

Cord continued, "Lucille, this is my mum, Mia's grandmother, Eileen."

The smartly dressed woman, tears in her eyes, hugged Lucille, saying a choked "Welcome."

Mia ran to the elderly man, smiling broadly.

"Gramps!" she said, hugging him tightly.

"Hi, sweetheart."

He took Lucille's hand, "And you're her mother. Look at you, two peas in a pod."

Cord broke in, "My twin sister, Corrine. Aunty Corrine, Uncle Mark, and their two children, Cameron and Jessica."

Corrine came to Lucille and held her hands. "I've heard so much about you. I felt I knew you then, in Penang, and now with Mia. I'm so happy. Welcome home."

Lucille smiled uncomfortably. Home, Lucille thought. This isn't my home.

Eileen spoke quickly and put her arm around Lucille as if to read her thoughts.

"We're your family now. Do you like seafood? The crayfish thermidor here's delicious."

"I do. Thank you."

"I recommend a glass of our down south Chardonnay," Keith added.

She looked across the table at Cord and he winked. He was her man and so this was her family. In its completeness, it was the only extended family she'd ever known and her daughter was part of it. It was a fact; better to embrace it than reject it. The cool wine helped her relax.

The family were full of questions about her work, living in America, her hobbies, her interests. It was mid-afternoon when they broke up the gathering. She felt more comfortable and Cord suggested a walk in the park to take in the view. An afternoon sea breeze fluttered her skirt and she felt his eyes on her. Was it too late for them? But America was calling and she had to go.

Mia convinced her to stay in the guest room for the remainder of the week. Lucille reluctantly agreed only because Cord was away attending to business at a Pilbara mine site and she wanted to avoid close contact with him. Mia made plans.

"Pa agreed I could have a gap year. I got into Uni, so it's no problem. I want to be a ringer in the next Dry."

"Ringer?"

"I'll explain later, but I don't need to go up north till May and Pa says I can go to America with you till then."

Lucille was surprised. "Sure, that would be wonderful, *anak saya*, but I have to work. I wouldn't see much of you. There are several projects that'll take me away."

"I could be with Pa. He said he could come too."

Lucille felt her heart surge, "Oh, he did, did he?"

Mia took her to the surf club with Corrine.

"She's a strong swimmer and enjoys the surf. I wish I could be with her more, but now you're here. I've never seen her so happy."

Lucille didn't want to say it but thought, here, but not for long.

"You know Cord went searching for you in New York. Things would have been different if he'd found you."

"I suppose so."

The morning Lucille left, she didn't say goodbye; she didn't leave the Chocolate Sailor. Only the leather bag she had bought for Mia and a note on the side table saying she was glad everything was now in the open.

*****

Two weeks later, as arranged with Lucille, Cord and Mia flew into Washington. It was a freezing day, the roads awash with melting snow. It was sleeting so hard, that Cord thought it was a wonder the cab driver taking them to Lucille's apartment could even see.

The doorman, under instructions from Lucille, let them in. She wore a beaded yellow sarong housedress and her breathtaking loveliness took Cord back to when they first met. The apartment was inviting, tastefully furnished, comfortable and secure.

"*Selamat dating ke rumah saya, keluarga saya.*" She hugged Mia who replied, "*Terima kasih ibu, saya tidak sabar untuk Anda lagi.*"

The delicious aroma of stir-fried cooking filled the air.

"Unpack, have a rest and we'll talk later," Lucille said, showing them to separate bedrooms.

"What did your mother say?" Cord asked quietly.

"She said welcome family and I said it was good to be here, or words to that effect."

Showered and refreshed, they sat and enjoyed the meal.

"I'll wash up," said Mia.

Lucille opened a bottle of Californian red wine; she and Cord retired to the sofa facing the flickering embers of a gas log fire. The weather continued to sleet outside.

"How long do you plan to stay?"

"That depends on you."

Out of politeness, she said, "You're welcome to stay as long as you like."

Cord decided he'd come a long way to the other side of the world. The weeks had gone by and he'd maintained a decorum, but the time to act was now.

"I'll stay till you come home with me."

Lucille sipped her wine, lay back on a cushion, tucked her legs under her and half-smiled.

Cord thought, that's how Mia sits. Finally, she spoke, "You don't really mean that."

"Try me."

"Cord, my life is here. I've a job, responsibilities. I can't leave."

"Then I'll stay."

"Don't be ridiculous. You have a business, a family and what of Mia and what she wants to do?"

"Don't you be ridiculous. You have the same family now that you have Mia. Come home with me. I need you. Let's make up the years we've lost."

He reached for her, but she pulled away. Mia came from the kitchen.

"What have you two been up to?"

Cord sighed, "Just talking about old times."

Cord moved from the sofa and Mia went to sit with Lucille, also tucking her legs beneath her.

"Mother, you're crying."

"It's just that I'm happy you're here."

*****

Lucille was highly sought after on the Indigenous Women's Rights circuit and left two days later to address a seminar for Aleut Eskimo Women's Culture in Anchorage, Alaska. Mia went with her, leaving Cord to wander the streets of Washington alone.

The weather broke and adequately outfitted with winter wear, he was able to stroll to Lafayette Park, where there was always some group advocating their democratic rights to protest on the doorstep of the White House. Standing in the newly fallen snow, listening to the chanting protesters, he thought of Albert, the quiet, still majesty of Mammoth Gorge, the boundless beauty of Jacana and even of his peaceful southern city on the river by the sea.

A stranger came and stood near him. He was sporting a wiry moustache and wearing tall leather boots, well-worn jeans, a huge duffle coat with a fur collar and one of those leather peak hats with fur trim, rounded off with red woollen mittens.

"Look at those motherfuckers. Fuckin' refugees, comin' here demandin' rights. They fucked up their own country, now they wanna fuck up ours."

He was swarthy-looking, probably of Italian descent and had a Bronx accent. He clapped his mittens together in the cold; snow dust filled the air.

"Fuckin' refugees," he said again and then moved on.

Cord watched him go and thought, the First Nations people could easily say the same about you.

He wandered back to the apartment, dejected and alone in this big city. He knew he couldn't stay; it was pointless to say he would. It was too much to hope Lucille would come with him.

The doorman let him in. "There's more bad weather on the way. Excuse me, Sir, Miss Cao didn't mention it, but do you mind my asking, are you Australian?"

"Yes."

"I thought so, Sir. From Sydney?"

"No, from Perth, two thousand miles on the other side."

The doorman nodded and whispered, "Jeez!"

Cord mused, he thinks I'm from another planet. Perhaps I am.

Mother and daughter returned, their bonding confirmed. Lucille was relaxed and effervescent and Cord, as always, was captivated by her smile. Mia was exuberant.

"We went to Denali National Park. It's spectacular. Mother and I had a snow fight. There were lots of Caribou and I saw a Brown Bear with a cub. We bought this beanie for you. See, it says 'Snow Man' on one side and 'Tuff Guy' on the other. You can wear it any way you like."

Cord was grateful for the beanie and glad to see Mia so happy.

"You will come home, won't you, Mother?"

"We'll see."

Cord found is difficult sleeping in a separate room, thinking of Lucille so close.

*****

A few weeks before her Alaskan visit with Mia, Jerome had called Lucille to his office.

"I had a call from a high-up in the Department of Interior. Seems your name's been mentioned as a likely candidate for a job they want done. I don't have the full brief, but it's to do with Indian land rights and that case the Commission considered a few years ago."

"Why me?"

"Why not? You have a presence in this area. They see your involvement in Indigenous affairs as an advantage."

"I can't see why! The case is cold. The government rejected the findings of the Commission. I thought that ended it."

"Yes and no. I gather petitions from Native American Tribes seeking land rights have grown and the Commission is lobbying to reopen the case. Lucille, you have a great track record with the Indigenous people and the Department is counting on you to head them off at the Pass. Those up top reckon you can talk to them, get them to back off. Everyone's frightened there'll be an avalanche of claims if the case succeeds. There'll be goodies attached all round."

"Bribes?"

"No, no! Incentives. A step up for you and financial assistance to the tribes."

Over dinner, Lucille explained the importance of the mission and Cord could see the writing on the wall; it was a *fait accompli*. Mia was proud of her mother's achievements and he noted the excitement in their voices as they discussed the consequences of the case way into the night. He realised his position was hopeless; there'd been no intimacy between them and it was unlikely there ever would be.

"It's all talk," she said. "Nothing's official yet."

"So, you'll be against land rights for Indigenous people?" Cord asked.

"No, just unreasonable claims."

"Surely there are no unreasonable claims for Indigenous people. Land is a finite resource. The earth belongs to everyone, doesn't it?"

Lucille mocked him. "Whatever you say, Landman."

Cord knew he shouldn't have belittled her. What did he know of the claims? They could be frivolous and unwarranted.

"I wish you well in your case. I've got to go home. I can't let the business run by itself. Mia can stay with you till the Dry. She'd like that."

Lucille was taken aback by his admonishment and the thought of his leaving so soon. At the same time, she felt foolish at her sarcasm and uneasy at the questionable ethics surrounding the task looming before her.

Changing the mood of the conversation, she said, "I'd like to go to Kuala Lumpur with Mia to see Mother and Father. They're not well. I'd like you to come too, for them to meet you as Mia's father."

Cord wanted the break to be impartial and clean, like when they parted in Penang.

"I'm sorry. It's best you two go."

Mia tried to persuade him, and Lucille was clearly disappointed as her iciness matched the sleeting weather outside.

On a frosty April morning, Cord hugged and kissed Mia goodbye and shook hands with Lucille. The touch of his work-hardened hand sent a quiver through her body. His blue eyes sought hers and the clean, clear smell of his aftershave lingered as he whispered in her ear.

"I'm so glad you're her mum. Take care."

"You too."

And he was gone.

The jet rose from the tarmac and he wondered when he would see Lucille again. They would keep in touch as Mia's parents, but how long would that last? The hostess came with drinks. A gin and tonic would be good; it would help him sleep and dull the ache in his heart.

*****

Cord found it hard to return to work and shied away from the office for several days. He sought Keith's company, turning wood into toys in the backyard shed.

Keith smiled wryly, "It must be hard for a woman to accept there was another woman in a man's life and vice versa."

"I know, Dad, but it's all so long ago."

"Son, I don't have the answers. There's one thing for sure, you chose two fine women, beautiful, intelligent, independent, and now there's only one. Hopefully, Lucille will see there's no challenge there anymore. She has a daughter with you, after all. She may come home to you, or the other option is you go to her."

"I can't, Dad. This is Mia's home. We're a family. America and Lucille's lifestyle is not for Mia."

Over the following weeks, communications were short, cursory texts from Lucille, although Mia texted almost every day.

'We went to all the Smithsonian Museums and saw the Native American clothes you told me about. Pa, I love you.'

'We went to the snowfields and bussed to the Appalachian Trail, but it was too difficult to walk with the snowdrifts. Love you, Pa.'

'KL was busy; Mother spent a lot of time with lawyer Hahn. Grandfather and Grandmother are both well but frail. See you soon, Pa, I love you.'

On her return, Cord decided to accompany Mia to Jacana for the start of the Dry. He wanted to personally tell Ted, Joan and the family that she was his daughter. Maggot flew them to the station; he was there for the muster.

"So, you're a ringer?" he asked as the bright red chopper lifted from the tarmac, swirled and pointed north towards Jacana. Mia smiled and nodded. Maggot chuckled, "Are you a ringer too, Landman?"

"Not this time. I'll leave it to the top guns."

As usual, the Bells were pleased to see them. May was first to hug Mia and Sofie cradled her in her arms before whisking her away.

"Should be a good season," Barry remarked. "The boys reckon there are lots of cows with weaners in the bottom paddocks this Dry. We'll have our work cut out to separate them from the rough mob before we start the main muster. We need good ringers." Earlier, he had hugged Mia affectionately and said, "We're lucky we've got some good recruits this year."

After dinner, over a glass of red wine, with Mia retired for the night, Cord told the family of Rodney's admission and, consequently, of Lucille's and Mia's heritage. They listened in stunned silence. He explained he hadn't seen or heard from Mia's mother over the years and had no idea she was pregnant; it was only a brief affair. Now that Lucille had suddenly appeared in their lives, circumstances had changed for the better in that he now had undisputed parental rights. It could also be detrimental if her mother got nasty and meaningfully exercised her right.

"We agreed on one thing, though. Mia could have a gap year from study and join the muster with you. It's something she's always wanted."

"So her brother brought Mia to you without you knowing she was your daughter," Joan said.

"Yes, it's incredible."

"Then, really, Kathy was more than a guardian. She was Mia's stepmother!"

They all nodded at this revelation.

"Where does Lucille live?"

"In America. She works for the Federal Government and has a high-up position. Mia is so proud of her and they've quickly bonded."

"Where do you stand with the mother?"

"I don't know. It's been overwhelming, taking the three of us by surprise. Mia wants us to be together as a family, but it's all up in the air."

"Crikey!" exclaimed Ted.

"Wow," said Barry.

"Congratulations," said Sofie.

*****

Before Cord made his way back to Perth, he and Mia saddled up Tuppence and Dollar and rode to the graveyard where so much of their lives were buried. The cliff face was teeming with wheeling and nesting seabirds. Vigilant black Crows kept an eye on empty nests. The Flinders grass was green and lush. The wind gusted and white fluffy clouds raced across the sky. It was a noisy place alive with nature, a fitting place for their beloved Kathy and larger-than-life Boris to rest. They placed a sprig of Bush Apricot on each plot before it was time to leave.

Dexter arrived at the homestead the day before Cord left for home. A new truck displayed the motif 'D & D DELIVERIES'.

"It stands for Dexter and Doreen Deliveries," he explained proudly. "Got three vans now. Ya know Clint an' Colin Collard? They're on the payroll an' drivin' for me. Doreen did me books, but when we got bigger, we had ta' get a bloody bean counter to do me bits an' pieces. Crikey! Then we had ta' get an ABN to boot. Aussie Business Number, they call it. Lotta bunkum if ya ask me. Ya got one of those Landman? Bloody ABN, bloody Aussie Bumblin' Numbskulls, load a' crap. Ya break ya back earnin' a hard quid an' the buggers over East want ta' take it off ya. Bloody tax wanka's!"

Dexter winked, "Maggot says cutie's ya dinky-di daughter. I told him I knew it all along. I says to Doreen right at the start that little Sheila's the dead spit of the Landman, a chip off the ol' block. I got an eye for these things. Ya can't fool ol' Dex."

318

Mia departed for the outcamp in the Toyota Troop Carrier. She hugged her dad tightly before waving goodbye. Cord was happy for her; he thought, she's in her element.

On leaving, Albert took Cord's hand in a strong grip. "Stay cool, Landman. Keep that Waddy near ya."

Maggot flew him out. Cord looked back at the homestead receding from view and could see the dust billowing from the tracks of the station vehicles heading south to the outcamp, carrying Mia away. It was a wrench to leave, and for a moment, his eyes moistened before that too passed. At the airport, the two men shook hands.

"If I need a good wingman to help me flush out a few buffalo, I'll give ya a buzz," Maggot smiled.

"Do that. Keep me in mind."

Signs
2016

Lucille felt good returning to America, to be back in comfortable surroundings with no personal responsibilities, only those relating to her job. Here, in familiar territory, she could sit back and assess the new domestic situation.

It was exciting being recognised, sought after and upwardly mobile in an important organisation. It was a career goal she'd always aspired to. The appointment wasn't yet official, but Jerome arranged a dinner with the stakeholders. It was clear the occasion was merely a formality to acknowledge the team she'd selected and to familiarise everyone with the objectives of the new post.

Following the short time with Cord and Mia in Washington, the weeks passed and Lucille began to feel uneasy in her new role. The question of conflict of interest began to nag her. On one hand, she had her brief to present and safeguard the government's interest; on the other hand was her role to protect the rights of the Indigenous people, a cause she had championed for so long. Cord's parting words, "So, you'll be against land rights for the Indigenous people?" disturbed her.

It was the first sign of her discontent and other clues emerged over the following weeks.

The weather hadn't let up for days and snow had built up around the buildings. Workers were shovelling it from around the restaurant door as she entered the building for the dinner meeting. Jerome greeted her in the foyer.

"I've got the nod, congratulations. The job's in the bag. Let's just relax and enjoy the day. I recommend the lobster thermidor; the chef's an Aussie who brings crayfish in from Australia. It's absolutely delicious."

She thought of Perth, the southern city far away and the cool, crisp taste of a Margaret River chardonnay. Visions of Eileen, Keith and Corrine flashed through her mind.

The dinner went well. Everyone was positive and looking forward to the new challenge.

The ride home in the cab was slow through heavy traffic. The taxi inched alongside a metro bus and emblazoned on its side was a photo of a magnificent sunset over an azure sea with the caption 'Australia – Relax in the Suntanned Country'.

She gasped at the thought of Mia, her lost child, the *Bibbulmun* Track, white beaches and rolling surf.

The cab stopped at traffic lights. Off to the left, a billboard was lit with the image of a laughing woman holding a popular brand camera and highlighting a massive coloured butterfly. She thought of the Chocolate Sailor and that happy day with the man she loved. She gasped again at the thought that the laughing woman could be her.

The driver looked back through the rear vision mirror. Concerned, he said, "You all right, Ma'am?"

"Yes, okay."

They waited for the lights to change. Lucille asked, "Do you believe in signs?"

"Signs? Are you kiddin' lady? Ya can't drive in this rat race without signs."

"I just got some signs."

"Good ones, I hope."

"Very good ones."

In the morning, she would tell Jerome of her decision.

*****

The weeks at Jacana were the tonic Cord needed to brush away the turmoil of the past. The land embraced him in a shawl of freedom and respectful silence; the outback welcomed him again. He rode Dollar to Apricot Springs and stood watching the water gushing into the pools. The Jacana birds were treading the lotus pads and at the third pool, he could see Kathy in her orange bikini calling him, but it was all a dream. He couldn't forget her. Above all, he wanted to forget Lucille and get on with life, but in his heart, he knew he never would; the spell she'd cast was still upon him.

It was late afternoon when he returned to Perth after a long and tiring flight. For a while, he stood alone, a solitary figure breathing in the tranquil river scene at his doorstep and watching the ferries as they passed close to each other. When he entered the building, the delicious aroma of cooking filled the air. He'd rung Marie earlier to let her know he was on his way. He thought how considerate of her to leave something warming in the oven and probably a fridge full of food. He stumbled over a box lying in the doorway; it contained the Chocolate Sailor.

As he opened the door, he sensed there was someone there. He didn't have time to speak before Lucille was in his arms. He dropped his pack and the first sweet, delirious kiss melted away the dark abyss the previous few years had created. She nestled her head on his shoulder. He felt the sleek, warm touch of her body; the silky, soft feel of her skin was what he longed for. He pulled away and their eyes met; he rejoiced in the smooth curves and the hint of a smile on her lovely face.

"Did Marie let you in?" he asked.

"Yes. She said she'd already guessed how you felt and was sure you'd be glad to see me."

"She was right," Cord said, then kissed her passionately.

Lucille murmured, "I thought about the land, where you are and where I want to be. It's here, on your land. It's where I belong."

Cord said the first thing that came to his head. "Marry me."

His tiredness evaporated; he picked her up and carried her into the bedroom.

*****

At the same time, at Jacana, it was approaching dusk. The last rays of the setting sun slowly receded, leaving a hazy blanket of purple lingering over the vast grassland plain. Albert sat perched on the cottage step, smoking, as May approached, her jobs done for the day. She took his large, weathered hand in hers and sat on the step beside him.

"Ya should give that up, ol' fella, it's no good for ya."

He extinguished the cigarette and grinned through his fluffy silver beard.

"What ya grinnin' about now?" she asked.

He nodded, squeezed her hand and said, "I feel the Landman's landed."

Wedlock
2017

On a sunny spring day in Kings Park and under the shady canopy of eucalyptus trees, Cord and Lucille exchanged vows. Lucille wore a vintage-inspired white knee-length lace wedding dress with a flared skirt cut around the hips to flatter her trim figure. She wore white braided high-heel shoes and the Malay-style bridle crown headdress her mother had worn as a bride. It was encrusted with rubies and emeralds set in gold clasps. The outfit encapsulated beauty and elegance.

Cord wore navy slacks and a light grey jacket over an open-necked pale blue linen shirt. His joy knew no bounds seeing his bride and listening as she pledged her life to his.

The guest list was small, just immediate family and the Bells. Barry and Sofie attended and it was understandable that Ted and Joan declined, given that station life stopped for no one, but they sent a small gift. Cord invited Albert and May, but they too declined, sending a gift of singing sticks, which Albert said contained the song of Mammoth Gorge. John Keep was the Master of Ceremonies.

Lucille wished to honeymoon at the Smokehouse Hotel at Tanah Rata, where their intimacy began, so they went. The long, winding, single-lane mountain road from Ipoh to Tanah Rata was still laden with the continuous stream of overburdened lorries that presented a hazard at every turn. As usual, lightning flashed from itinerant thunderstorms. It was a relief to enter the cobblestone drive that wound its way to the hotel door, fringed by blooming roses and vines. The building was enveloped in light, misty rain, a hospitable haven with its high-pitched thatched roof, tall chimneys and timeless Tudor architecture.

They had the same apartment. It had been refurbished in a similar vein as before, with a double four-poster bed, a soft pillowed lounge facing the crackling log fire and a shaggy wool carpet covered with oversized cushions that straddled the hearth. A porter brought a tray of light food, shortbread biscuits, cashew nuts and a bottle of Pinot Noir.

"Will you be eating in, Sir?"

"We'll have our meal in the room, thank you."

"Very good, Sir."

He left nodding and bowing to Lucille.

They showered together as lovers do. This divine woman who had returned to Cord excited him, as always. He traced the faint image of the caesarean scars that lingered on her abdomen and thought of Mia, the little girl born to them and then spirited away. Lucille never spoke of the anguish and pain she'd suffered; her only comment when he raised the subject was, "It's all right now." Her bitterness towards Rodney had subsided, as had Cord's; it was all in the past and best forgotten.

It still astounded Cord that Rodney had escaped being party to the fraud. The blame lay entirely with Kim Li, with no tangible evidence connecting Rodney to the crime. Kim Li was extradited to Malaysia on a tax evasion count and sentenced to twenty years in prison. Miriam Manx advised Cord that the Australian Government had recovered the fraudulent funds from Kim Li's assets in Australia.

The Coroner reported Rodney died from alcohol poisoning. The report revealed he'd been diagnosed with a heart murmur and was listed for surgery to replace the faulty valve and cited this as the probable cause of suicide. Lucille accepted that, but Cord knew otherwise and kept it to himself.

The porter knocked at the door and brought in the evening meal on a trolley tray. The bay shrimp and fried noodles were satisfying and delicious, the wine heady. After making love, Lucille watched over Cord as he dozed on the cushions by the fire.

Twins
2019

Mia went to Jacana as often as she could. The year she went as a novice ringer, she met Rhett Abbot, four years her senior, who'd completed a degree in Animal Science. He was of kind nature, affable, a skilled horseman, fearless and light in the saddle. It was clear Mia and Rhett were attracted and maintained a close relationship over the years.

The Abbots had a small spread in the Tablelands breeding Hereford cattle for the domestic market and Rhett went to Jacana to learn and work with Barry on his breeding program. Mia finished her degree in Veterinary Science and after a long courtship, the McCullum and Abbot families met to discuss wedding arrangements.

It was a rushed wedding as Mia had obtained an overseas scholarship in biological chemistry, focusing on animal venom and nanotechnology to resource beneficial drugs for human application. At the same time, Rhett would be able to pursue further studies in bovine genomics. Mia's parents proudly acknowledged her research would result in a doctorate.

Cord reflected that perhaps Boris hadn't died for nothing. He missed his friend and meditated on the hard days they laboured together, sweating under the fierce, unyielding outback sun. He thought, how about that, you crazy fuckin' Spaniard? You might get a life-saving anti-venom drug named after you.

Cord and Lucille were on their balcony having breakfast, contemplating the logistics associated with weddings. This was to be a lavish affair and the guest list was daunting, with invitees from around the country. Lucille was in her element organising the celebration, unlike the low-key affair when she and Cord married.

"It's hard to believe we have a twenty-year-old daughter," Cord said.

"And a beautiful one, too," she added.

"Just like her mother. How about a coffee? I'll get you one."

Lucille smiled and nodded, pondering over the guest list.

"I want Father and Mother to come, but travelling is beyond them. I'll get Mia to send a special message on the day. Perhaps we could record a video, professionally, I mean, with music and Mia's dialogue."

"Okay."

Cord went to the kitchen, filled the electric jug with water and spooned Starbucks medium roast, Lucille's favourite blend, into the mugs. He gazed out the window. It was about to rain and clouds covered the slowly meandering river in a dull grey blanket.

He mused how strange it was that history had a way of repeating itself. He thought about their honeymoon at the Smokehouse at Tanah Rata, where Mia was conceived. Cord was now forty-one years old and Lucille thirty-eight. It was no surprise that Lucille conceived at Tanah Rata again; as before, they hadn't used protection. Except this time, they were having twins.

Doctor Graham, their obstetrician, explained that a child of older parents could be born with complications and was even more concerned when twins were confirmed. He remembered their joy was filled with trepidation at the doctor's foreboding.

The months passed and Cord watched his love grow bigger. Eileen and Corrine fussed around buying and knitting baby clothes and preparing the nursery, which was converted from Cord and Kathy's old bedroom. He smiled as he thought of Lucille renovating the spare room soon after she had arrived, refurbishing it as the main bedroom.

Mia was overjoyed at the prospect of twin siblings; a brother and sister or two sisters or two brothers, whatever. She bustled around her mother, busy and attentive. It was, "Mother, can I get you this? Can I get you that?"

The jug continued to boil and from the window, Cord observed passengers scurrying from the incoming ferry onto the slippery wet quay. He smiled and reflected that the diagnosis of twins had been quite a shock.

Cord was at Lucille's side when she gave birth. It was a quick delivery of a healthy boy and girl, both at five-pound weight and squawking noisily. Nevertheless, he remembered waiting apprehensively for the medical assessment and getting the all-clear before publicly announcing the births of Roland Cordon and Spree Lucille McCullum.

The McCullum clan rejoiced and Eileen, whose prejudice subsided when she realised Mia was actually her granddaughter, proudly paraded the twins before her lady friends. She'd pompously declared, "Twins run in the family, especially pigeon pairs."

Keith said, "Now I have an even better reason to make toys."

Lucille's mothering instinct kept her at home with the twins and she and Cord never ventured far afield except when they visited her parents in Malaysia with Mia and the twins.

Cord recalled her mother's delight as she hugged and kissed her, saying, "*Anak perempuan saying.* I knew you could have children."

They went to Penang and the old family home in the jungle. Cord explained to Mia that the Moongate Trail was where he first walked and fell in love with her mother.

The jug finally boiled; the hiss and click of the vessel woke him from his reverie. The sun shone through breaks in the clouds and the river became blue again. He added milk, poured the hot liquid into the mugs and went out to the balcony.

"That took a long time."

"I overfilled the jug."

A child cried; one of the twins had woken.

"I'll go," Cord said.

Landman
2020

It was January and summer in Australia.

Cord and Lucille sat on the balcony overlooking the river. It was a balmy Sunday morning, with only the occasional ferry crossing the calm waters. A small flotilla of racing yachts with spinnakers flying criss-crossed the river, each vessel vying for the lead. The grassy esplanade foreshore was alive with people exercising. The faint, pleasant aroma of roast coffee floated into the air.

The twins were awake and playing on a blanket at their feet. Spree tugged at a red plastic boat Roland had in his hands. He cried and Lucille intervened.

"Takes after her mother," Cord observed.

Lucille ignored the comment.

"Mia's up. I can smell the coffee."

Mia was visiting with her husband, Rhett. She placed the tray of coffee cups on the outside table, then picked up her little brother and walked to the balcony rail. He snuggled in her arms as she pointed to the yachts.

"Look, Rols, there are real boats for you," she said, kissing him on the cheek.

Spree was content she now had the plastic boat.

"Mother, you and Pa should take a break. We can look after the business for you. We don't need to be back up north for a couple of weeks."

Lucille sipped at her coffee and looked across to Cord.

"Hmm. What do you think? Where to?" he said.

"I don't know," Lucille replied. "We could take a break, perhaps to Adelaide. You've always said a lot happened because of Torrens. Rodney's case, the investment review board; it's certainly affected our lives. I haven't been to Adelaide. We could go and take a trip down memory lane."

In the afternoon of another hot day, they strolled from their hotel in the city along the promenade, skirting the banks of Lake Torrens. They purposely waited till late afternoon when it was cooler for the twins in their tandem pusher. Under the shade of a tall gum tree on the water's edge, there was a shiny metallic bench, the type that resisted graffiti. The seat was warm, so Lucille spread one of the baby blankets over it. Cord sat back, raised his arms and cradled the back of his head.

"Just think, Torrens was here a hundred and sixty years ago. He wouldn't recognise the place."

A downstream dam had converted the seasonally dry Torrens River into a fine lake. People jogged, strolled and rode bikes along the pathways in the parkland. A girl on a scull quickly rowed by. A small boy tugged a boat tied to a string along the water's edge, watched closely by his father, the mother following, holding their daughter's hand. Cord thought they looked like twins.

Roland was playing, talking to himself as he handled a wooden tugboat Keith had made. Spree was sleeping; petal eyelids fringed with long black eyelashes covered her closed eyes, her delicate beauty already apparent.

"She'll want his tugboat when she wakes up," Lucille chuckled.

"Just like my Corrine," Cord said. "What was mine was hers but not vice versa."

He gathered Roland in his arms and carried him to the water's edge.

"Boat, Daddy," Roland said, pointing to the young boy.

"When you're older, we'll put your tugboat in the water. Gramps says it will float."

Lucille called Roland to have a drink. He ran up the slope as fast as he could into his mother's arms. Spree was awake drinking an orange juice. Cord sat her on his knee and bounced her up and down.

"Don't, Daddy," she laughed as he covered her with kisses.

The day before, they had ventured into the old parliament building where Torrens had introduced his land bill. Cord reflected that many countries had adopted the land reform in one way or another. Yes, the system had stood the test of time.

The afternoon waned. The twins played with their toys in the pusher. Lucille rested her head on Cord's shoulder and he could smell her sweet perfume. It was time to go.

"You know, my love, it's strange. On the *Spree*, with Gert and the guys calling me Landman, I felt uncomfortable, the odd one out and a bit humiliated. Now, after all these years, I feel honoured with the tag. I reckon everyone wants a plot of their own, and good or bad, I've been involved in the process. It's a valuable commodity, land. Despots invade and take it, others buy it and unfortunately, some can only rent it. I've always considered Torrens the original landman, but really, there's never been just one. We're all landmen. We all want a piece of Mother Earth."

Lucille pulled away and turned towards him, her deep brown eyes searching his. Her lips brushed his.

"Maybe so, but you're my Landman."

Acknowledgements

These are the people I owe.

My wife, Dianne, for her faith in me and who first urged me to put pen to paper.

My editor, Barb Clews, for her patience and wise words.

The people I have met along the way whose personality fragments I have drawn on.

The First Nations and Indigenous people of the world who have provided flavour for the tale.

As an author, I would like to think the plot and characters portrayed are real but, in fact, are just figments of my imagination. The only reality is the beautiful, fragile Planet Earth.